Stratford Library Association
2203 Main Street
Stratford, CT 06615
203-385-4160

THE SURVIVORS

To my parents, Cade and Anneal Havard, for giving me
nearly everything so I could get everything else

To Meghan Hannigan, for the willingness to live
inside worlds I create

THE SURVIVORS

Amanda Havard

Chafie Press
A division of Chafie Creative Group, LLC

CONTENTS

AUTHOR'S NOTE

𝔍n 1692, in the rural farming village of Salem, Massachusetts, twenty-four people died accused— and some convicted—as witches. Though there are over five hundred existing documents that tell the story of the massacre of the famed Salem Witch Trials, there are no official transcripts of the trials of the accused witches, and there is evidence to suggest that even the limited unofficial documentation recorded only segments of the process in order to conceal the sordid truth about the unjust trials. The deaths of the twenty-four victims of the witch trials were never recorded into the public record, likely in an attempt to expunge the existence of these individuals entirely. Because of this, the exact number of accusations, trials, convictions, and deaths, as well as the identity and fate of all of the accused, is entirely unknown.

Was a long and dark December
From the rooftops I remember
There was snow
White snow

Clearly I remember
From the windows they were watching
While we froze
Down below

When the future's architectured
By a carnival of idiots on show
You better lie low

If you love me
Won't you let me know?

"Violet Hill"
Coldplay

PROLOGUE

Salem, Massachusetts
December 1692

"We are decided then," he said, but doubts plagued his mind. "You take them, captain. Away from our homes. Away from this place," Reverend Parris demanded. The six men standing before him nodded.

"We will rid you of the miscreants," the captain assured him.

"How far is the chosen destination?" Parris asked.

"Far enough," the captain said.

"And the length of your journey?" Reverend Parris inquired again. He pressed his thin, pale hand to his forehead and clenched his jaw. It would be but a moment until his doubts overwhelmed him.

"We are not sure," the captain said readily. "We have heard only rumors that we can go so far west. I expect we may return when this winter gives way to spring. At worst, we may return with the summer sun." He swallowed uncomfortably at the falsehood, his conscience guilty for telling such untruths. None of the six envisioned surviving the journey ahead of them.

Reverend Parris hesitated. Then the governor spoke. "It is far enough that they could never return to Salem. They would die on the journey."

"If they shall die by God's hand in the wilderness, then why shan't we bestow upon them justice ourselves?" the reverend asked. The governor crossed his arms and narrowed his eyes. He and Parris both knew it was imprudent to ignore the allegations but outrageous to condemn them all to death.

"Enough is enough," Governor Phips said in a stern voice, and placed his hand on the reverend's shoulder. "I will not hang another unless His Majesty says so, and he does no such thing. We are already impugned for our crimes against the other nineteen."

Parris obliged. "Take them now, captain. Before this night has passed. You take what you need, and you leave now," he said roughly. He had half a mind to kill each of these children, these *witches,* himself, before anyone could stop him. He knew in his heart it was the Lord's way.

They could all sense this. The captain led his team of horsemen out of Parris's home hurriedly. In the street, thirty-two horses waited: one for each of the six, and twenty-six more, each with an accused witch shackled to it.

The horsemen were as prepared as they could be for the journey ahead. Their only regret was taking so many of the small community's horses with them, but they dared not question their purpose. To them, it was worth risking their lives. They believed that witchcraft had no place in Salem, that there should be no room for it in God's world at all. But they were quiet vigilantes, these six, who could remain complacent no longer. They were charged with keeping their town, their *religion,* from murdering any more than it already had. Many in Salem could not bear to witness the massacre that would result if these children were put on trial, but these six men were motivated not solely by beneficence. Instead, they were driven by purpose, acting as if God Himself had sent the word to them to remove the accused from Salem and bring them to safety.

In the seasons preceding this midnight ride, nineteen souls had hung from the gallows of Salem, accused and convicted as witches, and five more had died in prison. And now, just months after the most recent execution, this mass accusation had arisen. Twenty-six children were believed to be witches. The grievous claim was legitimate and was taken very seriously by more than just the zealous reverend. Alexander Raven, a respected member of the community, had made credible accusations about all twenty-six.

As an act of forbearance, Sir William Phips, the governor of Massachusetts, had decided to exile the accused instead of hanging them, which outraged the Reverend Samuel Parris. But the decision had been made. It had been only one week ago that these twenty-six had been taken from their homes and imprisoned, and now they were shackled, shivering from fear and frost, and certain that they were being marched in some uncommon fashion toward death.

Reverend Parris and Governor Phips stood in the lane, watching as the accused and the horsemen disappeared into the frozen blackness of night.

They headed westward with no plan but to continue on until they had gone far enough. It took a season to reach the point where the men had decided to drop these children, defenseless against the elements.

Their ride was treacherous. Their horses labored in the frigid winds as they trekked across uneven terrain, slowly climbing through mountain passes, struggling on steep declines. The sky shone a glaring white-grey as if snow that never dissipated hung in the sky. Each day they followed the path of the setting sun, driving the horses until their hooves could take no more. The accused witches were silent, save for the sounds of their quiet prayers.

Seven of the twenty-six died en route. A girl with brown hair and blue eyes and freckles was the first to pass on, still upright on her horse until they approached a sharp incline and her rigid, frozen body fell from the horse. It was dragged, hooked to the saddle, for fifty meters before the chains broke loose. A rosy-cheeked fifteen-year-old boy, whose father was friends with Reverend Parris, began to shake late one night, convulsing and crying out into the dark as he labored for each breath, until he labored no more. A horseman's nose, fingers, and toes began to sear in hot pain in the cold wind, turning black before he met his end. A second horseman had lain on the ground one night, too far from the fire. He never awoke.

On the seventy-fourth cold morning, they reached a clearing flanked by shallow hills. Frozen streams lined the grey and icy earth. The sky was white with frost. The team of horsemen decided they had done all they could.

The remaining four men released each of the accused, one by one, and let them off their horses. They freed the youngest, Hannah, who was just twelve years of age, first. She stood shakily on the ground and began to walk, looking like a newborn colt as she struggled to remember how to move her legs.

Each of the survivors felt a mixture of fear and relief as the captain removed the shackles. They looked at the dead, frozen ground around them in terror, certain that this would be their end. From their eyes, they had been sentenced to a slow and painful death. There was no mercy in this gesture.

As the last of the accused, nineteen-year-old John Surrey, stepped off his horse and into his new freedom, he turned to the captain and spoke. "You tell Parris that his conscience shan't be any clearer for sending us here than for hanging us from the gallows. This is surely a death sentence," he said, his face raw from the icicles forming on it. The fierce expression on the eldest boy's face reinforced his meaning, as he gestured to the dead land around them. "If this be not Hell, I know not what it is."

The young people roamed around, looking out into the distance at the perpetual nothingness. The captain remounted, and the three others followed. They drove the other horses together, not saying a word to any of the nineteen youths they had freed as they turned their backs on them. They galloped back toward the rising sun. None made it back to Salem.

The circumstances in the following months were austere. It had been a cold winter, colder even than the winters in Massachusetts, with more snow and wild air that stabbed through the skin like daggers even into months that usually felt like spring in Salem.

By their sixty-third day in the bleak wilderness, with no food or drink, only fourteen of them—eight girls and six boys—remained. They had become desperate, wandering in the wild, terrified. Each of them prayed at night, some asking their Lord to end their suffering, others begging for their lives.

And by some miracle none of them understood, the fourteen survived.

They had gone on to live in the desolate land for nearly two more years before deciding to travel farther west in search of a less exposed terrain. They had lived through impossible conditions, from frigid temperatures and ice storms in the winter, to blazing heat in the summer, in open plains that flayed them against the battered earth like meat beaten with stone. Their move west was a search for comfort. They hoped that a more mountainous, secluded environment might prove more hospitable.

They hiked in a bright spring and summer across lush landscapes, thick forests, and rocky inclines before they reached a green mountain range they would declare their home. They never left.

Since they were abandoned, the fourteen survivors had been able to go without food or water for weeks at a time, and despite the fact that it had taken them months to learn to start a fire with snow-covered wood or build a shelter with no tools, each of them was, in fact, strong. None had fallen ill or lost limbs. It never occurred to them what an impossibility this had been. Instead, they wondered why so many of their number and two of the horsemen—even so many of their community in Salem—had fallen ill and died in conditions less severe than the ones they had endured. They idly mused how fragile those lives must have been in comparison to their own.

They counted off their time in days, unsure of what day it was when they left Salem or reached their new home. On the 671st day since they were abandoned, an older girl, Sarah, voiced something many of them had noticed: Hannah had not grown or changed in any way since they had arrived. Her clothes still fit, unlike many of the others, whose clothes had grown slack as they had grown thinner, or too short once they had grown taller. But her young physique had remained; she was no more womanly than she had been when they left, despite having been born fourteen years before. She also began telling fantastical stories of happenings in a land not far from theirs, of things she saw that would happen, describing events in the unknown land or

speaking truths about what would become of the fourteen survivors.
They began to wonder if it was more than an active imagination.

Nor had the oldest of them, Lizzie, grown or changed since
their exile. But she had been born in 1670, so it was more difficult to
determine what changes should have occurred. As their 671 days
turned into nearly 1,300, and they had settled in their newer, greener,
mountainous homeland, they began to notice that many of the boys
who began as the youngest of the group now began to look older and
bigger than Andrew, who was seventeen when they left Salem. They
theorized as to why this was. The consensus was that the harsh conditions had caused Hannah, Lizzie, and Andrew to be smaller, malnour-
ishment impeding their development. But all three were strong, almost
impossibly so. Little Hannah could carry logs as thick around as she
was. Andrew could pull tree stumps from the ground with his bare
hands. Lizzie was always awake when others fell asleep in the wilderness and when they rose in the mornings. They thought this was because she felt a need to protect them, but it was because she never
slept.

One late autumn night, fourteen quiet survivors laid calmly on the
mountainside, asking God why He would keep them alive only to live
in such misery. It was then that a cool breeze turned quickly to a cold
wind. It rained at first, and then snow began to dance in the air and
cover the ground around them. All the survivors hastened to find dry
wood to burn to brave yet another cold night. A fire would not keep
them warm, but it did make the wind feel more like a dull pain rather
than the sharp stab it usually was. But this night they had not made it
in time. All the wood they found was wet and slick and snow-covered,
and it would not ignite.

They cursed at each other, launching screams of anguish and
insults at one another, each of them frightened at the idea of spending
another night in darkness and frigidity. They had not yet grown
enough accustomed to the cold to endure it without pain.

Overcome with frustration, from his failed fire building and from his existence, Andrew threw his hands up to the sky. In an instant, the wood they had piled together erupted violently into flames.

I

HUMAN

I sighed. My car sped angrily across the smoldering Mississippi pavement as I watched the temperature display on the dashboard click over from 98° to 99°. It was unseasonably warm, even for June. The road in front of me disappeared quickly under my tires. I was charging toward the hazy lines that sizzled off the pavement, making it look like there was a reflective pool off in the distance that I could never catch, like I was chasing a mirage.

That felt right, of course. Most of my life felt like chasing a mirage. I was always sure I was near to catching something, something I needed desperately—an answer, a person, a break—but I always ended up scrambling toward a deceptive vision with all my energy, only to be met with more disappointment, more isolation, or more rejection. More of the same.

As I crossed the city limits of Tupelo, the thermometer clicked to 100° and I could barely breathe. The heat radiated through the windows in my car; even the blasting air-conditioning no match for the sun's penetrating rays. What was I doing here? On this road, in this car, on this journey? I was going to Corrina's wedding, of that much I was sure. But as I drove farther and farther, I'd catch myself reaching my hand across the center console into the passenger seat as if I expected it to land on someone's leg. Of course, some stupid part of my mind thought he was still sitting there next to me. He wasn't. Invariably, my hand dropped onto the smooth, hot leather of the empty seat, and I'd be startled yet again. I recoiled my hand every time this happened, angry that I had again let myself forget that I was going it alone.

That's when I'd wonder what I was doing going to Mississippi to be a bridesmaid. This event was only going to remind me of what I would never have. It was so stupid of me, trying to have a life like this, trying to be so *human.*

He had left me, of course. It had been an unseasonably hot day then, too, and I wore shorts and flip-flops as we walked into a pizza joint in downtown Nashville. I hadn't seen it coming. I was embarrassed; I would have dressed better had I known. If I were going to go down, I would have liked to go down in style. But I was not perceptive enough to sense such things in advance. The trouble was, I had spent the first 141 years of my existence living in ridiculous isolation, in a culture that did its best to keep the intricacies of relationships between mortals outside our protected walls. As the youth, we were not to be distracted from our work, our life, our dedication to God and family. This really meant, of course, that they didn't want us to know what was out there, what life could be like. They preferred us only to know what it was like for us. If we learned what went with humanity—the passion and the torment, the freedom and the oppression—then at least some of us might be lured away from the family and our carefully crafted world. Conversely, it might scare some of the lesser ones into staying there forever, paralyzed in fear by the uncertainties that lay outside our walls, but most of us—those like me—were intrigued every time we had even half a glimpse into some bit of human life. The elders saw that, too, so they did their best to isolate us. This was effective for the most part. I was, after all, the only one who had ever left.

It made the adjustment to human life difficult for me when the time came, having experienced so little of it (if even I had read much about it) before I left. I had stopped visibly aging sometime between my nineteenth and twenty-first birthdays, so when I obtained an identity in the human world—birth certificate, driver's license, passport, Social Security number—I had said I was born in 1990. So now, I was more or less twenty-one years old by mortal standards. The problem was that people expected twenty-one-year-olds to know things about themselves and about the world that I could not possibly have known, despite my best efforts to prepare. It had been a rough transition.

Even so, I didn't want to go back. I was tired of being repressed. I had lived for nearly two lifetimes before I walked away from the city walls practically empty-handed. I never looked back. I had decided that I would take no more direction from them, that I would no longer relinquish my control of my life to anyone. So far, I hadn't.

I'd gone south immediately, believing they would send no one into uncharted territory to look for me. I'd been passing as a human for three years. Unlike some of my kind, I had the control of my inhuman faculties to do so. I had practiced it for years before I ran away. I even had a much wider knowledge of the outside world than my peers—I read every book I ever got my hands on, researched humans in any way I could—but that still didn't make the transition easy. I was entirely unprepared for the experience. People, it turned out, were not known for their thoughtful or good-natured intentions. Consequently, I had been hurt in so many strange ways I never expected that I could barely stand most of the people I met. I had not realized, either, that so much of human life was filled with monotony and duty, with the same moronic rituals I'd been trying to avoid by leaving my family.

Particularly, I had not understood that in this world, you could give yourself to someone completely, but they might never return the favor. I learned this with Todd, my ex-boyfriend, the hard way. We had spent seventy-nine days together, and then he was gone. As I came to learn, seventy-nine days was not any kind of major commitment—even to mortals whose life spans were so short, each day making up a greater percentage of their lives than mine—but he had said a lot of things in that time that made it seem like this was headed toward forever. And I believed him. Consequently, I was heartbroken, though he seemed unscathed. It floored me. I added to my growing list of human tendencies a simple line:

They do not feel loyalty, not the way we do.

I had yet to meet a human loyal to anything other than himself or herself. In Todd's case, he was loyal to his own impatience, his human drive to run.

I bit my lower lip absently at this thought. I understood the urge to run. That urge was what had landed me here, in this car, on this road, alone in the world, passing as something I was not.

Coming out of my trance, I quickly realized the next exit was mine. I began to more consciously and closely appraise my surroundings. The ground was mostly flat. The cars were old or cheap or both; I had seen the last Mercedes like my own 128 miles ago. It was the first thing—aside from the unbearable heat—that made me so sure I was driving into a place I didn't belong. The second was an unmissable billboard featuring an attractive, athletic-looking teenage boy with the words CHOOSE ABSTINENCE plastered across it. This seemed odd to me for many reasons. The human world, I had surmised, was a place where sexuality was not openly discussed. It was considered inappropriate, a taboo topic of discussion, even despite the fact that it happened so frequently and more casually than I cared for. So why the billboard? More than that, wasn't the message counter-intuitive? To show young girls an attractive boy only to tell them they ought not have him? I frowned. I feared that this sign's very existence was communicating a complex intent that my simplified understanding of human morality could not process. But I couldn't be sure.

The wide tires under my shimmering flint-grey coupe rolled to a stop as I exited the highway and was met with a red light. I looked around. Tupelo seemed nice enough. This street—Main Street—was wide and smooth. I idly noted that there was a lot of open land surrounding the main drag. The buildings—this was downtown, wasn't it?—were just a few stories high and I could see they only ran for four blocks or so before tapering off. There was little traffic.

I closed my eyes and filtered through the buzzing and humming in my head. I turned right and went toward the reception venue, where I would find Corrina. When I arrived, though, there were only workers there. Corrina had just left; it had been my mistake to tune in only for a moment and then tune out again. I should have kept my focus on finding her.

I went around the block and turned back onto Main Street, toward the hotel. I looked at the clock. It was 3:41 PM, a good time to check in to my hotel. I realized as I turned into the parking lot that I should really locate Corrina and the others by phone at least. It was the polite way to do things, rather than dropping in on them just because I could sense their whereabouts.

I parked the car close to the entrance, something I usually avoided, so that weak humans would have to walk a shorter distance to their destination. But I detested the heat, so I broke my own rule. Despite the suffocating weather, I pulled on a cotton Tahari blazer over my tank top. It made me more uncomfortable, but it would keep people from staring.

I lifted my suitcase, garment bag, and tote bag out of the trunk, balancing them all on one arm. I searched for my phone, which had slipped out of my bag and into the abyss of the car. When I looked up, I caught the eye of a young boy in a baseball uniform looking at me with his head cocked to the side. *Damn.* I quickly set the bags down and stacked them the way I had seen it done in airports, and rolled the flimsy bag behind me.

The air conditioning blasted me as I walked through the automatic glass doors and into the shiny lobby of the four-story hotel. My hair blew all around my face, but I didn't care. It felt so nice. Like home.

At the front desk, I met the invasive gaze of an employee. I knew what she was staring at. This happened every time I went into a small town, and it was still a regular occurrence even in very large, glamorous cities. It had taken me at least a year living among humans to understand it. I did not look like the typical girl, I admit. I was nearly six feet tall, had smooth, long, dark brown hair running to my waist, its black walnut color a contrast to my fair complexion. My skin had the texture of porcelain, and it was the isabelline color of espresso foam marked with heavy cream. Most noticeably, it glowed—subtly enough that it didn't cause trouble for me, but obviously enough that you couldn't *not* notice it. Every inch of my lean body hinted at a well cared for musculature that seemed out of place in a world full of extremes instead of perfect mediums. And my eyes were the strangest shade of clear purple, almost indigo. People always noticed my eyes, even when they noticed nothing else. I often got the feeling that they were not only struck by my appearance as a thing of beauty by their standards, but that it was more than that. *Should I know her from somewhere?* it felt like they were asking. I never understood this. The attention made me uncomfortable, and it seemed ironic considering all I was hiding. I assumed they stared because I was not what they were. Only it wasn't entirely new—they had stared at me at home, too, where *what* we were was the same. I was wholly odd.

I tried to pretend I didn't notice the look the woman behind the desk gave me. "May I help you?" she asked when she finally got past her internal speculations, her voice coated thick in a Southern accent.

"Checking in," I said. This exchange had become commonplace, a habit. I was sometimes reminded of how much work I had done to master humanity.

"Last name?" she asked, one eyebrow raised, the humming emanating from her filling my ears. These days, the humming I heard in the back of my mind was starting to sound different. It was less like a distant echo of hollow sounds radiating off my skull and more of a muffled mix of voices. I couldn't make out any of the voices, but I knew things—like how the woman behind the counter was hoping she would recognize my last name to know who I belonged to.

"Matthau," I said, and spelled it out for her.

"Sadie?" she asked, looking intently at the screen and then up at me. She was disappointed she did not recognize my name. It was so odd to me that I knew this. I could sense her in such a real way—each feeling as she felt it, each idea as she thought it.

"Yes. Should be three nights," I said.

"You're with the Meyer/Williams wedding, I see," she said, eyeing me more carefully now—still trying to determine my connection to this town, to these people, I imagined.

"Uh, yes, I am," I said. My speech was not so eloquent just then. I frowned.

"Are you one of Corrina's friends?" she asked. I paused. This question was not a part of the conversation I rehearsed in my mind for checking into hotels.

"Er, yes," I said.

"How close a friend?" she asked, still eyeing me. I was confused.

"I'm a bridesmaid. I know her from Nashville," I said, hoping that would satisfy her curiosity. I met her strange stare, and returned it with my own stiff gaze. She looked sheepish immediately, reacting quickly to my intimidating glare as people always did, as if I had shot them with something more venomous than a look. I imagined they thought I was some spoiled princess or celebrity cursing their incompetence behind my eyes. That was entirely inaccurate, but it worked well as a defense mechanism.

"I'll need your credit card," she said. I obliged, sliding a thick, black, titanium credit card across the counter. She eyed it in her hand before she swiped it and then handed it back to me, then slid a slip of paper onto the counter. "I need you to sign here," she said, pointing to the sheet, indicating the line marked with an X.

I scribbled my signature in exactly .46 seconds—I counted. She wasn't looking, and I hated slowing down if there was no reason to. She took the slip and examined it before sticking it in the file next to her right hand. She handed me the room key, and indicated the room number on the folder she gave me. I thanked her and turned to walk away.

She spoke again. "Corrina is my cousin," she said. This took me aback; it, too, deviated from the script of these conversations I was so used to. Why was she mentioning this? And did everyone know everyone here? Were they all related in some form or fashion? "I hear the wedding is going to be real nice," she smiled. "I'll be here on Saturday though," she said with a frown. She was embarrassed, I understood now, that she had pried to find out who I was.

Awkwardly—I'm sure—I smiled and backed away, unable to think of anything at all appropriate to say.

I rode in the elevator with three teenage boys who were smiling at me nervously and giving each other sideways glances they thought I couldn't see. I could feel the lust rolling off them in waves, and it made me uncomfortable. This was one of the most unpleasant things I had experienced in the time I was acting as a human, that men of all ages turned their energy toward lustful feelings of conquest in my presence. It made every part of me tense. It was so inappropriate. I had never thought of myself that way, and I had never felt those things, despite my age. It was another way I felt isolated among the humans, another way I didn't understand them. It didn't matter that I could strangle all three of these boys by the time the elevator doors opened on the next floor; it still irked me in a way I couldn't explain even to myself.

When the elevator dinged and the doors opened, the boys and I exited the elevator together. Their thoughts and feelings were still aimed toward me as I walked down the opposite end of the hall. I found my room and put the key card into the door. I dragged the luggage across the rough burgundy carpet and whisked myself past the generic stiff, patterned hotel bedspread and reddish fake wood furniture to the air conditioning unit. I turned it up as high as it would go. I stood in front of the icy blast and took a deep breath. It soothed me instantly.

I could tell Corrina was faintly east of where I was now, at her parents' house. I called her to announce my arrival. She squealed when she spoke to me. I could tell that she was glad that I had actually made it here. There had been some part of her that wasn't sure I'd come, my aloofness always a source of doubt. It meant only one thing to me: I wasn't doing a good enough job playing human.

I went quickly to her house. As I pulled up the steep drive, I saw cars everywhere. Before I even got out of my own car, I heard a distinctive humming from the house, and I knew there were many people inside. I inhaled deeply.

Corrina ran out the front door to meet me, and jumped up and down and then into my arms. She was considerably smaller than I was, and she often ended up jumping on me, assuming my strength could handle her, I suppose. Her curly red hair whipped wildly a foot into the air as she bounced, and her cool jade-green eyes were smiling. She really didn't think I was going to come, I thought, but here I stood. I felt a longing as she grabbed my hand and led me inside. I had missed her more than I thought I would. I hadn't ever felt this way about a friend, but Corrina meant the world to me. I wondered if, on some level, she knew I was different. She had always taken such good care of me, sometimes explaining things that other humans would neglect, able to perceive I wasn't following. And she had been protective of me. She had no idea how protective I was of her, too.

There were four other bridesmaids sitting around her living room while the rest of Corrina's family was scattered throughout the house. Everyone seemed to have a million tasks to complete. Nerves and excitement were in the air, but I couldn't tell which emotions belonged to which bodies. Corrina held my hand as she introduced me to the other bridesmaids, who eyed me incredulously. That look of confusion, suspicion, sometimes awe, sometimes envy had gotten old fast.

Corrina's mother heard us and came bursting out of the kitchen. She threw her arms around my waist. I felt such warmth from her! Corrina was like her mother in stature and in heart. I was glad to have her hug.

We spent the rest of the day touring the church and the reception venue—a spectacular mansion—learning about our roles, and getting everyone's schedule set for hair and makeup on the day of the wedding.

The next day, Friday, ran smoothly. We had a traditional bridesmaids' luncheon, complete with every female on Corrina's side of the family and some of her fiancé's, and spent the afternoon getting our nails done. I had very little time to spend alone in my hotel, for which I was kind of grateful. It was always a catch-22 being around people. I was so nervous the whole time, especially in a group this size, that *someone* would be watching me, notice I wasn't like them, notice I didn't have their posture, that I didn't fret about my hair or skin, that I didn't sweat even in the unbearable heat. But if I actually got to spend time alone, it was never as enjoyable as I'd hoped it would be. It had been a little over two months since I had last slept, and the hours spent in my own company were getting to me. There was a lot of unnerving quiet in my life. So I was grateful to these people for filling my hours.

But by the time I returned to the hotel on Friday evening to get dressed for the rehearsal dinner, I was mostly ready to be alone. I had hit the point in my capacity for social interaction where I couldn't comfortably do it any longer. And I wished so badly that I could sleep. I was so tired. Perhaps tonight I would finally feel the release of sleep.

I sat still on my bed for exactly five minutes before I sighed and got ready for the rehearsal. I slid into a sand-colored, long-sleeve jersey J. Mendel cocktail dress that closely mirrored my silhouette and had maybe a bit too daring a neckline for me to pull off. In a brash moment of self-confidence, I'd ordered it from Bergdorf's especially for this evening after seeing it on the runway. I grabbed my black and brown zebra Diane von Furstenberg clutch, and slipped on the black Prada suede platform sandals Corrina bought me as a gift. I smudged a kohl liner into a cat-eye on my eyelids, ran my fingers through my hair, decided I looked enough like a human, and I was out the door.

The rehearsal was the first place he noticed me. If he had been around the mansion where the reception was going to be held or at Corrina's house earlier in the day, I hadn't seen him or sensed him. But as the whole wedding party, attendants and ushers, families, and musicians filed into the church, he saw me. We were introduced to everyone. I smiled at them when Corrina pulled me forward and told everyone who I was. I had to smile, of course—that's what a human does in such a joyous situation. But it wasn't so simple for me. I was trying to block out everything I was feeling, everything I was sensing from the eight groomsmen and ushers who were in overdrive. I felt a giant surge of lust overcome them when Corrina was introducing me. Corrina's groom, Felix, never had a thought he shouldn't have, good man that he was.

I did not know Corrina's groom as well as most of the others here did—at least I hadn't spent as much time with him. Corrina and I had met in Nashville when she was finishing up college. Felix had already graduated and gotten a job in Dallas, where Corrina later moved when she was done with school. She had friends, of course, but in his absence she needed someone with whom she could spend all the time she had with Felix. By happenstance, I became that person. It meant that, second-hand, I got to know Felix very well, and, from what I could tell, he was the greatest guy Corrina could ask for. It made me happy that they were getting married. It seemed right.

When we took our places in the back of the church, Corrina came up to me and said, "You're going to walk with Cole." She locked her arm in mine. Hers was the only human touch I ever received. She touched me without any fear or hesitation at all. The thin jersey of my dress sleeve pulled at the beading of her Alice + Olivia strapless cocktail dress that she had secretly purchased only because she saw Taylor Swift wearing the same dress in an ad. "He's a really nice guy, Sadie. And very, very polite." She smiled.

"Thank you," I smiled back, relieved that she picked a polite one for me to pair up with.

She laughed and waved her hand. "Not a problem. You know I wouldn't throw you to one of the dogs."

I smiled again. I was right in sensing that Corrina would protect me, in believing that she knew something about me was different. I never felt sympathy from her though, just love. That made me love her even more.

She called out for Cole. He immediately flew to her side. I understood now that she was going to introduce me to the groomsman I'd be walking down the aisle with, though I noticed that she didn't do this with the other bridesmaids, all of whom seemed fine without the help. "Cole, this is Sadie Matthau. Y'all are walking down the aisle together," she said brightly.

Cole's eyes widened, but I felt no uncomfortable feelings from him. "Oh, hi! Yes, Cole Hardwick. Hi," he repeated, obviously nervous. "It's a pleasure to meet you, Sadie." He smiled. His clear blue eyes were genuine, and his thinking was pure. He was excited, to be sure, but he kept his thoughts above the belt.

"A pleasure," I said. He extended his hand to me. I hesitated for a fraction of a second. The hugs I received from Corrina and her mother were gross exceptions to my normal routine. I very rarely touched humans, though today was starting to seem like the time for it. Handshakes were tricky for me; I was always afraid the feel of my skin would give me away. My skin was neither warm nor cool but usually matched the temperature of the room I was in. In the warm church, it would not have alerted anyone, but in other settings it definitely would have. Finally I put my hand out to him, and I tried to shake his hand lightly so I would not hurt him, but not daintily. I didn't like being thought of as dainty.

"You kids have fun. I gotta go be the bride and all," Corrina smiled, squeezing my arm. She leaned into Cole, kissed him on the cheek, and breathed, "Be nice, please," which she thought I didn't hear. I wouldn't have if I weren't...me.

"So you're the famous Sadie," he said, his face still sweet, his faint Southern drawl endearing.

"Am I famous?" I laughed. I was at ease considering the circumstances.

"Only in that we don't know you. You came around after we left. All the guys at least, we graduated with Fefe," he mused. Fefe was their endearingly emasculating nickname for Felix. He earned this title, if I remembered correctly, when he cried during *Titanic*. I smiled at that image.

"The girls don't know me either," I said, having to focus to sound sociable, casual.

"None of them?" he asked, surprised.

"I've met Lara a few times. She hung around Corrina a lot that last year, but we never spent time together," I explained. Good. This was *so* good. I was sounding very normal.

Cole looked around, to make sure Lara was out of earshot, I presumed. "Lara's a crazy one, I hear," Cole said under his breath.

"*The* crazy one," I corrected him. He laughed. I liked Cole Hardwick. He was very nonthreatening and his thoughts were very respectful. We turned to face the front. A few moments passed before the rehearsal actually began, but we didn't speak again. This was very interesting to me. Humans were terrible about trying to fill silences with nothingness, unable to stand the quiet. In the company of humans, I rather liked not saying anything sometimes. When they were around, there was always the buzzing in my head, so it wasn't too quiet, the way it was when I was alone. But we stood there for at least two more minutes in silence, clearly capable of communicating but not having to, and I realized this was yet another thing I liked about Cole.

As we got ready for our turn, I heard the wedding coordinator remind everyone to walk slowly. I had to focus very hard on this because I was the least likely to do so. Cole bent his arm at the elbow and offered it to me, and I slipped my arm through it. Even with my high-heeled wedding shoes on for practice, my arm fit nicely into his. He was tall, too. We appeared to match.

As we took deliberate steps down the aisle through the mostly empty church, Cole must have sensed my tension at the eyes resting on me, because ever quietly, he whispered, "We're doing great." A smile broke across my face at his effort to reassure me, and I was relieved. We parted ways at the altar, and he winked at me. He could make me relax, even in a moment of fear. Another point for Cole Hardwick.

At the end of the rehearsal, in the hustle and bustle of leaving the church to head for the dinner, Felix called for me and guided my arm until we were out of the way of the rest of the group. I quickly scanned through the memory of all the conversations I'd ever had with humans. I had never spoken to Felix alone.

"Hey Sadie, I hadn't even gotten to say hi to you yet," he said as he leaned in and kissed me on the cheek. So much contact today! Maybe it was good it was so hot outside, the heat making my skin feel as warm as a human's. His thoughts were still pleasant. I could feel his love and excitement for his impending marriage radiating off him.

"What's up?" I asked.

"Hey I just wanted to tell you...about Cole..." he began, trying to say what he'd planned to say but having a hard time getting the words together.

"What about him?" I asked.

"I know you just broke up with Todd not too long ago, who, as far as I'm concerned, is a serious jerk," he said. I hadn't heard Todd's name spoken in three weeks. It hurt both more and less than I expected it to. "But Cole is the nicest guy here. He's the nicest guy in the world. Corrina told me about how that idiot didn't like that you were..." he paused, uncomfortable, "traditional," he choked. I saw why this was an awkward conversation for him. Corrina had told him that Todd had finally gotten tired of being in a relationship where I wouldn't let him cross lines he thought he had the right to cross. And for some reason I couldn't understand, Felix was trying to bring this up. "I just wanted you to know," Felix continued, sweat on his brow, "Cole is really...traditional, too." He smiled, relieved that it was over with. "Just give him a chance. At the least, maybe he'll restore your faith in the lesser kind," he kidded.

"Thank you, Felix," I smiled, able to relax now that our awkward interaction had passed. But interested too.

I quickly understood what was going on when I arrived at the rehearsal dinner and the place card with my name on it was next to Cole's. At the least, Corrina was trying to make sure I had someone to entertain me all weekend so I didn't sit silently by myself because she knew me well enough to know that is exactly what I would do. Cole was already hovering around the table when I arrived.

"Sadie," he smiled. He was very relaxed. I was jealous.

"Cole," I smiled back. My smile seemed to put him even further at ease. I had noticed this at the church, too.

He was holding a cocktail. "Can I get you anything to drink?" he asked.

"Sure. What you're having," I said. I had seen girls do this at times, and the men they said it to always interpreted it as some sort of compliment about their choice of beverages. It seemed strange to me that that mattered. It didn't matter to me, of course. Though I didn't need it, I could eat or drink anything and it all tasted about the same. Since it was irrelevant to me, I thought I'd try it on Cole. I didn't feel hunger anymore, but I could eat (as I would tonight, for appearances) and I could drink anything I liked as well. Since alcohol had no effect on me, it was safe to drink without fear of losing my inhibitions.

He returned a few moments later and pressed a cloudy, pale drink into my hand. It smelled like lemons—a smell I liked—and alcohol—a smell that burned the inside of my nose. I took a sip. "It's great," I said, sensing he needed reassurance.

People around us were beginning to sit down. This part made me nervous. Standing alone, I managed to avoid people's direct eye line and thereby usually avoided speaking to them. At a table, it wasn't so easy. We all faced each other, a design that forced communication. But I did look forward to those around me talking to each other, giving me the chance to be completely quiet unless someone asked me a question.

Cole pulled my chair out for me, sliding it underneath me as I sat down. "Thank you," I said.

"Of course," he said. I looked down at the table, unsure of how much longer I could continue this one-on-one conversation. I hoped someone would speak to him so I could just listen politely.

I wasn't so lucky. "So you know Corrina from Nashville," Cole said, his body angled toward me. I didn't feel anything radiating from him, no emotion at all, though earlier he was easy to sense. I looked up at his eyes to get a read. They were smiling at me, but I couldn't sense anything else.

"Right," I said, still getting nothing from him. It was very weird.

"But you didn't go to school with her?" he asked. He knew the answer to this question, his tone demonstrated, but I wasn't sure how he knew it. I looked at him very intensely for a moment, trying again to get a read. Nothing.

"Right again," I said. I was having to focus on keeping my facial features in a friendly expression. I'm sure the mix of my actual emotion and the one I was trying to project made me look a little strange.

"So how'd you meet?" he asked.

This one was easy, the truth. "We met at a coffee shop. Her credit card wouldn't go through, and she didn't have any cash on her. I was next in line, so I bought hers."

"Sounds like you were trying to hit on her," he joked.

"You've seen right through me," I sighed, and he laughed. "She thanked me, and I asked her if she wanted to join me," I said, but Cole cut me off.

"Again, trying to hit on her," he interjected. I laughed this time.

"Obviously," I said. "And we just got to talking. It was right after Felix had moved from Tennessee, and she was pretty upset about it. I guess I'm pretty good at listening because she started telling me her whole story. She talked about everything. And you know, she is marrying Felix tomorrow, so my attempts at picking her up were all in vain," I joked, then laughed at how this was coming to me so naturally. I sounded more human than I ever had.

"So why were you in Nashville?" he asked. This was a harder question to answer. I was the first to admit that I didn't know how or why Nashville had become my home base. I felt drawn to it for reasons I couldn't explain. It wasn't even practical; there were no direct international flights in and out of it, and it was often warmer than I liked. But two days after I arrived in Nashville, when I was in a coffee shop just to be around people—something I did often to sharpen my sensing skills—I met Corrina. She was the first human friend I had made, and I was hesitant to abandon that relationship. So I rented a suite in a hotel near Corrina's school, and I made that my home. I stayed there until Corrina graduated nearly a year later.

"Family," I said to Cole, thinking that was a weird reason for me to choose. Funny that no one else had ever asked me *why* I was in Nashville, not even Corrina.

"Are you from Nashville?" he asked.

"No, I'm from up north," I said honestly, knowing that was enough of an answer for this Southern boy not to press the issue any further.

"But you've got family down here," he said, confirming.

"We're spread out," I said sheepishly. That was the biggest lie I had told him yet.

"What do you do?" he asked.

"Travel, mostly," I said. I had standard answers ready for these kinds of questions, a lot of which were truthful on some level. They gave people a mistaken impression of me, but I didn't much mind that.

"For your job?" he asked.

"No," I said. I had not yet mastered being able to tell when I needed to add more to my answers and when it was okay to say little. My inability to further interpret Cole's responses by sensing him was making that even more difficult.

He frowned. "You don't work," he said. It was a statement.

"No," I admitted. This was the precise moment when people got the wrong idea about me. One of Todd's friends had referred to me as a trust fund baby, and I had no idea what he meant. When I learned later that, as best I could gather, trust fund babies were people who didn't have to do much—at least not what they didn't want to—because their families had set them up financially, I was amused. This was not my case at all, but I did understand that living the life I led, traveling as I did, driving the car I had, even dressing the way I did, had added to people's perceptions of me in this light. I had not bothered to correct any of them, but I could see that many of them found this highly unfavorable. I was hoping Cole wasn't one of them.

"What do you do?" I finally asked, when I couldn't tell what he was thinking at all.

"I'm into I-banking," he said. I had no idea what this meant.

"Where do you live?" I asked, following his lead.

"I'm out of New York now, but I don't know if I can stay there. The city's tough for me. I miss my family a lot," he said. It was endearing that he missed his family, even though it alienated me a bit.

"So why don't you come home?" I asked.

"And do what? I come from a town in Tennessee with fourteen thousand people in it. Not exactly the investment banking capital," he mused. Investment banking—that must have been what he meant by I-banking.

"Oh," I said. I wasn't sure how to react to this. Happy for him that he had a job that was important to him? Sad for him that he hated the city and was homesick? Admiring of him because he was going to stick it out?

"Is there one place you always visit, or do you go all over?" he asked, going back to me.

"I go...a lot of places," I said, vaguely.

"Like..." he said. This was one of those odd cues humans gave each other: one-word prompts to continue. When I wasn't careful, I'd miss them.

"Like all over. A lot of other countries," I said. He scrunched his brow together a little, like he was thinking very hard. I had no idea what was going through his mind, and that killed me.

"You don't like giving anything away, do you?" he said. His words stung, but I was sure he didn't mean them to. Todd had said the exact same thing when I had returned to Nashville from my most recent trip, tight-lipped about what I had been doing, only accidentally slipping on where I'd been. He, of course, had said it with more frustration and had drawn an obvious parallel to something far more personal that I knew Cole and I were not talking about.

I bit my lip. "What do you want to know?" I asked. He was about to speak, and I added, "Specifically."

He frowned. "Last place you visited," he said.

"Tupelo," I smiled.

"Doesn't count," he said. "Last place you went to on a plane."

"Last plane I was on was from LAX," I said, and this was true. What did I have to lose by admitting this? Cole was barely more than a stranger, and I had learned that strangers were a special kind of confidant; after all, one of the most peculiar things about humanity was how much you could trust strangers when you kept so much from the people you loved.

"You were in LA? Or you connected through there?" he asked. He was quick. It made my job more difficult, but I liked that about him. That was five points for Cole Hardwick—I had been counting— six if you counted Felix's highlight of "traditional."

"Connecting," I smiled faintly, relenting. This brought a grin to his face. I was playing along.

"So you flew into LA from..." he let his words hang. Another cue for me to finish his sentence.

"Sydney," I said, now totally smiling. Why did he make me smile so readily?

"Interesting," he said. He leaned back and crossed his arms, arched his eyebrows, and let his eyes linger on me. "Sadie, answer me this," he said, leaning in so close I could feel my face warm from his breath.

I gulped, an unnecessary instinct. "All right," I said, watching him carefully.

"What do you want most out of life?" he asked, his voice a whisper. He had to be joking. Who would ask a question like that of a girl he just met? I didn't suppose people could answer that question on the spot.

I, of course, knew the answer. *To die,* I thought. No, that wasn't it. "Mortality," I said, freezing as I realized too late that I had said it out loud. Time stood still around me. I was aware of every emotion in the room, every fork clinking, every burst of laughter radiating in the air. What had I done?

But Cole Hardwick only laughed.

The rest of the night went smoothly. Cole and I talked to each other, and he talked to the people around us. I was much more guarded after I had made the grievous error of answering Cole's last question honestly.

I spent a good amount of time watching Corrina and Felix. They were having such a lovely time together, both so genuinely excited to be close to one another. Neither of them was having even the slightest bit of anxiety about marriage; it was pure joy.

I thought about Todd as I watched them. I was worried when my thoughts went in that direction, but I seemed to be okay. I didn't even miss him as much as I had. I think I'd been scared that I'd had my only chance with humans, and that in losing him, I'd lost my chance. But sitting there at that dinner, I understood it wasn't like that. It was more that Todd and I were absolutely wrong for each other. And I wasn't much of a girlfriend. In the less than three months we were together, I was out of town for over two-thirds of it. We hadn't had any kind of intimacy, really; we just had a few good dates and late night movies and wine—wine that had done nothing to me, but that made him sleepy and for that I was grateful. But I had let myself fall so fully for him. It was irrational and immature, and it was certainly not love.

What Corrina and Felix had, what they felt when they looked at each other, that was love. As I let the warmth of their affection envelop me as it rolled off them in waves, I knew I had never felt that feeling in my life. I was almost certain I could never be with a human, and every one of my kind was sitting together in a walled city somewhere in the northern Rocky Mountains, a place I would never return to. Another wave of pure adoration hit me as Felix leaned in and lightly kissed Corrina's lips. I had definitely never felt that. I swallowed hard as I realized I probably never would.

I thought, too, about how odd it was that I couldn't read Cole. Lately, my senses were always in a heightened state. I could read people more easily than I ever had been able to before. But in my longest one-on-one conversation with a human other than Corrina, I had no idea what he was thinking. In some ways, I was grateful for how little I was feeling from Cole. It would make it easier not to feel anything for him, not to be attracted to him because he was nice and he was gorgeous. In fact, I spent the last few minutes of the dinner listing the reasons in my mind why I didn't feel anything from Cole. At the top of that list was the most obvious one: I couldn't feel anything from him because he wasn't feeling anything toward me.

The others began to file out of the large banquet room. Corrina and Felix had already taken off—separately—with their families. Only the bridesmaids and groomsmen were still mingling when I saw my chance to leave inconspicuously. I grabbed my clutch and headed for the door.

But Cole stopped me. "Leaving so soon?" he asked. This time I clearly felt anticipation surge toward me as he spoke. I was flooded with immense, powerful emotion, bombarded with all the fuzzy thoughts and feelings I hadn't been able to feel for the last two hours. He felt what I could best describe as a complete desire for me. I panicked.

"Yes," I finally got out. The waves of disappointment came instantly. Too gentle to leave it at that, I added, "Early morning, you know." I made a sound that was a cross between a laugh and a sigh. It came out awkwardly.

He shrugged. "Have a good night then," he said, his eyes deceptively upbeat for the sadness he was feeling. I had done so well to be so human tonight, and for what? So that I could ruin it all in this moment?

I walked swiftly to my car. I felt a tension in my gut. I hated hurting him.

The purr of the engine rang in my ears as I turned the key in the ignition. I hated having to try so hard to act human when stupid human emotions came to me so easily, without my permission or acceptance.

MEMOIR

The Survivors' City, Montana
Summer 1883 (give or take)

I was walking on the outskirts of the main square of our tiny town. I looked out over the twenty-some-odd grey and red and faded yellow wooden houses that ran along narrow roads we'd cleared to the east of the main square, wondering whether this spot was as secluded as I'd hoped if I could still see the main square so clearly. I took a few more steps for added safety, and then I dropped to the ground. I was alone.

I had filed a piece of flint until it was sharp enough to carve into wood without my having to try. And then, on the back of a tree in a thick block of forest, I began making a list of all the questions I had about my life so far that no one would answer. The sun was warm on my skin as it crept through the breaks in the overgrown forest.

This was my sixteenth summer in my family's town. This late in the afternoon, after we'd been let out of our lessons, most of the kids from my generation were running around the rugged terrain just outside the city walls, closely supervised by an elder from our family, one of the original Survivors. I relished being let even an inch outside the city walls, but I savored time alone even more.

Our lessons were monotonous. We studied passages from a Bible I was sure was outdated—its version of our language sounding different from our own—and we talked extensively about the evils of the outside world. On rare occasion, we'd discuss primitive mathematics and archaic scientific principles. We did this day in and day out, five days a week, for the last ten years of my life. I remembered every word I had ever heard and every sentence I'd ever read, so repeating these ideas over and over again grated on my nerves. I hoped that I would stop aging soon. Once we stopped aging, we didn't have to go to lessons in the rotted-wood, flat-roofed room that functioned as our schoolhouse. By then our powers would be matured, our talents determined, and our futures set.

It would also be time to start building the next generation. This idea thrilled me less. From what I knew about it (at the time)— the whispers I had heard from my sisters and the quiet and polite sentiments I'd heard from Lizzie, the elder I was closest to—I knew it involved being extremely close to the boys in our generation. But I had always been unnerved by the touch of others, unable even to hug my family members without trepidation. As a Survivor, though, our fundamental principles were simple: praise God and continue our line so that we might do God's work—an arbitrary purpose that was, as of yet, undefined. And I couldn't argue with work I had been put on this Earth to do. At least, I couldn't then.

We spent our Sundays, of course, in the small, dilapidated, chapel opposite the square from where I sat. It was the first building the elders had erected when they chose this pass as their homestead over 190 years before. They were waiting for the boys in my generation—only the third generation since they had settled—to grow old enough and strong enough to build a new church that would accommodate our growing village. We had seventy-eight family members spanning three generations, and when the church was built, there were just the fourteen of them, though, if I counted correctly, Rebecca and John Surrey were already expecting their first child when they arrived in Montana.

I had been sitting quietly in the forest for some time, my list on the tree bark seeming paltry but still bolder than any words I had ever spoken aloud in my life.

My first question: *Where did we come from?*

The elders in my family believed that we had survived treacherous events that would have killed humans because God had willed us to. In our Bibles, there were stories of Abraham and Sarah welcoming a child into the world when they were each nearly 100 years old and of

Noah taking over a century to build the ark. They referred to these stories to speak of instances in which God had done this in the past. And I didn't doubt that it could happen so much that I doubted that it had. Hadn't Abraham and Noah had special relationships with their Lord, special purposes to fulfill? We lived in an isolated town with walls erected to protect us from the outside world. What purpose were we fulfilling here? And why those fourteen Survivors? Twenty-six of them had been exiled from Salem so long ago. Why hadn't God willed the other dozen of them to live? I couldn't accept it the way they could, but to say this to them was a risk I could not take.

My second question: *If the world outside is evil, should we not bring the word of God to them?*

This is one I never understood. For all the time we'd spent with Bibles, talking about God's Word, and about the evils of the outside world, why, then, did we not evangelize as the Book told us to? Like so many other hushed traditions in my family, it was illogical, conflicting directly with some of the more loving messages in our revered text. I believed, quietly, that we had reason to venture into the world outside our walls, that we needed to fulfill the purpose they were so convinced we were put here to do. I also believed that outside those walls there was a greater world.

My third question: *How do we know there are no others like us?*

The elders had always maintained, without even the slightest wavering on the matter, that we Survivors were the only ones of our kind. But they had taken it so much further than that, insisting that there were no other supernatural creatures in this world, nor had there ever been. Recently, in late night discussions with Lizzie and Sarah, elders with whom I felt close, they had told a few of us tales of how the outside world believed in creatures that God did not create. They had given us some aging copies of literature that a select few from my generation—Noah, Benjamin, and me—were allowed to read. We each got one book that, in turn, we'd end up sharing with each other. Until then, we had only ever read the Bible. Noah received a copy of Shakespeare's *Macbeth*, Benjamin got a copy of *Beowulf*, and I got a tattered, gold-lined compilation of Hesiod works including *Theogony* and *Works and Days*.

I took in the stories of mythology from the Greeks, sordid tales of creatures unlike man and unlike us, blasphemous talk of gods and idols, of violence and trickery that startled me. Lizzie and Sarah wanted us to know that, outside our walls, man sometimes believed in such ridiculous creatures. They had been satisfied enough to believe that all those legends of superhuman creatures across history and in every culture big and small were just examples of tall tales and idolatry. They admitted it was possible that we had ancestors like ourselves, but they believed that, because so many of them had ended up together in such a small town at such a precise time—Salem, at the height of the witch trials—and had escaped unscathed, then they must surely be the last remaining Survivors of their kind. Always surviving. This belief is the reason we never sought out another name for ourselves. To my family, surviving that first winter had made them Survivors in every sense of the word—they had endured, and they had been given a chance to continue the line of this rare species. This made them believe that God had chosen them, those fourteen children, to save this unique breed of immortal superhuman. That belief developed our basic principles.

My fourth and final question: *How could we be destroyed?*

This was, of course, the darkest of my questions. Though I was reticent to admit it, I wanted to know how to die. This did not seem like an outrageous idea to me since death appeared to be universal across all cultures except for ours. So I believed that surely we could die, and I wanted to know how it could be done.

Needless to say, since their exile in 1692, not a single Survivor had done anything other than...survive. The youngest member of my family when I was sixteen was a three-year-old girl named Anna. The oldest member, by birth year, was Lizzie, who looked about eighteen years of age but had been born in 1670, over 210 years before. And we accepted this as normal: We expected immortality from each new addition to the family, we assumed invincibility against all circumstances.

But I had wondered. What if this ever got out of hand? What if ever there were an evil Survivor, a force that needed to be stopped? What would we do then if none of us knew how to destroy the other? I understood destruction as a necessary evil in God's world. My family saw it as a blessing that we had been so peaceful—with the world around us and among ourselves—in all our years that no one had ever had to find out what destruction was like. We never saw eye-to-eye on this.

I had eventually given up with the flint and rested against the tree, absorbing the quiet surroundings. Abruptly, I heard footsteps— rather, the unmistakable whir of a young Survivor running at top speed. In a fraction of a second, Noah was sitting beside me on the ground, his hair windblown and his clothes disheveled from the run.

"Hi, Sadie," he said, his chest heaving a little bit. Noah had not yet stopped aging, so he was capable of getting tired or short of breath with exertion. He was precisely my age and, though I wasn't especially close to anyone in my generation, I guess I was closest to him. Noah and I had grown up hearing the story about two babies being born at exactly the same time at a stressful moment in our history. Other than that, no one ever talked about the process of childbirth. And they never let on who belonged to whom.

"Hi, Noah," I said, perturbed that my time alone had ended.

He lay back on the twigs and leaves on the ground and tried to catch his breath. Noah looked exactly like Lizzie. His hair and eyes were fair, his skin rosy. I don't know whether Lizzie was still having children when Noah and I were born, but if she was, it meant that she was definitely his mother, which hurt me a lot to realize that meant she wasn't mine. Then he eyed the tree I was leaning against. "Interesting list," he said, nodding toward the carvings.

I shrugged. "You wouldn't say anything about it, right?" I asked.

"Wouldn't dream of it," he said. "You have enough trouble, as I see it."

I shrugged again. "I don't think it counts as trouble that I don't have an active power yet. That can't possibly be something I've done wrong."

"I didn't say it was. I just know they're giving you a hard time about it. I wouldn't want to make it any harder on you than it already is, especially since John seems to be the most concerned about it," he said. He sat up and pulled his knees to his chest, his posture mirroring my own. I felt some ambivalence in the air between us, and then I could sense some tension. This extra sense had been developing lately, and I believed it was the beginning of my so-called powers. But it didn't seem to fit with any of the powers of any of the original elders, so I had yet to mention my budding talent to anyone. It was useful in learning some things, though, like how Noah was starting to envision a life where he and I would end up together in some form or fashion or how the tension in that moment stemmed from his concern over what he perceived as my rebellion. I couldn't place how I knew this, I just did. Unfortunately for him, these feelings became more articulate at the precise time at which I had decided I would, one day, live outside the walls of this city. I had realized that this would mean going against part of the purpose of this family (rebelling, as he feared), and I knew I could not bring anyone into it with me. In essence, at sixteen years of age of what was destined to be a very long life, I had decided that I would spend my life alone.

For better or for worse, I had kept that promise. I regretted it every day.

2

MATRIMONY

It was nearly midnight when I got back to my hotel. Walking across the parking lot, I took a deep breath and surveyed the empty streets around me. There wasn't a soul in sight. The night had cooled off some, and a gentle breeze had picked up, so the air was more bearable than it had been.

I passed through the hotel without seeing anyone. When I got to my room, I felt relief immediately. Despite how I hated being alone as often as I was, it had been so much work trying to be normal all day! I had never spent this much time with so many people, and I was exhausted. I kicked off my shoes and dropped my bag on the dresser. I shook out of my cocktail dress and into a camisole. I collapsed on the bed.

For a few fleeting moments, I was still. My breathing was even, and my eyes were contentedly closed. I didn't risk doing any of the normal things I typically did—taking off my makeup, putting my cell phone on its charger, even turning out the lights—for fear that I would wake myself out of this trance. It was so quiet in my head. I wondered if maybe I was already asleep and hadn't realized it yet since the feeling was so foreign.

I waited patiently as my muscles began to relax one by one. I saw faint images dance across my mind. I was relishing the peace. I had not been this close to sleep since the last time I actually had slept, over two months before.

I wasn't sure how long I laid there, but it was long enough that I felt the impulse to move. I resisted, confident that stillness would bring me closer to my goal. I felt the rhythm of my breath increase, interrupting the peace, and I squeezed my eyes closed even tighter. But it was too late. My body had fought off the sleep. I sighed and opened my eyes. Every inch of me was instantly awake. *Damn it.* I just wanted to sleep. It wasn't so much to ask.

I glanced at the clock: 12:49 AM. My little almost-sleep had lasted less than an hour. I stood up out of bed and began my nighttime routine. After I had completed my rituals—removing my makeup, washing my face, brushing my teeth and my hair—I grabbed a worn book and soft-covered Moleskine journal from my bag and lay on the bed. I rubbed my smooth thumb along the gold-tipped pages of the ancient book, letting my mind wander. The book was my copy of Hesiod, which I pulled out most nights, and the notebook had become the place where I kept information that I needed to let out of my head— lists of things like human tendencies or my family members' powers, important or striking memories from my life, notes and anecdotes from my travels.

I reread my old questions. It was brash, cutting them into a tree where others could see them. But Noah had come behind me and touched his palm to the wood, searing the bark until there was no sign of my carving. He didn't care for my impetuous attitude, but instead of confronting me, he spent the 141 years I had known him quietly righting my wrongs.

I picked up Hesiod and thumbed through the worn pages of the mythology book, the sensation of the linen pages against my old skin the only thing anchoring me to this world. The rest of me was lost in memories.

As I held the tattered book Lizzie had given me nearly thirteen decades before against my chest, I remembered clearly the time in my life when I convinced myself that love was impossible. My eyes stared at the bland white ceiling over the hotel bed. Why was I trying now—128 years after making the decision to stay alone—to partner up? I still hadn't understood my pull to be with Todd. I didn't even particularly like him—evident now by how little I missed him, though I did miss the companionship. I remembered from *Theogony* that Eros—desire—had come to being entirely out of nothing. As if it couldn't be controlled. As if none of us—god or man in Hesiod's version, Survivor or man in my own—could avoid it.

Lying on the hotel bed, I realized that I was envisioning a life with Cole Hardwick, violating the terms of my own treaty with the world.

I suppose I counted love as a human thing. Somehow I had convinced myself that finding love while trying to pass for a human was acceptable, a part of the persona I was creating. But it was foolish to relegate these desires to some form of humanity as if love had never been a part of the world I came from. Survivors fell in love, too—albeit rarely—and lived even longer, more dedicated lives together when they did mate, so it was strange that I would choose now to think about love, neck deep in a culture practically defined by the uncertainty of affairs and divorce. At least where I came from things were straightforward. Either you loved each other forever or you never loved each other at all. There was not this kind of security among humans. Todd had been the first painful reminder of that. I hoped that Cole Hardwick wouldn't be the second. Only, in so many other ways, I did.

I closed my eyes again and brought the book closer to my face, inhaling its antique smell. What was I doing here? Why was I trying so hard? I opened my eyes again, gently separating the pages of the book. On the inside cover, it was dated beneath the typeface in elegant blackletter: 1696. Once I was in the outside world and could Google the witch trials in Salem, I had figured out that this was after the elders had been exiled. I thought about how they had lied and told us that they had never left those city walls until the twentieth century. But they couldn't resist the outside world. We had that in common, the elders and I. The difference between us was that they had come back.

This book that I had in my own possession since 1881 was proof of their lies, one of many lies I had already discovered, part of a multitude I likely hadn't.

I wondered how much they knew about the outside world. When Lizzie gave me this book that summer over 130 years ago, did she know of the Civil War that had raged two decades earlier, of democracy, of the abolition of slavery? Did she know of westward expansion, or even of the Revolutionary War? Had she ever heard the words *The United States of America?*

I wanted to ask her these things, but I'd never get the chance. I sighed heavily, thinking of Lizzie, missing her. She was the only one I ever missed. But, painfully, I knew I was never going to see her again. I had run from my family, broken their hearts, spit on their traditions—all because I wanted to be a human. I was still a Survivor, but I was likely dead to them.

When my cell phone started playing Chopin at 9:45 AM, what seemed like an eternity had passed.

"Hey, gorgeous," Corrina's voice cooed over the phone.

"Hey, bride," I said. "How's the best day of your life going so far?"

"It's going okay," she said. "It would be better if you were here instead of twenty-five middle-aged women from my family who are poking and prodding me and trying to give me wedding night advice." She laughed. I knew she wasn't kidding, though.

"Want me to come over?" I asked. "I will neither poke nor prod, and I surely have no wedding night advice to give," I said. "Scout's honor." As I said that last line, I wondered where I had picked that up. I knew what it meant, but I had no context for it.

"Would you really brave it? There are so many people here!" she said, stressed. It was clear, even over the phone, that she really needed me to come but didn't want to come out and ask because she knew how I felt about being around a lot of people. Though I was using my talents to know this for sure, I could have guessed it just by knowing my best friend.

"I'd brave anything for you," I said. I meant that. She smiled, I could tell. She also swallowed to hold back tears. I realized her emotions were running high. It was, after all, her wedding day. "Do I need to bring anything?" I asked.

"Hmm," she said. "I wonder if... Hold on, Sadie."

"Okay," I said, not able to tell clearly what was going through her mind. I couldn't read things through the phone as well as I could in person. I didn't realize how much I relied on context and other kinds of communication to supplement what I could read from people until I was on a phone and cut off from my other senses. With the phone pressed between my shoulder and my ear, I walked around my room making sure I had everything ready for the day. I slid into my favorite worn pair of Citizen jeans, pulled on the low-backed strapless bra I needed for my bridesmaid dress, and layered a Tory Burch tunic over it. I slid into a worn pair of Rainbow flip-flops, and grabbed my giant Fendi Spy bag. I hoped, daily, that no one noticed that I learned to dress half from *Vogue* and half from the girls at Corrina's school. I ran my fingers through my hair, dabbed pale lip gloss on my lips, and was ready to go by the time Corrina got back to the phone.

"Play along," she breathed, almost too quietly for a normal person to hear.

"What?" I asked.

"Have you eaten breakfast yet, Sadie?" she asked, her voice louder and brighter now.

"Oh, I'm good..." I began, but Corrina cut me off.

"Oh, you haven't? I've got some downtime here before we have to go to the salon. But we just ate here, so we can't feed you. If you don't *mind* picking me up, though, I can totally go with you to get something to eat," Corrina said.

I finally understood and laughed. "Oh good, because I'm so starving and I couldn't possibly find something to eat in this whole town by myself," I said.

"You sure you don't mind having to come out here to get me?" she said.

"Of course not, Corrina." I was giggling. She had just clicked me onto speakerphone. "I don't mind at all. I never get to see you, so I want some serious Rina/Sadie bonding time." Corrina said, "Aww" and a few other female voices I didn't recognize echoed.

"Now, Sadie, you listen here," I heard Corrina's mother's voice. "Go find one of the boys staying at the hotel and tell them where y'all are going for breakfast. Tell them to make sure Felix does not go anywhere near there! He cannot see Corrina today, or we will call off the wedding, do you hear me?" Corrina sighed in the background, and I laughed.

"Will do," I said. "Rina, I'll be there in about ten minutes. I'm already dressed. I just need to find a boy."

"Wonderful. Cole is in room 322. You could try that," she said, pushing her agenda. I rolled my eyes. "Tell him to keep Felix away from Finney's."

"Got it. Thanks," I said. "See you soon."

Grabbing the hanging bag with my dress in it, my giant tote bag full of shoes and other things I might need at the wedding, I threw the Spy bag over my shoulder and hauled out the door. Cole's room was one floor down, and I took the stairs so I could move more quickly. I didn't know how long Corrina would last.

I found room 322 and took a deep breath before I rapped twice on the door. A few moments later, it flew open. A very nice-smelling, clean, and still dripping-wet Cole was standing in front of me with only a towel wrapped around his tanned waist. With all my social anxiety, I had seriously underestimated the shape he was in; his body was phenomenally fit. He was gorgeous. He looked as surprised to see me standing at his door as I must have looked to see him half naked.

"Well, hello," he said, his voice pleasant, almost cocky.

"I have a message for you," I said as soon as I regained my faculties. Just like the night before, I couldn't get a read on him. It was so frustrating.

"Oh?" he said. With one hand holding his towel—what I hoped was firmly—in place, and the other on the open door, he still managed to relax his posture and lean against the doorframe. He was flirting! Reading ability or no reading ability, he was definitely flirting.

"Corrina and I are going to breakfast," I said.

"I see your attempts to claim her for yourself will never cease," he joked. "Will you stand up and object at the wedding, or will you draw the line at that?"

His joke brought me back to the night before. I smiled, suddenly lighthearted. "I suppose I will let Felix have her," I said. "We're going to a place called Finney's," I said. "You're supposed to make sure that Felix goes nowhere near it so they don't see each other. This is your job. I leave it in your capable hands."

"Wait just a minute, sweetheart," he cooed. *Sweetheart?* "I thought Finney's was a lunch place."

"I've never heard of it. For all I know, it could be a karaoke bar, but it's where Corrina told me to keep Felix from going. And, by default, it's where Corrina's mom told me to tell you to keep Felix from going. Now can I go get the bride?"

"I suppose," he said. He shook his head a little to clear the hair from his eyes. Then he dragged one of his hands through his saturated sandy brown locks. It was an absent-minded mannerism I'd seen him do a couple of times already.

"All right then," I said, turning to go.

"Wait," he said, reaching out to my arm. I had already turned to walk away, so I couldn't see but wondered earnestly whether it was the towel or the door he had let go of to catch me. I wasn't sure which I was hoping for. "If you're going to play bride's-right-hand today, and you came to me to control where Fefe goes, thereby sort of making me groom's-right-hand, have you just made it so that we can't possibly see each other all day?" he asked. I hadn't thought of it that way. I hadn't thought of it any way.

"Perhaps. Or," I said, throwing him a bone, "maybe I made each of us the point person for our respective teams. That way no one talks to the opposite team except through us. So I may just have made it so that we're going to see each other all day, no matter how much we wish we could avoid each other," I joked. I was smiling broadly now. I couldn't help it. He had roped me in.

"Really?" he said. His voice actually cracked.

"Maybe," I said, deciding not to commit. It was the safest way. (How the humans were rubbing off on me!) I realized then that he was still holding my arm. He realized it at the same moment I did and dropped his hand.

"Well, see you soon then," he said.

"Not if I see you first," I said as I had already made it several doors away from his. I didn't have to turn around to know that he watched me walk away until I was out of sight.

I pulled up to Corrina's about five minutes later. There were as many cars as there were the day before, but I didn't recognize many of them apart from Corrina's parents' cars. I took this to mean that none of the bridal party was here, and I wondered how they'd feel about that when we showed up together at hair and makeup. I didn't care. Corrina had called me to save her, and that was all that mattered.

Corrina was already out the door. "You're going to bring all the stuff, right, Mom?" she yelled to her mother, who was standing in the doorway as she came bounding down the walkway.

"We've got it. Have fun. And don't see Felix, no matter what you do!" her mom warned. Corrina plopped down in my passenger seat, but her mom was still talking. I rolled down the window. "Hi Sadie!" she waved. "You take care of her!" she yelled as I started to back out, waving back at her.

"Oh, thank God," Corrina said as we drove out of sight.

"That bad?" I laughed.

"Worse, probably. Literally my grandmother trying to talk to me about things to keep in mind now that we'll be trying to get pregnant," she laughed. My stomach tightened into knots. The idea of pregnancy—human or otherwise—terrified me more than any topic I could think of.

"Oh, man." I forced out a laugh. "So where to?" I asked.

"Can we just go hide in your hotel?" she asked. "Unless you really want food, then we can go wherever. But if you aren't hungry we can wait and get milkshakes at Finney's later when we go get our hair done."

"Sounds like a plan," I said, and drove the few blocks back to my hotel. "I did warn Cole to warn Felix not to come near there if his life depended on it."

"Did you say it just like that?" she asked, laughing.

"Scarier," I said. She laughed again. I loved Corrina like this. She was so calm, so relaxed, and she was just so happy. It was easy to be around her.

"I bet you could be scary if you wanted to be," she said, her face a little more serious now. I felt some odd sensations from her just then. Like she wanted to ask me something but was afraid to. I couldn't tell what, just that she wanted answers. That was a vibe I had never gotten from Corrina before.

"How so?" I asked, taking the bait so I could have a little longer to get a read on her.

"I just bet, for all your meekness, you have a sharper edge to you," she said. I replayed the last few seconds of the conversation in my head. Weren't we just laughing?

"Oh, I bet not. It's hard to be edgy when you're so awkward. You can be creepy, yes, but not actually scary," I said, now sidestepping whatever it was she had going through her mind. I wanted to get back to safer waters. She shrugged and appeared to let it go.

Corrina and I ended up spending an hour in my hotel room before we went to Finney's. She had asked a lot of questions about Cole and me. I realized that she and Felix had wanted very badly for Cole and me to connect on a serious level. This wasn't about this weekend; this was about getting us together for real. I wasn't sure how I felt about that, but it didn't matter because I had spent most of the sleepless night reminding myself of reasons I should be alone.

As predicted, when Corrina and I arrived together to get our hair and makeup done with the rest of the bridesmaids, we were greeted with a chorus of cross thoughts and jealousy. Why was I the special one? They had all known her for longer. They should have been the ones she spent her wedding day with. I was happy, for Corrina's sake, that she couldn't tell what the girls thought the way I could. It would have ruined her perfect mood.

Corrina's early evening wedding went beautifully. The bridal party looked beautiful, walked down the aisle slowly, and undershone Corrina, who looked stunning in a floor length cream-colored ball gown with a train half the length of the aisle. Each bridesmaid wore a dress Corrina had had designed to flatter each of us, all in a surprisingly pretty orange silk. Mine was closely fitted to my body, cut to my knee. It scooped off my shoulders and across my collarbones in the front and dipped so low in the back that it was almost backless. The dress sat so far down the curve of my shoulders that it had to be held in place by double-sided tape, but it had well-tailored, super long sleeves. I had never asked, but Corrina knew. Another reason I loved her.

Cole and I had ended up spending a lot of the day together. Whenever anyone from his camp needed something from ours, we were the go-betweens. This worked out surprisingly well for me since I didn't feel the need to touch up or primp after my makeup and hair were done for me, and it worked out for Cole, I guessed, because he wanted to spend time with me. When we were relaxed during the day, I had no trouble reading his emotions. If I stayed focused on my reading—instead of on those clear blue eyes—I did fine. I knew what he was thinking, how confident he felt, how he couldn't wait for this to be him. I tuned out a little then, to give him some privacy. As my readings on people were becoming clearer, I was going to have to learn how to control them so I didn't overstep my bounds. It's not like I had asked permission to feel their innermost feelings and know their innermost thoughts.

At the reception, I was never alone. Either I was tending to Corrina—filling her glass, primping the dress, or touching up her lipstick—or I was side-by-side with Cole. His feelings for me were growing so quickly that it seemed impossible. I wasn't even saying that much. I wasn't sure how his affection could swell at such a pace.

When we sat down to dinner at the reception, I was not surprised to see Cole's name next to mine once again. I was a little sad to realize that I would have to eat again, though. It wasn't something I did often, particularly this much food in so little time. I felt like I might burst open.

Several of Corrina's family members incorrectly assumed that Cole and I were together. How obvious the affection between us—however imbalanced—must be if complete strangers were reading our interactions as romantic! After the third person said something, I stopped correcting them. I could feel a strong satisfaction from Cole when he noticed this, but I was just tired of correcting people. It was easier to be what they expected. That had been my philosophy on being human since the day I started passing for one.

At random points in the evening, I was glad that he did not leave me alone to brave the sea of people on my own. He was being protective. And I was grateful.

After we watched Corrina and Felix dance their first dance, Corrina's father spin her around, and Felix dance with his mother, a surprisingly large number of people sauntered onto the dance floor. They were playing music a couple might actually dance to together— not the hideous stuff I'd heard at parties that evoked in young people the need to rub up against each other no matter where they were, and with no regard for the company they were in. This made it less scary to accept when Cole asked me to dance, but it didn't take away all my fears.

As he took my hand and guided me onto the dance floor, his hand felt warm, and I realized that, after days of unbearable heat, I had finally started to cool off. I was worried that he had noticed my odd temperature, but if he had, he didn't react to it or even think about it enough for me to be able to sense it. He walked me to the very center of the dance floor and turned to face me. I stood a few inches away and gently placed one hand on his shoulder, the other hand in his. He lightly held my waist, and looked at me very carefully for a moment before we began, as if he were trying to decide something. Just then, he wrapped his arm more tightly around me, pulling me toward him so the length of his body matched up with mine. His hand was high enough and my dress was cut low enough on my back that he was touching the bare skin. I felt a tingling like an electric shock travel through his warm hands as they lay on my cool skin. No one had ever touched me there before.

"You aren't nervous, are you?" he asked, speaking directly into my ear. His heartbeat was more elevated than it had been all day. His breathing was uneven. He was nervous.

"Why would I be nervous in the company of such a perfect gentleman?" I asked. I took the high road to remind him that's what I expected him to be. He smiled, and I felt a surge of pride float off of him. All Cole Hardwick wanted to be was a perfect gentleman. "Ah, a good point you make, mademoiselle," he said as he spun me out and then pulled me even closer to him. Our hands were in each other's now, resting against his chest. I felt comfortable being so close to him, which was an entirely new feeling.

I wondered what it would be like to spend a lot of time with Cole Hardwick, to be this close to him every day, to be able to dance with him in his kitchen or someplace equally ridiculous. I looked up at him and studied his face. I'm sure he noticed, but he looked away as if to let me have my moment to look at him. I even wondered what his lips felt like. They seemed soft, inviting. He smiled, as if to emphasize my subject of study.

"What?" he finally said.

"Just looking," I said. That might have been a little too honest. Surely I could have come up with something better?

"Are we allowed to look?" he asked. "'Cause I've been dying to get another look at those gorgeous violet eyes of yours."

I bit my lip, a little embarrassed. "I suppose looking is within the realm of appropriate behavior, yes," I said. He met my gaze. I hated these moments. I had been in them so many times with Todd. Struggling desperately to figure out what was okay and what wasn't—letting Sadie-the-twenty-one-year-old-in-a-new-millennium act normally while not forgetting that I was still Sadie-who-was-born-in-1867. My boundaries were not as set in stone as I once thought, but I still didn't want to disappoint myself. And I didn't want to disappoint Cole Hardwick either. He was still looking directly into my eyes, and I softened under the warmth of his baby blues.

"What is it?" he asked, genuinely concerned.

"Nothing," I said. He didn't buy it. His brow creased the same way it had last night when I wouldn't answer his questions. He wanted to know what thought I had that made me look away. I'd give him something close enough. "Just thinking about how much harder this weekend would have been if you hadn't been here," I said. It was true. In spite of my awkwardness, I was having fun. His eyes seared into mine, connecting. I suddenly thought I should dance with Cole for longer. I thought I should stay here with him all night. I thought I should let myself—and my inhibitions—go.

Cole seemed to sense that my guard was momentarily down because he took this opportunity to lean in and press his lips ever so slightly against my forehead. It was very endearing. I could feel the heat of his lips on my forehead for several minutes after he pulled them away.

I was sad about this. The heat of his lips against my cool forehead made our differences so apparent. He was one thing; I was another. More importantly, he was a human, and I was not. Like oil and water, we would never mix.

When I leaned my head back to see his whole face more clearly, I knew exactly what he was thinking about. He saw my small, heart-shaped mouth and longed for exactly the same thing I did when I watched his soft lips part. He hesitated for just one moment—I felt it—and it was just long enough for me to come to my senses. I released my body from him. He looked confused, as I would have been too.

This was so much harder than I anticipated! But I would always be something else entirely, something Cole Hardwick would never understand. I was a Survivor. But with Cole, I remembered why I wanted mortality so badly.

This was so troubling. My chest tightened. As we stood a foot apart on the dance floor, I put a palm to my forehead and squeezed my eyes tight, trying to make all of it go away. I spun on my heels and walked away. I could feel him close behind me.

What did I do wrong? I heard.

"Nothing," I said, turning to face him.

"Nothing what?" he said.

"You..." I began, but stopped. I played the last few seconds over again in my head. He hadn't said anything. But I heard him; I was certain of it. Was I hallucinating now, too?

"Sadie, what's wrong? What did I do?" he asked. Okay, that time he spoke. I was sure of it. But I had heard him as clearly as that a few seconds before.

"You didn't do anything," I finally stammered, massaging my forehead. My jaw was clenched, residual tension traveling up my head.

"Then what was that?" he demanded. He was very stern, but I knew—somehow—that he wasn't angry. He was only concerned. What I thought of his actions meant a lot to him. He wanted to be seen in a good light. *I'm trying to respect you, Sadie. I know what Felix said, but you seemed so into it out there, but now...*

There it was again. I could hear that. I knew for a fact that I heard those words.

"It's me. I just have a lot going on," I said.

"Is this about your ex-boyfriend?" he asked, almost wincing. He knew more than I thought he did.

"No!" I snapped, more harshly than I intended. He thought I was going crazy because of some stupid human *drama*. I wished it was that simple. "I'm sorry," I finally managed to say. His eyes were so hurt. The one human male on the planet who thought the way I did, who seemed to understand my boundaries, who put me at ease was standing in front of me, and I had managed to hurt him because of things beyond our control. Because I couldn't adapt to a world designed by humans. Because I could never be who or what he wanted me to be. I was a mess.

"Sadie, I just..." he began. I put my finger to his lips, silencing him. He recoiled a little bit, probably at how cold my finger was in the air-conditioned space. I exhaled and closed my eyes. I needed a minute to think. When I opened them again, he was still looking at me with the same perplexed look on his face. I dropped my icy finger from his lips, grabbed his hand and steered us through the crowded reception to the back doors of the mansion. His thoughts were coming faster now, feelings of anticipation and hesitation alternating with a protectiveness that surprised me.

We cleared the door and passed the small crowd around those who had gathered at outside tables before we were standing in the open space behind the mansion. It was nearly nine o'clock at night, but the sun had just set. The sky was a bright navy, covered in diamonds. There was no moon.

"Cole, I like you," I said. *Really?* I thought. "And I'm not great at liking people. I'm not great at being social. I'm not very good at a lot of things." He tilted his head slightly to one side, excited by my first sentence, confused by the rest. "But I have a lot of stuff going on in my life right now, stuff I can't and don't want to explain," I said quickly. It wasn't true, though. Really, it was just my life. I was completely incapable of balancing my own insecurities, fears, and differences with my insane desire to be like a human. I couldn't make it work, and I needed an out. Abruptly, I said, "And even if I didn't have all that, tonight I'm getting in my car and driving back to Nashville, and tomorrow I'm sure you'll fly out to New York, and then we'll be operating on our different planes anyway. So it doesn't matter that I like you. It doesn't matter that you've been so wonderful this weekend. There are too many complications. I'm sorry. I shouldn't have egged you on the way I did." I took a deep breath, glad that I got all that off my chest.

"Are you finished?" he asked. I nodded. "Good," he said. "Sadie, there was no egging. I visited Corrina and Felix months ago and somehow we got to talking about you. The things they said...man, I couldn't get you off my mind, and I had never even met you. I'm tired of all the girls I usually date. I'm tired of the stupid stuff they expect. I just wanted to meet you and get to know you. No pressure. I, more than anyone, was shocked that it was going as well as it was. I never expected you to actually like me back. I wasn't expecting anything. I just thought it'd be nice to know you. So even with all your crazy life stuff, you think that much would be okay? You think I can be one of the people who knows you?" he asked.

I thought about it for a moment. It seemed like a reasonable request. After all, there weren't many people who knew me, and even those who did didn't know me particularly well. I could have another friend, another person like Corrina in my life, maybe. That wouldn't be so bad. And that way no one needed each other, and no one would hurt when the other had to leave.

"That sounds fair," I said.

He smiled, relieved. "Good," he said. "Now, I'm guessing we need to get back in there to throw some birdseed or something like that because the happy couple should be making their exit any minute now." He put his hand on my back and guided me toward the party inside.

We were getting closer to the back door when he spoke again, "Are you really leaving tonight?" he asked.

"I was planning on it," I said, half-lying.

"Why the rush?" he asked.

Because I'm terrified. And when I get scared, I run, I thought. "Not sure," I said. "I just need to get back to get some things done, I guess."

"Oh," he frowned.

We reached the back door, and he opened it and stepped back, holding it for me. Felix and Corrina were nearing the front door as others were hurrying out ahead of them. We reached them just in time for Corrina to give me a giant hug, her feet lifting off the ground. Felix and Cole hugged. Felix squeezed my hand affectionately, and Cole kissed Corrina on the cheek. More of the bridal party had gathered around us to say goodbye, and then we filed out the door so Corrina and Felix could make their exit. After the happy couple was in their limo and down the block, Cole spun around to face me.

"You're going now, aren't you?" he asked, his disappointment clear.

"It would seem so," I said, coolly.

"I had a fantastic time," he said. "And I hope if your life stuff calms down so we can talk again soon. I got your number from Corrina. I hope that's okay."

I smiled. "That would be nice," I said, ambivalence in my head. It wasn't that I didn't mean the words as I said them, but talking to him would likely make it difficult to stay away from him.

He put one hand lightly on my arm, leaned in, and kissed my cheek. I swallowed hard when I felt the surge of heat his lips left on my cheekbone.

"Thanks for everything," he said.

"Ditto," I said, and I walked away. I retrieved my keys and bag and then quietly departed out the back to my car without any more goodbyes.

I put the keys in the ignition, and pulled out of the lot behind the mansion smoothly. I went back to my hotel and changed out of the dress and back into the jeans and tunic I had on earlier. I packed up the remaining things in my room and checked out, leaving the man at the desk with a quizzical look on his face as I departed at ten o'clock at night.

My tires found the way back to the highway that had brought me here, the pavement cooler in the dark. I drove out of the city limits of Tupelo, my Mercedes 63 AMG engine a powerful purr against the quiet surroundings, and disappeared into the night.

3
OTHER

At the pace I was driving, I would make it back to Nashville in less than three hours. The roads were nearly empty, so I sped across them, cutting through the night air at speeds unsafe for the average driver.

I felt freer on the road, and being away from Cole made it easier to focus. He had an uncanny ability to cloud my judgment and my senses—a dangerous combination. I needed my nonhuman side to be in control at all times so I wouldn't slip up and expose myself, or, worse, hurt someone.

The streets of Nashville were not as quiet as the roads in Tupelo had been. It was, after all, Saturday night. I pulled off West End Avenue into the Hutton Hotel a little after one in the morning. Ever since Corrina had left Nashville the year before, I had been trying new places to stay when I returned to Nashville from each of my trips. When I had returned from South America earlier in the year, I had found the new Hutton open, and its east-facing penthouse had become my new home base. As I drove up, Sean, the overnight valet, greeted me.

"Welcome back, Ms. Matthau," he said. I had noticed that all the employees knew my name. I appreciated them for that. It made me feel like I was coming back to a home instead of a hotel.

"Hi, Sean. I've got luggage. I just got back from a trip," I said, popping the trunk.

"I'll bring them up," he said, flashing me a smile. He was flirting, of course, but in a polite, socially acceptable way. I knew the real reason he'd see to bringing the bags up himself was for the tip I would give him. I kept a stash of twenties and fifties inside the side table in the foyer of my suite. I arbitrarily chose which to give when. It made everyone here like me a little more.

In the lobby, I was again greeted by name by every member of the graveyard shift skeleton crew. I liked the Hutton's main lobby. It looked less like a hotel lobby and more like an upscale living room. It added to the charade that this was my home.

"Welcome back, Ms. Matthau. Anything you need brought up to you?" Veronica, a small, round woman with thick black-rimmed glasses asked as I made my way toward the elevators.

"Pillows?" I said, imagining barricading myself into the bed on all sides. I longed to be able to sleep.

"How many?" she asked, scurrying behind me to match my long stride.

"Lots," I said, smiling as I reached out and pressed the elevator button.

"Certainly, Ms. Matthau," Veronica said as she backed away.

The hallway on the top floor was silent. I trod lightly, sensing that others were sleeping. I was relieved when I opened the door to my large suite and felt cold air rush over me. The housekeeping staff had left the air on as low as it would go, no doubt something they noticed I did. It was a small comfort they provided, and I was grateful for it. Some members of the staff were intrigued by me, but others felt a certain amount of pity toward me. They all wondered why I was alone, and why someone so young seemed to have no family or even friends. This wasn't an uncommon thing for people to wonder about me.

I went into the wet bar. Though I never needed to eat or drink anything, I often liked to drink water. It was soothing to be cooled from the inside.

There was a knock on my door. I sensed the feelings from the other side of the door: anticipation. It was Sean with my luggage.

"Here you go, Ms. Matthau," he said, bringing each piece in and setting them down in my bedroom.

"Thanks, Sean," I said, backing out of his way so he could do his job. "You know," I said, "you can call me Sadie." He had to be a few years older than I was in human terms. Surely I didn't need the title.

He smiled. "Sweet of you to offer, but boss's rules," he said shrugging. I nodded. "All set," he said and headed for the door.

I already had the bill in my hand. "Thanks again," I said, slipping a fifty into his palm. His heartbeat picked up a little bit. I sensed he needed the money.

Veronica came and went with the pillows, thanking me profusely for my generous tip. I understood that the way people reacted to the sort of money I threw around was something that should alarm me or at least encourage me to change my habits. Instead, I liked bringing them joy. Money was a means to an end to me—a way to live my life without being tied down to many human constraints. It didn't bring me joy despite the fun I had with it. It didn't relieve any stress. But it always did that for other people when I tipped them, so it was a habit I'd never break.

I turned out all the lights and slipped into my most comfortable clothes. I barricaded myself in with pillows so that every inch of my lean frame was supported. I was dying to sleep. It seemed cruel that I, who had limitless time on Earth, would be the one who didn't have to—and couldn't—sleep. The irony was not lost on me.

I worked hard to still my breathing. But just like the night before, it was no use. After a while, I sat up, pushing pillows aside so I could crawl out of bed. I flipped on the lights and sauntered around the penthouse, trying to decide what to do. I had spent so much time anticipating the wedding that now that it was over and I had a monotonous eternity to look forward to, I wasn't sure what to do with myself.

I settled on going for a run. It was about 3:00 AM, which was tricky on a Nashville Saturday night. There were still enough people milling around the streets that it was impossible to run in the city like I wanted to. I decided to drive to the Natchez Trace and run there. It would be pitch black and deserted, perfect for discretion. I'd be able to run as far as I wanted, as fast as I wanted, and no one would be there to see me.

I slipped into the kind of clothes I often saw humans wear to exercise—this puzzled me because I could run in anything—and made my way back downstairs to the lobby. I sensed the suspicious feelings coming from the staff as I passed by them, and I tried to block out the negative thoughts.

The tail end of the 444-mile Natchez Trace Parkway was a straight shot down West End. After driving painfully slowly on deserted city streets, I finally saw the old neon sign for the Loveless Café, the last landmark before I merged onto the Trace. The ramp for it was marked with a road sign I had seen nowhere else: "No Commercial Vehicles of Any Kind."

I drove around the twisting road lazily. As expected, I couldn't see or sense another soul. A few miles in, I stopped in a small parking area where there were other cars—they belonged to campers, I was sure—and got out of the car. I slipped off my shoes and left them in the car—the bottoms of my feet were the only soles tough enough to endure the speed at which I ran. I secured my car key remote in the tiny pocket in the back of my running pants and took off.

The mild night air whipped past me, cool on my skin. The moon had risen since I was at the wedding nearly six hours before, and now the waxing moonlight coated the world around me so that it seemed to glow faintly. I ran for twenty minutes at my top speed and then twenty more at a slower pace. When I hit the Alabama state line, over a hundred miles southeast of where I started, I turned around and headed back to Nashville.

Just past the sign for the exit at Waynesboro, I heard the humming. It was distant, but it was clear. Suddenly, I felt thick curtains of fear hanging in the air, so far away that they only dusted against my skin. As I got closer, the fear swallowed me the way the sea swallows rocks.

I came to an overpass on the Trace and stopped, the humming ringing loudly in my ears now. It was below me. I followed the sounds and moved closer to the edge of the bridge, looking for the source. I looked down—it was about a sixty-foot drop to the ground below. I decided I could jump it. I wanted to be closer. This, I understood, was completely adverse to the typical reaction of a woman alone in the middle of the night. Had I possessed any human instincts at all, I would have run away as quickly as I could. But I didn't have human instincts. Instead, I was a girl who could tempt fate, who wondered just how much I could endure before being a Survivor became less an inborn trait and more a condition easily changed. I tested my limits, quietly searching for the way to meet my end.

I launched myself over the rails and landed hard in thick brush. The humming quieted for a moment—the source of it had heard me— but then it picked up again. I was close enough to hear voices now. There were people here. I felt their feelings, too. I was wrapped up in a cocoon of terror and anxiety, of anger, and—very distinctly—of homicidal rage. I stayed low to the ground, shielded by the wild grass, but I couldn't see what was happening from there. There was a tall line of trees above the road. Though I knew I might get caught, I would see better from there. I decided not to consider the consequences just yet. Crouching low, I launched myself over the roadway and into the trees. Neither of them saw me.

From my new perch, I saw a girl with black hair and brown skin lying on the ground and sobbing hysterically. She had to be the source of the fear and anxiety I felt. The rage came from the rugged man on top of her—ripe with alcohol and filth. He was screaming at the girl to shut up, holding her down by her neck. She was fighting him with all her strength, and I could tell by his feelings that he was intent on killing her.

I knew I had to do something. I surely could fight off this man; I was more powerful than any human alive. But if the man fought back, I'd have to defend myself, and I would hurt him. I would do what it took to save this innocent life, but there'd be some kind of fallout I didn't know how to deal with. I had never actually attacked a human, but I could imagine the mess.

In a moment, I had examined all the angles, formed a game plan, and was ready to pounce. But out of the darkness, another body—a guy about my age, maybe even younger—appeared. His skin was pale and glowed in the moonlight, much like my own, but his features were dark. He looked menacing. I couldn't tell where he came from. My senses were momentarily blinded by his presence, and though the impairment quickly remedied, I could get no read on him specifically.

"Clarence, you get off of her!" the young man yelled, his voice unclouded by the Southern drawl of the older man. He charged at the drunkard. The girl screamed, her fear upgraded to full blown terror as the young man ripped Clarence off her and flung him off the road and into the tree line below me. The young man sped off into the woods toward the old man's hunching form, his figure a blur as he moved at speeds that rivaled—if not exceeded—my own. I blinked twice, sure I had seen it incorrectly.

I could see the men from my place in the trees, but I had to remember that my original goal was to save the girl. She was shaking on the ground, clearly in shock. I was torn. I so wanted to see *what* this younger man was, but I was scared for the girl, too. I dropped to the ground next to her. She screamed when she saw me. I put my finger to my lips to silence her, grabbed her up in a swift motion, and sprinted as fast as I could toward the town. In the few seconds I had her in my arms, I drowned in her terror, her disbelief, and her gratitude for these strangers who had come between her and death. I set her down gently in front of a 24-hour McDonald's with two police cars parked out front, and before she had time to react at all, I sprinted back to where I had been, hoping I hadn't missed seeing anything too important.

I had to ask myself why I was running back. My goal had been to save the girl, and having ensured she made it to safety, my part in this was over. But I couldn't pull myself away from seeing what the young man would do. I made it back to the tree line and watched from behind a low branch dangerously close to the men. The old man was standing against the trunk of a giant oak, struggling as if he were bound though I could see nothing holding him.

The rage I had sensed earlier still hung in the air, but it was evaporating as the old man struggled against the invisible chains. The young man paced with intent, seeming to calculate his next move. I knew the old man was going to die. I struggled over whether to get involved. It seemed like an opportunity for me. Morbidly, the danger in this situation was an incentive to get involved. I wanted to find my breaking point. But I willed myself to stay still. Painfully, I understood these urges meant that I was as eager to die in reality as I was in the abstract. The old man yelled, a gurgling, painful sound erupting from his throat. Unable to turn away, my eyes were glued to the scene.

Then the young man growled. I gasped at the sound—it was the kind that came from an angry lion, not a human being. The young man thrust his arms out toward Clarence, and he began to writhe in pain. His legs twisted underneath him and went limp but he remained upright. The younger man pressed his wrists together with his palms fanned out. When he twisted his hands, the assailant let out a cry. He was gasping for breath. I could feel his pain.

"Clarence, Clarence, Clarence," the young man said, a mocking tone in his voice. "Why didn't you believe me?" His question was clearly rhetorical. The assailant could not answer, overcome with his pain. "I told you that was your last shot. I swore if you touched a hair on another girl's head, I'd kill you. I offer every man a chance to change, Clarence. A chance to make his peace with God. But you didn't do that, did you? You thought I wouldn't find you here, but here I am, keeping my promise." He began to pace back and forth again. His body looked almost relaxed. Apparently, it took no effort for him to restrain the old man this way. "If you'd listened to me, I wouldn't have to do this."

The assailant choked out a laugh. He was trying to be defiant, scoffing at the young man's abilities, attempting to look brave in the face of death, I suppose. Laughing, though, was not the right thing to do. It angered the young man considerably.

He raised his left hand and held it as if he were pressing the old man against the tree though he was several feet away from him. The man's chest became pinned to the tree. Then he raised his right hand and clenched his fist, crushing the man's windpipe. I felt my own throat close as he did this.

The young man was taking Clarence's life without even touching him. I was shocked. It wasn't the violence or the power that was unbelievable. I had seen comparable talent before—Mary and Catherine, two of the elders of my family, were capable of the same thing. What stunned me was that this was not a human capability. As I watched this young man torture the assailant, I understood that, without a doubt, I had met an Other.

Another one like me.

The assailant was almost entirely drained of life when the young man stepped toward him and hissed, "When you get up there to Saint Peter, before he sends you to Hell, tell him Mark Winter sent you." And just like that, the man's head twisted in a way it shouldn't be able to, and a loud snap resounded in the air. I felt a sharp pain in my own neck and then all the tension released. Mark Winter's hands fell to his sides, and Clarence slumped to the ground. He was dead.

Mark Winter took a few steps back, scrubbed his face with his hands, roughed up his hair, and walked deeper into the woods he had come out of. I was just about to start breathing again when I saw him pause and turn back to the heap on the ground. With a wave of his hand, the body burst into flames. When he was satisfied, another wave put the fire out. Then he stepped backward and dissolved into the blackness.

What the hell had just happened? It was clear Mark Winter was not a human. I had only spent three years among humans, but I knew there was no way a human could do that.

If it weren't impossible, I would have sworn Mark Winter was a Survivor.

My mind was in turmoil as I raced back up the Trace. Once I was back inside the car, I clenched my fists and screamed at the top of my lungs. I slammed my fist down on the center console and the trim cracked. I instantly regretted it. I had a soft spot for—and a real attachment to—nice cars, specifically my own. I started the engine, slammed it into gear, and hit the road, speeding uncontrollably back out of the Trace, barely keeping my wide tires on the narrow pavement. I had to get it together.

I was angry that I had seen this. My family had spent over three centuries insisting that, in this world, there were humans and there was our family of Survivors, and that was it. They didn't believe in all matter of supernatural creatures, and they refused to acknowledge even the possibility that there were others like us. Our onliness was at the heart of our beliefs. But what I had seen Mark Winter do tonight made it clear that they were wrong. Or they were lying.

And what was more, Mark Winter was violent. In the 319 years since they were exiled from Salem, no Survivor had ever turned on a human or on one another. But Mark Winter had gone to a deserted stretch of road outside a small town in Tennessee in the middle of the night to hunt down a human. He may have been justified, having killed evil and to save an innocent life, but we had never been destructive in any way, so I perceived him as a threat.

And he was so much more powerful than any of us! Not only was he one of us, he was better at it than we were. There were people in my family who could do the things that he could do, but each of them could only do one. All of us were fast, all of us had superhuman strength, and all of us—except for me—had exactly one power. But Mark Winter had several completely separate powers. And where did his talents come from? Each Survivor had a power that roughly related back to one of the fourteen elders. Of course, my situation was a little fuzzier. My family had whispered that my talents were underdeveloped, and this made them pity me. But I never minded that my powers weren't kinetic or active ones, that I couldn't throw a brother or sister across a field or freeze things in midair. My strengths related to knowing people, to knowing the world around me, and I much preferred that.

It was just one more way that I was unlike them. And so, of course, it would be me who had seen this. I was the only one who had ever left my family, and now I was the only one who knew that there were Mark Winters out there, that there were more like us. Didn't they need to know that? What if Mark Winter's violence was not limited to vigilante justice but included, instead, all matters of hunting and attack? What if he found my family? What if he knew something that I did not about how we could be killed? What if he belonged to a larger family like I did? What if they were all violent? What if they massacred my family?

I screamed inside my car again. I suddenly understood I had to warn them. And to warn them, I would have to go to back.

But I couldn't go back! It took me 141 years to leave the first time. I couldn't get stuck back there again! They might not even let me back inside the city walls. And, more than likely, they wouldn't listen to me.

I had to slow down when I got to an area with other cars. It was hard to do, though. I had trouble controlling my mind and body when I got this upset. I peeled my fingers off the steering wheel so I didn't break straight through it.

When I pulled back into the Hutton around 5 AM, my forehead was so tense it felt like I had a headache. A headache! We weren't supposed to feel pain! This was ridiculous.

I climbed out of the car, and Sean looked at me warily. "Are you okay, Ms. Matthau?" he asked.

I nodded, my palm to my forehead. "I'm fine," I said, dismissing him. He looked very concerned. I must have looked as bad as I felt.

In the lobby, I ran into Veronica and the morning chef. "Ms. Matthau?" she asked, peeling away from her conversation with the chef, though he followed her. "Are you all right?"

"I'm fine," I said again, having to concentrate on walking at a human pace to the elevator.

"You don't look okay," she said. Nervous that she had over-stepped her bounds, she added, "Ma'am."

"Really fine," I repeated, waiting impatiently for the elevator to arrive.

"Maybe you need some sleep," she said.

"I would love that, believe me," I said under my breath.

"Perhaps we could send you up some breakfast? Maybe you'd feel better if you ate," the chef suggested.

I shook my head. "I'm really okay. I'm going to lie down," I said. Finally, the elevator doors opened. The chef whispered to Veronica that he'd send me a tray in a few hours. I admired them for trying to take care of me, and I wistfully longed that my troubles and rough nights could be soothed like other people's by sleep and a good meal.

Back in my room, I didn't know what to do. I paced back and forth across the suite, trying to piece together what I had seen, and tried to think of a way I could avoid telling my family about Mark Winter. What if he was not a threat? What if he was just a quiet young guy—albeit an extraordinary one—who traveled alone like I did? Would that be so bad?

But he wasn't like me. He was more powerful, and it terrified me. His face when he killed that man, his movements, his lack of hesitation—it made me think that Mark Winter was a monster.

I was going out of my mind. I took a shower to relieve my muscles and to clean off the dirt from hiding in the brush and climbing the trees. I closed my eyes and let the water fall over me. I convinced myself that I could pretend that nothing had happened.

So that's what I did. When I got out of the shower, I got dressed and sat at my computer. I spent almost all my alone time researching. The Internet was my single favorite thing about the human world. I loved the immediacy of it, the expanse of it. There were so few questions I couldn't answer with my computer at my fingertips. After a few months, I got pretty skilled at circumventing the unpleasant and offensive material that so often appeared at random. I remember being worried the first time I had realized that even very young humans used the Internet. I thought of all the horrific things I had seen inadvertently, and I wondered if children had seen the same things by accident. It rubbed me the wrong way that a culture would put offensive things out for all to see when they knew innocent eyes might happen upon them. I considered that carelessness, that irreverence for innocence, a telling characteristic about humans. I had scribbled this on the list I was keeping in my Moleskine journal.

My research was centered on one thing: mythological creatures. I had been shocked to learn that almost every culture on the planet had legends about creatures that haunted or graced their kind at one point or another in their history. Many of the creatures in cultures around the world were close to human form, and a lot of them had similar traits that my kind had: apparent invincibility, super speed, heightened senses, and immortality, to name a few. I took an interest.

I had started researching mythology as soon as I started living among humans. I had a background in it, already having become so familiar with Hesiod's works from ancient Greece. I was trying to uncover where these creatures came from, and, morbidly, how they could be destroyed. We would need to know how to stop one of our kind, even if it meant destroying them. And, I hated to admit, on a personal level, I wanted to know that there was a way to end this—my pain, my existence—if I ever wanted to. I hadn't lied when I told Cole Hardwick that, more than anything, I wanted mortality.

I had left off my research on a creature called the *Abarimon*. I was unsure what culture the legend belonged to, having found conflicting information. I knew only that the *Abarimons* were thought to live in isolation in the Himalayas. They sounded more like my family than any of the others I had read about. They were very similar to humans (though they had backward feet and we did not), but they were too strong for humans to hunt, and they had super speed. I hadn't yet discovered their origins or how they could be killed. My only clue was the belief that the air in the valleys where they lived was so special that any other air would be like poison to their lungs. Apparently, it was a defense mechanism, a way to protect their kind by not letting any of them ever leave the valley. This frustrated me. They sounded a *lot* like my family.

I combed through literally thousands of Web pages about these and similar creatures, but I didn't find any more information, so I added *Abarimons* to my list and moved on.

I combed through historical mythology sites for hours, looking for a new lead. But I was getting nowhere. It had been my experience that primary sources were the most descriptive, and there was no better way to get information than by talking to the people who believed the myths themselves. In the last three years, I had set foot on six continents looking for answers to my questions. I was hungry for knowledge, and desperately trying to get it any place I could. Now I was looking for a new creature to pursue. I had returned from my most recent trip—to Australia, to speak with several Aboriginal tribes—about a month ago. I hadn't planned another trip because I was taking a break for Corrina's wedding, and I planned to spend time with Todd. But that was quashed the day after I returned when we ate lunch at that stupid pizza joint I'd never go to again.

Todd was the last place I wanted my mind to go. I had officially lost my concentration now. I checked my Twitter page—yes, I had Twitter. It was a strangely satisfying human thing I had picked up on. Corrina had complained that she never knew where I was, so I added a Twitter application to my iPhone and every time I set foot in a new country, I'd tweet about it, much to Corrina's delight. I saw that Corrina had been my most recent update. *@Corrinarina: Excited to FINALLY be Mrs. Felix Williams!!!!* I decided not to say anything. I mean, what would I say? *@SadiesTravels: Watched a guy kill some psycho tonight. Wonder if he's a superhuman freak like I am...*

I snapped my laptop shut. The quiet of the room was startling.

Then there was a knock on the door, even more startling because I hadn't sensed anything. I assumed it was Veronica or someone from the restaurant with breakfast, so I opened the door without even looking through the peephole.

So when I found myself face-to-face with Mark Winter, I was, to say the least, taken aback.

I blinked several times to make sure he was really there. I still couldn't sense anything from him. He was completely still. His shoulders were hunched and he was leaning toward me. His eyes were angry.

And he was wearing the same leather motorcycle jacket I'd seen him wearing hours before, which stood out because it was so out of place for June in Tennessee. I wondered if he, too, hadn't slept since his midnight murder.

I'm not sure how long we stood there in silence before I decided he should come inside. I finally turned sideways and gestured for him to pass. It was at least ten solid seconds before he took a step into the foyer—trying to decide if he wanted to come in, I assumed. When he passed me, I noticed his movements were fluid—more like mine than a human's, only even more graceful. He crossed the room and looked out the windows at the city.

I waited for him to sit or speak or just do *something*, but he was silent and stood aloof in the corner. Admittedly, his posture had relaxed.

"How did you..." I began, but just then he faced me, his stare enough to kill the words in my throat.

"You saw it all, didn't you?" he asked.

"If you're referring to you saving that girl's life, then yes," I said, deciding not to vilify him.

"You aren't scared of me? Aren't terrified that I followed you and waited to get you alone?" he asked. It seemed he was trying to intimidate me.

I laughed, stifling this. "Why would I be scared? What are you going to do to me?" I asked. He looked perplexed.

"You saw what I did to that man. You know what I could do to you, how I could snap your neck and end your life by just imagining it.

That doesn't scare you, *Sadie?*" He said my name in a hiss, another scare tactic. He was being so dramatic! It wasn't surprising he knew my name considering what else he could do.

Two could play that game. "No, Mark, it doesn't," I said to provoke him. And snap my neck? Really? Did my spine even have a purpose? Would it even break? And what if it did? I'd already decided that the worst-case scenario was that he would actually hurt me in some way, which would only bring me closer to my goal.

He narrowed his eyes and cocked his head to one side. Then he took several careful steps toward me. I didn't react. He put his hand out, as he had before he hurt the man, and he closed the distance between us. He stopped when his hand was inches from my chest, and looked into my eyes. I stayed still and kept my expression neutral. Blind without my powers, I couldn't tell what he was doing.

He very gently placed his hand against my sternum. His skin was colder than mine. He held it there for several seconds, and then his eyes widened. I assumed the absence of a heartbeat startled him.

"What are you?" he asked. I could hear the panic in his voice.

"I was hoping to ask you the same question," I said.

He backed up. "You aren't human. Of course! That's how I missed you last night. I couldn't even tell you were there until it was too late."

"And you aren't human either," I said. "Clearly."

"You're a tracker, aren't you?" he asked. I had been called this before, but I was not sure it was the most accurate term.

"I follow my senses where they lead me," I said.

His face was angry again. "Well don't track me," he hissed again. He stepped toward me quickly, his mouth almost grazing my ear. "If you value the lives of the ones you've left behind, you won't," he said. I shivered. Now *my* eyes widened. Was he speaking about my family?

And with that, he left, the door closed behind him.

My head was spinning. I guessed that, since he found me, he was a tracker, too. That meant that his powers were more extensive than I had even seen. He could start fires, control people's bodies from a distance, and he could track. And something he was doing kept me completely out of his mind and blocked his feelings.

But above all, he had just threatened my family, so now I didn't have a choice. I had to warn the other Survivors. I had to go back.

4
NOMAD

I spent most of the day with my eyes closed, sitting on the bed, trying to focus on anything I could about Mark Winter. I had never encountered someone I could not read, though clearly Mark was unlike all the humans I had spent my time with for the last three years. I could always sense my family, though, so why couldn't I sense Mark? After he walked out the door of my penthouse, it was as if he'd evaporated.

I needed to be able to see inside his mind because, despite his warnings, I planned to track him. First, I would tell my family of his existence, and then I hoped to provide them with his whereabouts. Then I would go, my part in this ended. But I had to find a way to sense him first.

In the meantime, I got ready for my journey. I had to pack everything I owned, which was not quite the feat it would be for a typical person. Despite using Nashville as home base for some time, I was still a nomad. I didn't travel as lightly as the typical nomad, true, but I could fit everything I owned into a large set of Hartmann luggage that fit in my car. I had never had the desire to stay in one place, and I had used up the resources in Nashville, so it was time to move on. Now that Corrina was gone, I had no ties here.

The next morning I gathered all my things and called for a bellman. I took the elevator down to the lobby and asked a young girl behind the desk to get the general manager so I could speak with her. I explained that it was time for me to leave, and assured her that they had done all they could have to make this hotel feel like home to me. I meant every word I said.

She shook my hand and thanked me graciously for my patronage. She inscribed her private cell phone number on a business card and encouraged me to use it should I need anything. I handed her a stack of sealed envelopes, each marked with a hotel employee's name. I had made a mental map of everyone I had met here, and I put at least a $50 bill into each envelope, along with a thank you. For those I perceived needed or deserved more, I threw in a little extra.

The valet pulled my car around, and the bellhops loaded my luggage, puzzle-pieced to fit in my trunk. I thanked them graciously, pulled out of the lot back onto West End, turned left, and quickly merged onto I-40. I wove my way out of Nashville's giant roundabout of interstates, onto I-65 northbound, then I-24 westward, and finally left the city in the rearview mirror. As I saw the last of the city's skyline fade away, my stomach caught. It had been the only human home I'd ever had, and now this was it for Nashville and me.

I had 2,000 miles to think. I spent the first 500 miles trying to convince myself there was a reasonable explanation for Mark Winter's powers so I could turn my car around. Was there a technology I wasn't familiar with, perhaps? Was he a superhero like those I saw in comic books and in movies? Couldn't he be something other than what I was? Because if he were like us, then that would mean there were others roaming the earth, and I refused to believe that. Why would the elders lie about that?

But secrecy wasn't out of character. My family had kept us isolated in a walled city in Montana, and had banned the reading of books from the outside except for evolving translations of the Bible (with the exceptions of the books Lizzie and Sarah had given Noah, Ben, and me). And why? They never offered explanations for the isolation.

As I chased the sunset near Sioux Falls, South Dakota, thirteen hours after I had said goodbye to Nashville, I began to get nervous.

When I had walked out the gates of my family's settlement in Montana three years earlier, I had never envisioned returning. I found it difficult to imagine what it would be like.

This felt very much like I was returning for good, a white flag flying above my head. But that was not my intention. I had made it out once, and I was desperate not to jeopardize my freedom. I could never go back to the life I had lived there. I was returning this time out of loyalty, and temporarily.

My family began as fourteen children, abandoned and left for dead in the frozen hell that was now South Dakota. They had retreated to the northern Rockies in Montana, and by some miracle, they had survived. They had lived together under a God they knew existed—who else could have saved them?—and taught each new generation dedication to God, to family, and to the land. But ours was not a family held together only by bloodlines. We cared about where we came from and where we were headed. We were dedicated to each other, to our purpose. In the human world, I had heard of only one culture that had a virtue approximating this: It was part of ancient Confucian ideals, set in ancient China as far back as the fifth century BC. They were the only ones who valued the notion enough to name it. They called it filial piety. These ideals were rooted in the same sentiments on which our family philosophy was based.

Our undying bond to one another may have begun because we were a species all our own, because we needed each other in a world where we were different, or because our still-living ancestors believed so heavily in the Puritan doctrine they had been born into. Whatever it was, it was effective. No one ever strayed from the family. At least, no one but me.

My leaving meant that going back to warn them might be useless. I had left without even a goodbye, adding insult to injury. In their eyes, I had stomped all over our values. I couldn't imagine they would welcome me back. I wondered if, initially, they thought it was a temporary exile. Did they wait for me to come back? How many sunrises and sunsets passed when they thought, *Any day now...*?

I knew they would paint me forever as someone who threatened all our family was based on, as a causeless rebel and a disloyal child. I hated that this was my legacy. I guess that by now my family had translated my actions into a cautionary tale for all of the youth, telling them stories of how God had smited me when I left, and possibly insinuating I hadn't made it past the pastures around the city walls. They'd tell them how I was a slave of Satan now, condemned to an eternity of servitude and torture. And some of them might believe that.

This made it difficult to drive toward Montana, but I still had the ache in my bones. Something inside of me *belonged* to that place, and I had to go back to make sure my family would be protected from threats outside their walls. I knew there could be threats. If there were more Mark Winters out there, if he had come from a family like mine, and if they had any of the human urges to conquer or reign, then we were in trouble. And Mark's threat had been clear. He knew who we were, likely even where we were. And I couldn't set my family up to be massacred by a war-hungry version of ourselves out there. I had to protect them. In a strange way, because I had left, I was the only one who could.

I wasn't sure what to expect, but I was certain it wouldn't be pleasant. If they had told all the young ones I had been destroyed, they would be frustrated that I proved them wrong by bursting through the city gates. Not wanting to pour salt in the wound, I planned to arrive as quietly as possible. It didn't matter, though. I assumed that Hannah, our original elder, either had already seen me coming, or she would soon enough. And as soon as the first one of them spotted me, all 164 would swarm the center of our village at supernatural speed to see what the cat had dragged in. I squirmed as I thought about the attention.

I intended to stop at a small bed and breakfast about a ten or fifteen mile run as the crow flies from the city walls so I could stow my car and luggage and prepare. I had dressed comfortably for the trip, so I would change into more appropriate clothes to meet my family again. There were rules and expectations, and I would be respectful of them, within reason. My sleeves would touch my hands (they always did), and my legs would be covered. My chest and back would be covered up to my neck. I would not wear makeup. But I wasn't going to wear a dress, nor pull my hair back and tuck it into a bun or a braid. I'd be covered, but I had every intention of walking into the village in a modest top and jeans, hair free flowing as I always wore it. They were going to hear me out and take me as I was or not at all. I had no plans to return to the life they had made for us, and I refused to give anyone a moment's doubt about that by dressing the part. I had already broken all the rules anyway.

It was around noon on Tuesday when I wound down to the two-lane Montana highway that hugged the coast of the deep blue Swan Lake in the northwest part of the state. As I passed the small houses and sparse landmarks inside the town of Swan Lake, I felt tension. I hadn't seen this road, this water, this place since I'd gone.

The Laughing Horse Lodge, a tiny bed and breakfast of eight rooms, which I had passed on my way out, was exactly where I remembered it to be. My tires crunched against the gravel as I pulled into the rocky drive. I had been able to go very fast, headlights off, through the winding highways during the night, but in daylight I had to drive at legal speeds. Despite that, I had traveled over 2,000 miles in the twenty-seven hours since I had left Nashville. It still hadn't felt like adequate time to prepare.

I got a room key and drove my car around to the side of the small building. I pulled a small suitcase from my car and put it in my room. The rest I'd leave in the car in the likely case of a necessary quick exit. I changed into my favorite pair of jeans, layering a long-sleeved T-shirt under a hoodie. I would be warm in the mild air of the Montana summer, but I wanted the hoodie to blur the edges of my figure. I pulled on socks and tied on a pair of Pumas. I examined myself in the mirror, satisfied that the only skin showing was my face and part of my hands and neck.

I tucked the room key into my jeans pocket, slid my cell phone into my back pocket, and picked up a bag containing things I'd bought that my family would need if they believed me.

I strapped the bag to myself and walked around back. Behind the lodge, there was hardly anything. The landscape blurred quickly into mountainside, which blurred even faster into nothingness. Confident no one was looking or could even see me between the tall trees, I took off running. If I ran at my absolute fastest pace—about three miles a minute if I sprinted across even terrain—I was not likely to be seen by humans. There was a fair chance I wouldn't pass anyone on the way there anyway.

After five or ten minutes, I slowed my pace to a walk among the tall trees some 6,000 feet up the isolated mountainside. I was close now, and I suddenly realized I had never decided on how I wanted to enter the city. I walked more slowly as the forest grew so dense that it completely obscured the light of the sky. I was also stalling.

Ahead, I could see bright sunshine filtering in at the edge of a clearing, obliterating the darkness created by the forestation. Just beyond where the sun shone in, maybe fifty yards further up the mountain, I knew, were the gates to my family's city. Approaching the clearing but still hidden by the heavy shade of the trees, I quickly tried to devise a plan.

But once I was in full view of the gate, coated in glaring sunlight, I knew my decision had been made for me. Spread out like a wall in front of the village were the furrowed brows, folded arms, and narrowed eyes of all fourteen original Survivors.

Memoir

Bigfork, Montana
Autumn 1985

One fall, I was permitted to leave our village for a short trip for supplies. I had gone with two of the elders, Anne and Jane, and another girl from my generation, Beth. It was the first time I had ever left the city walls except for running around in the green mountain pasture right outside of town. This time I was really, truly *leaving*. Beth and I were the first two aside from the elders ever permitted to go.

Anne and Jane were making their biannual trip for clothing, and Beth and I had begged for so long to be able to go outside the walls that the elders had finally complied.

Some time in the early twentieth century, several of the elders explored the world outside. They liberally took the step of dressing like humans while they were walking among them, and they brought back clothes for us all to wear. Every few years, there would be more trips by only a select few, and we would get more updated. They did this with technology, too, to an extent. In the 1980s, they brought the first computers, and they spoke of the existence of phones for years but never brought any to us. There were no lines running to our town, and we had no one to call. We had radios as early as the 1950s, but they kept them away from us, likely shielding us from news of the world outside. Soon we had record players, and cassette players, and, eventually, we would even get CD players. Of course, none of that compares to the amazement of the iPod. It turns out that "60 gigabytes" of music...whatever that means...is a *lot*. I don't think I could ever live without it now.

So when they let us out, Jane, Anne, Beth, and I visited Bigfork, a town about a hundred-mile run from our family's settlement. Its

most noticeable feature was its location, nestled on the northeast corner of Flathead Lake, just above the Flathead Indian Reservation.
There wasn't too much there in the eighties, but there was enough for
me. The majority of the town concentrated on Electric Avenue, a tiny
main street comprised mostly of small cafés, tourist shops, and art galleries. I wandered the town's narrow sidewalks, astonished by the tiny
galleries that dotted the lane. I stopped in front of several and just
stared, completely in awe. I had never seen anything so beautiful. I had
never known art.

Beth had been unimpressed by the town and by the art, and she
ventured away from me to join Jane and Anne. I continued, walking in
each storefront, overwhelmed by all I saw. Then I came across the
bookstore. It was at the bottom corner of an old two-story building
with aging dark shingles and a glass front that touched Electric Avenue. The building backed up directly to a cove of Flathead Lake, with
an alley on one side so that you could see the lake from the front of the
building. The glass door had an OPEN sign hanging in it, and the
numbers 480 printed over the doorframe, tucked under a narrow over-
hang. At eye level, hand-painted words read:

Books & Ladders

Inside, the shop was small but lined floor to ceiling and wall-to-
wall with books. I had read only four books in my life—the Bible, the
book of Hesiod works that Lizzie had given me, Noah's copy of *Macbeth*, and Ben's old *Beowulf*. But inside this tiny shop there were
thousands of books, some tattered and some shiny and new, and each
one different. There was a standing shelf imprinted with glossy, hand-
painted words that read "New York Times Bestsellers" (now I know
what that means, but I didn't have a clue then) and there were a number of books on the stand. I chose the first one, *The Cider House
Rules*, and flipped through it, reading a few pages. I wondered if these
words were written about real people or if someone had imagined
them. It was all so foreign—even the few pages I read standing there—

but it was so intriguing. Humans were so complex! They felt things so strongly, and they had such conflicts! I sat in an old chair in the corner with the book in my hands, flipping madly through it, my eyes flashing across the words, taking them in at a supernatural pace. Twenty-five minutes later, I had read the entire book, and I was hungry for more.

Lizzie was the only one I told about the book when we returned. She listened patiently as I repeated the whole story back to her, nodding politely for me to continue through some embarrassing or confusing parts, smiling at my enthusiasm. I asked her if I could go back to the bookstore to read more. She had said the other elders wouldn't approve of what I had done, but I could tell she felt sympathetic as my enthusiasm faded quickly into disappointment. She said she would speak with Andrew about it, and, privately, they would decide. The next day, she told me they would allow it if I didn't mention my miniature vacations to anyone else. I agreed, thrilled.

I returned to the bookstore countless times after that. Lizzie had given me some bills, explaining to me how they worked, so that I could purchase some books. It was my first glimpse into the world of human procedures. I wasn't sure I understood the idea behind the money, but I tried it the next time I was there. The shopkeeper was excited by my enthusiasm for literature and hadn't seemed to mind that I sat in her store for hours every day, just reading the books. I never bothered any other customers, so she was patient and kind. But, after Lizzie gave me the money, I bought one book to take with me each night. I read those books with care, much more slowly than I stormed through the others since it had to last me all night. I always returned to the shop the next day with the book read, and offered it in trade for another used book. That first summer, I read everything from Jane Austen to Karl Marx.

That's how I learned of wars and violence I never knew existed, of other religions, of things people would fight for. I began to understand love as it applied to mortals. In some ways it was so much scarier and unpredictable than the kind of love those in my family felt for each other once they mated. Some parts of it seemed inappropriate or embarrassing, but none of it was without passion. I was confused by the feelings that came to me the first time I read a Danielle Steel novel. There were descriptions of things I hadn't imagined, and they caught me off guard nearly as much as the idea of weapons and fighting in wars had. It became clear to me that all of human life was foreign to me. All of it, a mystery.

Each book was its own experience for me, and each experience was a new feeling. I wanted to feel each of those things in my life and not just in the pages of the books. I suppose my desire to become a mortal began there.

In just a few short months in my century-and-score of living, I had learned so much about the world outside our walls. That was when I made a promise to myself that I would end up in the human world as I had always wanted to, living among them, *as* one of them, some day.

Another promise kept.

5
HOMECOMING

There was a mix of emotions radiating toward me from the elders. All of them were relieved to see me, though many of them tried to mask it.

Lizzie, Sarah, and Hannah were glad, happy and eager to hear my stories. Lizzie and I had always had a good relationship, and though I didn't know Sarah and Hannah quite as well, I knew Lizzie was close to them among the elders, so I trusted that they were good. If I had any allies here, it was these three.

Ten of them—Thomas, Jane, Rebecca, Andrew, the sisters Catherine and Mary, Joseph, Anne, James, and young William—were ambivalent, unsure whether my return was a relief or an outrage, or if forgiveness was possible, though they were unwilling to hold grudges that God would want them to pardon.

Two—Andrew and Lizzie—radiated parental love out toward me. They were the only ones. I was grateful to them both. I was pleasantly surprised to feel these things from Andrew. Perhaps he would be an ally, too.

Only one, John, had hatred directed at me. It was so strong that it was clear he wanted to make sure I felt it.

I was moving slowly, focusing my attention on them one at a time to make sure I knew who was feeling what. As I got closer, the humming in my head picked up with every step. It was different from what I usually heard, though. If the humming I heard from humans was like a diatonic scale on the piano, this sound was like someone screaming a pentatonic scale in my ear—it was foreign.

As I got close, unspoken words hit me all at once.

Clear as day, a voice screamed in my head. *Terrible ingrate. Of course she came crawling back. Even the humans wouldn't put up with such a traitor, such scum.*

Why couldn't you have dressed properly? another voice pressed.

Say something! a third voice said.

Just apologize. Apologize and never speak of it again, and our life will return to peace! another said.

I never thought I was going to see you, again. Praise God, came from the softest, sweetest of them.

I was able to hear all fourteen voices, the same ancient voices I had always known. It was like at the wedding when twice I heard Cole speak to me when he had never even opened his mouth. But this was clearer still. I scanned the line of faces, glancing at each. No one's lips moved. I was actually *hearing* what they were thinking. I was reading their minds.

I smiled in spite of myself. This did not help John's sentiments. *That little bitch is smiling?* he screamed in his head. I didn't know he knew words like that.

I was standing slightly downhill from all of them, but I was so intrigued by being able to hear their thoughts that I had completely forgotten my fear, even with all their eyes staring down at me.

Say something! one of the voices said again. It was Rebecca, John's wife. She knew his temper better than anyone. She was the most afraid for me. I obliged.

"I see you were expecting me," I said, closing the distance between us. I had assumed a very relaxed posture, my weight forward on one hip, my hands in my back pockets, my elbows out. They all shifted mentally and physically toward John, waiting for him to speak. I wondered if they had appointed him spokesman or if he had appointed himself. I could have guessed.

"Surely, child, you haven't forgotten your family's power in such a short time," John said, his tone scathing. *Child?* I scoffed in my mind. We had stopped aging at about the same point in life, and were equals as far as I was concerned.

"Oh, John," I said, speaking to him more directly and casually than I had ever in my life, "how could I forget you?"

The voices in my head spun. They didn't like the way I had addressed him.

Such disrespect! This is why we don't live among the humans! one shrieked.

Our children would never speak to us in such a disgraceful way, another hissed.

"Sadie, Sadie, Sadie," he spoke again, shaking his head. "It was bad enough that you left, but worse that you shame yourself by returning. But bringing the remnants of that vile human world with you? That's an insult we won't tolerate," he said.

"Please, I'm sure you think everything I do is an insult. What do I care?" I laughed darkly. I knew my attitude wasn't helping my cause, but I couldn't shake it. I felt irrationally angry around them, and I was on the defensive even though I hadn't intended to be.

Sadie, please, Rebecca's voice pleaded.

"Let me remind you of your transgressions, child," John hissed, charging toward me. "The way you speak to me with disrespect is reprehensible. This bag you carry with you, bringing their world in here, is intolerable. But the way you dress and the way you wear your hair like a true Jezebel, that is the real indecency. And you seem to know how you insult us, which is worse still. Perhaps if you were unable to remember your heritage, we could forgive such transgressions," he said. He brought the tips of his long fingers together. "Yes, nothing, Sadie, is as insulting as you standing here, in front of God and your elders, looking like a *human*, when you were once a Survivor."

"Am," I said.

"Pardon me?" he said, surprised.

"I *am* a Survivor. I was borne of you, raised among you, by you. And here I stand, alive and well." *Not for lack of trying,* I thought. "You may hate me, or think that Lucifer has imbedded himself in my soul, but I am a Survivor still."

John's eyes were dark with anger. I sensed that if he knew how to kill me, he would have. I threatened everything he held dear.

It was quiet for a moment, then Lizzie spoke up. "John, she may not behave the way we want our children to, but she is our family. And despite our fears, she stands here before us, apparently healthy and good-hearted. We couldn't have expected her to live among humans and not have assimilated somewhat," she said calmly. She walked toward him as she spoke, breaking their careful formation. When she said "despite our fears" she had thought clearly "despite our fears for her," censoring herself to say it in a way that didn't convey their concern over me. I assumed she had done this to appease John.

"Couldn't we?" he asked. "Couldn't we have expected that we raised her well enough that she would uphold her values, even among heathens? Couldn't we expect her to respect this family, our values, our God?" he argued.

"I do," I said carefully. I was less defensive now. The chorus of thoughts in my head had picked up, moving in favor of John's sentiments, so I quickly had to compose myself. I had to act. "I have maintained our values, though I'm sure my appearance doesn't communicate this to you. But I show no skin. I do not speak ill of our family. And I respect God still. I know His role in my life, in all of ours. I have not forgotten where I come from." John was thinking carefully about my words, trying to decide if he believed them. "And I certainly have not lost respect for this family. That's why I'm here," I said.

"So you are coming home?" Andrew asked. His voice was hopeful. He had let John lead this because he hadn't the heart to feel malice toward me for leaving. I was shocked as I pulled this thought from his mind. I wondered how many of them had felt the pull to leave at one time or another, how many of them felt it now.

I looked at the ground. "No," I said clearly. At least I was being honest from the start. Andrew's face dropped, along with the others, except Lizzie, who was the most disappointed of all of them but not at all surprised.

"Then why did you come?" Catherine spat. "Yeah!" and "Amen" rang out from several others as they joined in a chorus of support. I had never cared much for Catherine. I had never liked either of the sisters, but she had always been bitter toward me. We had never been cordial. But now others were feeling what she was feeling. I was losing support fast.

"I came to warn you," I said.

John laughed. "Oh, child. You think you know so much, but your ignorance would astound you," he said. "Have you forgotten Hannah's powers? That she can see our future, and foresee dangers? And what dangers are there for Survivors? We can only be hurt in our hearts, and you are the first to have committed this sin against us. What could you possibly warn us about?" he prodded.

I had not expected this to come up so soon. I thought we'd sit around the long oval table in the cloisters of the chapel where they all met to talk. I thought I'd tell them quietly and calmly. I hadn't expected to speak over the wind, out in the open, not even protected by the city walls with the rest of the town on the other side of the gate listening to every word.

"She clearly has no reason for trespassing here," William said. William was so young. He had been only fourteen when he stopped aging. I was at least a head taller than him, and looked down at him, surprised.

"Is it trespassing to visit one's family? To seek fellowship? To worship together?" I asked. I hadn't necessarily envisioned sitting through a service with my family, but it was not something I would object to. It might be the only thing that would get them back on my side.

"You see, John. She has not forgotten the Lord. She knows Him still. I can feel it in my bones!" Lizzie said with enthusiasm.

"That much is true," Hannah called from her perch at the end of the line. "I have seen her in my visions. She is still a woman of God." I was winning back some support.

"Maybe we should go inside..." Andrew began.

"Silence!" John snapped, unable to tolerate their sympathy toward me any longer. His thoughts flipped through his mind so quickly I couldn't completely catch them. They were all colored with rage, though, so I got the gist. "She can fool us!" he screamed. "She can lie to any one of us. She has the devil in her!" He believed this. "You listen to me, child. Look at these, the faces of your family, one last time. You will turn around and run from this town like you did the first time you abandoned us, and you will never, never come back," he seethed. He turned his back and walked up the short hill to the gates of the city. Nine of them followed him, but Sarah and Hannah looked at me and only slowly shifted their bodies toward the gates. Andrew doubted John's decision, and Lizzie looked at me longingly, and remained still.

"There are others like us!" I cried out. Everyone froze. The quiet humming I had heard from the other side of the wall erupted into whispers and gasps.

All the elders looked at each other then at me. I expected them not to believe me, or to think I was trying to deceive him.

But to my surprise, John quietly said, "Come with us." It took me a moment to realize I would have to move my feet for this to happen. They waited until I reached them, then we walked into the city as if they were strolling...or marching me to death row. The gates closed behind us. Perhaps I should have thought twice before blindly following them.

The entire family was waiting inside the gates; they had all come to see the show. No one spoke to me when I entered the city—they only stared—but their thoughts told me the story clearly: They had been ordered not to speak to me under any circumstances. They had also been assured that the elders had had no intention of letting me inside the city walls.

Many of the older generations were appalled that I was walking the streets of their hallowed ground again. I caught Noah's eye. He look bewildered. Others of my generation and those below me had mixed feelings. Some of them were happy to see me, some of them were jealous of me.

We proceeded slowly down the main road to the church. The saunter through the streets had been intended as a parade of shame, designed to embarrass me. It hadn't worked. No one here knew how detached I was from them. It was filial piety that had brought me back here to warn my family of Mark Winter's threat. There was nothing more to it.

Down a long hallway to one side of the chapel was a row of rooms used for various purposes. At the end of the passage was a dark, wood-paneled room dug out of the ground. It had a thin window along the ceiling and only one door that faded into the woodwork once it was closed. You'd have to know where to look for it to find it. There was a long, oval table cut out of a gigantic slab of marble that was getting worn around the edges. Eighteen wooden chairs—carved when they had settled here three centuries earlier—surrounded it. I had been in this room only once, when I had taken a few things I knew I'd need before I left. Some things the family owned had great value in the world outside our walls but no significance inside of them. I was certain that they had no idea of the worth of these items, so when I stole a handful of very small things from their stash upon my departure—a sin, I admit—I didn't think anyone would notice, much less understand what I had taken from them.

We walked single-file into the room. As I crossed the threshold, I felt my senses drain and my mind go quiet. I could no longer feel anything radiating off the elders. The intensity with which I could see the world faded into what looked somewhat like normal sight. I tried to envision Corrina's mind, but I could come up with nothing. I felt panicked. Lizzie walked me to a chair at the far side of the table, her arm around my waist, and she sat to my left. Andrew sat on my other side. I faced John.

"What is it?" I asked, feeling uneasy without my powers.

"Never you mind that," Catherine said. She was enjoying my fear.

"Honestly, Cattie," Lizzie said. "The room is protected, Sadie. Your talents are stopped at the door. They'll reattach to you when we leave," she explained. I nodded quietly, more timid than I was before. I realized I hadn't noticed it the last time I was here because I had been alone. I slid my hand under the table and pressed my fingers into it. The marble gave way as my fingertips sank into the stone. I still had my strength, then. It was our individual powers that were stripped in this room.

Catherine rolled her eyes. "A pity the poor little traitor can't sense what we're feeling," she mused. Catherine and the rest of them had no idea that what I had lost was the ability to read their minds. They had assumed my powers would have remained stagnant in the time I was gone, as theirs had remained the same for over three centuries. "Ah well, she needn't her talents here. She knows we all detest her."

"Not all of us," Andrew corrected. I smiled at him.

John began to speak first, but Andrew raised a hand to silence him. He studied my expression, then slid his hands toward me, and took one of my hands in his. "You have nothing to be afraid of," he said.

I was very lucky to have him on my side. As one of the three original elders—he, Lizzie, and Hannah had been the first to evidently stop aging—Andrew was the patriarch of our family. When he asserted his rightful place, they were obliged to listen. Having been the eldest boy when they were exiled, John had taken a piece of power for himself. He more outwardly seemed to be our leader—he enforced rules, created discipline, was feared. But, still, Andrew came first. There were many in the family who never understood the distinction, but it was shockingly clear to me in that moment.

"Sadie, you said there are others like us," he said, his voice very soothing. I nodded. "Can you tell us more?"

"I saw something," I said, "something that only one of us could do." I looked around the room at the expectant eyes and began to explain.

I told them the whole story. I described in detail how Mark Winter killed the man just by willing it so, and of how he had set the body on fire. I told them about how he had come to see me in Nashville. How he warned me not to follow him. How he knew that I was not a human either. Quietly, apologetically, I shared his ominous threat against them.

They listened intently. I expected them to be outraged, concerned, even shocked, but they remained quiet, calm.

When I finished, it was silent. I squirmed in my seat.

"I have a question," Rebecca began. "Your talent, Sadie—how you can find people? What is it you feel from a creature to be able to find it again?"

I tightened my brow. This was a loaded question. I chose my words carefully, trying to find a way to answer her question honestly without explaining to them all I could do.

"I suppose it's mostly something I hear and partly something I feel. The sounds are the most unique—they make people easy to find. Sometimes there's a deep tug in my stomach, though, pulling me some way, guiding me to what I'm looking for. That part is harder to explain," I said.

"So did Mark Winter sound normal to you? Did you get the same things from him you usually get from humans? Or from us?" Rebecca asked.

"I could not feel anything from him at all," I said. Their expressions instantly grew wary.

"Is it because the filthy human world has deteriorated your powers?" John asked pointedly.

"No," I said. "I have gotten much better at reading humans," I said. That was true except for emotional moments like with Cole. "When I returned today, I found that I have an easier time reading *us*, too," I explained, counting myself among the group in front of me. A corner of Andrew's mouth turned up when I made the distinction. No matter how much I wanted to be a human, it didn't change what I was. Even I could admit that.

"Why do you think you could not feel anything from Mark Winter?" Andrew asked.

"I'm not sure," I said. "My skills are not flawless, I'll admit, but no one has ever been completely blocked from me. But Mark Winter is so tightly guarded that it feels like he isn't even really there."

Andrew spoke. "I think we must find Mark Winter. We must bring him here and ask him of his heritage and his powers. He has many talents, and it would be beneficial for us to know how he received them. It would be unwise to continue in ignorance now that we know he exists," he said. Then he turned to me. "Sadie, will you give us a moment to discuss our plan of action?"

I nodded and rose from my chair and made my way to the door quickly.

"I'll join her," Lizzie said, catching up to me, "if no one minds?" she asked, looking at Andrew.

He nodded. She opened the camouflaged door, and we stepped through it together. Once outside, the door sealed itself shut. There would be no way to get back in until someone opened it. I immediately felt clarity in my mind and my senses.

I picked up on Lizzie's thoughts and feelings. She had not imagined this reunion would ever come. When I left, I hadn't told Lizzie I was going. Her responsibility as an elder would have forced her to warn the others. This was the first time I had a chance to even partly justify my reasons or to apologize at all.

"Oh, Sadie! I can't believe you're here," she said, wrapping her strong arm around my waist and tucking her head into my shoulder. I squeezed her back.

"Did you miss me?" I asked, smiling.

"So much, my dear," she said, tightening her grasp. "I was so worried about you. We all were."

"Oh, yes, I could tell how glad John was to see me," I joked, with traces of hostility in my voice, as we emerged from the church into the fresh air.

"You're a daughter of this family. Whether we agreed with your choices or not, you are still our flesh. We didn't know what would become of you," she said.

"I'm sorry I worried you," I said, choosing my words carefully. "That was not my intention. I just had to go."

"Are we that terrible?" Lizzie asked. Her voice was light but her question serious.

"It isn't that. I wanted to know about the world out there. Humans interested me. All we care about here is procreating, building the family for whatever purpose God has in mind. I wanted something else," I said.

"I should have known the night you told me about the book you'd read in Bigfork," she said. "I guess I did, in a way." Memories flashed across Lizzie's mind. "I suppose we made a mistake letting you go," she said. I looked at her with heavy eyes as intense waves of guilt washed over me. I hadn't anticipated that she would blame herself for my leaving. "The books led you away from us," she said sadly.

"Lizzie, I hadn't lived until that day. And I didn't leave until twenty years later. If it were the books that made me go, I would have left immediately," I said, hoping this would convince her that she was not the cause of my exodus. In truth, I would have gone that first day if I had felt ready. But I waited until I had read enough to understand what I would be walking into. My twenty-five-year excursion to the bookstore in Bigfork, reading four or five books a day, meant I had read over 35,000 titles by the time I left—at least every one that ever cycled through the doors of Books and Ladders. And yet, somehow, I was still unprepared.

"What made you go, then?" Lizzie asked. I felt a bit of hope in her mind.

"I wasn't turning out to be what I was supposed to be, Lizzie. Some of the others—the elders, I mean—were getting impatient. They wanted me to mate. I could sense it. They were growing hostile because I hadn't had a child for them yet."

"And what's not what you wanted," Lizzie said. It wasn't a question.

I sighed and bit my lower lip, trying to decide what to tell her. Having children was considered more a responsibility than a choice in our family. Just before I had left, I overheard several of the elders talking about me. I was the only girl in my generation and in the generation below me who hadn't given birth to several children. They thought something was wrong with me, spoke quietly to each other about how to determine such a thing. Of course, they never entertained the possibility that I had just never done anything that could lead to having a child. And so they began making plans to experiment on me, to poke and prod until they determined just how much of a freak I really was. Then one of them asked what would happen if nothing were wrong with me, if I just hadn't gotten pregnant yet, and John had answered coolly, "Then we will see to it that she gets pregnant and has the child without any complications." I hadn't been able to believe what I was hearing. At that point, I had been planning to leave for quite some time, but that was the thing that pushed me over the edge. I left that night.

But I couldn't say that to Lizzie. I would have to soften the blow. "It isn't something I see for myself. I can't explain why," I said. Lizzie was hurt. She was a perpetual mother, care-giving her greatest strength. I sensed her dismay.

"You have no plans to marry?" she asked.

"You've never married!" I said.

"But I am not alone," she said. I gave her a surprised look. She hesitated. The elders decided early that they could not make a marriage commitment to one another for fear that they could not sustain their culture if they were committed to each other individually, especially because there were fewer men than women among the original fourteen. With Hannah and William too young to bear children, their numbers were even more strained. Given that they were convinced their purpose from God was to build this society and keep it here to-gether, these were serious concerns. I suspected it was a very difficult time for them, reconciling their supernatural circumstances with their human-life morals. It was exactly the opposite of my struggle.

In the end, Rebecca had been the first to get pregnant, by John, and he decided he couldn't bear to let her go through it alone. He asked permission to call her his wife. Sympathizing, they allowed it. The compromise was that their child had to be raised by all the elders equally. After that, no one knew who belonged to whom. No one knew their parentage, and parents weren't allowed to care for their own chil-dren until the child was old enough not to identify anyone specifically as a parent. They had done this to ensure loyalty to the whole family, and so individual immediate families wouldn't break off together. Their plan had worked.

"How's that?" I asked.

"I have Andrew," she said. Suddenly, Andrew's alliance to me made far more sense.

I smiled lovingly at Lizzie. "I'm so happy for you. It makes me feel so much better that you have someone here with you, someone who loves you so."

"And you don't want that?" she asked.

"I have never met a man I would want to be with," I said. But then a sparkling face glimmered across my mind.

Cole.

Just the idea of him—embarrassingly, I most vividly remem-bered his wet body in the towel—made my breath catch a little. I smiled, thinking of the way he dragged his hand through his wet hair, shaking it out of his eyes when it fell again. I thought about the elec-tricity I had felt when his hand had touched the bare skin of my back when we danced, when his lips had so gently pressed against my fore-head. It was a moment before I realized I had stopped breathing en-tirely.

"What is it?" Lizzie asked, trying to interpret my rapt expres-sion.

I inhaled. "Nothing," I said, trying unsuccessfully to wipe the smile off my face. I was very glad that no one in my family could feel my emotions the way I could feel theirs. I was even gladder that no one could read my mind.

"I wish you didn't have to go," she said, pulling me toward her. Her grasp was strong. I hadn't felt that strength, that security, in so long. When I hugged humans, they always felt breakable.

We heard the door inside open. Lizzie and I glided back inside and down the hallway at an exceptional pace. We were anxious to hear the elders' plan.

As I took my seat, I looked around the room, reminded of how strange the group of elders was. The one who had stopped aging first, Hannah, appeared to be only twelve years old, William not far ahead of her. The oldest, per se, was James; he hadn't stopped aging until he was sixty-two years old. Among the fourteen faces staring at me, there was a fifty-year age range in their appearances. It was hard, after living among mortals, to recognize all these faces as those of my elders, as authorities over me. The world outside our walls was influencing my perceptions more than I thought, just as they had feared.

Andrew spoke. "We want to express our sincerest gratitude, Sadie. We recognize that you did not have to come back and tell us of this development, but we are glad you did. Even though we do not understand your choice to live among mortals, we know that we have instilled in you some of what is important to this family. This was made evident by your return," he said. I had always liked Andrew, but I liked him so much more now that I knew about his love for Lizzie.

"I am still a member of this family. I'll always be a Survivor. Nothing will change that," I said.

Andrew swallowed hard. My conviction was making him emotional. "We agreed that we would like to find Mark Winter and bring him here," he said, regaining his composure.

I nodded. I had anticipated this. I had that in mind when I purchased the things I brought with me. "If I could interrupt, I'd like to show you…" I pulled the bag off my shoulder and emptied it onto the table. They all looked in wonder at what I had brought, things they had never seen. "These are satellite phones. One has a direct connection to another, if you know what code to put into them," I explained. "They work like the phones you've all seen in town, I'm sure, but there are no wires. They work over the air." I had bought five satellite phones to bring to my family, knowing full well there would be no standard cell signal where they were. I'd also brought two cell phones, the kind I saw advertised on TV for grandparents because of their simplicity. I had guessed that they would send some members of the family after Mark Winter, and by giving them satellite phones to keep in their town and cell phones for whomever they sent to look for Mark, they'd at least have a way to communicate with each other.

"How peculiar," Jane said, as she picked up one of the boxes and turned it around in her hands.

"I'll show you how to use them. That way you can talk to whoever you send after Mark," I said.

"Do you have one?" Andrew asked me.

I slid my iPhone out of my pocket and held it up. "It's a little different. It does other stuff, but it works as a phone, too," I said.

Some of them turned their heads in curiosity at what probably just looked like a shiny black block to them. "Other stuff?" Anne asked.

"Um, yeah," I said, clicking the button to make the screen come up and then unlocking it. As the phone made a tiny click sound and twenty icons appeared on the screen, many of them gasped. "It has a calendar on it," I opened the calendar and flipped through it, "And it can play music," I said. I played the last song I had been playing, a favorite of mine by The Killers. The loud electronic sound made them jump back. I looked over at their horrified expressions, and I couldn't help but laugh. "It has a camera, too. See?" I snapped a photo of Lizzie and then showed it to them. They looked at it with narrow eyes, an equal blend of confusion and startle on their faces. Deciding today would not be the day to explain the Internet to them, I shrugged and slipped it back into my pocket.

"But it is still a phone? We could reach you, too?" Andrew asked. I hesitated. I hadn't considered that.

"Um, you could," I said.

"This is perfect then," he said smiling. "Sadie, we have a monumental request of you. We understand that you might not agree to this, but we would be grateful if you did. Possibly a way for all of us to make amends?" he offered. I was very surprised. I hadn't envisioned anyone suggesting that we come to terms with each other. I had envisioned something more like the standoff at the gate than I had this.

"Anything," I said, my enthusiasm apparent. I felt my own excitement, and it surprised me. Perhaps I wasn't as detached from them as I had imagined. I could live my own life apart from them with such a clearer conscience if I knew that they didn't harbor any resentment. I could do whatever they asked of me to achieve this.

"We would like you to find Mark Winter and bring him here," Andrew said.

But I hadn't expected that. "M-m-me?" I stuttered.

"Mark lives among humans the way you do, so he might respond better to you. Maybe you could persuade him," Andrew suggested. "You know that world better than we do."

"But how would I find him?" I asked.

"You could track him, of course," Andrew said.

"But he threatened you! And he told me not to track him," I argued.

James responded, "He will not be able to hurt us. We are immortal. What harm could possibly come to a Survivor?" he scoffed. This unnerved me. I had come all this way to warn my family of danger, and they saw no danger in the situation at all.

"I'm not actually a tracker, you know," I said. I was getting anxious. "You have much better, *real* trackers. I know you do."

James stepped in. "You weren't born with that gift, true," he said. "But you are capable of so much more. Our trackers—Noah, Ben, and the younger ones—they all work only off their physical senses, tracking scents and sounds, like animals preying. But your talents exceed this.

You sense the creature itself. And you can sense from far away, can you not? We think you are more likely to locate him."

I shook my head. "I can do it from a distance, sure, but that's only if I know his mind. I couldn't get any read on Mark. There's no way to find him."

Lizzie chimed in. "You said that you were surprised you could get stronger reads on us than you could on humans," she said. "Do you sense anything different about us than you sense about people?" I thought carefully about her question. Their humming, I had noticed as soon as I walked up to the gates, had sounded entirely different then a human's.

"Yes. There is a difference," I said, still not acknowledging the existence of my new power.

"Can you use that to track him?" Andrew asked. "Can you track someone who, theoretically, would feel and sound more like a Survivor than a human? Maybe he can block you when he's standing in front of you, but whatever it is you feel from creatures—their thoughts or feelings—surely he exudes that when he is relaxed."

"I've never tried," I said. "It would take some time."

"Do what you need," Andrew said.

"Maybe I need to be away from you, from anyone who feels the same way he would," I said. This made some of them nervous; they thought I was abandoning them. "I have a place to stay in Swan Lake. I'll stay there until I figure this out. If that's okay with everyone?" I added.

"That will be fine," Andrew said. I didn't wait for anyone else's reaction.

"Thank you," I said.

"Would you mind if Lizzie went with you?" he asked. Lizzie smiled adoringly at him. Andrew was such a diplomat. He didn't believe that I would run, of course, but he saw an opportunity to keep me in his favor, satisfy the other elders who were afraid I'd abandon them again, and make Lizzie happy. He had a gift.

"I wouldn't mind at all," I said. I rose to my feet and Lizzie followed. "I'll teach you more about the cell phones tomorrow," I said as I made my way to the door, a parting promise that ensured my return.

Andrew rose and stepped close to me. He put his hands on my shoulders and looked me in the eye. "Thank you, sweet girl," he said tenderly. It was strange to hear such things coming from his baby face. He was, after all, only seventeen years old by human standards. He pressed his cool lips to my forehead. In some ways, Andrew was a father to me. He had been, at least, the closest I had ever come to one.

I said my temporary goodbyes to all of them, and Lizzie and I sprinted to the city gates, jumping over them in a bound. I hadn't wanted to talk to anyone else while I was there, and she understood that. I would avoid the attention as long as I could.

We bolted over the green mountains, westward, toward the tiny town of Swan Lake. I was running at full speed, but Lizzie almost matched my pace. She was as limber as ever.

We talked all afternoon. I told her of many of the adventures I had had out in the world. She hung on every word, asking questions about everything. I had refrained from mentioning Cole. I didn't want to get her hopes up.

At about nine o'clock, as the sun was setting, Lizzie and I walked around the lake. I had missed this part of the world. I loved how green everything was, how cool the air felt on my skin, even at this time of year. The land had an earthy, piney scent to it, too. I loved it all.

Lizzie and I were sitting on the ground and looking out at the water when my phone rang. She jumped, not knowing what it was. I pulled out the phone and laughed. "That's how you know someone wants to talk to you," I said. "It makes this sound."

I looked down at my phone. I didn't recognize the number, but the phone said it was from New York. My stomach tightened. I knew who I knew in New York.

"Hello?" I asked, trying to keep my voice even.

"Hi stranger," the voice on the other end cooed. I heard the smile. It was Cole Hardwick.

We spoke for nearly an hour as my surroundings turned dark, twilight passing into night. Lizzie had returned to the lodge to give us some privacy. I wandered through the trees near the lake as we spoke. We didn't actually talk about much; we were just spending time together on the phone. I told him I was visiting my family up north, but I didn't explain any further. Respectfully, he didn't pry. The conversation sent me spinning back to the place I had been at the wedding, his lips on my forehead, his hand on my back. I lost all the clarity I had gained since that day.

When I hung up the phone, I sat down and closed my eyes. I put my fingertips to my temples and rubbed softly. I was listening. I could feel humming from those around me—the several hundred people in and around Swan Lake. Their buzzing was all the same, save for one quiet exception. I assumed that was Lizzie.

I flew through different the sounds in my mind, skipping over the loud countermelody coming from my family's village. Out of nowhere, my senses were pulled westward. I scanned as far as I could, projecting my thoughts across the terrain, through Montana, past the narrow pass at the top of Idaho, where it turned southwest, and I sped over Portland and out to the Pacific Ocean. I had gone too far. I moved my senses back to the coastline, tracing it in my mind as I'd seen it on maps, passing by the humming of several million human minds that all sounded exactly the same. And then, in central California, I heard something distinctly different. It was nowhere near as powerful as the hum that came from my family's village, but the unique sounds were definitely there.

I tried to refocus, and I found it again. It was faint because of the distance, but it was definitely the same foreign scale I'd heard when I came upon my family earlier in the day. It had to be coming from another creature like us. It had to be coming from Mark Winter.

I rushed back to the lodge. "I found him!" I told Lizzie as I came crashing through the door.

"The man you want to marry?" she asked with obvious excitement.

"What? No! Mark Winter, I found him," I said, sliding my laptop out of its case. I pulled up a map of the California coastline, examining it from the top downward. I closed my eyes and envisioned what I had seen when I had heard the unusual humming of Mark's mind.

Then it was staring back at me from my computer screen. It was the half-moon shape of the coast I'd seen in my mind, halfway between San Francisco and Santa Barbara: the Monterey Bay. I tightened my view of the bay and found the exact place where the humming was coming from.

I knew where I had to go.

6

PACIFIC

It was dusk on Wednesday evening when I left the city walls and approached my car at the lodge. My family had thought it ridiculous that I was going to drive to California. They thought it was a waste of time, but I insisted that I would need a dependable form of transportation that was human-appropriate once I arrived to face this strange kin.

As I drove, I thought what a strange thing it was for my family to know where I was again. They knew where I was headed and that I was coming back to them. They could call my cell phone! Much had changed in the last seventy-two hours.

I was fixating on the elders' underwhelmed reaction to Mark Winter's existence. Either they had been lying to us, and they knew all along there were others out there, or they had realized it was a plausible truth. But they certainly hadn't been surprised when I told them what I had seen. They weren't afraid of him either. They sent me to this creature apparently without concern. Perhaps he was not the threat I imagined.

But as my tires rolled to a stop in Monterey, California, on Thursday afternoon, I thought, *They sent me.* What if they saw the danger this strange young man presented, and instead of risking a member of the family they cared about, they sent me because I was expendable? Maybe they were hoping to send me away forever. Maybe I was sitting at a stop light off the Pacific Coast Highway in California, about to face something they hadn't wanted anyone else to face. Maybe this was the end I had been seeking.

Realizing how close I was to Mark Winter, alone and possibly vulnerable, my thoughts began to race, my nerves surfacing. What was I driving toward?

As I rolled through the intersection in heavy traffic, I tried to calm myself down and focus. Though I didn't know the limitations of my ever-developing powers, I did know that the more emotional I was, the harder it was to use them. I needed to be calm for this meeting. That was easier said than done.

I had focused on only two things in my life outside the city walls: learning to pass for a human and finding a way to destroy my kind. The latter had always meant more to me. I had traveled, searched through academic and historical documents, stalked caves and pyramids and ruins in an attempt to find art or language that spoke of the mythological creatures of that particular culture, all to answer one question: How could you kill them?

How did the Australian Aborigines believe the Mokoi could be destroyed? Did the Romanians believe wooden stakes and holy water could kill their vampires? Could werewolves really be killed with a silver bullet through the heart? Did it only take finding the right spot on Achilles' body to kill him? Did the Mayans and Aztecs believe that dismemberment would kill anyone or any*thing*? Did the heart have to burn, or did it have to be eaten? Could modern day tales, pulled from the pages of *Twilight* or *Harry Potter*, have truth in them? Were the witches in Salem actually witches, and were they really killed by hanging?

This is all I wanted to know—how we could be destroyed. So why, as I weaved through the streets of Monterey into Pacific Grove and a greying fog, was I afraid for my life? I had been on a highbrow suicide mission for three years, never explicitly trying to kill myself, but testing theories with enough fervor that I had grisly scars all over my body, and covering my arms—something no other Survivor could claim. Why, then, was I afraid to die at the hands of this *other*? I had always sought mortality.

I stopped at the far end of Lighthouse Avenue, Pacific Grove's main street, and realized that I wasn't afraid of dying. I was afraid for my life. There was quite a distinction.

Realistically, this other wouldn't be able to kill me. But he could torture me, and though I never knew instances of other Survivors having felt pain, I knew I certainly could. I had felt it with every wound—self-inflicted and otherwise—that had left a scar. And he could capture me. And, if he did, I would lose my freedom, the very thing I cherished above all else. It was the threat of losing my freedom that was the final straw that made me leave my family, the reason I allowed myself to go at all. I understood, now, that this stupid boy could ruin my life. He could wave his hand casually and set me on fire, leave me hanging and bound, midair. He could create a literal hell for me, and I'd have no idea how to stop him.

I could sense his presence so strongly that it sounded like a fire truck siren was blaring inside my car, the same strangely-pitched humming I had heard with my family. Only it was louder.

He wasn't alone.

I sighed. I suppose it had been foolish of me to imagine that he would be. I had had romantic visions of him as a wanderer, of someone who had run from his family or had no family at all. I had thought him to be like me. But I was all wrong. He wasn't alone at all, and, so, he wasn't like me.

I followed the road that hugged the coast, passing the Asilomar Beach, and eventually turned left on one of the small streets that went inland. A beautiful home, large and elegant, sat on the crest of a rise overlooking the ocean, and I knew instantly that it was his—or that it was *theirs*. I pulled my car to the side of the road across from the house. I would walk up the long driveway.

The buzzing had become more pronounced. I sensed they were feeling anticipation. There was some hostility, too, and some fear, but mostly ambivalence. They didn't know what to think. The most important was the anticipation: It meant they had seen me coming, and so at least one of them could track in the special way I could or possibly even see the future. Maybe both.

I sat there for a few minutes trying to get my head clear and work up the guts to go in. I closed my eyes and hunched over, resting my head against the steering wheel. Behind me, I heard a car and a crescendo of the off-key buzzing. I sat up just in time to see a sleek onyx Maserati Gran Turismo S turn into the driveway of the house.

The driver's door swung open. A stiff, black Gucci boot was set firmly on the ground, and then another. Then he emerged from the car.

He was taller than Mark or me, and his shoulders were broader. His hair was a deep chocolate color and blew messily in the sea air. He smoothed it out of his face and slung the door closed behind him.

I had never seen anyone like him. He was easily more beautiful than I was, his skin a paler, creamy, aged ivory color. Its texture was like velvet. He turned his head in my direction, looking directly at me for only a split second. The movement was odd and so fast that it was obviously inhuman, but whatever he saw looking at me or my car incited a reaction in him. Of course, looking at him was inciting a reaction in me, too. Something I couldn't read flashed in his eyes, which made me nervous. Was that hate? Fear? *Attraction?* He quickly made his way into the house, spinning his car keys on his finger the whole way, and never looking back at me.

I couldn't stall any longer. I got out of my car.

I turned to the ocean. If I had a running start, I could jump into it from where I was.

Instead, I smoothed my skirt and tugged at my jacket sleeves to make sure they covered my arms, tucked my hair behind my ears, and went up the drive past the black Maserati and a glistening cypress green Bentley convertible and up to the glass façade of the long house. My breathing was shallow, and I tried in vain to slow it. I wanted to present a calm front. As I broached the front steps, I looked down one last time. *Deep breath.* I raised my hand to the doorbell, but before I could press it, the door opened.

Mark Winter stood before me in that same roughed-up motor-cycle jacket—Burberry Prorsum, I now recognized—he wore in Nashville. I realized it was something of a signature. "You can't take a warning, can you?" he said with a sigh and with far less hostility than he'd shown before. There was a hint of sarcasm in his voice—he was talking like we were friends, almost joking. And, suddenly, I couldn't remember what I had been afraid of.

But I quickly turned to the creature standing next to him, the driver of the Maserati I'd seen only minutes before. Up close, I could see he had golden-green eyes. They met mine and transfixed me. His arms were crossed on his chest—likely a deterring signal to me, but I ignored it. He cocked his head to the side to look at me and grinned deviously. I couldn't tell at all what he was feeling, but I didn't care. I just liked what *I* was feeling.

My breathing sped up, and I'm sure he could tell. I never even blinked; I would not miss a moment of looking at this face. As several moments of silence passed, he raised one thick eyebrow at me, making his whole face crease endearingly. A few loose strands of hair fell forward into his eyes, and he slicked them back. I smiled at him, hypnotized.

Mark sighed. "If we could get back to *this*," he said, waving his hand between the two of us, "at a later time, that would be excellent." I finally broke the gaze. Get back to what? I wondered.

"Are you coming?" a female voice called from inside.

"Yes," Mark answered, spinning on his heels. "By the way, Sadie, this is my brother, Everett. Everett, Sadie." Everett parted his thin, peony lips as if to speak but closed them and turned to walk inside.

Then I remembered why I was there. I bit my lip. *All* my focus had gone, and I tried to regain it, but even a glance in Everett's direction made it impossible. I could not hear their thoughts or feel their feelings.

I followed Mark into the living room. Everett walked behind me. I should have been more concerned that they had me surrounded in the narrow hallway, but I was still too ruffled to think straight.

Seven pair of eyes looked up at me, most with the same golden-green glisten Everett's had. Had Mark's eyes always looked like that, or had I just been too scared to notice in my hotel that night? Suddenly that night felt like a lifetime ago. Everything before meeting Everett thirty-eight seconds earlier felt like a different life. Those eyes! Those lips! Who *looked* like that?

I looked at him again and smiled sheepishly. He smiled back. I was mesmerized.

"This is Sadie," Mark said. His hand hovered over the small of my back and guided me toward a chair. He was being tender. Were they possibly not a threat to me? Or was this a ruse to disarm me? "Sadie, this is my mother, Adelaide," he said and gestured to a striking blonde, blue-eyed woman who looked to be in her early thirties. She nodded cordially in my direction. "And my father, Anthony," he said. Anthony, who looked about fifty, did not acknowledge me. He was a tall man of about Everett's stature and had the same deep brown hair Everett did, only his was edged in silver, and there were soft lines in his face. His eyes flickered back and forth between Everett and me suspiciously. Mark sat across from me, and Everett stood, unable to relax, or so it seemed. Was he feeling what I was feeling?

Mark continued. "This is Patrick, my oldest brother." A Mark look-alike—with the same hair and eyes as his brothers and father—lifted his hand in my direction, a careful greeting. "And his wife, Madeline." A thin, timid girl with a pallid complexion stared blankly at me from behind copper-brown hair, her eyes the strange color of my own. Her gaze was severe, made worse by the dark circles under her bright eyes and the harsh angles of her face. She was beautiful, though, even in her severity. Was she one of them, too? I wondered, but I was not in a position to ask questions of that nature. "And this little gem," he laughed, gesturing to the gorgeous blonde he had left out, "is Ginny."

Ginny laughed just then. "I'm the sister," she said, answering a question I had in my head. "No confusion." *Is she seriously wearing the Nimue suit from the Thakoon Spring/Summer runway in my living room? I could get used to this,* I heard in the same voice. Was I reading her mind? Could she read mine? That was a talent no one in my family possessed, and I had been beginning to think my abilities were unique above all others. But maybe not. Ginny was very enthusiastic, bouncing where she sat and grinning widely. She immediately reminded me of Corrina. I smiled at her, her warmth putting me at ease. Instantly I began to get a read on the feelings in the room. The relaxation helped my senses. Plus, I wasn't looking at Everett. Had I been, my focus would have been shot again.

I noticed that these creatures, like me, seemed so human. They lived in this house, in this town among mortals, and they interacted with each other like regular people. There was real affection surging between them, and their emotions were very complex. I felt a million different things pressing in on me, though I wasn't sure who in the room was feeling what—but I really hoped that muted feeling of longing was coming from Everett. I also hoped that he didn't have the talent for sensing that I did. It would give away more of me than I had already given.

There was an awkward silence while I waited for someone to speak to me. After everyone had done their best to look me up and down and pull anything from me they could, Adelaide finally spoke.

"You've come to speak with us," she said, making it clear that they were waiting on me.

"Yes," I said. I was still thinking about Everett. I shook my head quickly, trying to erase the thoughts of him from my mind. *Come on, Sadie. Focus!* I began. "I didn't know if you would be angry that I came here. Mark told me to stay away, not to track him. But my family...they wanted..."

Everett laughed, startling me. I looked at him and felt my bones go soft. I realized that *this* is what girls meant when they said they *melted.* I was pathetic. "If you stick around, you'll learn Mark only *tries* to be tough," he said. It was the first time I'd heard his voice. It sounded like an angel's. I felt more of the tension ease from my body; he was a natural analgesic. I played that line in my head over and over again. Specifically, I liked the part where he said, *If you stick around...*

Mark narrowed his eyes at Everett. "Oh, come on, little brother," Everett said.

"Boys!" Adelaide snapped, her soft, creamy face creased in anger for a moment. "Let her talk. Poor thing is about to convulse from fear we're going to eat her or something, I'm sure, thanks to Mark's little stalking incident." Adelaide smiled and her face glowed, matching her golden hair. This lightened everyone else a little, but I shrank in my chair.

"It's true," I said carefully, "that I didn't know what to expect. What I saw Mark do to that man... I've never seen anything like it. We don't have but one power each."

"Why don't you tell us a little about who 'we' is," Anthony said. His voice was deep, but its cadence was smooth and melodic.

"What do you know already?" I asked them.

"They know what I know," Mark said. "That you are one of us. That you saw what I did that night in Tennessee. That I tracked you to Nashville and told you never to track me."

"Well," I began, "I have a family. There are one hundred sixty-five of us. We live in the middle of nowhere in Montana, near the Canadian border."

"That's a huge family," Patrick said.

"We've been around for...a while," I said, not knowing exactly how much to divulge about my family's history right now.

Patrick smirked. "So have we."

"Then what were you doing in Tennessee? Were you on a quest of some kind?" Adelaide asked.

"Well, *they* all live in Montana. I sort of...don't," I admitted. If this family were anything like mine, admitting I had run off would not impress them.

"You left them?" Patrick asked.

"It's complicated," I said.

"Try us," Mark said.

"Three years ago, I left. I couldn't take it anymore. I had been learning about the outside world as best I could for some time. And I knew there was more out there. I knew that we could live among humans, that we could try to have real lives, but they just wouldn't hear of it. And then..." I stopped myself. It was clearly not the time to bring up the fact that I was a freak who wouldn't or couldn't reproduce. "I just wanted to see what was out here. So I left."

"You've been alone all this time?" Adelaide asked, worry coloring her voice.

"Yes," I said. "But I've made friends, and I've been as normal as possible. I don't sit in my hotel room all day and stare out at the sky." Everett shifted his weight, and I immediately lost my focus again. I looked up at him, surprised to find that he was looking at me. I smiled. He smiled back. I looked away, but I could tell he didn't.

"You mean to tell me that your entire family lives *apart* from humans?" Anthony asked.

"Religiously," I breathed.

"And even still you took it upon yourself to leave and try and live among them, with no one to help you?" he asked. I nodded, unsure of what to say. "And on top of *that*, you managed to make *friends*?" he asked. His tone was incredulous.

I shrugged my shoulders sheepishly. "Well, yeah." I had never thought of it that way. I spent too much time beating myself up for leaving in the first place or for not acting human enough ever to notice that what I was doing might be considered a feat. I had no point of reference.

"That takes guts, my friend," Patrick said.

"Does it?" I asked, and they laughed. I hadn't meant it rhetorically. I wanted an answer.

"She's amazing," Ginny said to her family, grinning, almost in disbelief. I noticed Madeline still hadn't spoken. What did she think of all of this?

"How many did your family start as?" Anthony asked.

"There were fourteen original Survivors," I said. "They're our elders now, but they all appear to be different ages by human standards. The youngest-looking is twelve, the oldest is sixty-something."

"Survivors?" he questioned. I paused. I hadn't thought about this. If there were more like us, what did they call themselves? Had they identified themselves in some other unique way, as we had?

"That's what we call ourselves," I said carefully.

"You must have quite a history if that is your epithet," Anthony said.

"Well, we have a history," I said, not sure if it was *quite* a history, considering that it may not be as impressive to others who likely had a similar story.

"Why don't you tell us about it?" Anthony said. I looked around the room. Was this why I had come? To give away all our secrets? I frowned.

"What's wrong?" Everett asked. He creased his brow, clearly concerned.

"Could you sit down?" I asked him.

"Am I making you nervous?" he asked, a playful smile breaking across his face.

"Very," I said. He sat in the chair closest to mine. Everyone else was staring at Everett and me, trying to evaluate our interaction. I was embarrassed. Our four-line conversation had given them the impression that Everett and I thought we were alone when clearly we were not. I bit my lip.

I decided to bring the awkward moment to a close with the story they were waiting to hear. "The original fourteen Survivors figured out what they were in the late seventeenth century. They had been abandoned somewhere in what would be South Dakota now, as best they can tell. They were from Salem, Massachusetts."

"Salem?" Adelaide gasped. She quickly looked at Anthony. "Were they...?"

"Accused as witches," I said. "Twenty-six of them. Several people in Salem lobbied for them not to be killed since they had already
killed nineteen people in the previous months, and the twenty-six were
all children. By some stroke of...luck, I guess, they were exiled instead
of executed. Six horsemen brought them in shackles, as far west as they
could go. After two and half months, they arrived. In the dead of a
South Dakota winter, the horsemen unshackled them and left them
behind. To die, they suppose."

"But they didn't," Mark said.

"No. Twenty-six became nineteen on the journey, and nineteen
quickly became fourteen. Not all of them were like us. But those that
survived, who lived through the winter, were shocked that they were
alive," I explained.

"Needless to say," Anthony added.

"They journeyed further west after a while, looking for a place
that would shield them a little more. They ended up in the Rockies. It
didn't take too long to figure out something was up. After the first two
years, they saw that some of them had stopped aging. Andrew, one of
ours who can manipulate the elements, set a bunch of wood on fire one
night when they couldn't get a fire going because it was raining. The
other stuff came after that. One, Thomas, can astral project. Another,
Joseph, can make things out of thin air, anything—food, water, clothes,
whatever. Two of the girls—sisters—Mary and Catherine, can control
bodies. They figured it out on each other first, but they can do it to anyone. They figured out how fast they could run entirely by accident. It
went on from there," I said.

"No one has traveled or left that place?" Adelaide asked.

"They go out every now and then. The elders go in pairs, sometimes threes, to the outside world to learn what's going on. We have
technology there—some of them can control electricity, so we've had it
since before the average house did, and we have some really old computers. We aren't living like it's still 1692," I explained. "Though it feels
like it sometimes," I added quietly. Everett looked concerned again.

He had heard me, the sadness in my voice. He was sensitive to the slightest change in my mood.

"The same fourteen are still there? Or have you lost some along the way?" Anthony asked.

"No, we haven't lost any," I said coolly. But I wanted so badly to ask him if he knew how we *could* be lost.

"How old are you, Sadie?" Adelaide asked.

"I was born in 1867," I said. "But I stopped aging sometime between nineteen and twenty-one." I said. It was so strange to say this out loud to someone, even if she were like me. Ginny giggled.

"Was it ambiguous when you stopped aging?" Adelaide asked.

"It was, kind of," I said, knowing that didn't completely answer her question. For some reason, talking about the two years in which I felt my body harden, and the anguish that came as any near-humanity I had slipped from my fingers felt too personal to share with these strangers. So I redirected. "What about you?" I asked. "What's your story?"

Mark spoke. I could tell they had planned what to tell me. "Adelaide and Anthony have been traveling together since the mid-sixteenth century. They started in England, but they've been all over. Adelaide had a family there, but, like you, they left them," he explained. I was relieved to hear that they understood the need to leave one's family. "They started...er...procreating a little before you were born. Patrick was born in 1840, and he stopped aging at twenty-seven. Everett was next," he said. I was relieved to have an appropriate excuse to look at Everett. "He's about twenty-four now. Ginny was born, like you, in 1867, and is also twenty-one. That leaves me. I'm nineteen for good."

"The spoiled baby," Everett joked. "A teenager forever, if you can imagine it. Polly is our twentieth-century baby," he added.

"Who?" I asked.

"Thanks," Mark spat sarcastically.

"His middle name is Apollo," Everett joked.

"And we call him Polly to piss him off," Patrick added. I laughed.

"Hey, I was named that because I'm a warrior," Mark defended himself.

"That's enough," Anthony said. They quieted down.

"Is it common for siblings to end up about the same age?" I asked.

"It's not uncommon," Mark said. "Is it not that way with your brothers and sisters?" he asked. I didn't want to tell them the truth—that I didn't know. I was sure that the fact that we had no specific parents was not normal, and would upset this family, who was so close.

"No, it's not like that," I decided to say instead of explaining. I wasn't ready to admit how strange my family was. "What can you do?" I asked to change the subject.

"A lot of things," Mark said.

"I know what *you* can do," I laughed toward Mark. "I saw you. But what about the rest of you?"

"A lot of things," Patrick repeated. "You say you can each do only one thing?" he asked.

"More or less," I shrugged. Ginny raised one eyebrow at me, and I immediately felt waves of suspicion hit me. I ignored them. "We've all got speed, strength, and very sensitive...senses." It was so weird to list them off like this, openly. The whole situation felt very surreal.

"Do you eat?" Anthony asked.

"We can, but we don't have to," I said. "And it isn't processed the same way it is for humans. It seems that anything we eat or drink burns up in our bodies in some way. We're not quite sure on that one."

"Us either," Patrick said.

"Do you sleep?" Mark asked.

"We can," I said.

"But?" Everett asked, sensing there was more that I wasn't saying.

"But I don't," I said.

"Have you ever?" Mark asked.

"Yes."

"What made you stop?" Everett asked.

I squinted a little. "I don't know," I said, lying. "Do you sleep?" I said.

"Yes," he said.

"Have you ever been sick?" I asked, turning back to face them all.

"Never," Ginny said. "What about you?" she asked.

"None of us ever has," I answered. I had been injured, but that was a story I didn't want to have to tell them.

"Do you feel pain?" I asked.

"Supposedly we can, but none of us ever has," Mark said. "I mean, it would take something really strong to hurt us, right?" They all laughed. I joined with them, sure it was not at all the time to tell them about my morbid quest.

Adelaide finally said, "Okay. You're one of us, we're one of you. What do you need from us?"

"My family wants to meet you. They've believed until now that we were the only ones like us. They're a peaceful people, that I can promise. We've never hurt one another or humans or anything. But they just thought we were alone, that there were no others like us. They wanted me to determine if you were peaceful—which you clearly seem to be—and if you would come back with me," I explained.

Everyone looked at Anthony. "Do you think we will be safe, Sadie? Or should we keep our distance, as you do?" he asked.

That was a good question. "I went back," I said. "They are not terrible. What they wanted from me...why I left...well, that isn't applicable to you. They just want to know who you are, to form an alliance, or, at the very least, to establish peaceful coexistence. I think they're apprehensive."

"But they sent you alone, so they must not be that scared," Anthony pointed out. Of course, they were very scared. They sent me alone because they didn't care if anything happened to me. But I couldn't tell him that.

"I think it would just be better if we all knew each other, really," I said, trying to be as diplomatic as possible.

"I can see the benefit of that," Adelaide said.

"All right," Anthony said. "We'll come."

"Road trip!" Mark enthused as he hopped up and high-fived Everett. I laughed.

"When can we leave?" I asked.

"Well, that depends. How much of California would you like to see before you go?" Ginny asked, zeroing in on my thoughts again, more evidence that my original conjecture that she could read minds might have been the right one. But I didn't know about anyone else. They hadn't clarified who could do what. They were protecting themselves, no doubt, but it still made me uneasy that in our quick conversation they had sidestepped things I asked. Then again, I hadn't told them what I could do either.

Everett smiled an achingly beautiful smile at me, flashing white teeth between rosy lips. He was heartbreaking, and he wasn't even trying. I had never been so drawn to anyone or anything in my life. I thought of the way Cole felt about me at the reception. I had thought it ridiculous that someone could feel so much after just one day. And here I was, starry-eyed over a man I had known for fifteen minutes.

I grinned like an idiot when our eyes met. My breathing was shallow again, and my skin was tingling. My focus had come entirely back to him. Everything around him was a blur.

7
ROAD TRIP

Spending time with the Winters had been a relaxing reprieve. It was hard to believe that I had come to the tiny town on a tiny peninsula on the Monterey Bay only four days before—fearing capture or torture, or worse. Instead, I had been met with a close-knit family who had opened their arms to me, and brought me in as their own, displaying the most positive attributes of human hospitality.

We had at least one big meal together every day. All of them slept with regularity. Anthony and Patrick had jobs of some kind. It made them very human. Adelaide had explained that they determined long ago that if they kept up with typical mortal habits and schedules, it was easier to pass as humans.

Ginny and I had become fast friends, spending the majority of our time together exploring the Monterey Peninsula. She helped me do a few errands I wanted to accomplish before we got on the road to Montana. We spoke little of the strange circumstances that had brought us together, or of our lives as Survivors. I still wasn't sure what her powers were, but I was leaning toward mind reading. There were many questions I wanted to ask her, but I felt I should follow her lead.

I was disappointed not to have spent one moment alone with Everett. I knew his thoughts were not quite as syrupy as mine—until I smiled. Then he cracked. I was having an effect on him.

Every night, I studied his features as he sat in the family living room, reading a book while his siblings gathered around—Mark and Ginny battling each other on a Wii, Patrick and Madeline usually playing games of some kind. He read books at a human pace, which I discovered he did to enjoy them. Inconveniently, he was never the last to go to sleep. If he had been, I would have had time alone with him. But inevitably Ginny or Mark stayed up playing a video game or watching a movie until after Everett had gone to bed. He would kiss every member of his family on the cheek—they all did this—and nod in my direction. "Sadie," he'd say coolly. I'd smile.

"Sleep well, Everett," I'd reply. Then he'd rub his face and run his hand through his hair nervously. He wanted to say more. I did too. But it never progressed.

We discussed the best way for us all to get to Montana. Only four could fit in my car, so that wouldn't work. The Winters—more seasoned car enthusiasts even than I was—had amazing cars. There was, of course, Anthony's Bentley Continental GTC, and Everett's beautiful Maserati, which was perhaps the sexiest car I'd ever seen, and I never describe things as sexy. Adelaide drove a midnight blue Lexus SC-430 her sons had bought for her. Mark drove a powerful black Audi R8, and Patrick and Madeline had matching silver Mercedes CLK-55 AMGs. Ginny, whose fabulous albeit outlandish attitude didn't end with her platinum blonde hair or fondness of Christian Louboutin stilettos, drove a candy apple red Lotus. But none of those seven fantastic cars had a useful backseat, so we'd have to take at least three cars to Montana, which I thought was ridiculous. I had been toying with the idea of buying my family a car, and this made my decision. A few of my family members knew how to drive, and if their readiness to approach the Winters was the first step in letting the family come and go with more liberty, I wanted them to have a normal form of transportation. Mark and Everett went with me to select a nice but subtle Range Rover—it was a hybrid of my taste and a more practical car for the Montana weather. So we'd only have to take my car and the Range Rover.

When it came time to buy the Range Rover, I pulled my checkbook from the giant Spy bag I carried with me everywhere and wrote a check for the full amount. The boys were stunned; I read their thoughts easily.

What the hell? I thought she just dropped into this world three years ago, Mark thought.

She's got to be brilliant to have mastered every intricacy of her life in such a short amount of time, Everett thought as he watched me write the check.

I smiled, a little embarrassed.

Mark, uncharacteristically, waited until we were about to drive the new car off the lot before he grabbed my arm and asked, "How does a chick who is basically a glorified nomad end up with a checkbook?"

I looked down and smiled. "I have my ways," I said coyly. I liked knowing that the Winters were as intrigued by me as I was by them.

On Sunday night, we packed up the cars. We crammed in five giant boxes of books I had bought for my family at the Barnes & Noble in Monterey. If even one of them started to think better things about the outside world by reading these things—a healthy mix of classics and contemporaries, thought-provoking literature, to things like *Gossip Girl* for the young ones—then I'd feel like I had done right by them. I steered clear of the popular supernatural literature, though. They would do best not to know what the world thought of creatures like us unless it became absolutely necessary.

We sat around the dining room table and planned our route, something I never did. I had a GPS I trusted, and I never had a need to stop. But they didn't travel that way. It would take me only about eighteen hours to drive the 1,400 miles from Pacific Grove to Montana. But the Winters were dedicated to acting human, and they would not drive round the clock the way I would.

"Where are we going to stop?" Adelaide asked.

"I hadn't thought about it," I admitted. "I've never stopped before. I always drive straight through. You can go faster in the middle of nowhere at night."

"You drove all the way here without stopping?" she asked. I nodded.

"And she drove to Montana from Tennessee like two days before that," Ginny added.

Adelaide gasped as Mark chirped in, "And she drove from Tupelo to Nashville the night before that."

"And you still can't sleep?" Adelaide asked, her hands on my arms. She was rebuking me the way an angry mother would an unreasonable teenager.

"It isn't that easy for me to sleep," I admitted.

"How many miles was that?" she asked, trying to get a grasp on my stamina.

"I have no idea," I said. I didn't keep track.

"Wait, hold on," Ginny said, holding a finger up to us as she typed furiously into her BlackBerry. "Google says 3,650 miles, give or take."

"In how many days?" Adelaide asked.

I rolled my eyes. "Honestly, Adelaide, if you can't sleep, it's not that big a deal."

She shook her head. "I worry about you, Sadie. I worry, worry, worry about you," she said. I knew what she was thinking. *If you don't have a mother to take care of you, I'll do the job myself.*

Later that night, after the Winters had gone to bed, I took a walk down to the beach. In the early summer, thick fog covers the shoreline and the hills of Pacific Grove and Pebble Beach. It was hard to see the beach from the Winters' back porch, and it was only just across the green belt in front of the Winters' home.

I strolled down, pulling up Twitter on my phone as I walked. *@SadiesTravels: Looking out at the Pacific in CA, heading to Montana tomorrow.* I hoped this would satisfy Corrina for a few days.

The ocean had mesmerized me since the moment I laid eyes on it days before when I topped a hill in Seaside before I got off Pacific Coast Highway. I was floored by it up close. I had only ever seen the ocean from the window of a plane. It was more powerful and more beautiful than I'd imagined. Alone in the fog, I walked barefoot across the sand, making memories of what the beach felt like, and what the ocean smelled like. It was pitch black, and the cool, damp air on my skin was comforting. As the water crashed up on the beach, time after time, I wanted to touch it. I knew it would be icy, but I wasn't worried. I walked across mushy wet sand before the next cold wave came in and splashed across my feet.

My thoughts drifted to Everett. I had replayed my arrival and our introduction maybe a million times in my head. I let my mind run away. My breathing caught, and my empty stomach tightened. I felt dizzy.

I imagined laying my head on his muscular chest, in a place where a heartbeat might have been. I imagined my body pressed against his as his arms held me close to him. He would never want to leave me, and I would never want to leave him. I sighed. What would it be like to be next to Everett Winter every day of my life? To touch his skin, his lips? To travel the world with him?

That thought interrupted my blissful reverie.

I wondered, would I still be drawn to the morbid journey I was on if I had someone to love? More specifically, if I had an immortal someone to love? I had obviously never envisioned this as a possibility, since I thought that every immortal in the world was living peacefully inside my family's city walls. And in my three years of wandering, I had imagined falling in love with a mortal or not at all. (Truthfully, always not at all until I met Cole. The closest I'd come had been Todd and there wasn't anything real or lovey about that.) If I fell in love with a mortal, my quest would only intensify. If love between mortals was like the books described it, then I wouldn't be able to detach from it when the object of my affection grew old and died and I was left alone and no closer to release from this world. I would have to become mortal myself.

This was, of course, problematic. There was no way.

I walked farther up the beach to dry sand and dropped down onto it. I let my head fall forward onto my knees and released a grumble of frustration. I had started this conversation with myself about Everett, and now I was thinking about Cole. I pulled my cell phone out of my pocket. 3:38 AM. It was 6:38 in New York, and I was sure Cole would be getting up soon. I closed my eyes to focus on him. I sensed him quickly. He was sleepy, but he was definitely awake already. I could call...

No. No. That would not help. I had had my chance with Cole, hadn't I? And I ran. *I ran.*

I always run.

I made new rules for myself. No mortals! What if I killed him? I hadn't even let myself entertain the idea of really kissing him for fear of what I would do! In a moment of love or lust, I could lose my mind completely and kill him—crush him, maybe poison him—entirely by accident. Then where would I be? He was fragile.

Everett was so different. I thought of the description in *Theogony* of Eros coming into being out of nothing. I had thought it meant that desire was bigger than us all, and now I could believe that. This thing I felt for Everett was something I could not control. I knew it could consume me the way nothing ever had—save for finding freedom from the chains of immortality. And it was so stupid! I had never even spoken to him alone. Every time he was near me, I became irrational. Even now, I was considering forgoing my fight for mortality if I loved an immortal. If I loved *him.* The rhythm of *his* breath, the timbre of *his* voice, the color of *his* eyes, and the texture of *his* skin were a mating call I couldn't ignore, a love letter I couldn't refuse.

I remembered that I had not thought much of sweet and beautiful Cole Hardwick until we had talked and touched, albeit in the most chaste ways. Did this mean that when I spoke to Everett Winter alone, or when my skin met his, even in a haphazard way, my feelings would magnify? What might I feel if I danced close to *him*? Joked with *him*? Felt *his* hand on my back, *his* body against mine, *his* lips against my forehead?

I stood up quickly, trying in vain to keep myself from thinking about it. It made me squirm uncomfortably in ways I usually did not. I turned to walk back up the road to the Winters' home and tried to clear my head.

But I couldn't stop! I wanted many things I had never wanted before—things I had never even dreamed of. I wondered if this was what people felt when they fell in love or even what drove them to do stupid things out of lust.

And so, relenting, I let my mind run free. I laid in a hammock on the Winters' back deck and stared at the cloudy sky. All I could think of was what it would be like to kiss Everett Winter.

On Monday morning, the whole family went to Toastie's, a diner in Pacific Grove. They wanted a good meal before they got on the road. I drank some water to cool myself, but otherwise I just watched them eat. Just this morning, they had informed me that Madeline wasn't coming, and I was surprised they would leave her behind. I didn't know what to think about her; we hadn't spoken to each other yet.

We didn't arrange who was going in what car until we finished breakfast. I was driving my car, and Patrick was starting the drive in the Range Rover. Anthony and Adelaide chose to go with him, and Mark opened the rear door and hopped in. That left Ginny and Everett with me. I was thrilled as I anticipated this long journey with Everett in such proximity, but Ginny grabbed my hand and pulled me toward my car.

"Give us girls some time," she said to Everett. "Maybe we can switch around wherever we stop first. You good with that?" Everett nodded. I was crushed.

Reluctantly, I climbed into the front seat of my car as Ginny followed suit. I eased out of the parking spot in front of Toastie's, made a U-turn to head back the way we needed to go, and drove out of Pacific Grove with the Range Rover on my tail.

Ginny flipped through the channels on my satellite radio until she found something she wanted to listen to. She didn't talk until we got on the highway. Then she suddenly shifted into high gear.

"Man, do I have some questions for you," she said enthusiastically, turning down the music a little.

"Like what?" I asked.

"This is the first time we've been totally alone. No family overhearing. No obvious topics to avoid in public. I want to know everything!" she squealed.

I had plenty of questions for her, too, but I had assumed they were off limits. "Okay," I said. "What first?"

She answered immediately. "Who is Cole Hardwick?"

I was caught off-guard. "What? No, no. Let's not start there. Me first. What are your powers?" I asked.

You haven't figured that out yet? she said clearly in her head.

"You know I can read minds," I said out loud. "Can you? Is that how you knew?"

"Is that how I knew what? That you could read minds or about Cole Hardwick?" she goaded.

"Both?" I asked.

She laughed. "When I'm around you, I can read minds. I'm a mirror," she said.

"What is a mirror?" I asked.

She laughed again. "See, I thought that was pretty self-explanatory. I mirror other people's powers when I'm with them. When I've been around them long enough—like my family—*sometimes* I can use their skills when they aren't there."

"Whoa, what a talent!" I said. I'd never heard of that one before. I assumed it could be useful but possibly very overwhelming. "What's your favorite?"

"Definitely mind reading," she said. "We've never met anyone who can do that." Just as I had thought. I wondered how much of a freak that made me.

"You're not a freak," she said, responding to my thoughts. "I think it's a good thing. Can anyone else in your family do that?" she asked, flipping the satellite channels again.

"No," I confirmed.

"What do they think about that?" she asked.

"They don't know about it," I said. I realized we could be having this entire conversation silently, but that seemed unnerving, so I was glad we were talking.

"Whoa yourself. You've hidden that from them?" she asked, sounding impressed.

"It's a new thing," I said. "I couldn't do it until this week." She doubted me in her mind. "No, really. I've always been able to sense things from people. It used to be just emotions, kind of like I was an empath. But then I started to hear the stupid humming in my head which has turned into voices some of the time."

"Is *that* what that is? Man, it was about to drive me insane. Every single person is thinking something all the damn time, and I could not for the life of me figure out how to turn it off," she laughed. I did, too. I knew the feeling.

"My family knows about the senses. They know I can sense minds from afar, too. That's how I found you guys in the first place, looking for Mark's mind," I explained.

"But you couldn't sense Mark's mind when you met him," she said.

"How did you know that?"

"You shouldn't have been able to get any read off him," she said. "He was projecting both times you saw him."

"Astral projection? *That's* why? I thought he was just impervious to my skills. I hadn't even thought of that," I said. His actual being wasn't there. "What can't he do?" I asked.

"I don't think there's much he can't do, though he can't read minds, so you're one up on him there," she smiled. "And ever since you've been around, I've been one-up on him, too. I thank you for that." Her voice was so sincere. She was thinking she wished she had a sister instead of three brothers who didn't understand her. She was glad I was here.

"Ginny, you're so sweet," I said, responding to her thoughts and dying to know why she was having more fun with me after four days than she had with Madeline in however long they had known each other. "Do you have to focus to do the mind reading?" I asked, wondering if she had my powers exactly as I had them.

"Oh, yeah. It's doesn't work all the time yet, but when it does, it's golden," she said. "Does your family know about the perfect memory thing?" she asked.

"You've already picked up on that?" I asked. "Perceptive."

"I've never been particularly observant," she admitted, "but four thousand yards back, there was a wildflower growing parallel to the ground instead of upright like all the others, and two days ago a girl dropped her sunglasses two blocks away from where I was, and, well, now I notice and see everything and can't forget it. I'm sure I got that from you."

I laughed. "I don't think they know. It's turned out to be useful several times," I said. I thought back to when I was lost in the rainforest in Costa Rica and had managed to find my way out just by having run through there at my top speed days before.

"You'll have to tell me about the rainforest later," she said. It was going to take some getting used to her seeing so clearly into my mind. I was glad we were friends; it would have been scary for me if we weren't.

"Do they know about the languages?" she asked, again surprising me.

"No one knows about that one either," I admitted. She had already picked up on my ability to speak any language that was spoken to me. "How did you figure that out?"

"I was trying to talk to the guy making my burrito at Chipotle," she said. "He didn't speak English, and I was getting frustrated, and then all of a sudden I said everything I'd been trying to say, but in Spanish. I was amused, so I found people at the mall who were thinking in another language and came up with a reason to talk to them. Turns out it worked in three different languages in twenty minutes, so I knew it had to be one of your powers."

"Do you not have any powers if you aren't around others who do?" I asked.

"I have no specific talents, no. Just the basics. I'm sure I could go without food, too, but why bother?" she asked. I shook my head. I didn't see eye-to-eye with them on this. "Have I missed any of yours?"

"That's it," I said. She had nailed every one.

"I thought you said you each only had one power," she prompted. "What was that about?"

"Everybody else does have one," I said.

"So you always knew you were special, different than the other Survivors?" she asked.

Um, was I? "Not exactly. My powers aren't active powers like starting fires or throwing people, so they think I'm pretty weak. And most of them have only developed recently, though typically our powers are set by the time we stop aging. I feel like something's wrong with me," I admitted.

Ginny laughed. "Nothing's wrong with you. You're increasing in strength because of the time you're spending with humans."

"Spending time with humans *helps* powers?" I gasped.

"I wonder if your elders know this. Your powers become more potent when you spend time among humans, like it refines them. Didn't you know that? Like for you, all your powers have to do with tapping into the world around you—what people think and feel, what you see, and so on—so the more time you spend in new environments with new minds to read and new things to see, the stronger your powers get," she explained.

"This is insane," I said, still shocked. "Does it work that way for all powers?"

"It should," Ginny said. "One way or the other, your powers change around humans. Think of it like a chemical reaction."

"Do each of you have different powers?" I asked.

She shook her head. "There is some overlap."

"What can everyone do?" I asked. She hesitated, as images and explanations filtered through her head. "You don't have to tell me," I said. "I understand." I didn't want her to feel uncomfortable, but the truth was that before I offered to drop it, I had already gotten a glimpse into Ginny's mind. I could see that Anthony could see the future, and that Mark had more powers than I had already seen. I also sensed there was a connection between those two things, but I couldn't see what it was.

"It's weird, isn't it? Just being able to talk about all this stuff?" Ginny said.

I nodded. "I was thinking the same thing earlier," I said.

"Where do you get your powers from if no one in your family has them?" she asked.

"The jury is out on that one," I said. Ginny was focusing hard. She thought I was hiding something.

"Others in your family get their powers from their parents, though?" she asked.

"We think they're hereditary, yes," I confirmed.

"Think? What can your parents do?" she asked.

Here we go. "I don't know," I said.

"How is that possible?" she asked.

I was scared to talk about this. "I don't know who my parents are," I said.

"Sadie," she said, choosing her words carefully, "you said that your whole family has remained together for over three hundred years, that no one has ever been destroyed, and that they're all still in the same place. How is it even possible that in a community that small, that connected, you don't know who your parents are?"

"We do it differently," I said. She raised an eyebrow, so I went on. "The elders decided a very long time ago that our family would never survive unless all generations were loyal to the clan as a whole. They worried that individual family lines would emerge and become more loyal to each other than they would be to the family as a whole.

So before any of them even had children, they decided that they would raise each child as if that child belonged to all of them. We are literally raised by the village," I explained.

"No one knows whose parents are whose?" she asked. Her thoughts and the tone of her voice told me she thought this was very bizarre, even troubling.

"Right," I said.

"So you believe powers are hereditary why, then?" she asked.

"Aren't yours?" I asked.

"We're born with some version of powers our parents already had, yes." I noticed that was a very careful way to phrase it. I also wondered how true that was since at least one of the children could do a lot more things than Anthony and Adelaide could. Ginny tried to re-route my thinking.

"Everyone in my family has a power that closely approximates one of the powers of the elders," I told her. "One of our elders, Andrew, can control the elements, for example, and there are several in my generation who can manipulate maybe only one element, but with greater control. There's this guy I hung around growing up, Ben, who can manipulate water. If there's moisture in the air, he can freeze it. If we're near a body of water, or if it's raining, he can do almost anything—pull the water together and up into the air to make a wall of water. Or vaporize it to make steam. And he can move it around, too. Like send a wall of water toward you or shoot steam in a certain direction. Anything. Presumably, Ben is in Andrew's line somewhere. Or Noah can control the temperature of things, heating them up. He can touch something and turn it to ashes though he can't actually manipulate fire. He's probably Andrew's line, too."

"But your powers don't resemble any of the powers of your elders?" she asked.

"No," I said.

"And that doesn't concern them?" she asked.

"I think everyone in my family thought I was useless, that something was wrong with my powers. So no one's ever thought twice about it."

"But even if you don't know about who your parents are, couldn't you trace the line back to the two elders who started it? I mean, how hard could that be?" she asked.

"You wouldn't know which two elders to start with," I said.

"Wait. What do you mean you wouldn't know which two elders to begin with? I mean, your elder with the control of elements, who is his mate?" she asked. I had hoped this part wouldn't come up.

"They never married," I said, slightly embarrassed. "They just sort of did whatever they needed to ensure the family grew."

"You mean to tell me that you are a family founded by fourteen Puritans, and they've all had children without being married?" she asked enthusiastically. She made it sound like celebrity gossip.

"So it seems," I relented.

"That's the weirdest part," she said. Then she laughed. "That means every one of you, in Puritan-speak, is an illegitimate child."

"Not everyone. Some in the later generations married, and stayed committed. Once two of us do decide to commit, it's a mate-for-life thing. But until that decision is made, they're no better than humans," I said. I so disapproved of this part of my family's culture. I couldn't understand any more than Ginny how we held so many Puritan values, but ignored that part. I much prefer a life alone than a life of uncertain and uncommitted love or—worse—lust.

"So ironic," she said.

"Can we move on from this topic, by any chance?" I asked.

"Yeah, sorry," she said. "Okay, I've got another question about your human life."

"Shoot," I said.

"Well, we're driving in a Mercedes CL 63 AMG, which, if I'm not mistaken is give or take a hundred fifty thousand dollar car," she began.

"That's not a question," I said.

"And two days ago you paid cash for a Range Rover," she continued, her voice leading.

"Uh-huh," I said tentatively.

"And that Fendi you carry around with you is worth, give or take, three grand," she said. "And I've been able to recognize every dress, piece of jewelry, pair of shoes, jeans, everything I've seen on you since you got here."

"Right," I said.

"Do you see where I'm going with this?" she asked nervously. She was afraid of offending me. I had learned that humans considered it impolite to discuss people's money with them. This was fine by me because it meant no one ever asked me how I had everything I had.

"So do you want to know how I have money or why I blow it?" I asked, laughing.

She grinned. "I'm not judging the way you spend it, girl. I just want to know how you got it," she mused. "I got my money the old fashioned way—I was born into it. What's *your* story?"

"As it turns out," I said, "red diamonds are incredibly valuable. I got a little over six hundred thousand a carat for mine." I smiled at her playfully.

Her jaw dropped. "How did you come by them?" she asked.

"Joseph, one of the elders, has the power to generate matter. Yes, yes, I know. It goes against the laws of physics and all of that, but somehow he can do this. And a long time ago, they figured out they might need money if they went outside. At first, he made cash, then he experimented with minerals." Ginny's face was full of disbelief. "When I was getting ready to go, I found their stash and took a few of them. I didn't want to take the diamonds because I thought they were too valuable. So I took a few red stones—rubies, I thought—to get started with. I got one of them appraised and found out it was a flawless red diamond. Christie's auctioned it for me, and I was, as it were, set up," I said. I had never told this story before, but it was one of my favorites.

"How big was it?" she asked enthusiastically.

"Big enough," I said, deciding it was time to be discreet. But Ginny could see it in my head.

"Forty-two carats!" she squealed. "Sadie, that's like twenty-five million dollars for just one of them!"

"At least I don't have to worry," I said. This is what the money had meant to me: a way to keep from being tied down. That way, I didn't have to find a ridiculous job, or commit to living in one place. Of course, I also had fun with it.

"My next question was going to be how you could afford all that travel, but now I know. Instead, how about telling me why you travel?" she suggested.

"I plead the fifth," I said.

She was too amused to be annoyed with my evasion. "How have you mastered every colloquialism and social reference in the last three years?" she asked.

"Talent," I said. She laughed.

"How about the long sleeves?" she asked. "Don't think I haven't noticed."

"The fifth on that one, too," I said. I focused hard to keep the image of my scar-covered arms out of my head. "My turn," I said. Ginny indicated she was listening. "What's the deal with Madeline?"

"On behalf of my family, I plead the fifth, too," she said. She immediately felt bad. She hadn't wanted to make it so obvious that there were many things the Winters hadn't been forthcoming about. I didn't mind, though. In fact, I sympathized. I wanted to be honest with them too, but there were some things that I wasn't ready to admit either.

"It's okay, Ginny. I understand," I said to relieve some of the guilt I felt emanating from her.

"Thanks," she said uneasily.

"I've got one I'm sure you can answer," I said, lightening the mood. "What's the deal with the ring?" On Ginny's left hand, she always wore a giant black and cream cameo-style ring with a woman and a deer in a forest on it. This was the way the goddess Diana was usually portrayed in Roman mythology.

"You seem to have that one figured out. I assume you're awfully well-versed in mythology if you recognize this as Diana," she said.

"Diana is an interesting choice," I said. "She's the Roman equivalent to the Greek's Artemis, said to have the strength and wit of Athena coupled with the beauty of Aphrodite. I see the Aphrodite part, clearly, but should I expect the Artemis-like skill or Athena strength out of you as well?"

"Mark gave it to me. I suppose that's how he sees me," she smiled, a clear hint of cockiness in her expression. "Now. My turn. That brings us right back to Cole Hardwick."

I wasn't sure what I wanted to say about him. First, I told myself, there was nothing to say. Secondly, I didn't want Ginny knowing any more about him than she already did in case she was reporting back to Everett. I know he probably didn't care, but I didn't want to risk it. Third, I realized she was hearing these thoughts as I thought them, so it was time to talk.

"I just met him. He's a friend of a friend. He was at a wedding I went to in Mississippi," I said. "Nothing more."

"You danced," she said. I really didn't like that she could see in my mind just then.

"It was a wedding," I said.

"You felt something," she said. I shrugged. "It's okay, Sadie. He's hot. Just be careful not to break the poor kid's heart."

"How's that?" I asked.

"I mean, it's not like you can do anything with him," she said in a tone that suggested what she was saying was something so obvious even a child would know it to be true. "He's a *human*," she said, her voice degrading.

I had thought the exact same thing the night before on the beach, but it still hurt to hear her say it. I wasn't sure why. I had already discussed with myself how much more I was drawn to Everett, and, more importantly, how I could and would be fine on my own.

Ginny gasped. I looked at her but then realized too late that she had been reading my mind just as my romantic thoughts turned unequivocally to Everett. She grinned wide.

I frowned. "I think you're better at the mind reading than I am," I muttered. "Ginny, if you could not mention..." I began.

She cut me off. "Done and done."

8
TWIN FALLS

Our scheduled stop, the rough halfway point, was Twin Falls, Idaho. We arrived at about ten o'clock that night. We had stopped a few hours before to eat dinner when we got off I-80 and onto the 93 in Nevada.

We checked into a Best Western we had booked before we left, just outside of the city. I had reserved four rooms, so that Ginny and I would share a room. I knew she would sleep and I would not, but I planned to escape the hotel and the family for a little while that night anyway.

A little after midnight, Ginny laid down and closed her eyes, and I let myself out of the room. As Adelaide had grown more and more protective of me over the last few days—in thought if not in action—I knew these nights spent wandering foreign cities and towns would make her unhappy.

I got little research done in California; the beach had been too tempting. But I had begun to read about Eastern European vampire lore after picking up *The Historian* by Elizabeth Kostova when I was at Barnes & Noble in Monterey. It was fiction, but it had an academic element to it, so I thought the legends it was based on might be worth looking into. Many of the classic and modern vampire stories contained obvious similarities between vampires and my family, like those about the *Abarimon*.

I planned on spending this night learning more, but the drive with Ginny had been exhausting. My mind was overworked from trying to keep her from reading it. She must have felt the same way, so I tried to keep out of her mind for most of the trip. But she wasn't returning the favor. It would be good to get away for a while.

I walked out of the hotel through a side door as I always did late at night if one was available. I hated everyone giving me sideways looks as I walked through a lobby, out of the parking lot, and into the night by myself at such hours. I also hated to hear what people thought I was doing, so I avoided them.

The land was mostly flat, but I could see hills in the distance. After walking until the paved road ended near the Snake River just above the deep falls, I jumped over it, and then leisurely ran north for about ten minutes until the plane of the earth began to shift upward under my feet. I found a lush, green hill that provided privacy, and a gentle slope to lie on. I looked up at the stars. I was far enough away from the town that I couldn't even hear the falls. The quarter moon was setting, but the sky was clear enough that it was still casting a faint glow.

I don't know how long I had been lying there when I heard rustling in the earth behind me. I was concerned that an elk I'd seen in the distance was wandering in my direction, so I sat up to appraise my surroundings and get out of its way. But I didn't see anything, up or down. I topped the hill, walked along a row of trees, and looked down the other side. When I heard a low humming coming from behind me, I spun around.

Even in the pale moonlight, I could see every feature of Everett's face. He was slightly breathless. At least an eternity passed before he said anything.

"I hope you don't mind that I followed you," he said.

"I don't," I said plainly. I did not assume he was here for the same reasons I wanted him here, and so I wanted to maintain a safe distance. I didn't want to be disappointed.

"You do this every night, don't you?" he asked.

"Most," I admitted. "I can't help it. There are too many hours in a day for me, even though people always say there aren't enough." I smiled. I could tell that disarmed him.

He grew quiet. I suddenly empathized with all the humans I had met who couldn't leave a silence be. I felt the need to speak. "But what about you? You sleep, so what are you doing out here?" I asked. I began to stroll across the hilltop. Standing still was an impossibility.

He followed me. "I don't *need* to sleep. I am not as different from you as you think I am," he said.

"I don't think you're all that different from me," I said. "You're more like me than anyone I've met since I left my family. The differences seem minute."

"Are they?" he asked, his pitch high. I shrugged, not sure what he meant.

"I wanted to talk to you," he said. "We haven't talked. I mean, maybe you haven't noticed," his voice sped up, "but you and I..."

I interrupted him. "I've noticed," I said. He exhaled in relief. "I'm not sure what took so long."

"It just seemed like the right time," he said.

"Was there something you wanted to talk about that requires the privacy of nighttime in a field in the middle of Idaho?" I asked.

"I suppose not," he shrugged. "Sadie, you have to be the bravest...person...I've ever met. I would never have it in me to take off alone."

"Oh, you would," I assured him. "You've got such a wonderful family that you wouldn't have to, though. If Anthony and Adelaide had been my parents, I would never have left. There's a lot of hypocrisy and secrecy in my family, but mainly there's isolation. And I never liked or understood it. I felt imprisoned every day of my life."

"Was it really a prison?" he questioned, his voice implying I was being dramatic.

"More than it will seem when you see it, yes," I said. "I'm not sure what would have become of me if I'd stayed."

He laughed softly. "What do you mean? You'd have been fine. Maybe not happy, but fine. You are immortal, are you not?"

"You see it like they do, I guess. You think of our immortality as a privilege, while I think it's a curse," I said.

"What would you prefer instead? Death?" he asked incredulously.

I shrugged, unsure of what to say and hesitant to lie to him. I could sense his alarm, and I couldn't look him in the eye. I sauntered down the far side of the hill and sat down. He followed me.

I pulled my knees to my chest, crossed my arms over them, and rested my chin there. "I can see the virtues of mortality," I said, avoiding his gaze. "But I worry that we're too powerful. Does God want a force so powerful in the universe? One that no one, that nothing, can destroy? What if we turn evil? Shouldn't there be a way to stop us?" I asked.

"Are you afraid of becoming evil?" he asked seriously.

"It's not that," I said. "But just what if it did happen?"

He shrugged his shoulders. I tried to focus on pulling thoughts from his mind, but I only heard white noise.

"You're reading my mind, aren't you?" he asked. He sounded offended, as if I had invaded him.

"No," I said, truthfully. I had been trying, yes, but I had been unsuccessful.

"Bull," he said. "Don't lie to me, Sadie. I know what you can do."

"I can't do it all the time," I said. Sighing, I added, "But I was trying, yes."

Still offended, he didn't respond, so, on instinct, I reached out to him. I put my hand on his bare arm. That was it. I felt the electricity I knew I would. I closed my eyes and took a deep breath. Warmth radiated through my body, and my head began to swim.

"Are you okay?" he asked.

I tried to speak, but the words died in my throat. I nodded.

"What is it?" he asked. He leaned in toward me and put his hand on my shoulder.

The spinning began again. Every nerve ending he touched was on fire. My body made a strange movement resembling a shiver. I think I had stopped breathing.

"Sadie?" he asked again.

"I'm fine, I promise," I said. Although he wasn't satisfied, I brought us back to the conversation. "I'm not lying when I say that I can't read minds very well yet. Like right now I can sense that you're concerned about me, you might even think you've done something wrong. But that's all I've got. I can't tell anything else," I explained.

"Will you tell me when you can read my mind? Just so I know?" he asked. I understood his concern. I was frustrated and insecure about Ginny being able to read my mind, so I couldn't imagine an intimate moment like this if he could read mine.

"Agreed," I said.

Ever since he had turned to me in concern, we were sitting much closer together than we had been at first. I felt the heat radiating between our arms even though we weren't touching. Even though we weren't warm. I was dying to know if he was feeling what I was feeling, thinking what I was thinking.

I looked at him, and saw that his golden-green eyes had a faint glow, even in the darkness. I started counting so I would remember how long we held each other's gaze. One, two, three, four. I counted slowly. Five, six, seven, eight, nine, ten. He smiled. Eleven, twelve, thirteen, fourteen, fifteen, sixteen. He looked down, finally.

"What are you thinking?" I asked.

"We are not as alone as your family believes," he said. Sadly, this had nothing to do with professing an undying love for me, so I was disappointed.

"Of course we aren't. I'm here talking to you, aren't I? That already proves their beliefs to be fallacious," I said.

"No, Sadie. That's not what I mean. There are other immortals out there, not just your family and mine," he said.

"I inferred," I said.

"It's as hard for us as it is for you because we're predominantly alone," he said again. "I have my family, but you and I are the same in many ways. After all, who is there for us to love?"

I said nothing. I found it interesting that he had the same questions I had. Only I had surmised that I could love him, whereas he had made no mention of the possibility of finding solace in me.

I laid back into the grass, trying to keep a poker face. Then he lay back, too, rolled onto his side, and propped himself up on one elbow to face me. I cradled my hands under my head and focused on the stars. Anytime I looked back at his face, I got a rush that made it hard to converse normally. I was going to have to control myself.

He began again. "I guess I'm trying to say that you intrigue me."

"Because of a lack of options?" I said, my tone implying offense.

"No!" he said quickly. "That wasn't what I meant at all." Tension billowed off him in thick clouds. He was frustrated I didn't understand what he was trying to say.

I decided to let down a bit of my wall. "Ditto," I answered. "And not for a lack of options," I said, truthfully. I was afraid that I had been too honest, so I added, "Because I could always go for Mark."

"Please tell me you're kidding," he laughed. He slid his hand across his face and then through his dark, thick locks.

"There are three billion mortal men on this earth and several dozen Survivors I could choose from. Your competition is fiercer than you think," I said.

"I'm not concerned about the mortals," he said, "unless you're more sadistic than I think." He said it just the way Ginny had when she said I could never be with Cole. They clearly believed that our kind and humans could never mix. "But the Survivors, well," he paused and grinned at me, "you didn't pick any of them in the last century and a half, so I say my odds are pretty good."

"A good point." Satisfaction and excitement emanated from him.

He reached out to me, and lightly traced the skin of my temple down my cheek and along my jaw line with his fingertips. I didn't move. Then his whole hand stroked my cheek. I had never felt anything like it.

I was drawn to him so strongly it was painful. I could see a life I had never envisioned forming in my mind. I imagined walking down the beach near Everett's family's home, holding hands and laughing on a night much like this. We'd chase after each other in the moonlight, splash into the water and eventually fall to the ground, bodies intertwined, lips entangled. Then he'd pull my face to rest on his chest so he could kiss my hair. He'd whisper that he loved me, and he would mean it. And I would want him to say it because I loved him, too.

The vision felt like a fishhook in my stomach as I came back to reality. We were not in that world.

"What is it?" he asked.

"Just thinking," I said.

"About?" he asked lightly.

"You," I said. I could feel his smile. But I was getting scared. This was so unlike me! I was a cool-headed person, but when I would take one look at his beautiful face I felt oddly soothing flames engulf me. I knew I was falling in love with him, and it was happening too fast.

I stood up. The moment was too perfect. It gave my imagination too much to work with.

"What'd I do?" he asked, jumping to his feet. I felt his protectiveness hit me, like what I had felt from Cole at the wedding. Did I really seem that fragile to them?

"You didn't do anything," I said. I began to walk away, but he reached for my waist and turned me around, his eyes asking permission. I relaxed my body, and he pulled me in close.

He was so strong, so solid, and so much bigger than I was. But even in such a passionate moment, I felt only pure and respectful emotions coming from him. He was every bit as wonderful a man as I had thought.

"You've never..." I said, an unspoken question hanging between us.

"Never," he said, his eyes earnest.

"So it's new to you, too?" I asked.

"And terrifying, of course," he said.

"You aren't like Mark, then?" I asked.

Everett pulled away. "Um, what do you mean?" he asked nervously. Instantly I had ruined our moment by mentioning Mark.

"I can hear his thoughts. Do you know what he thinks when he looks at girls?" I asked.

Everett laughed. "Do you know what he *does*?" he countered. I was instantly embarrassed.

"Are you more like humans than I gave you credit for?" I asked him. My voice was light, but it was a serious question.

"Mark is. Ginny's got a little bit of that in her, too. But Pat and I are cut from a more traditional cloth. He had never even kissed another girl when he married Madeline," he said. "He did dance with one at a wedding we went to in like 1890, but that was it, no joke. He felt bad about it afterward, like he shouldn't have been able to touch her waist like that if nothing was ever going to progress between them," he laughed. I bit my lip. Was Everett laughing because he thought it was ridiculous? This concerned me. Maybe I had misread him. He sensed my discomfort.

"What is it?"

"Nothing," I said.

"Something," he said, not letting our eyes part.

"I'm wondering if you're really more twenty-first century or nineteenth," I admitted. It was the best I could come up with.

"Definitely nineteenth," he said. "There are just things to do and things not to, I guess. It may not be the way things are done today, but it's the way I am. Mark embarrasses the hell out of me sometimes. He's worse than most human nineteen-year-olds I meet."

I wasn't sure what to make of this. I was definitely glad that Everett seemed to think Mark's behavior was too explicit, but it made me realize that there was a real chance that Everett might not be a mate-for-life kind of person if his own siblings weren't. Then again, based on my family's moral transgressions, I could appear guilty by association, too. A Bible passage flicked into my head. *Judge not, lest ye be judged.*

"And you, princess?" he asked.

"Nineteenth, as well," I said. "Though I'm sure that's obvious."

"It is," he said. He pulled me closer again. We stood there for a while, holding each other. I sensed he was afraid of doing anything that would make me pull away.

"Can you do something for me?" I asked, my grasp on him tight.

"Anything," he said.

"Can you kiss my forehead?" I asked. If he thought my request was strange, he didn't let on. And he didn't hesitate.

He gently pressed his lips against the thin skin below my hairline, then pressed his brow into the spot he had just kissed.

"Thank you," I whispered.

Eventually we broke apart and walked down the hill to an old split-rail fence. I hopped on it, but Everett stayed back, watching me look at the stars. He was unapologetic for the way he admired me, and so he was not careful how he looked at me. This should have bothered me more than it did.

"You definitely can't read my mind?" he asked.

"Not yet," I said.

He grinned deviously.

"Why? What *are* you thinking?" I asked.

"All the things I've wanted to think since the moment I met you and been afraid you would hear," he said.

"You didn't know I could read minds then!" I protested.

"Ginny could read your mind the minute you walked in the door. I've known since the beginning," he admitted.

"Well," I said, feigning agitation, "I hope you aren't being any less of a gentleman than you usually are," I said. Realistically, I only halfway hoped that was true.

"I'm doing my best, but no promises," he joked. "You're so beautiful," he said.

I looked at my feet. "As are you," I said.

"That's not a very girl thing to say," he said.

I kept my eyes down. "Sorry, I'm bad at this," I said.

"I didn't mean to say you were bad at anything," he clarified. He looked down at my dangling feet. "Your toenails are grey," he said.

"Ginny did them," I said.

"Mmhmm," he mumbled. He wasn't listening. We weren't really talking about nail polish.

He lifted his eyes slowly from my toes to my knees to my thighs to my hips and on up my body. They stopped at the skin above my tank top, and he gently touched my collarbone. He traced my neck with his fingertips until his hand cradled my jaw. He closed his fingers behind my neck.

"Sadie," he said, his voice low and heavy.

I couldn't breathe.

I swallowed, and managed to get out, "Yes?" He closed the distance between us, pushing my dangling legs to either side of him.

"You'll tell me if this gets too twenty-first century, right?" His breath was sweet and cool.

"Mmhmm," I mumbled. Even with my lips pressed tightly together, my voice cracked. Our foreheads touched. I closed my eyes.

I counted again. I made it to eleven before he kissed me.

His lips were hard but smooth like sterling silver. I reached my arms around his neck, and he slid his around my waist. My lips parted against his as I heard a soft moan escape from my throat.

This was an out-of-body experience. It was much more intense than anything I had imagined on the Winters' patio the night before. It was more than anything I'd imagined in my entire life.

I ran my fingers through his hair. He shivered and leaned back and looked at me, a cautious grin on his lips.

I hopped off the fence, knowing that if I didn't exhibit some self-control, I might never leave. I turned to walk back to town. He slid his hand around mine.

Everett walked me to my room.

"Thank you," he said, as I opened the door.

"For what?" I asked.

"For introducing me to a part of myself I've never known," he said.

I looked down, embarrassed.

"I suppose I owe you a thank you, too, then," I said. Was this really happening? Hadn't it only been a few hours ago I had left this room in a different place, as a different person entirely?

He leaned in and kissed my cheekbone. "I'll seen you soon," he said, taking a few steps backward before finally turning around and walking away. I watched him walk all the way down the hall.

I crept into the room quietly so I wouldn't wake Ginny, but I heard the shower running.

"Sadie? That you?" I heard her call.

"Yeah," I called back. I opened my suitcase and looked for something to wear. I wasn't going to cover myself the way I had the first time I went back to my family. This time I had done them a favor, so I was going to come as myself. Nor had I told Ginny or Adelaide that they should take any precautions. We were going to see my family on our terms.

I picked out tattered but close-fitting jeans, a pair of Reva ballet flats, a coral tank top and a thin sweater and dressed while Ginny was still showering.

I pulled out a curling iron and my makeup bag and went to the sink and mirror outside of the bathroom. I used a washcloth to wipe my face clean, and then I applied my makeup. When I started living in the normal world, makeup was one of the first things I learned how to do, right up there with learning to dress. Looking right was a huge part of passing. Most of my family had never seen a woman wear makeup, but they would today. Regardless of what I did, Ginny could be counted on to be dressed and primped to the nines every day of her life, so I might as well match.

She emerged from the bathroom, one towel around her body, another in her hand, blotting at her bottle-blonde chest-length hair. I was wrapping a brightly colored scarf around my neck, and watching her in the mirror. Her skin was deeper than mine and flawlessly smooth. I imagined her in the California sun, arms and shoulders bare, glistening like the picture of West Coast ease. I tugged at my sleeves, cupping the edges of them in my palms. I would never be that girl, and I had only myself to blame.

She laughed when she saw the curling iron. "I didn't know that was an option on this journey," she said. "I thought we were packing light."

I shrugged. "That's the nomad lifestyle, kid. Everything I own I have with me on every journey," I said. "You can borrow it if you'd like."

"Done and done," she said. I realized this was one of her catch-phrases.

We spent the next hour or so chatting and getting ready like we might have on any other day if we were sisters or roommates. She hadn't asked where I had gone, and I didn't tell her, though I was sure she'd fish it from my mind at some point.

I had never felt more like a human girl. I had had moments like this before with Corrina, and even a few conversations with girls in my family. But I had never felt like I was among people who understood me, like I was part of a real family. Secrets out. Defenses down. But now I felt a longing to be a part of *this* family, no matter the cost.

Over breakfast, Mark and Everett decided to come with Ginny and me. She had insinuated that our car was for the younger, hipper crowd. Patrick glared at her when she said it, and I heard a low rumble from his chest. It was that same growl I'd heard from Mark that night on the Natchez Trace.

Ginny called shotgun as we walked toward the car. Mark groaned, but Everett grabbed her and looked her in the eye.

"What?" she said, obviously annoyed with him. He put his hands on her shoulders, almost shaking her, and stared into her eyes. "Wha-at?" she repeated, dragging out the word into two syllables.

"Focus!" Everett snapped. Then her face brightened, and she looked at me with a smile. He had just told her something in his mind. I hadn't focused in time to hear it.

"Fine, you get it," Ginny said. She walked toward the car and crawled into the cramped backseat. I hadn't planned on carrying passengers when I bought this car.

"Hey!" Mark called. "Why's he get shotgun?" he whined as Everett slid into the front seat with me.

Ginny flicked Mark's arm. "Shut *up!*" she hissed.

"Now, children," I said, jokingly.

We pulled out of the parking lot and made our way back to the main highway. The three siblings were arguing over whose iPod we should listen to. Ginny won and Everett opened the glove box for the connector and hooked it up. We were blasted with the sounds of Katy Perry singing about kissing a girl.

The boys both protested. "Fine, fine," Ginny said. "Put it on the 'Road Trip' playlist." I obliged, fingering the steering-wheel controls. The first song was Van Morrison's "Brown Eyed Girl," which seemed preferable to all involved.

I felt the same way I had in the hotel room, so comfortable, and like part of this family. It was one of the best things I had ever felt.

Not long into the journey, I began to hear Ginny's thoughts effortlessly, and some of Mark's thoughts became clear, too. He was annoyed with being crammed into the back of my two-door.

Didn't we buy a Range Rover so this wouldn't happen? he asked himself, trying to rearrange his long legs into a more comfortable position.

I laughed. I couldn't help it. "Mark, do you want to pull over and get in the Range Rover?" I asked, meeting his eyes in the rearview mirror.

"Lame that you can do that," he said. Ginny and I laughed.

"What? You're mind-reading?" Everett asked in a panic. I bit my lip and nodded. "What about our deal?" he hissed.

"Deal's a deal. I haven't gotten into that thick skull of yours yet," I said, tapping the side of his head. I was surprised at myself for how casually I was touching him.

"I'm holding you to it," he said.

Ginny squealed in her mind. *You have SO much explaining to do!*

I smiled. *You knew what was going on. What'd he tell you to get you to give up the front seat?* I asked her back. It was our first silent conversation.

He brought me into the loop, she said, her eyes coy in the rearview. She flashed an image of me and Everett on the hill from last night: his arms around my waist, his forehead to mine. I was instantly embarrassed.

Boy can't keep his mouth shut, I said.

More like can't keep his mind shut, she retorted. Then she laughed out loud. I laughed, too.

"What?" the boys said in unison.

"Nothing," we replied in unison. Maybe the connection to Ginny was going to be more fun than I had anticipated.

It was quiet for a little while save for the music. I heard Mark's running dialogue with himself about what he would do if he, personally, had the kind of money I had. Ginny was envisioning a frilly wedding for Everett and me.

Then I heard, *Don't freak out. Don't freak out. Don't freak out.* It was Everett. I wasn't sure if he was talking to himself, to me, or to his siblings, but he slid his hand quickly toward mine where it was resting on the shifter. He picked my hand up and flipped it over, interlocking his fingers into mine. *This* was why he'd wanted the front seat.

My chest tightened the way it always did around him.

Be cool, he said, clearly to himself in his mind.

"Oh!" I said. I realized I had broken a promise.

"What?" Everett asked. *Oh no, she didn't want them to know...* Everett began to pull his hand away. I tightened my grip.

"No, that's not it," I said. I looked at him apologetically. "Deal's a deal," I said.

"What? Now? You couldn't read my mind until right now?" he asked. *Lovely timing.*

"Sorry," I said, frowning a little. Everett creased his forehead when I did this.

Oh, no, Sadie, don't frown... he said, very tenderly. *Wait! Shit! She could hear that!* I looked at him, raising an eyebrow. "Sorry," he mumbled. "This is going to take some getting used to."

"Are we going to pretend nothing is happening?" Ginny asked.

I looked at Everett. "I don't know what you're talking about," I said.

Mark moaned. "I mean, I get that it was inevitable and all, but still," he said.

"Inevitable?" I asked.

Shut up! A chorus of Ginny and Everett's thoughts rang. There were a few expletives, too, but I tried to tune them out.

Ginny elbowed Mark hard in the ribs. "Jerk," he said, and pushed her back. Soon they were fighting like little kids.

You'll get used to them—eventually, Everett said to me in his head.

I smiled at him when he said this. He was accepting my abilities. And he alluded to my continued presence in his life just like he had the first time I met him. In a bold move, I raised his hand to my lips and kissed it softly.

9

JULIET AND HER ROMEO

It was nearing dusk when we got to Bigfork. We checked into a chain hotel several miles up the road from Bigfork, halfway to Kalispell, and then we headed toward the Survivors.

We drove the same way I'd come the week before, down the same small road lining Swan Lake. I pulled off behind the Laughing Horse Lodge and got out of my car. "We're going to have to go together in the SUV," I told them. "My car won't make it up the road."

Crammed together, two to a seat and three in the cargo space, I took the driver's seat in the Range Rover and put us back on the main road. Quickly, I turned onto a National Forest trail that was just wide enough for (though perhaps not meant for) a car.

"Is this a road?" Ginny asked, trepidation in her voice.

"We're on it, aren't we?" I replied. The road was rocky and uneven. Inches from the sides of my tires, the road sloped sharply down. It wound up and around the mountain, and, at the top, there was a trailhead. Beyond it, the road became even rougher, looking less and less like a place someone should drive. It wound further, until finally, the path flattened and abruptly stopped. When we emerged from the Range Rover, we were surrounded on all sides by mountains taller than the one we were on, now somewhere near the edge of the Flathead National Forest and anonymous peaks on a contiguous mountain range that reached all the way to Colorado. I had found this road before I left for California, so I'd know where to bring a car back to. It was only six miles, but it'd taken us nearly half an hour to reach the end. As best I could tell, this was the last sign of man-made anything within 20 aerial miles of where my family was hidden. We had to travel the rest of the way on foot.

"They weren't kidding with this isolation bit, were they?" Mark asked.

"You all thought I was being dramatic," I huffed. The boys laughed, and we all took off running.

I was getting slightly nervous about this encounter. I knew Anthony had the ability to see the future, and I wondered if he had already seen how this meeting would go. I tried to tap into his mind, and I heard his deep voice clearly.

Forgive us our trespasses as we forgive those who trespass against us.

He was reciting the Lord's Prayer. This was probably more to block me than it was anything else—he didn't appear to be praying. Still, it was an interesting choice. As the descendent of accused witches from the Puritan era, the Lord's Prayer had a very specific connotation to me: The ability to say it was, supposedly, proof that one was not a witch. I wondered if he were sending me a message.

We were fast approaching the gates to the city. I scanned through the Winters' thoughts. Their minds were all very serious, focused. They each had a conviction that this visit was part of their path, but I couldn't imagine why their thoughts were so intense. I suddenly considered how little I knew about the family that stood around me, the one I wanted badly to be a part of. Should I have found out more before I brought them here, putting my own family at risk?

Before I had long to consider this, we reached the clearing and, upon entering it, the gates opened. They had seen us coming. That was a relief. I hadn't decided how to explain why I brought the whole family instead of just Mark.

Andrew and John emerged first. The sisters, Catherine and Mary, were on their heels.

As we got closer, Andrew smiled and stretched out his arms. "Welcome home, Sadie," he said, embracing me.

"Um, thank you," I said awkwardly. That was an interesting, deliberate choice of words. I pulled away and gestured toward my traveling partners. "Andrew, family," I said, "these are the Winters."

"It's our pleasure to have you here. It was gracious of you to travel all this way," Andrew said. His façade was calm, but I could sense his inner tension.

The Winters did not respond.

I looked at Ginny, catching her eye so we could speak. *Say something*, I said.

Dad doesn't want me to, she said.

Then make him talk! I said. *Do something!*

She looked at her father and searched his face for direction, but there was nothing there.

I tried to convey my need for them to say something, *anything*, to Everett. *I can't, Sadie,* he apologized, *I can't do anything until he says something first.*

Anthony was still reciting the Lord's Prayer in his mind.

I couldn't take it anymore. "Family, this is Mark." I grabbed his arm and pulled him forward. "He is the one I met in my travels. This is his father, Anthony," I gestured, "and his mother, Adelaide, and his brothers, Patrick and Everett, and his sister, Ginny." Each of the Winters nodded. Still, no one said anything. I couldn't let the awkward silence hang there, so I added, "They provided me with great hospitality."

Andrew didn't even try this time. Everyone was silent. I was getting stressed and losing my focus, and it wasn't long before all I could feel was tension radiating toward me from each of them. "Maybe we should go inside?" I asked, touching Andrew's arm. He nodded.

"Come, friends," he said, coolly. "Let me introduce you to my family."

I hung back for a second and found myself between Ginny, Mark, and Everett. "Guys, why are you being like this?" I hissed.

"Sadie, just don't worry," Mark said. In her head, Ginny caught my eye and said *I don't know why the cloak and dagger.* At least my connection to her was back, but that still wasn't an answer.

Everett very gently hooked our fingers. He whispered, "Deal's a deal?" and raised an eyebrow. He wanted to know if I could read his mind so he could talk to me.

I shrugged. "Try."

Dad is appraising the situation, he said.

Apparently he was not convinced they were safe from danger. And he was being rude, which wouldn't help at all.

We got to the main square. "Sadie," Andrew's voice called. I walked to his side. "Daughter, I'd like you to focus very hard on sensing me," he said. I was unsure what he was getting at, but I obliged. His voice came to my mind immediately.

Do not be alarmed that I know you can hear me, he said. *Hannah saw this mind-reading in your future, and I realized the talent has come to you. It is a secret that will remain between Hannah, Lizzie, and me,* he said calmly. *Please nod if you understand.*

I did.

Do we need to know anything about this family?

I shook my head.

Are they violent? he asked.

I shook my head again.

Can they read minds like you?

I nodded and grabbed a strand of my hair, curled it around my finger and held it to my chest. He understood I meant Ginny.

Do they have other powers?

I gestured as if I was fingering a beard.

The father? he asked.

I nodded my head and quietly said, "Hannah."

He can see the future. Others?

I didn't know any of the other Winters' powers other than Mark's. "The one I was looking for," I said aloud. "Mary and Catherine and you."

Yes, he said, *you saw those talents before.*

"Thomas, too," I said.

He can astral project? Is he projecting now? Andrew asked.

"No, he's here," I said.

Thank you, Sadie, he said. I was more nervous now, this going nothing like I had seen it in my mind.

We reached the amphitheatre. The other ten elders were there, along with a large crowd. I scanned the faces and immediately realized it was my entire family.

Andrew pulled me toward the center with him. "Family!" he cried. "Our daughter, Sadie, has returned to us yet again. Praise God. We are truly blessed!" A chorus of "Amen" from my family filled the air. He held me close. He was making me their hero. "She has returned with the other we spoke to you about, and his family. We have come together to meet and learn from one another," he said, his voice booming through the space. "I would like Sadie to introduce this family, the Winters, to you."

I did as I was told, motioning for each member of the family to come forward.

Then Andrew introduced every member of my family, by generation. Each group rose and bowed their heads as Andrew called their names out, one by one. It was a powerful gesture.

When he was finished he said, "I'd like to offer Anthony a chance to speak to us."

I thought it was risky, perhaps even presumptuous, that Andrew would put Anthony on the spot like that. But Anthony stepped forward. Perhaps this was what he had been waiting for.

"Thank you," he said to Andrew. Then he addressed the family as a whole. "Survivors," he called, his arms outstretched. "My family and I have traveled here to meet you because we know we are a small community. Until today, you had never met any of your kind from outside your walls, and my family has never met as many as we are meeting now. It is a privilege to make so many new friends. Our two families are part of one family, together.

"We have traveled this earth for many years. We have seen many of God's wonders, and we hope that we will have a chance to tell you about the world that lay outside the mountains that surround you," he said in earnest.

At these words, a thousand loud thoughts swarmed in my head from the Survivors, clouding my hearing and thinking. Survivors of all ages began reacting to Anthony in their minds. *Heretic!* They screamed. *Lies!* I heard. *He'll tear our family apart,* one sobbed. My breathing hitched. But then a quieter, more distant echo: *Oh, thank God,* some said. *What we've been waiting for!* one of them said. *Thank you, Sadie,* one said. It surprised me the most.

But those softer voices of support did not outweigh the rage coming from the elders and from the traditionalists. These were things my family did not want to hear. I could feel John behind me, the white-hot anger building in him, permeating my skin. The crowd leaned in toward us, their eyes telling their feelings. Andrew was fighting to stay calm. Lizzie prayed quietly, asking the Lord to forgive me for what I had brought upon the family. The Winters were trying to maintain a calm façade, pretending they didn't hear the whispers or notice the stares.

Anthony spoke again. "We have been so pleased to know your daughter and sister, Sadie. She is the picture of bravery and progress. We hope that you will feel her strength as your own so that you, too, might one day seek a life exploring God's wonders across this globe." I stopped breathing as the silent intensity of my entire family rose. "It is our pleasure to meet all of you today. Blessings to you all."

The Survivors began whispering to each other, a quiet roar of suspicion and outrage coming from the crowd. But as soon as Anthony finished speaking, Andrew stepped forward, not missing a beat. "Thank you for your words, Anthony," he said. "Family, friends, we invite you now to a feast and bonfire. Let us celebrate and get to know our new friends."

He closed with the Lord's Prayer.

Several of the elders, led by John, began to circle off to the side. It didn't take my senses to feel the animosity radiating from them. Soon several circles formed as I walked through the crowd hand-in-hand with Everett, flanked by the Winters. Survivors from all the generations backed away from us.

For fifteen tense minutes, I stood near the bonfire with the Winters as night fell, trying not to discuss the obvious. Then a small group from the generations below mine approached us.

"Sadie?" one of them, Cassie, said. She was in the youngest generation and had stopped aging at about sixteen. "Can you tell us stories?" She nodded to the two girls and one boy behind her.

Noah walked up behind them. We hadn't spoken yet. He watched me carefully, waiting to see what I would say, how far I would take this. Would I tell the youngest of them what I had seen in the world outside? Would I tempt them more than I already had, alienate the elders more than I had?

He knew what I knew. The message of Anthony's speech would resonate most with the youngest members of my family, the ones who had not experienced centuries of life in our family, who were not content with isolation. I couldn't bring myself to be upset that this was the case—hadn't I wanted to spark their curiosity? But I was worried. None of them had practiced trying to control their powers the way I had for years before I left. They hadn't read thirty-five thousand books or spent decades learning and preparing to live among humans. If any of them walked away from the family, they would be more frighteningly unprepared than even I was. How would they get along then in a culture they could never understand? In a wholly different world? It would be disastrous.

I suddenly wondered what I was doing, why I was here, and why I had come back at all. I wanted my whole family to have the opportunities I had given myself, but at what price? I wasn't trying to destroy the family my elders had created; that had never been my intent. But I did not understand why my family had isolated themselves. Maybe the elders had no choice. Maybe my family needed to stay where it was and as it was to stay safe. I realized only then that I had always assumed isolation was about naïveté, but what if it was about more than that? What if they simply couldn't protect their family in a world they knew nothing about? Or what if there was more, a reason for being inside these walls I could never have imagined?

But what if it were possible for my family to transition to living in the real world? They wouldn't be able to do it alone. Maybe I'd been called back to my family so that I could help them. Maybe this was my purpose. I realized this could be God's work for me to do here.

Before I could answer Cassie, John intervened. He had been watching the interaction carefully. "Cassie!" he bellowed across the square. "Stay away from Sadie and her heathen friends!"

Anthony snapped his head around. "Heathens?" he screamed, overreacting. Patrick and Mark jumped to attention and faced John, their gazes menacing in the flickering firelight. Adelaide looked at me and then turned to face John with her family. Ginny and Everett stared at me, panicked. "We are not heathens, you self-righteous son of a bitch," he hissed.

"Anthony, don't do this," I pleaded. I could hear his thoughts, feel his outrage. I suddenly saw how disastrously—how violently—this could go. I looked at Everett in a panic. He gripped my hand tightly.

Anthony ignored me and walked toward John. Noah grabbed the young girls and backed away until they all stood with the elders. Soon they were all on one side and we were on the other, staring each other down.

"Godless and depraved home wreckers, that's what you are! Did you come here just to destroy my family for sport?" John spat.

"We came here for all the reasons I said," Anthony defended. "You cannot ignore the world out there. There are six billion humans on this earth. For every one of you there are four million people that your God created. There is art. There is love. It is time to see it. If you loved your family, you would let them go."

"We stay here!" John screamed. "That is a part of being this family. We stay here! Together!"

"Tyrant!" Anthony growled, charging at John's chest.

"Barbarian!" John roared.

I couldn't stand still. I launched myself into the fight, and Everett followed. He pushed his father backward, but I was no match for John.

"Andrew, help me!" I yelled, pushing my weight against John. Andrew hesitated, horror in his eyes, and he didn't move. None of the elders did. "Noah! Anyone!" No one came to my aid. "Stop this!" I screamed.

"These vile people!" John screamed, his mouth foaming. "Coming into our home and insulting our family!"

"Your home? This is a prison!" Anthony seethed. I instantly felt terrible. I had called it that myself. "You've trapped your family here for long enough. If they want to go, you should let them! You cannot protect them forever!"

"We can! We will!" John snapped back.

Sadie, make it stop, Ginny pleaded in her mind.

Trying, I said.

Anthony and John continued to throw insults back and forth at each other.

"You ridiculous child of Lucifer!" John barked.

"Bible-beating despot!" Anthony roared.

"Stop!" I screamed as loud as I could manage. "Stop fighting! Listen to me! I know better than anyone how hard it is to be loyal to a family like this and be part of a world like that," I said, throwing my hands in the direction of the city gates. "But we don't need to tell the Winters how to live their lives and they don't need to tell us how to live ours," I said, as forcefully as I could. "The last thing outcasts like us need is a rivalry. Surely we can find a way to understand each other."

"Don't lie, Sadie," Patrick yelled. "You can't count yourself as one of them. You're the only one who has seen the error of their ways!" This definitely did not help my family's view of me.

"I am a child of both worlds," I said. "We can find a way to reconcile our beliefs."

"I'm sorry, Sadie," Anthony said. "We cannot condone what's happening here. We're leaving," he said roughly. "Now."

"Good riddance!" John yelled to a chorus of support.

"No!" I cried.

"Let them go, Sadie," John spat.

"You are welcome to come with us, Sadie. We would welcome you as a member of our family," Anthony said. These were the kindest words he had ever spoken to me.

"If you go with them," John warned, "you will be dead in our eyes." His words were a crushing blow. I looked to Andrew, who wouldn't meet my gaze. Lizzie was crying into his shoulder. "You may have left us once and received forgiveness, but we will not extend the favor again."

"Please don't make me choose," I said. I had left my family once, and that had been nearly impossible. The last few days of knowing they had not forgotten me meant the world to me.

But in those same short days I had begun to feel so normal among the Winters, a real family. And Everett! Every bit of me ached at the memory of his touch, of that kiss. How could I stay?

I was dancing on the drawn line in the sand, watching the Capulets and Montagues staring each other down.

I looked at Everett, fearing I was about to lose him. Me, his fair Juliet. He, my Romeo.

"Decide, Sadie," Anthony snapped.

I hesitated.

Anthony snarled. My hesitation was enough to alienate him.

Everett took a step toward me, but Anthony and Patrick grabbed him, and without another word, the Winters ran away.

I'm so sorry, I heard Ginny say. *I love you, Sadie. We all love you. Find a way to come back to us.*

I watched them bound over the city walls out of my sight and into the darkness.

I fell to the ground and pounded my fists into the dirt. I was so close to the fire that its heat burned my skin. "No!" I screamed. "No! No! No!"

Lizzie emerged from the crowd and came to my side. Hannah and Sarah were on her heels. "Andrew, take care of that," she said gesturing to the fire. The huge bonfire was out in an instant, and I felt the cool air take its place. I couldn't move. My knees and forehead were pressed into the dirt. I couldn't lift myself from this position.

Lizzie tried to lift me up, but I fought her. I didn't want to look at the family of Survivors standing there in the darkness, the glowing green eyes missing from the pack. I didn't want it to be real, so I stayed down.

"Sadie," John said. I hated him. "You made the right choice. Your place is with your family. You have been following Satan for too long. But now you are home. You have proved your loyalty to God and to this family," he cried, his voice excited and proud.

I finally stood up, my face and hands and legs covered in dirt. "You know nothing about what I've been following. You know nothing about me!" I charged. If John were ever proud of me, I had done something truly wrong. "You think you've done right by driving them out of here? You think you have saved us? You've just alienated these youths who want to go even more now, shown them that you can't even make peace with those like us from the outside. You've shown them you are everything they were afraid you were, and so now they'll want to go. And they will leave, John, just like I left. We could have had allies out there, but now you've run them off!"

John grabbed my shoulder. "Take that back, child! Don't you tell me that my family will fall apart!" I fought him off.

"Your friends left us, too, Sadie. Aren't they to blame?" Catherine argued, coming to John's side.

But a dark smile grew on John's face. "Oh, I get it now," he laughed cruelly, his tension draining. "Don't you see, Catherine? They didn't leave us," he smirked. "They left her."

I shot my arm directly at his throat and picked him up off the ground, stronger, then, than I had ever been. "You've ruined everything," I hissed as he squirmed in my grasp. I threw him forcefully to the ground.

I dug the Range Rover keys out of my pocket and threw them on the ground and looked at the youngest generations. "There's a car for you parked on the road. There are books in it. You want to learn about the world, that's a good place to start," I fumed. "I'm sorry, Lizzie," I managed to say.

Before I knew it, I was running.

It was too late to join the Winters. My hesitation had turned Anthony against me. But I couldn't stay here anymore.

This morning I had two families, and now I had none.

I ran at my full speed through the trees and across the mountains, the underbrush tearing at my skin, ripping violently at my clothes. I ran until I hit the glassy, black water of Swan Lake. I left myself sink into its icy depths. I wanted so badly to be released from this body and from this life.

I might never see Everett again. The thought cut at me like razors. I had waited almost a century and a half to feel love and in less than twenty-four hours of having it, it was already lost.

I couldn't get the look on his face as Anthony and Patrick dragged him away from me out of my mind. It cut at me, too.

I felt the weight of the water pressing in on me. I breathed it in through my nose and mouth until I puked it back up in the water. And I prayed—literally prayed—to drown.

I closed my eyes and thought of Romeo and Juliet. At least they got to die at the end.

10

PATIENCE

I lay submerged at the bottom of the icy lake until my skin started to swell and feel slimy. I waited until dark to drag myself onto the beach and out of the murky waters. I made it only a few feet out of the water before I gave up, exhausted, my body splayed out on the isolated western coast of the lake. My temperature was so low that my muscles were seizing. I had never been so cold in my life.

I knew I had to get out of the wind, out of the cold, and out of those clothes, but I could not will myself to move. There was a bright waxing moon in the cloudless sky. On the day of Corrina and Felix's rehearsal dinner, the moon had been in its first quarter. That was only thirteen days ago. My life had turned completely upside down in less than two weeks.

Now, with the evening wind turning the water to ice on my skin, I tried to feel the pleasant heat that came from my memories of Everett. It wasn't working.

I felt my senses dulling and imagined this is what it must feel like to die. So when I heard Mark Winter's voice in my head, I knew was hallucinating.

"Damn, Sadie," his ghost voice said. I didn't respond. I felt something large and soft and warm around me, and suddenly there was no earth below me and the moon was moving in the sky overhead.

This was real.

Mark had picked me up off the ground in one, fluid movement, and now he was carrying me away. He ran impossibly fast, my entire body covered in a blanket, protecting me from the forest he ran through. I could tell when we stopped climbing and descending and knew that we'd reached the even terrain of Flathead Valley. As the blanket draped away from my face, I could see the blur of light and houses, cows, barns, and fences as we sped by them in the dark. He took me to the hotel I'd come to with the Winters, halfway to Kalispell. But why Mark? Where was Everett? Wasn't this exactly what my knight in shining armor was supposed to do? (How quickly I had been reduced to the damsel in distress.)

I was mildly aware of the thoughts of hotel employees who were incredibly concerned that this man was carrying this woman, nearly passed out and visibly shaking, up to a room. They did nothing, of course. Another strange human quality that made it to my list— knowing something is likely going terribly wrong and doing absolutely nothing about it.

He brought me to my room and lay me on the bed.

"Sadie," he said again, shaking me. "Sadie, come on," he said. I could only hear his voice. He was projecting; that's why he was here instead of Everett. "Snap out of it," he urged.

I couldn't move.

"Ahhh," he said, frustrated. "This isn't going to work. You need to be dry first." I became aware of him rummaging through my suitcase. "Sadie, you need to get into dry clothes." I could hear how stressed he was. "Sadie, please. You probably can't feel how cold you are, but even for you, it's not good."

I wanted to get into the dry clothes, but I couldn't move. I couldn't speak. He rubbed his face and hair with his hand. "Please forgive me," he said, partly to me and partly to himself. "Sadie, I would love your help on this, but you aren't responding, so I'm going to change your clothes for you," he said.

He sat me up and cradled my body in his arms. I heard an echo in the back of my mind. It felt far away, like someone was calling to me down a long hall. The sound got louder, as if the voice was running toward me. *Sadie, no! He's going to see you* naked*! He's going to see your scars!* It was my voice. I was screaming at myself. I knew the voice was correct, but my body couldn't respond. I was helpless.

Mark fumbled with the hem of my shirt. He knew how modest I was. He knew I would not have wanted this, but I had heard the helplessness and the concern in his voice. I hadn't left him a choice.

He lifted the sweater and tank top over my head and tried to move quickly, the dry shirt already in his hand.

But he froze. "Oh, my god," he said. He had seen what no one else ever had. The voice in my head went crazy. *You're too late! Look what you've done!* His arms gently released me, so he could explore my arms. He rubbed his cold thumbs over the scars, then, very tenderly, he turned my palm over to look at my wrists. He gasped.

He had completely forgotten the modesty. He had been derailed by the forty-seven scars on my mangled arms. I was sure he was not even registering that the most modest girl he'd ever met was sitting in front of him in jeans and a bra.

"What happened to you?" he whispered to himself in disbelief. He very tenderly ran his fingers over them as if checking to see if they were real. As he felt each scar, even with my eyes closed, I could envision each one—a roadmap of the damage in my head.

After a moment, Mark shook his head as if trying to purge the sight from his mind, and resumed dressing me. Soon I was wearing a soft hoodie and sweatpants and wrapped up in dry blankets. I opened my eyes as he walked to the bathroom with my wet clothes, where I would later find them hanging dry.

He came back and saw my open eyes. He climbed into bed next to me, pulled me toward him, and wrapped his arms around me. "Sadie," he said. "I know you can hear me." I could. "Were you under the water the whole time?"

I nodded, able to control some of my faculties again, just in time to have given away all my secrets. He pulled my head into his chest, gently placing his chin on top of it. I felt nothing. He was not

Everett, and it was not the same. "You scared me," he said earnestly. He was holding me this way because he was so worried. It was affectionate, and a brotherly posture.

I opened my mouth to try to speak. "How did you find me?" I asked. My mouth and lips ached, the air from inside me burning my lungs as I spoke. The words came out in a whisper, but he could hear me.

"Ginny was in your head when you went into the lake," he said.

"But that was a while ago," I croaked.

"Two days ago," he said, grimly. "I saw your stuff here when I came to look for you. When you weren't here, I went to see if you were still where Ginny had last sensed you. Thankfully I found you when I did." He rubbed his hands up and down my back, trying to make me warm.

Why did people always say that? *Thankfully.* Like something was going to happen to me if he had just left me. I was not so fragile. Or lucky.

"Why'd you come?" I asked, my voice regaining strength.

"Worried about you, like I said," he shrugged.

"Just you?" I asked. He knew what I meant.

"We all are. Everett especially," he said.

"Really?" I asked, excited to hear that he missed me.

"I've never seen him like this," Mark said, obvious pain in his voice. "It's textbook, I guess. He won't eat, won't sleep. He blames Anthony for ruining his life every chance he gets. Some bullshit about Romeo and Juliet."

I smiled. I couldn't help it. "I thought of that. Our dueling families trying to keep us apart," I said.

"It's just dueling fathers," Mark said. "We all still love you."

"Hey," I corrected, "John is not my father."

"Fine, dueling patriarchs," he amended. "I suppose it fits that you tried to drown yourself. Suicide attempts are hallmarks of the Romeo and Juliet story."

"They aren't suicide attempts if you can't die," I said.

"Can't you?" he asked.

"Do you know something I don't?" I asked.

"Well, clearly you are not as indestructible as we thought." He was talking about the scars. I knew it would get here.

"I am, too," I said. "I'm still here, aren't I?"

"Not for lack of trying, it appears," he said. He slid his hand inside the cuff at my wrist, pushing the sleeve up my arm as he felt his way up, fingering some of the scars.

I shrugged.

"Sadie, I've met a lot of people like us," he said, his thumbs still on the scars. "I've never seen a scar on any of them. What the hell happened to you?"

"It's hard to explain," I said. I didn't want to divulge anything about how I acquired them.

"You could try me," he said, his voice gentler than it ever had been. I was grateful that I couldn't read his mind just then. I didn't want to know how messed up he thought I was.

"But I don't want to," I admitted. Surprisingly, he let it go.

I thought about asking him not to share his discovery with his family, but I knew it would have been useless. The existence of my scars was too jarring to our kind to conceal.

We lay there quietly for a while. He had closed his eyes, and his breathing had slowed. I nudged him. "Mark," I said.

"Hmm?" he responded immediately.

"Were you sleeping?" I asked.

He let out a soft laugh. "You want to hear a secret?" he asked. "It's only fair since I stole one of yours, uninvited."

"Sure," I said, curious and appreciating his sense of justice.

"We can't sleep, not really. Mom's the only one who can. But we're so into this idea of acting human that over the years we've done our best to tune out everything around us, lay still, close our eyes, and slow our breathing down for a few hours a night," he explained.

"No way!" I exclaimed. "All those nights you could have been hanging out with me?"

"Yeah, sorry. When we're at home, we've got to do it. Mom's rules," he said. "But that's when I project."

"So that's why I saw you in Tennessee in the middle of the night," I said.

"And that's why I'm here now," he said.

"Why can Adelaide sleep if you can't?" I asked.

"How come your family can sleep and you can't?" he countered.

"Guess it's something I inherited," I said. "I wouldn't know."

"Then it's best to think of it as something Dad gave us. He hasn't slept in centuries," he said. "What were you going to ask me?"

"Oh," I said. "How mad is Anthony?" I asked.

"You mean, will he stop hating your family enough that you and Everett can go off and be happy?" he asked playfully, easing my tension.

"Something like that," I said, rolling my eyes a little.

"Yeah, he will," he said, "but it's going to take some time. Anthony is going to have to wrap his head around a lot of things."

"Like what?" I asked.

"There are some visions of the future that he's had for a very long time, and they've been shifting since we met you. Well, before we met you, actually," he said.

I looked at him expectantly. "Go on," I urged.

He hesitated. "I think there's stuff I can say now and stuff I can't. We know that you and Everett will get your chance. Dad saw it. He'd seen what you two would become—way beyond what you are now."

"You think we're nothing now," I said, my disappointment clear.

"That's not it," he said. "But be real, Sadie. A moonlit stroll and a hot kiss is not the same thing as a real relationship."

At first I was hurt that he didn't put any stock in the feelings I had for Everett. But then I got what he was saying, and I shot up into a sitting position to face him. "There's more? Like, we know for sure that Everett and I will get more?" I asked.

Mark laughed. "I can't be rid of you, it seems."

"Oh, man," I said. "Why didn't you tell me this before?" I snapped the back of my palm against his chest.

"I can't believe you didn't get it from one of our heads. You're a useless mind-reader," he kidded.

"So what now?" I asked.

He frowned. "Now you wait," he said.

"For what?"

"For us to come to you. And we will come, you'll just have to be patient." He laughed again to ease my tension. I didn't want to wait. I wanted Everett to be here now. I wanted to hang out with Ginny. I would miss Mark when he was gone.

"How long?" I asked. I was upset about this.

"I don't know, but I don't think all that needs to happen will happen overnight," he said. "Come on, Sadie. Patience is a virtue," he smiled.

"*You're* telling *me* about virtue?" I asked, cracking a smile.

"Give me a break," he said.

"So what do I do in the meantime?" I asked.

"You do whatever it is you always do. We'll find you. I can do that, you know. Find people," he said.

"Ginny sent you here, loser," I joked, giving him a hard time.

"Found you in Nashville, didn't I?" he argued.

"Found you in California, didn't I?"

"Touché," he said. He rose to his feet. I joined him. He was leaving.

"Thank you for coming," I said. "I appreciate it...a lot," I fumbled.

Mark slung his arm around my shoulders and roughly pulled me toward him. This was the way he handled Ginny. "Don't mention it. I couldn't leave you hanging."

"You'll tell him I'm thinking of him?" I asked nervously as we reached the door of my room.

"He already knows, but yeah, I will," Mark said reassuringly. I threw my arms around his waist and squeezed hard. He laughed and said, "I'll see you when I see you, little one."

"Little one? I'm older than you!" I protested.

"You're the newest to us, so you get to be the baby," he countered. He gave me one last hug. "See you when I see you."

MEMOIR

The Survivors' City, Montana
Summer 1987 (For sure. I could tell what month and year it was better after I started going to Bigfork.)

We were deep in the woods, making our way to the city wall. Noah and I had been talking when Ben solicited us to come with him out here to show us something. When we got to the wall, I looked around and didn't see anything. Then Ben jumped the wall. I was startled and looked at Noah. He shrugged and jumped it, too. I followed suit.

We didn't go far. Ben's about three years older than Noah and me, but he stopped aging when we did. He brought us to a stop in the middle of the woods. There was a large barrel that he had clearly made himself lying on its side, a small hole filled with a stopper on the top of it.

"What is this?" Noah asked.

"It's wine," Ben said. Noah and I exchanged troubled and incredulous glances. "What? Don't look at me like that. I've been working on it for literally years, and now I think I have it right."

"You made wine? Like what we drink for communion?" I asked.

"Yeah, I get grapes from David. He's gotten a lot better at being able to make stuff when you ask him. Just food though," Ben said. David was the youngest from the second generation who had stopped aging only in our lifetimes, and he could create stuff like James could, only in a more limited way.

Ben dipped a small wooden cup into the small hole at the top. A golden liquid filled the cup. "It's not the same color as the communion wine," Noah said. I nodded in agreement.

"I know. I think the grapes must be different than the ones they use," he said. "You have to try it, though. It will make you feel funny."

So we did. And, from what I could gather, it did make them feel funny, but I felt nothing. Soon enough, I was sitting on the ground, picking at the underbrush, and Noah and Ben were both leaning against trees and talking aimlessly. I had wanted to ask them something for years that I had never had the guts to ask, so this seemed like a good time to catch them with their guard down.

"Boys," I said, addressing them both, "I have a question."

"Yeah?" Ben asked.

"Why do you think they gave us the books when we were kids? Lizzie and Sarah... Why do you think they let us read things from outside?" I asked.

They both thought about it for a moment, strangely blank expressions on their faces, the corners of their mouths upturned, feeling the effects of wine. Noah spoke first. "I wonder if they trust us. Maybe they know that someone in each generation should know a little bit about the world outside, and they know we're not crazy enough to fall in love with that world," he said. This pulled deep in my stomach. I was already neck-deep in love with the complexity of it.

"Yeah, I think they wanted to make sure we knew how reprehensible things are out there. People killing each other, indecent with each other, those witches in *Macbeth*...it was all insane. And the worst was yours, Sadie. That *Theogony* was ridiculous. I cannot believe that people out there believed that stuff, that they thought that was the way the world was created, denying what God really did," Ben said. The pull in my stomach escalated to a stab.

"Why do *you* think they gave them to us?" Noah asked me.

I didn't say anything. I shrugged my shoulders, unwilling to admit the truth. I couldn't tell them that I had *hoped* it was because they were getting us ready for the outside, or, at the very least, that the three of us had some purpose, some need to know more about the outside world. I liked to think it was because Lizzie and Sarah understood what I did: I felt a need to be connected to the world outside our walls, even a century before Lizzie let me start going outside.

Finally, I said, "You don't think it's a little strange that you two are the only two ever to have been born with the gift of tracking in all our generations, and you just so happened to be two of the ones they chose?"

The boys looked at each other, obviously having never considered this before. Soon Noah's face cleared. "That can't be it. You're not a tracker," he said.

"Yeah," Ben said, backing him up.

"What if I might become one?" I said quietly.

Both boys laughed. "Look, we don't know much about the tracking, where it comes from, how we got it, but we do know that it is something you're born with, not something you get along the way," Ben said. "Besides, you stopped aging over a hundred years ago. Nothing about you is going to change."

Noah could tell they had hurt my feelings, so he tried to fix it. "Sadie, let's think about it. If the three of us were trackers," he began. Ben sneered in the background. "Or something," he said, glaring at Ben, "then maybe it's like Ben said. They wanted us to know how insane it is out there. That way, if ever we had to go outside these walls, because we have the skills of tracking, we'd also have no desire to linger out there because of what we've read."

Noah was trying to be reassuring and supportive of my tracking theory. However, his theory took exactly the opposite spin of the one I was hoping for. In my head, they gave us books, let us know about the outside, because they could tell that one day we'd need to go outside, and that way we'd be prepared. But thinking about what I knew about my family, Noah's version seemed far more correct. The three books had, after all, terrified Noah and Ben, scaring them further and further into loyalty to the family.

I didn't say anything else, but rose to my feet to go back into the city, wanting to be away from the boys, who didn't understand me.

"Sadie, you're a little weird," Ben called out to me as I walked away from them, his voice slurred. Then he broke out laughing.

INTERCONTINENTAL

I had been sitting in a hotel room for three painful months. Though I felt better about my future after Mark had comforted me that night in Bigfork, I was not satisfied. I missed Everett with every fiber of my being. The more time we spent apart, the more every molecule of my body desperately tried to reach out to him.

After Mark left, I gave myself a day to get my head together before retrieving my car from the end of the mountain road near my family's land. I packed everything in it and got on the road, heading west. I drove through the night to Seattle.

I booked a suite at the Four Seasons in downtown Seattle—if I was going to sit and wait in a hotel room, it might as well be a nice one. It overlooked Elliot Bay and had a view all the way to Puget Sound. I was happy to look at water again. I could sit on my couch and waste hours just staring at it, which was good. Because in three sleepless months, I'd had over two thousand hours to waste.

I explored the city by day and delved into my research by night. When I walked the busy streets, I was enthralled with what I could hear. My powers were getting stronger, my senses even sharper. I was able to hear clearly and even see into people's minds. I gained insights into humans by hearing what people were thinking, especially the way they phrased things to themselves before they said them out loud.

People were so interesting! They were more like the characters I had read about in books than I gave them credit for.

But my initial thrill with the city and with my developing powers wore off. After two weeks, I was useless. I couldn't focus on anything. By mid-August, I was a wreck—my nerves stripped, my soul aching. Some days I'd find myself combing iTunes and loading up my iPod to drive aimlessly around Washington, even into Canada. Most days I would waste time and money shopping or telling Corrina about my non-adventures on Twitter. Twitter was becoming very useful for feeling less alone. I began to update it incessantly. I didn't know if Corrina cared about everything I said, but I could pretend. It also helped that I had a forum on which I could share my thoughts and, if nothing else, pretend Corrina was listening because every forty-eight hours my cell phone rang and it was Cole Hardwick and it was getting harder to ignore him. I did ignore the calls ninety percent of the time, though. I was afraid of talking to him, afraid of liking it too much. Afraid of liking *him* too much.

And I tried to sense Everett. But I couldn't find him. I couldn't find any of them. I questioned my ability to track at all.

My research consumed me. I spent the majority of my time studying eastern European folklore concerning vampires, which I had stumbled upon in California. It was far more extensive than any other lore I'd ever researched. I focused on specific legends in which vampirelike creatures were born into their condition like I was. Many creatures in folklore were changed into their supernatural form in one way or another after having first been human and maturing or even dying. My family and the Winters had all been born the way we were. It seemed to set us apart.

I had realized that in my quest to find an avenue for the destruction of my kind, I had inadvertently been studying different origins, too. Many in my family believed that we were created by God, that we had started as humans and then were each chosen to be Survivors. But I couldn't imagine it. I knew there was some sort of lineage, that there was a line that could answer at least some of the questions I had. My search, then, had shifted to a strange place in which I was studying destruction and creation, side by side.

Some of the more obscure vampire lore out of Russia and Romania spoke of vampires who were born, not made, and it sounded promising. But the information was scant, and I kept hitting walls. I knew what this meant: I had reached this point in my research a number of times, and that's when it was time to get on a plane and go to the source. But this time, I couldn't.

I was waiting for the Winters.

Mark had assured me that they would find me when the time was right. Still, I was afraid of going anywhere too crazy. That fear had led me to stay in Seattle, pacing a hotel room for three months.

Finally, I decided to trust Mark. He had not led me astray yet. I determined where I might go, if I decided to go. I chewed on that idea for a while before acting. I lazily browsed flights to Moscow and Bucharest in coffee shops. I researched the areas I thought might be most pertinent to my quest. I made rough plans, looked up hotels, the weather, the terrain.

Then, on the first day of October, as I watched a cloudy and cold Seattle afternoon settle in around Puget Sound, I decided to go. I booked a plane ticket to Moscow, pulled everything out of the hotel closet, and dug deep for clothes that would be appropriate. The weather would be in the 30s and 40s, cold but mild temperatures compared to the winters at home, where it was already snowing and in single-digit temperatures at night.

Although I carried everything I had with me around the States, when I traveled for research, usually in obscure places, I went with the clothes on my back and not much more. I'd often run through the night across vast stretches of land, finding my own sources of information in the moonlight, straying from the cities for days, even weeks at a time. Even though I had grown accustomed to a high-maintenance lifestyle, I was still adaptable.

I left myself only three days to prepare for Moscow. I spent my time packing, making reservations, and preparing financially for time abroad. These trips got expensive quickly. My first class ticket from Seattle to Moscow (via London) cost $11,000 one way. I booked a month at the Hotel National in Moscow. Unfortunately, only one of the larger suites was available at such late notice, so it would be over $1,500 a night for a hotel room I might never spend a night in. That was more than $50,000 just to get to Russia and have a place to leave my things (albeit a nice place). I'd keep my room in the Four Seasons, too, so my things could stay here.

As I boarded my flight from Seattle to London on Sunday evening, I found myself in familiar surroundings. Before I had gone to the wedding in June, before I had seen Mark Winter for the first time, this was the life I had led. I lived entirely by myself, existing without a schedule or responsibilities, real companions, or even a support system. But three months had passed since then, and I was back to where I started.

My mind began to wander. I wondered if I was right to trust Mark. What if they were never coming back?

I spent the next nine hours growing more paranoid. What were they doing that had taken months to accomplish? What had been happening that kept Mark from visiting to reassure me? Why couldn't I sense them? I could read every mind on the plane. I could vividly see the dreams my fellow passengers were having as they slept peacefully or restlessly on the intercontinental flight. I could even sense Corrina's mind though I didn't know where she was. I could feel Lizzie. I could tune into Cole. I was so aware of everything around me. But I couldn't sense the Winters. They had blocked me out entirely. They were hiding.

What if they were never coming for me?

That's it. All along, that had been it. They were never coming back. And how stupid was I for waiting all that time in a hotel room in Seattle, thinking any day they return and I would get my life back?

My chest tightened. I clenched my fists, and I crushed a piece of the armrest by accident. Had that night in front of the bonfire been the last time I was going to see Everett? I twisted inside. This is what it had felt like on the bottom of Swan Lake. I wished I were there. Anywhere was better than being in an enclosed airplane with two hundred people and nowhere to hide—and, worse, nowhere to run.

I felt no release when I got off the plane in London. I found my way to an airport bathroom and closed myself in the tiny stall as I had seen others do. I pressed my fists against the flimsy walls and laid my head against them. I tried in vain to slow my breathing. I was terrified as I realized that Everett had left me.

I couldn't breathe. I felt my throat close up and my chest tighten further. My eyes stung. The bridge of my nose tingled. I was crying. There were no tears, of course. But it was crying just the same. I could barely stand the sensation.

A few long minutes passed before I calmed down a little. I composed myself before I emerged from the stall. I attracted enough attention as I hurried through an airport. I didn't need to look like a sobbing mess to complete my freak show ensemble.

Only when I walked back into the bustling corridor of the terminal to find my connecting flight did reality sink back in. I had a very tight connection, less than forty minutes to cross Heathrow before my next plane began boarding. Having stood in the bathroom stall for longer than I realized, I had missed it. I stumbled to the British Airways counter. Of course, they only flew to Moscow twice a day, and mine had been the second. I was so frustrated. I had had a stupid human moment, and now I was stuck in London for a night. I booked myself on the next morning's flight and staggered out of the airport with only my Longchamp tote—my luggage had gone on to Moscow without me—to find a hotel. I couldn't bear to spend eighteen hours in the terminal.

As I shuffled toward the taxi line, I heard a familiar humming and then an even more familiar voice, before he had even said my name.

"Sadie?" he first said to himself, and then, sure it was me, he exclaimed. "Sadie!" I turned around.

It was Cole.

It would be life's cruel joke to dangle Cole Hardwick in front of me at the exact moment I believed I had lost Everett forever. But here he was, the same piercing blue eyes, two behind me in line, sandy hair sweeping toward his brow, in a classic Brooks Brothers suit. The picture of perfection. I had done an excellent job of forgetting how gorgeous he was.

I thought he might be a mirage. This seemed like a legitimate concern in my current state, so I looked at the two people standing between us and tried to get a read on them. They were both young women about my age. They definitely saw him, too.

Of course! The gorgeous American from my flight has his eye on this supermodel. Leave some for the rest of us, sweetheart, one of them thought, looking me up and down. I closed my eyes, shaking off their cross thoughts.

I figured it was safe to speak now. "Cole," I said. The smile in my voice as I said his name surprised me.

Look at that smile, champ. She's missed you, too, he said in his mind. I saw myself in his mind as he looked me up and down— skimming his eyes over the thick red DVF coat to the silky, multi-print Tracy Reese dress with cinched waist and glancing just too long at the deep V-neck; fixating on the knee-high, laced-up English riding boots. Though subtly, he was checking me out.

I squeezed by the two girls behind me until I was standing next to him. He threw an arm around me, and I stood on my tip-toes, hugging his neck.

"What are you doing in London?" he asked excitedly.

I laughed. "Cole, I told you—all I do is travel. The better question is, What are *you* doing in London? You're the one with a normal job and all," I said.

"I'm here for work," he said. "I've got a major meeting in the morning," he said. In his mind, he said, *Please don't be busy tonight. Please don't be busy tonight! I've waited months for this!* We had stepped up a few spaces in the line.

"Actually, it was an accident. I've missed my connection, and there's not another flight until tomorrow," I said.

"So you're stranded." *Please need a place to stay.* I was a little uneasy with that thought. "What are you going to do?" he asked.

"Kill time," I said. "It's only just after noon, so I'll probably hit Harrod's or Harvey Nicks."

"You girls and your shopping," he laughed. "You're just like Corrina. Where are you going to stay?"

"I'll find some place," I said casually. Though it was nice to see a familiar face, I didn't want to give him the wrong idea.

"You should stay with me so you don't have to pay for a hotel," he said.

"I don't know," I said, letting the heavy concern weigh down my voice.

"Well, at least come with me while I get checked in. You can pull out your laptop there and find a place," he said. Nice save.

"That's sweet of you," I said. "That would be helpful."

Cole beamed inside and out. We had made it to the front of the taxi line. "Shall we?" he said. He opened the door of the taxi for me. Still a perfect gentleman.

Cole was determined to pull out all the stops. In his mind, he had exactly one chance with me, and this was it. He wasn't going to miss it.

I played dumb when we arrived at the Savoy and he upgraded his hotel room to a suite, paying out of pocket for the expense since his company would only pay for the regular room. He would act surprised when we got to his room and found that there was a foldout couch there. His company always treated him so well! Maybe I should think about staying?

I also pretended not to notice the plethora of—I assumed—work calls he ignored on his cell phone. Concerned that I was getting him in trouble, I probed his mind for more information about the meeting. It seemed like he was not neglecting any responsibilities, so I let it go.

I decided to stay with him. I would be out first thing in the morning anyway, and it would force me to lie down and pretend I was sleeping, something that would likely be beneficial to me in my current state. But I would have to purchase some things on our outing—he was going to go shopping with me—including but not limited to real pajamas.

Cole changed into nice jeans and a retro-feeling Thom Browne cut and sewn shirt with a Zegna sweater over it, a casual Theory blazer over that. Aside from the time I had seen him in a towel, I'd never seen him in anything but a suit. He looked so normal, so relaxed, in his jeans. He was also very stylish, which I appreciated.

Cole was more fearless than he had been months before in Tupelo. He was being forward. I'd hear him think about the consequences of each comment before he made it, wondering how much he could get away with without alienating me or offending me. He counted the hours until I had to be back at the airport, and reminded himself over and over again that that would be how much longer he had with me until I was likely gone forever. Unless he acted. So he acted.

He guided me through stores with his hand gently on my back. He made a joke, and I laughed, and he stroked my face. He slid his arm around my shoulders and pulled me close to him, and once, he placed a quick kiss in my hair. I pulled away, casually, but it might have been out of concern over my behavior more than over his: I liked the attention more than I cared to admit.

Cole Hardwick was exactly *what* I wanted. But he wasn't *who* I wanted.

He had offered to buy me a few things while we were out, but I refused. I knew for a fact that I had more money to waste than he did. I also knew he would have gone into debt to make me happy, and I couldn't let him do that. I understood that feeling; I would have done anything for Everett. This was another reason to keep Cole from buying me anything: My heart was in another place.

"At least let me take you to dinner," he argued as we emerged onto Knightsbridge.

I relented. "Fair enough," I said. "Where do you want to go?" I hadn't eaten at all in Seattle, so the idea of food was not so intimidating.

"Anywhere your heart desires," he said, his charming smile working hard to melt me.

"You pick. I don't know London," I said. This was untrue. For one thing, I had been here several times before. For another, I remembered everything I had ever heard or read about it, and I had a mental map of every place we'd walked past or driven past since we left the airport. Still, I wanted him to pick.

"Well, we could see if the concierge can get us good reservations..." he began.

I held up my hand. "No, no. I don't want to go anywhere you'd have to change back into your suit for. I like this version of you," I said, tugging on the lapel of his blazer. I shocked myself at how casual, how *flirty* my words and actions were. He smiled.

Wasn't this exactly the sort of thing I was trying to avoid? After just a day together, he was disarming me. I had to be more careful.

"I like every version of you," he said. I looked away.

We ate a late dinner at a popular Thai restaurant called Mango Tree. It was a brisk night, but we chose to walk from the hotel, passing by Buckingham Palace along the way. I was pleasantly surprised by the Thai food, which I'd never tried before. The swanky atmosphere and the rich food and wine made me feel more normal than I usually did. I wondered if there was something to the Winters' rule about eating and drinking and sleeping to be more like humans.

Cole's anticipation had been building all day. He so badly wanted me to respond to even the smallest of his advances. But I wasn't at all, and it was driving him insane. Though I wasn't exactly objecting. I should have pushed him away more sharply, or made up some lie about having a boyfriend (because that was a lie, wasn't it?). I should have made it clear I had no interest.

But I couldn't bring myself to do it. Everything I liked about Cole Hardwick at the wedding I liked now. Everything I thought made him unique from other human men was still true. He was soft, gentle, respectful, and charming. And he was so beautiful. That shouldn't matter, but it affected me considerably, so it did.

And I had been so alone. I often wondered why I hadn't just gone to Dallas and spent time with Corrina instead of sitting alone at a hotel in Seattle, torturing myself. And even despite the circumstances, Cole's was the first friendly face I'd seen in months, so I was enjoying myself.

"I don't suppose I can get you to tell me what's in Moscow," Cole asked as our server refilled his wine glass.

"It would be too easy that way," I joked. "Besides, I am not so interesting. Not like you think I am, anyway," I said, sipping from my own glass.

"On the contrary," he said. "You're fascinating. I have absolutely no idea why you travel, no idea how you end up where you end up, no idea where you come from, who your parents are, or where you get the money to do what you do. And you're only what, twenty-one?" he asked. I nodded, confirming what it said on my forged passport and birth certificate. *She's younger than Corrina... Does that make her too young? She was born in what...1990? I'm 1985...* He wondered if the five years between us was too great a difference for me. This thinking amused me. "So where's all this life experience come from?" he asked. "It's damn near impossible to think you got out of high school only three years ago." I legitimately had never thought of it that way.

He waited for me to respond, but I kept my eyes fixed on the wine.

So he went on. "What have you been doing since then?" he asked, this time knowing I wouldn't respond. He sighed. "You're a mystery."

I spun the wine around in my glass. "Answers aren't my strong suit," I said.

"Why don't you practice on me then? Start anywhere you like," he said, his voice insistent. He didn't want to let this go. "Like, let's say, why don't you tell me what's in Moscow?"

I kept spinning the wine, saying nothing.

His thoughts were frustrated. He didn't understand why I played these games. They weren't games, of course, but he couldn't know that. Because I could never tell Cole Hardwick the truth.

"Sadie, why do you do this?" he asked, his voice effortless but pointed. He was starting to get mad, in his own calm way.

"Do what?" I asked.

He crossed his arms. I understood his message. "Deflect me like this. I'm just trying to understand you, get inside your head a little. That's not so bad, is it?" he asked.

I bit my lip. "No." I recognized how unfair it was that I could read his mind when all he wanted was a glimpse into mine. I didn't say that, though. "Cole, I've had a strange life. The kind of life no one ever talks about because nobody would believe it." He began to speak, but I knew what he was going to say, so I lifted my hand and stopped him. "And, no, you wouldn't believe me. And even if you would, I'm not going to tell you. I don't have to explain myself to you," I said. "I don't even want to."

He had leaned forward, heated for a moment, but then he sat back. "I can't compete with that, Sadie," he said, his disappointment obvious. "I can compete with anything except you not *wanting* me to know you. I'll listen to anything you want to say. If it's tough stuff, I'll hold you while you cry. If it's strange, I'll believe you. If it's terrible, then I'll forgive you. I just want to know who you are. I want you to know me. I think we could really have something. I feel it in my bones. Sadie, I do," he pleaded. I knew that every word that came out of his mouth was honest.

"Your bones can lie to you," I said, the words cold in my mouth. He was taken aback. "And it's not as simple as telling you a story, as crying while you hold me, or letting you kiss me to comfort me," I said. His heart rate audibly sped up. "There are many reasons that we cannot, that we will not be together. More than I can explain. And I'm sorry for that. I'm sorry that you had your hopes up, that we ended up in London on the same day at the same time. I'm sorry this happened because now you're going to hurt, and I don't want that. I tried to walk away before you got hurt once already."

But it was too late. He was already hurt. The pain was radiating from him in heavy waves, swirling around me, hanging on like thick velvet curtains weighing me down. I couldn't handle it. I pushed my chair back, grabbed my shopping bags and my travel tote, and stood up. "Maybe this is my exit cue," I said.

"Sadie, wait," he said. He made a motion to stand up, too, but I dismissed him.

I knew this wasn't the smoothest or most polite way to do things, but Cole's beautiful mouth was in a tight frown and his blue eyes were filled with sadness, and all I could think of was Everett Winter's golden-green eyes and warm smile.

I just couldn't stay. Everett was the only one I wanted, the one my heart was breaking for, the way Cole's was breaking for me.

"Sadie, please," he pleaded. Now we were both standing, clearly causing a scene. "Don't do this."

"No, I should go," I said, my hand landing on his arm. "Cole, it's been so lovely to see you. Thank you for a lovely day and a lovely dinner," I said. "I wish you the best." He dropped back down into his seat and looked up at me in disbelief. The gentleman in him wanted to stop me from going, or at least escort me to the hotel. But then the rest of him couldn't make it happen. He was too crushed.

"I'm sorry again," I said, and I turned my back on him. I slid two £100 notes into the host's hand to cover the check and then some. I took one more look at Cole's pained face. He wasn't looking at me.

He let me walk away.

12

BLANK SLATE

I boarded my flight the next morning after killing time all night. And by the time I landed in Moscow, I had purged the images of Cole's pained face from my mind. I was focused and ready to begin.

The bright high ceilings of the Hotel National's lobby delighted me. Mesmerized by the architecture and classic style, I spent the afternoon wandering Moscow, getting my bearings in this foreign place, and speaking to as many people as I could to get used to the feel of Russian on my tongue. I had no idea what I would have done in my travels if I hadn't had the ability to speak any language I heard. And now that I could read minds, even more limitations had been lifted. When I couldn't read a sign—I could speak the language but I couldn't read it—or when I got confused, I could tune into minds around me and figure things out.

After I found some landmarks to depend on, I went back to the hotel and unpacked. Moscow at this time of year was not a sunny place. The locals told me it was light out for only about three hours a day. This meant I had to be careful not to confuse darkness with isolation—too often I'd feel protected by a cloak of darkness, content that most people were asleep or off the roads at night. Given that it could be pitch black at three in the afternoon, I would have to pay close attention to who could see me.

I dressed for a cold evening in rugged terrain. I stuffed myself into a long wool coat lined and quilted with down and fur trim around the collar, wrapped a thick scarf around my neck and pulled on my hiking boots. I strapped a tight-fitting messenger bag across my frame. I stuffed it with pencils and my Moleskine journal, my digital camera with three or four fully charged batteries, battery-pack boosters that I could hook up to my iPhone, and a tiny laptop that could pick up the Internet wherever there was cell phone coverage. I'd picked up several different kinds of maps, and I had a slim compass I took everywhere with me. I also carried an unsafe amount of cash—American dollars, Euro, and rubles. One of the truest things I had learned in my time passing as a human was that money talks. And because I wouldn't go anywhere without it, I slipped my old book of Hesiod in the bag, wrapped in a scarf for safekeeping.

I waited until the evening commute subsided, until most people were at home, and then I was ready to go.

I had planned to rely on my instincts. My new ability to hear the humming of a supernatural mind from a distance was going to be my guide. The Winters had opened up my eyes to the existence of others like us, so now I was looking for them. They would be the best sources of the information I coveted.

Once I made my way out of Moscow, I darted between towns and suburbs before I got to land empty enough that I could run at my fastest speeds. I was headed south toward the Ukrainian border, but somewhere near Voronezh I heard a distinct humming that sent me eastward.

By then, it was morning. I had to slow down when I passed towns and was close enough to be seen.

For several days, I wandered, following the elusive humming. I passed through several towns big enough to have museums or tourist destinations dedicated to their own mythology. I stopped at each one, finding everything from monuments dedicated to witches burned at the stake to locals who believed in burying their loved ones face down so they wouldn't come back from the dead as vampires.

On the third day, I was walking through the countryside when the off-key humming picked up full force. The weird pitch had come and gone over the past few days, but it was always on my mental radar. Now it was loud and clear. I topped a hill and was not surprised to find a sleepy village tucked into the small valley below me. The sound amplified in my ears. Surprisingly, there was no normal humming to balance out the rare sounds. Whoever lived inside this tiny village was entirely inhuman and entirely alone.

I went slowly down the hillside, flipping through the vampiric names I had heard in several towns over the last few days: purple-faced vampires who hunted only at night that some called the *myertovjec*, heretics reborn into haggard old women they'd named *eretica*, even the beautiful but lethal women they called the *vordulak*. More than one poor soul had looked at me nervously while explaining the *vordulak*, afraid that I was one of them. I was surprised at how many young people believed in the existence of these creatures. I hadn't expected that.

The town was all but deserted. Doors hung sideways off rusted hinges. Planks rotted off the sides and roofs of abandoned shacks. Grass grew high between the houses, and crowded the sides of the dirt road in the middle of town. I could hear a suspicious silence coming from one dilapidated shack at the end of the road. It was obvious that whoever was inside had each silenced one another when they heard me coming. I headed straight to it.

I called out loudly, "I know you can hear me, and I can hear you. I mean you no harm. I'd just like to talk," I said. I heard fierce whispers among the group. From what I could hear of their minds, I was fairly certain there were three of them, but I couldn't shake the idea that there was a greater presence.

"Who is she? Why does she not fear us?" one hissed.

"How did she find us?" another asked.

"We should trap her," another said. They murmured in agreement.

"Eat her," one said. I tried not to laugh.

I thought I'd level the playing field. "I said I can hear you," I called. "And if you want to eat me, you'll have to catch me first, which might be harder than you think," I said. They could hear the amusement in my voice, and it angered them.

I was standing in front of the tiny home now. The door swung open with such force that it teetered on its hinges. I was taken aback by an overpowering stench I had never smelled before. A rough, wrinkled woman with yellowed white hair down to her waist stood in front of me. I knew she was an *eretica*. She was hunched over and at least a foot shorter than I was. Her skin looked like crinkled tea-stained paper with gross irregularities in it. Her cheeks were hollow, as if she had no teeth. But she had unmistakably dangerous, long fingers that looked like hollow needles at the end. I could guess what they were used for.

"You shouldn't be here," she said, her Russian thick and slurred. *Not often we get your kind this way, witch. Most of them know to leave us be.*

"I would like to talk to you," I said calmly.

"We're not interested," she said gruffly. She stepped back to swing the door closed, but I stepped forward to catch it and got a foot and hand inside the doorframe. The smell was even stronger there, and I realized now that it was coming from a stack of at least ten dead bodies piled high on one side of the shack. I tried not to react, but she caught my eye. My horrified expression redirected her thinking. *Wait! She's a human! A special treat, for sure.* She squealed to herself, her inner monologue a much younger voice than her speaking voice. A terrifying amusement sparkled in her cloudy eyes. They were foggy blue like the pigment had gone from them, and had a red rim around the iris. She might be blind. "Are you scared yet, girl?" she asked.

"Why would I be?" I said casually. A raspy cackle erupted from her lips. She stepped closer to me and I stepped backward, out of the shack and away from the bodies. Two other women like her stood behind her and walked toward me. I backed all the way across the lane until I was pressed against the shack opposite them. One of them had fiery red hair and eyes but the same old, wrinkly skin. The other had solid obsidian eyes like I had never seen before. I prayed for protection in the presence of such devilish creatures. I had not asked God to help me in quite some time.

"We'll kill you, girl, that's why," she said.

If she's human, she's stupid, the one with red hair and red eyes was thinking.

Look at this pretty little girl. A witch, she must be. Who else would have that skin? No matter, the one with black eyeballs thought. *We'll catch her.* Did they think they could outrun me?

"I'm not a witch," I said, forgoing whatever game we were playing. "But I can read your minds," I admitted. "Like I said, I'd like to be fair. I just want to talk."

They reacted negatively to this. They were certain I couldn't read their minds, and they were offended that I would make such an excessive and outlandish claim.

"I know it's strange," I said, "but it's true. And I'm obviously not one of you."

"Then what are you?" the red-haired one asked.

"She's a stupid human who is good at lying. Can't you smell her? She's trying to trick us into believing she's not human so we won't try and drink of her," the first old woman said.

Oh, Annika, she's not human. Just look at her! the red-haired one said in her head. I wondered if they could hear each other thinking.

"Annika, is it?" I said to her. The three exchanged glances and then looked back at me.

"What is she, Annika?" the one with red hair asked, ruffled that I could read her mind.

"Something strange," Annika said, her eyes narrowing. My attention was focused on the *eretica* with the dark, scary eyes standing behind Annika. Her head was turned sideways and her hand was outstretched toward me. She was trying to decide if she should try to suck blood from me.

"I'm not any stranger than you," I laughed, but they did not. "We're a lot alike. My name is Sadie, by the way. And you're Annika.

What are your names?" I asked politely of the other two. They didn't respond. "No names, then? Should I just call you both *eretica?*" I asked, deciding to make clear I knew who and what I was dealing with. They hissed at the name.

"What do you want to know?" Annika finally asked.

"I'm looking for information on my kind and yours. Really, on any kind that's not human. Can you help me with that?" I asked.

Annika deliberated. The one with black eyes was still waiting to pounce, but the one with the red hair was growing curious. She spoke. "I can," she said. Her mind was less callous than the others'. "You walk this way with me?" she asked, nodding toward an open expanse of land just past the houses. There was a line of thick forest a few hundred yards beyond it.

Annika's thoughts were not pleasant. She hadn't wanted the red-haired one to talk to me, but she wasn't going to stop her either. She returned to the house with the bodies, and the ravenous black-eyed one went with her.

"I'm Ritka," she said as we walked. "I have never seen your kind before, so I want to know what you are. That's why I'm talking to you," she explained. She wanted to be clear that this was no favorable gesture, only a morbid curiosity on her part.

"I thank you, Ritka. I've never seen your kind before, either, but I have heard of you," I said. "You're vampires, are you not?".

She shrugged. "You say vampire like there's only one kind. We are *eretica.* We drink blood, yes, but that is all we have in common with the others. We don't have teeth, and we don't hunt. We don't turn into bats, either," she said. A gruff cough escaped her lips. I think she was laughing.

"Where do you come from?" I asked.

"We all three lived in this village. A strange man came maybe fifty years ago. He was of the devil, I suppose. He offered us immortality in exchange for our souls. The three of us were already condemned as heretics, shamed for not believing in the God they all believed in.

We thought we had nothing to lose," she said. Her voice grew raspier as she spoke. I sensed she didn't talk often.

"But you did lose something," I said, expounding on what she was thinking.

"We lost everything," she said. "Our souls first, but then we turned into this," she said, pulling at the loose skin on her cheeks. "It took a year or two before we were completely changed. But the blood-lust came before that. It happened to Annika first. She was making love to a traveler when she was overcome with a need for his blood. She bit at him but couldn't get it fast enough. She clawed at his neck till the blood poured out. And she drank it all. Soon her fingers began to change," she said wiggling the arthritic, hollow points of her own. "Eventually, we couldn't control it."

"What did the people in your village say?" I asked.

"Nothing they could say," she said. *We killed them too quickly*, she thought. I had figured as much.

"Have you known many of your kind?" I asked.

"No, but we had heard the stories, too, like you," she said.

"Have you heard stories of any of you dying?" I asked.

"They say we can drown in fresh water but not in saltwater. We have never tried, obviously," she said. I was disappointed. I knew I could not drown.

"Do you feel pain?" I asked.

"Only where I once had a soul," she said. "We are not like others either. We aren't fast, and we aren't strong. But the rest are."

"The rest of who?" I asked.

"The others you'd call vampires. They are always fast and strong. I bet you are like that," she said.

"I'm not a vampire, though," I said.

"Then what are you?" she asked, cocking her head to one side. "If you're not a witch and not a vampire? A shape-shifter?" she asked.

I shook my head. "I'm something in between, I guess. I don't know what you'd call me."

"Do you have a family?" she asked.

"I do," I said.

"And you were born this way or you were turned?" she asked.

"Born," I said.

"Maybe you're a *vieczy*," she said. I raised an eyebrow. "You haven't heard of them?" she asked. She made the same throaty sound. "*Vieczy* is the child of a witch and a shape-shifter. They say women shape-shifters can't bear children, but the men can impregnate. And everyone knows witches can have children," she explained. I reached for my pack, pulled out my notebook, and started scribbling furiously. "They are born, not turned like us. I think they may be the only vampires who are. Sometimes they grow old, but usually they stop around your age," she said.

"But they are immortal?" I asked.

"Of course," she scoffed.

"Can they die?" I asked. She looked at me strangely.

What kind of trouble are you in, pretty girl? She asked in her mind. "I suppose," she said. "But I don't know how. Some say cutting out the cold, still heart will do it, but *vieczy* I've met have skin too hard to penetrate. It's colder than a witch's or a shape-shifter's, and it's hard like stone," she said.

"That's not me, then," I said. I pulled up my sleeves a little to show some of the scars around my wrists.

She was taken aback. "You are sure you aren't a witch?" she asked. "They're the only ones who bleed like humans. They have heartbeats, too."

"But I don't have a heartbeat, and I don't bleed either," I said. "You can open the skin, and there is blood inside, but it doesn't pump, and it's thick like molasses."

"Are you sure?" she said. She looked at me with a new curiosity in her eyes, appraising my movements. "Witches can die, you know. You can drown them or burn them or break their necks. And we can take blood from them. We don't like it like human blood, but it will do if we need it to, when we can catch them."

She was thinking that I was a witch, and she was starting to picture the same things the one with the black eyes had. I tried to derail her. "How do you catch them?" I asked.

She squinted up at me to focus on my eyes. "We can paralyze them if they look into our eyes. And then we can have them. Sometimes they can still run after just a look," she explained. "But they die later." She, of course, was trying to do that to me. It wouldn't work, I knew. I was impervious to such powers.

She licked her lips.

"I'm not a human," I sighed, sliding the journal and pencil back into my bag. "And I'm not a witch," I said as I slid my coat off and rolled my sweater up to my elbow. "You can try, though," I said. I extended my bare forearm out to her.

For one second she looked at me in disbelief, but then she let a snarl escape from her mouth. She didn't hesitate after that.

She had to try several times, her brow tensed, to get the needle-like end of her finger through my skin. She inserted it parallel to my arm, the way I'd seen blood drawn on television. The pain was searing at first but subsided.

This was, of course, how it went when I traveled. If I were met with a village or a tribe with legends about killing creatures, I would tell them what I was so they would try it on me. Mostly they were vicious and extremely anxious to destroy any creature they came across. It had obviously never worked, but it had always been painful.

Ritka continued for a few moments. She was making gurgling sounds as her long fingers tensed and wiggled a little inside my arm. That made my stomach catch. She was getting frustrated. I assumed that meant it wasn't working.

"Ah!" she yelled suddenly, and she ripped her finger from my arm. That hurt much more than I anticipated. I looked at the pale skin of my forearm. There was a hole in my flesh about a quarter of an inch in diameter, and it burned. It was very deep and jagged, and would, of course, leave another scar.

"Didn't work?" I asked.

"You aren't *vieczy*," she said, breathing hard. It took her some time to recover. "They have no blood, and I wouldn't be able to break the skin, though it wasn't easy breaking yours. But there's nothing normal about you, either. Your blood is thick. It tasted good but it burned inside me like acid," she said, anger and disappointment in her voice. *Tasted?* I thought. Hadn't it gone in through her fingers?

"So you don't know what I am?" I asked.

"You are nothing we've met. There is a very rare creature we've only heard of that has no name. It is supposedly like the other vampires in ability, but the skin is softer, and they are beautiful, but no one knows if they drink blood or not. I've never met one. They're warm, too. Not like humans or witches, but warmer than us and the *vieczy* and the others. They live among humans because of their soft skin and beauty," she said.

That piqued my interest. "But you've never heard their name?" I asked. I rolled down my sleeve and picked up my coat.

She shook her head. "Some say they're like blank slates. They become like one of us—or something—sooner or later. Maybe good like the *moroi* who protect their living families, maybe bad like us or the *vordulak*," she explained.

"Where did you hear of these creatures?" I asked.

She looked embarrassed. "From some witches," she said, "before we killed them." She turned and started walking toward the house.

"Thank you for speaking with me," I said, calling after her. "I have money, if you would like. I could pay you for your troubles."

"We have no use for the money," she said. "Just leave us and do not return. I am not sure what you are, but it can't be good to have you near," she said. I understood. This was generally the feeling I left in my wake.

"I will," I said. I put on my coat. The sun had set in the time we were talking, and the land was deserted for many miles around. I ran as fast as I could out of the strange village, stopping when I was safely far away to write down a memory this strange encounter triggered. Then I raced back to Moscow.

MEMOIR

The Survivors' City, Montana
March 1992

It was a quiet, freezing afternoon. The snow had fallen in blankets for days without stopping. It was awful. But that day, it had finally laid off. The wind had stopped, too, and, because we didn't mind the cold, it was a perfect afternoon. About thirty of us had gathered outside the city walls to run in the snow. A massive snow fight had ensued. The others started to get tired or lose interest, but Noah and Ben and I had remained. Andrew emerged from the gate where he had been watching us, and he called for Ben. Noah and I followed, knowing we wouldn't be allowed to stay outside the gates alone. "No, no, you stay," Andrew called, waving at us. Noah and I looked at each other, not going to turn down a chance at staying outside the walls with no one to bother us. I took off running and then jumped off a little bank, diving into the deep snow. Noah laughed hard behind me and followed suit. It was one of the happiest, most carefree moments of my entire existence as a Survivor before I left.

Laying on top of the snow and watching the thick clouds move overhead, I decided to talk to Noah about something I had been reading about. I had not told him what I did in Bigfork every day, but he was the only one other than Lizzie and Andrew who paid enough attention to me to know that I left every day. He had kept that secret safe, so I thought of him as an ally.

"Hey, I have a question," I said, trying to act naturally.

Noah had been half-buried in the snow bank a few feet down from me. He pulled his body free and launched himself so he landed right next to me. "Shoot," he said. My speech had grown increasingly modern even with only limited time on the outside and with my extensive exposure to literature. Noah had picked up on it when he spoke with me.

"When you're with the elders, do you ever hear that really soft, pounding sound? Like someone rhythmically tapping against the inside of your head?" I asked.

He considered this. "Happens about a hundred times a minute, right?" he asked.

"Yeah," I said. "Do you know what that is?" I asked.

"I guess it's a heartbeat," he said.

I nodded, having read a lot about this. "I think so, too," I said. "Do you notice you don't hear that sound all the time?" I asked.

He sat up and looked down at me. "I hadn't thought about it," he said. "But I don't hear it right now."

"I don't either," I said. "I think we don't have heartbeats."

Noah thought intently about this for a minute. He stuffed his hand inside his shirt and laid his palm flat against his chest. "I mean, it's stupid that I never thought of this before now. But even when we read about heartbeats—I didn't know what they meant. I mean, I understand the concept of a heartbeat, but I never felt one," he said.

"Me neither. Even when we were kids?" I asked.

"Never," he said. "You think something is wrong with us?"

"I mean, it's probably not that weird. We are immortal. Who's to say our hearts could hold up for that long? This probably just comes with the territory of being...not human," I said.

"That bothers you, doesn't it?" he asked.

"What does?" I asked.

"It bothers you that there's another way you're not like humans. You always sound like you're disgusted or irritated or something when you say, 'We're not like humans,'" he said. I never thought of Noah as being particularly perceptive before that moment.

I sort of shrugged, ignoring his question. "Do you think there's something to it? To their hearts beating and ours not?" I asked.

"Well, maybe if it's just us then it's something weird. I mean, it's already got to be a little weird that we were born at exactly the same time," he said.

"You think there are others? I've been trying to tell, but there are always several people around, so I always hear the heartbeat sort of," I said.

"Let's find out," Noah said. I smiled. This is what I wanted, but I didn't know if I could enlist his help.

Noah and I spent the next two weeks slowly getting each Survivor alone enough so that we could tell if they had heartbeats or not. Noah could hear a little clearer than I could, but I didn't miss any.

Then we made a list. Of all the Survivors, we found twenty-seven who didn't have a heartbeat. Including the two of us, that made twenty-nine. I carved the list of names of the twenty-nine still-hearted Survivors into the tree like I did with my questions 110 years before. I did this because (just like right now) I like writing down things to think through them. I committed the list to memory, and then Noah touched his hand to the wood and the bark fell off in ashes. We talked endlessly about the meaning of a heartbeat, and I told him what I knew of them, of blood, and of the purpose of those things to the human body (breaking the rules Lizzie had set out for me, I suppose). We hypothesized on why hearts might not do the same things for Survivors.

Unable to really explain it, we decided it must be because, as time went on, Survivors were still evolving, and the need for a heart that pumped blood grew superfluous. (Then I had to explain the concept of evolution to him, which he didn't like. He called it blasphemous, so I laid off.)

13
BODY AND BLOOD

When I reached Moscow, I was exhausted. My body ached and my arm throbbed. I stopped at a drug store and bought some cleansing face wipes and a brush and hair bands, then I got a cab back to the hotel. In the car, I brushed through my hair and pulled it into a smoother ponytail, and I wiped the grit and dirt off my face, neck and hands, which made me feel considerably better than I had. Traveling the way I did, without bathing or resting or even going inside, was tough. I tried to make myself look presentable before I walked back into the nicest hotel in the city.

The manager of the Hotel National was in the lobby when I returned. He greeted me by name and then wondered, silently, where I had been. I ignored that and greeted him back, but he stopped me.

"Ms. Matthau," he said, in heavily accented English, "you have had a guest arrive for you," he said. My chest tightened. "He asked to see you, but we respect your privacy, so we did not tell him you were away. But because you are such a grand customer, we gave him a room, free of charge. He is there now," he said. I frantically searched the manager's mind for an image of my visitor, but his memory of the man's face was fuzzy. It could have been anyone.

"Thank you so much," I said. "I would like to see him."

"We could send him to your suite, if you like?" he suggested.

I nodded. "Please do," I said. "Thank you again."

I wanted to run full speed up the emergency stairs up to my suite, but I had to remain composed. So I just quickly went to the elevator and waited the eternity it took to get to my floor. No one was in my hallway, so I ran to my door and let myself in. I had only a few minutes before my mystery guest arrived. I stripped my dirty clothes and flipped through my suitcase to find something decent to wear. I could hear footsteps coming down my hall before I had even decided what to put on. I quickly threw on the dress I'd worn in London because it was lying out from before I left, and I pulled my hair out of the ponytail and smoothed it. I rubbed my lips with lip balm and dusted my face with powder and blush. The bell to my suite rang as I was jumping back into my boots. He was here.

I could hear absolutely nothing from the other side of the door, so either it was Mark projecting or I had completely lost my focus, which was possible. Without even checking, I flung the door open.

"Oh, thank God!" I yelped.

It was Everett Winter.

He was every bit as beautiful as I remembered him—the piercing green eyes, a broad smile on his face as I threw my arms around his neck. He squeezed me tight and lifted me off the ground.

"Sadie," he breathed into my ear, kissing the side of my head. "Oh, Sadie," he repeated. I couldn't bring myself to let go, and he laughed softly. He carried me farther into the room, closing the door behind us.

"I knew you would come!" I exclaimed. "I've missed you so much," I said breathlessly. As soon as I spoke the words, I knew how true it was. I couldn't stand to be away from him for one more second.

"I've missed you, too. I haven't been able to function without you," he said. We were still just standing there, holding each other.

"I thought you might hate me," he said. "I was so worried."

I jerked back from him. "Why did you think that?" I asked, concerned.

"Because," he said, "I left you behind. And no one has even so much as told you we were alive." I rolled my eyes at the colloquialism. "I can't imagine how that made you feel," he said. "I'm so sorry."

I put my hands around his waist and pulled him in, but I leaned back so I could see his face. "I'm not going to lie to you. It was terrible being apart from you. But this is all I was waiting for, all I ever wanted," I said. He was relieved. "I've just missed you so much," I said again, unable to come up with anything else to say. I sank my head into his hard chest. I couldn't believe he was really there. I had played this moment over and over again in my head, and now it was happening.

He wrapped his big arms around my shoulders and kissed the top of my head three times. I looked up at him and he bent his head toward me, cautiously leaning toward my lips. I freed one of my hands from around his waist and placed it on his neck. His skin was so cool, but just like it had months before, the contact felt hot. He closed the tiny distance between us until our lips met.

His sterling silver lips were exactly as I remembered them. His breath was just the same. The feel of his face was smooth and cool, too. It felt like perfection as I ran my fingers over it.

He parted his lips slightly, and I fit my lips between his. His tongue ran over my bottom lip. I shivered. I had never felt that before. I lost my concentration for a second.

He noticed it. "Everything okay?" he asked, his voice cracking as he said it.

"Everything's fine," I said. I pressed our foreheads together and then kissed him lightly again once and then again for good measure. Then I took his hand and stepped to the couch. I let myself fall backward, taking him with me. I forgot how exhausted I was. "I'm sorry," I said. "I'm so dead."

He smiled. "You were out exploring, eh?"

"Yeah. How long have you been here?" I asked.

"Since yesterday," he said.

I sighed. "A whole day of Everett just wasted!" I joked. "How'd you find me?"

"I have my ways," he smiled deviously. I swatted him with the back of my hand. "What? I can't give it all away. There'd be no mystery left in the relationship, and then where would we be?" He laughed again.

"Relationship?" I squeaked. I was instantly nervous. Had I misinterpreted that? Or did he mean *relationship*?

He righted his posture so he was hovering over me a little. "You think I came to Russia—a place that, it turns out, is just as dark and cold as I imagined it—so some other guy could sweep you off your feet?" he asked. He stroked my face and moved my hair out of my eyes. "Sadie, maybe I wasn't clear enough. I literally accomplished nothing for the last three months. I was a moody jackass to my whole family. I have spent every second wondering about you, worried about you, wanting to be with you. I lie in bed every single night and remember what it felt like to kiss you. I envision your face, your smile, your hair," he said, stroking the strands gently. "I just want to look into these pretty purple eyes every day for the rest of my existence. I get lost looking at you. It's some kind of nirvana I've never experienced before."

I swallowed hard, enamored. "I know exactly what you mean."

After I had looked at Everett long enough to believe he wasn't going anywhere, I told him I really needed to get cleaned up after my trip. He kicked off his shoes and propped himself up on several pillows on the bed and flipped channels on the TV. He looked like he was pulled straight from the pages of editorial ads in *Vogue*—Ralph Lauren Black Label, maybe Prada, or even some of the more subdued Dolce and Gabbana. His jeans were nice and dark but worn in—Dolce, I was pretty sure—and fitted. And he had on a crisp white Dior dress shirt. He'd removed his chocolate velvet sport coat—I recognized it from Ferragamo's fall catalogue from the year I came to Nashville—and laid it on the bed next to him. He looked effortless, but he had been very careful in the choices he'd made, right down to the silk Brioni pocket square folded in his jacket pocket. His look was classic, tailored, but fashionable. He'd always dressed this way, and I of all people hadn't noticed. I rarely got past his face.

He caught me staring. He laughed a little and kissed the air in front of him. I smiled when I realized how comfortable he must be with me to act this way. Then he turned back to the TV.

I gathered up everything I would need to get ready—from clothes to hair products—and went into the bathroom to bathe. It took me a while, I admit, to get half a week's dirt and dust off of me, to dry my hair flawlessly, get my makeup just right, and get completely dressed. I had chosen to wear jeans because he was, but I layered a tank with a striped, long sleeved Elizabeth and James T-shirt so I didn't look like I was going too over the top. I'd top that with a crazy leather, wool, and fur Helmut Lang asymmetrical jacket I'd picked up in Zurich the year before. I would wear boots but flat ones. I liked fitting into a very specific crook of Everett's neck, and that only happened if I wasn't wearing heels.

I thought about him all the while. I wondered, of course, where he had been and what he had been doing. I wanted to know why he had come to find me now: Could he just not take it any longer? Had something happened? Had Anthony finally relented, or did he come without his father's consent? He probably wondered why I was in Moscow, and I wondered what Mark might have told him about the night in Bigfork.

But as I was applying a thin layer of lip gloss to my lips, I realized I wasn't able to sense him. I hadn't heard any humming or read his mind, hadn't felt what he felt since he had walked through the door. I flung the bathroom door open and walked out.

"Whoa," he said. "You look gorgeous." He smiled softly, but then he registered the look on my face. My grand entrance had been ruined.

"Why can't I sense you?" I asked, heated.

He looked down. "Sadie," he began.

"You're really here, aren't you? You're not projecting?" I asked urgently.

"I'm really here," he said. "You know I can't project."

"I don't know anything," I said. "Why can't I, Everett?"

"It's a bulwark," he said, sighing.

"A what?"

"A mental defense. A blockade so you can't read our thoughts," he explained.

"You literally built a wall to keep me out of your head?" I asked incredulously.

He had been dreading this conversation. "It wasn't my idea. It was a Patrick and Anthony creation." He had never called Anthony by his first name. I guessed it meant he was mad at him.

"Why would you do this?" I asked.

"It's important to my father that you can't get in our heads. We've never actually met someone who could do it," he said. He'd sat up and slid to the end of the bed, his back hunched, his head in his hands. "Sadie, I can't explain it right now. I can just tell you that it wasn't my idea, and I didn't have a choice. I had to go along with it," he said.

Even though I didn't know for sure, I guess I thought Anthony had let Everett come here, like maybe the stupid family feud would dissolve before it became anything more serious. But now Anthony was trying to keep me out.

I sank down next to him. "Is it just you?" I asked.

"It's all of us," he said. I bit my lip. My eyes stung a little.

"Even Ginny?" I asked.

"No. Ginny's...special," he said. "She can't assume any new powers. It's part of being a mirror." I wasn't as relieved as I thought I would be to hear that. There were so many rules I didn't understand, so many things they knew that I didn't.

I turned and looked Everett directly in the eye. "What are you hiding from me?" I asked him. He closed his eyes to break the contact. "Tell me," I said.

"It's not that easy, Sadie," he said, rising to his feet. He hugged his arms across his chest, pacing.

"This is ridiculous," I said. "Why are you keeping secrets?"

"Wait a minute," he said, his voice a little hostile. "Where would you like to start on secrets?" he said, his tone not so forgiving. "How about what you're doing in Russia? Or why I smell fresh blood? Or why you really left your family?"

"Those aren't secrets," I said. "You haven't asked, for one. But, two, I haven't gone out of my way to hide those things. They just haven't come up." I knew as soon as I'd said it, it was a mistake. A defense like that would do nothing but put me on the spot.

He wasn't pleased. "Why'd you leave your family?" he said, testing me.

"Aside from generally hating them? They wanted to get me pregnant," I said quickly so I wouldn't chicken out. "Forcefully," I added.

He raised an eyebrow. He appeared to be as surprised to be getting answers as I was to be giving them. "You didn't approve of a child?" he asked.

I couldn't look him in the eye. "No," I said, pressing my lips together. "Or the way they wanted to do it."

"Russia?" he asked.

"Researching," I said. I had a headache. I put my hands back to my forehead and began to massage my temples. I was certain I would regret this honesty later.

"What?" he asked.

"World mythology, local legends about supernatural stuff, vampire lore. That sort of thing," I said coolly.

"And what's that to you?" he asked, his body suddenly tense.

"I want to know how we can be killed. I think it's ridiculous that we are all but invincible. I think it's wrong that we couldn't stop our kind even if we got dangerous. We could be out there killing innocent humans or something, and there'd be nothing I could do about it," I said, my voice passionate.

Everett was completely frozen next to me, his hands balled up into fists on his knees, his shoulders hunched toward his ears. "And that's all?" he asked, his jaw clenched.

"Maybe I wouldn't mind knowing how to die, if the time came," I said. I was going all in. He'd find out all of this eventually, so it might as well be now.

This information changed his expression. His face looked worried now. "So you're on a suicide mission?" he asked, concerned.

"That isn't quite it," I said. He frowned. "Do I get to ask questions too?" I asked.

"Momentarily," he said. "Does your research...does it have anything to do with the scars?" So Mark had told him.

"Of course it does. How else can I test the theories?" I asked.

"You are trying to kill yourself," he said quietly.

"It's not like that," I said calmly. Okay, it wasn't *totally* like that.

"How come you can scar? No beating heart, no pumping blood to heal skin. How is it possible?" he said.

"I have no idea," I said.

"What about the smell of blood? Did you try and off yourself today?" he asked bitterly.

"I didn't hurt myself, no, but yesterday I met someone who tried," I said, leaving out the details.

"Let's see them," he said, turning to face me. I had my eyes closed tight, my lips pressed tighter. I could feel him looking. I shrugged out of my jacket and pulled my sweater up an inch or two so he could just see the ones around my wrist. His breath caught, and I pulled my sleeve back down. "Hey," he said clasping my wrist. I looked up at him, my eyes pleading. "I need to see them all," he said. "Please," he added.

I didn't move. He reached for the hem of my sweater and pulled it up gently. I straightened my arms and let him pull it over my head, leaving me in just a tank top. My arms and shoulders were bare. My newest wound was still jagged and not healing as quickly as my skin usually did. I closed my eyes again, in some kind of pain from watching this happen.

He gently lifted my wrist and brought it to his face. I was shocked when the tip of his nose gently ran along the scar nearest my hand. Then his cool lips pressed softly against it. It was the most tender thing I'd seen in my life.

"Where's this one from?" he asked, his voice a whisper.

I hesitated, and he could tell. He looked at me out of the corner of his eyes, his face not leaving my wrist. His eyes were asking for the story as gently as they could.

I relented. "Cursed eagle talon to make the sorcerers bleed," I said quietly. "From the Cherokee in North Carolina."

His silky lips glided on my skin to a jagged, raised scar about an inch further up my arm. He kissed it gently. "And this one?" he asked.

"Burn of some kind from the Aborigines in Australia," I said quietly. "They rubbed something on it and then held smoldering wood to it." His eyelids fluttered, dusting his eyelashes against my skin as he kissed this scar. The images were disturbing him, I was sure.

He gently turned my wrist over and skimmed his nose along the length of a thin, shiny white scar that ran from the edge of my palm up my arm. "Dagger dipped in holy water," I said. "A trick used on the *stregas*—er, witches—outside the Vatican." It took seven kisses to cover the length of it.

We went on like that. He didn't say much, but he held me closer and closer as he made his way up one arm and down the other until he had kissed every single scar. It was the most intimate experience I had ever had. I was so vulnerable like that, my secrets so exposed. But he didn't pull away in fear, and he hadn't been repulsed. Instead, he took great care to show me how these scars hurt him, too, and how he cared for me—scars and all. I might have been blind without my second senses, but I was fairly certain in that moment that Everett Winter was in love with me.

He eventually wrapped his thick arms around me and pulled me onto his lap. I put my head in the crook of his neck. I liked this place—it was cool and smooth and smelled like him. We were quiet for a while. I had never felt so at peace.

"Sadie, you can't keep doing this," he finally said. "I'll go out of my mind with worry. I care way too much about you now." This pulled at me. If the tables were turned, I wouldn't want him out on kamikaze missions either.

"I just want to know if it can be done, Everett," I said.

"Do you know how hard people search for immortality?" he asked. "It's a millennia-old quest. People sell their souls for it. But you and me? We were born with it. And how extraordinary, right? Because you're a gorgeous young supermodel, barely more than a teenager, and I'm an energetic young twenty-something who is crazy enough to try and keep up with you, and we get to stay this way forever. And look what we've seen! What we've lived through! World wars. Women's suffrage. A civil rights movement. Revolutions all over the world. The Cold War. The music. Cars. Computers. Art. Do you know I was at a gallery opening of Degas's work before anyone had ever heard of him? Picasso, too. Don't you think it's a gift, Sadie?"

I put my hand against his chest. "You don't understand. I didn't live through all of that. I mean, even though it was happening in the world around me, I was incarcerated in that walled city in Montana. We didn't know about revolutions—political, sexual, or otherwise—because we didn't know about anything outside our walls. I didn't know any of it existed until I started reading books, until I started breaking the rules in the eighties, Everett. The *nineteen* eighties. And I still don't know it all. But what I do know is that I haven't experienced anything. I might have six iPods worth of music and have read more books than a library has, but it's not the same thing as living it. I don't have a romantic vision of immortality. It's been nothing but chains to me." I searched his eyes as I said this. I desperately hoped he understood, but I knew he didn't.

"That's all the more reason to appreciate your unending lifespan! It will never be too late to experience these things. You can do anything you want. You've got the time and the money. And it's not like the revolutions aren't happening now. And new artists who will be the next Degas and Picasso? They're out there right now. We'll find them. And new feelings? New experiences? We can track them down. I'll help you, Sadie. You can start now. You can start with me," he crooned. I leaned into his lips and kissed them.

This was the trouble with Everett. It was the trouble with any immortal I had ever known. They never considered what it meant to be without a heartbeat—a ticking clock counting down the days until time ran out. It would be suspenseful. It would bring things into perspective faster. And then it would be over. In death, there would be freedom.

He would never understand.

We got his things out of his room and brought them into mine. I thanked and tipped the manager profusely for taking care of him until I returned. Then we spent the rest of the day out in Moscow. We walked the cold, dark streets of the city for hours, wandering in and out of shops, stopping for him to eat. I ate a little to humor him.

I began to get pieces of the puzzle of where he had been and what he had been doing. Anthony had allowed him to come see me, knowing full well what that meant since he had been the one who had seen us together in a vision. Anthony, Patrick, and Mark had been out searching for something. Adelaide had many cross words with Anthony about this, a very rare occurrence in their five-century marriage. She had been angry that they had left me behind.

Over a quiet dinner at a small bistro near the hotel, I told Everett what I knew he would not want to hear. "I'm going to Romania next," I said.

His brow furrowed. He didn't speak.

"When I came to Europe, I planned to go to Russia and then Romania, so that's where I'm headed. I think I'll just run. It's far, but it's easier than trying to fly," I said. "With any luck, I should only be there a week." I was going to keep talking until the horrified expression on his face dissolved. "I might be able to find some more creatures like I did here. That was much faster than trying to dissect beliefs, village by village."

"You can't be serious," he said incredulously.

"I'm going, Everett. This is what I do," I said, standing my ground.

Everett rubbed his face, stroking it like there was stubble there even though it was inhumanly smooth. He was thinking something over. In the end, he sensed defeat. "Fine," he said, "but I come with you."

I raised one eyebrow at him. "Fine," I said.

We spent the night looking at maps of Eastern Europe. When the shops opened the next morning, we bought him clothes more appropriate for the kind of traveling we'd be doing. I packed him a bag like mine, pulled on coats and scarves, and put everything worth saving—mainly, the remaining red diamonds I carried with me—in the suite's safe. That evening, we were sprinting across Russia at close to two hundred miles an hour.

We followed leads and our intuition into the Ukraine and then into Moldova and back toward Romania again for two days. I had heard distant humming across parts of the Ukraine, but it wasn't strong enough to follow. But when we crossed into Romania, I felt something strange. I slowed at the base of a snow-covered mountain so I could talk with Everett.

"Something's here," I said.

"What?" he breathed, his voice winded from the very cold air penetrating our lungs. His hair was tousled from the wind, and it made him look irresistible. I smiled suddenly and kissed him gently. "You were saying?" he said. Suddenly I saw that his golden-green eyes had darkened to a brown that matched his hair. I closed my eyes and opened them again to make sure I was seeing right.

The humming swarmed in my ears. I'd have to ask about the eyes later. "There are creatures of some kind inside there," I said.

"Inside the mountain?" he asked.

"Possibly, or they could be in a valley between this mountain and the next. One way to find out," I said, and took off up the mountain, Everett on my heels. It was steep and icy and it took some time to reach the peak. The sounds and feelings were stronger here than they had been at the bottom. They were definitely beneath our feet.

"How do we get to them?" Everett asked when I told him what I'd discovered.

"Caves are a good place to start," I said. "Let's look down the other side," I suggested. We trekked down the slope. We heard the sounds of a large pack of animals as we descended. "Do you hear that? It sounds like lions," I said.

We had instinctively begun to whisper. "Yeah, but there are no lions in Romania," he said. "There are lynxes, though."

"Then I'd put good money on it that that's what they are. Listen to the snarls. I can feel them, too. They're certainly predators, and they smell us coming," I said.

"Of course they do," Everett scowled. "Are they alone?" he asked.

"I can't hear any humans," I said.

We saw a glow in the distance. "Is that fire?" he asked.

"I think so," I said.

"What kind of animals have a fire going?" he asked.

"A good question," I said. I was growing tense. Everett crouched a little as we walked, too, resembling a predator. That didn't relax me at all.

Then we saw one. It had a golden coat, sparse black spots, and a fuzzy white beard. Lynxes were supposed to be significantly smaller than lions and tigers and other big cats, but this one was huge, at least six feet long from head to tail. It must have weighed at least three hundred pounds.

More of them emerged from a cave below us to join him, forming a line to face us. "Are you seeing this?" I asked Everett quietly. He nodded. "For the record, this is an example of when the stupid bulwark is going to get in the way," I hissed.

There were about twenty giant lynxes in front of us. We had gotten close enough that the humming had clarified into more distinct sounds, words, and phrases. I realized how strange it was that I was hearing thoughts—very distinct thoughts—from animals. I knew that they were supernatural in some way, but it still surprised me that they thought like humans or like Survivors.

Everett hadn't gotten up from his crouching posture. He more closely resembled a lynx than a man. The foreign pose made me nervous and suspicious.

The girl can hear us, I heard a female voice say. I tensed. One of them could hear me the way I could hear them.

Then it's time to stop thinking, a deep male voice said. I fixated on the lead lynx's eyes. It had been his voice. They all responded, clearly able to understand his unspoken orders.

I decided to speak. "Can you understand me?" I called.

Everett looked at me sideways. "What the hell language was that?" he asked.

"Romanian?" I whispered.

He shook his head. "More like lynx."

We can hear you. You don't need to shout, the male voice said.

You think she's going to try anything? a quieter voice asked. I scanned the line and determined it belonged to a fuzzy, darker lynx down the row.

Surely not, a female voice said.

"I just want to talk to you," I said aloud. I knew one of them could hear me and translate, but this way I was addressing them all. I was trying to be respectful.

Is she American? one asked. *She sounds American.*

She looks French, another said.

She looks like one of those Russian witches, another said.

"If you could just stop speculating on my heritage for a moment, I'd like to ask you some questions," I said.

Everett had moved closer to me as I neared the pack. A loud growl escaped his chest. I flinched at the sound; it was more intimidating than the version of it I had heard from Mark and Patrick.

Anxious little vampire, one of them smirked.

"I'm not a vampire either," I said, frustrated. Several of them laughed, though it sounded like a growl in my ears.

Quiet, the lead one said.

She didn't understand what you meant by vampire, the one who could read my mind said, chastising me in some way.

Quiet! the lead one repeated. *Everyone,* he said, looking to his left and right. He stepped forward and closed the distance between us. His mind was blank to me. I wasn't sure how he could control it so well. He stretched his front legs in front of him, splaying his paws against the ground, and bowed his head. The muscles across his back rippled. He let out a low howl.

Suddenly his fur retracted into pale skin. His shoulders broadened and his arms shrank. Three seconds later I was standing face to face with a threatening, naked man.

A shape-shifter.

I deflected my eyes, not wanting to see him like that. "Witches aren't usually known for their modesty," he laughed. He was speaking English. "You can look back now." When I did, he was dressed in a pair of low-slung, worn out blue jeans and nothing else. The lynx who could read my mind had stepped up next to him and was nuzzling his hip. He fluffed the fur between her ears affectionately.

His body was very muscular, and he was larger than Everett. Veins clearly showed on his arms. He had white-blond hair the same color of his beard when he was in his lynx form; it hung messy and in his eyes, long past his ears. His skin was very pale but his eyes were a very deep, beautiful chestnut brown. His ears were pointed and his eyes were slanted and thin, just like they had been in his lynx form. I could hear his heart beating.

"I'm speaking English for your friend here. This is Narcisa," he said, indicating the lynx at his side. "And I'm Valentin." He stepped forward and extended his hand. Everett was eyeing him suspiciously.

"I'm Sadie," I said, speaking in English again. I shook his hand. Everett growled. "This is Everett," I said.

"She's not something we know," Valentin called to the other cats in what Everett called Lynx. I realized that once he touched me, he could read me in some way.

Not a witch? one of the cats thought.

Not one of us, surely, another said.

Cold like the strigoi, Valentin said in his mind. *Pretty like them, too.*

"What's a *strigoi?*" I asked.

Vampire, Valentin spoke to me in his mind. *A very lethal one. Not unlike your friend there.* I rolled my eyes. I was very used to our kind being mistaken for many things we were not.

I looked at Valentin meaningfully. Then I looked at Narcisa. *Can you translate for me? So Valentin can hear me?* I asked her.

Certainly, she said. I hadn't envisioned using my talents to keep something from Everett. I had thought it would be the other way around.

He's not a vampire, I said. Narcisa conveyed this message this to Valentin who raised a doubtful eyebrow.

Then what is he? Valentin asked.

He is like me, I said. I looked at Everett's crouching, snarling form next to me. How sure of that was I?

I think you're mistaken, friend. Though I do not know what you are, Valentin said.

"What's he saying?" Everett asked. His tension was rampant.

"He's asking me what I am," I said. "And what you are."

This upset Everett considerably. He crouched again and snarled wildly this time, exposing his teeth. My belief that he and I were the same was evaporating quickly. I heard a flurry of voices in my head: They were ready to pounce. They were only waiting for a signal. "Everett, stop," I hissed.

Valentin looked above my head and into the woods behind us, and then he looked back at the lynxes. "Sorry, pretty girl."

It all happened very fast.

Narcisa lunged first, able to hear Everett's own plans to attack. The other lynxes circled quickly, then piled on top of him before I could even scream. Then I was moving, being dragged across the ground by the lynx with the fuzzy darker hair, its powerful jaw clenching my side, its teeth searing into my flesh. I heard mangled animal screams as Everett fought against them, and the sound of claws and teeth shredding flesh.

I was feeling dizzy, and my vision was clouding over as my arms and legs went limp, being dragged across the rugged terrain, defenseless against the fuzzy lynx's jaw. But suddenly I saw two blurs of long blonde hair jump toward the pile, then three large men and another woman sprinting out of the woods. They launched themselves into the fray.

Valentin ran to me and swooped me out of the lynx's jaws and into his arms. I let my head fall backward and tried to see what was happening.

At first I thought I was imagining it, but something told me it was real. Still, it was hard to believe: All of the Winters were sparring against the giant lynxes. I couldn't understand it. Where had they come from? What had they been doing? They couldn't possibly be here! And what if they got hurt?

But quickly I understood my fears were misguided. The last thing I saw was Mark Winter rip the throat from a lynx that had pinned Everett to the ground.

I panicked. I tried in vain to call out to them, to fight my way out of Valentin's forceful embrace, but his strong arms were like a vice grip against my weakening frame.

"Sadie!" I heard a bloodcurdling scream. It was Everett. Valentin ran so fast, Everett's voice quickly dissolved into silence.

14
NOSFERATU

Above me was a rocky and cavernous ceiling. A fire nearby threw dancing shadows on it. My side ached, and I could hardly move.

"Ah, she wakes," a woman said to me. Her body was warm next to mine. I recognized the voice as Narcisa's. She was in her human form. She had alabaster skin, light grey-blue eyes, and long, ashy brown hair flowing down her back. Her coloring was the opposite of Valentin's.

She was tending to me. I sensed no danger—not that I had sensed it earlier either—and I even felt that she was very protective of me. It relaxed me.

"How did you knock me out?" I asked. I was disoriented—I hadn't slept in over six months, so waking from any sort of darkness was strange. I tried to push myself up, but my arms buckled under me.

"An old potion that always does the trick. Don't try to sit up just yet," she said, a gentle hand on my shoulder.

"How long have I been here?" I gritted my teeth. I was in a great deal of pain.

"About four days," she said. Her eyes were on the flames.

"Where are they?" I asked.

Your vampire friends? she thought.

"Not vampires," I murmured.

"They've gone," she said. My chest tightened.

"What did you do to them?" I asked. I was laboring to speak.

She scoffed at the question. "You mean what did they do to us," she said, facing me. "We outnumbered them, and they still killed two thirds of our family. They are quite the coven." She saw the shock on my face. "Don't be surprised," she said. "We are not immortals like you. Death is a part of us." She sighed quietly and turned back to the fire. "We saved your life, you know," she said.

"What does that mean?" I asked. "I couldn't have died anyway."

"You would have with that crazy lot. You aren't as strong as they are."

"They wouldn't have killed me," I said quickly. "Couldn't have," I whispered to myself.

"You didn't think they'd leave you either," she said, "especially not that handsome mate of yours. But here you are, alone with me. Where are they now?"

"I don't think they've gone," I said bravely, as if speaking the words would will it true.

Narcisa shrugged. "You can believe what you want," she said. She poked at the fire and then spoke aloud in Greek. "For men, we can make falsities and fallacies seem true, but when we want we're able to give truthful statements, too," she said. It was a line from *Theogony.* I looked at her wide-eyed. She laughed and nodded toward my bag; it was open and a few things were scattered about, including my thread-bare book with the gold-lined pages. "Before I became a person who couldn't control whether I was an animal or a human, I went to university to study classics," she said. "A favorite of yours if it came with you on this journey?" she asked. I nodded. She changed the subject. "You know I was impressed with you back there. You never let on to the coven waiting in the woods," she said.

"I didn't know they were there," I admitted.

She laughed grimly. "They keep you at a distance, don't they?" she said. "You know that shield in their minds doesn't work against everyone." I perked up, interested in this. "It was only one shield and they split it several ways to each get a piece. So they had to decide what

2

8 Amanda Havard

to shield. They chose you," she eased, pulling her knees to her chest. "I bet that feels good, knowing you're the only one in the world they don't want in their heads."

"That's not it," I defended.

"Isn't it?" she laughed.

"They had never met anyone else who could read people the way I could," I said.

"Pretty girl, you're off the mark. Mind reading isn't common, but it's out there. A coven that size has run into it before, I can assure you."

"You could tell what they were thinking?" I asked her. She nodded. "Can you tell me why they have the bulwark against me?"

"They have a secret they don't want you to know."

"Do you know what it is?" I asked, my voice gaining momentum.

"That's why you're here, Sadie," she said gently. "You must know the truth."

I could make out a murky shadow coming down a hall behind her; we must have been very deep in a cave. "Valentin," she said and stood up.

"My love," he said, walking up behind Narcisa. He wrapped his arms around her waist and kissed her neck. "You're awake," he said to me. I realized then that we were speaking Romanian.

"Where are my friends?" I asked, hoping to get different answers from him.

He sat by the fire, and extended his bare feet toward it. "You're in an awful hurry to get back to them," he said. An image of a group around a fire in icy fields shot through his mind. They knew where the Winters were, I decided. I had to get him to tell me.

He pulled some scraps of charred meat off the stones around the fire, and ate them. "You seem like too good a girl to be hanging out with the likes of them," Valentin said. He licked his fingertips.

"What is that supposed to mean?" I asked. I saw the image of Mark Winter ripping out a lynx's throat with his teeth flash through

Valentin's mind. Until then, I hoped that image was a nightmare, not something I'd actually seen.

"You're not violent." He looked at Narcisa and smirked. "Self-destructive and a bit of a nut job, sure, but not violent."

They knew a lot. I didn't know how, but I didn't care. "What does that have to do with them?" I asked.

"You don't know?" he asked.

I shook my head. "You'd be surprised how much they haven't told me," I said.

"In all of your morbid research, have you ever learned of the *nosferatu*?" she asked. I wondered how much of my journal of lists and memories and research notes Narcisa had read while I lay unconscious.

I shook my head.

"They are legendary here in Romania. They're said to be very dangerous creatures," she explained.

"What are they?" I asked.

"Shape-shifters," Narcisa said. "That's what they call us. We are born of humans. As the legend goes, if two people who were born out of wedlock produce offspring also out of wedlock, then that child will become a *nosferatu*."

"Are you immortal?" I asked.

She shook her head. "We aren't, though many legends say we're supposed to be."

"Why are you lynxes?" I asked.

"They're native to the environment. We can be anything with some practice," she explained.

"Was that group your family?"

"Not blood. We just travel together. In human form, our men are fertile, but most of our women cannot have children," she said.

Ritka, the *eretica*, had said the same thing about shape-shifters. "If the men can produce offspring, who do they reproduce with, if not other *nosferatu*?" I asked.

"There are many legends. Some say witches, some say humans. Some say *nosferatu* can't reproduce at all," she explained.

"Why are you telling me this?" I asked.

Her face grew grave. "Their patriarch," she said.

"Anthony," I offered.

"Yes," she said. "He is one of us. He denies it, and claims that he and his family are like you. But Valentin could read him—he can tell what a creature is by touching it—and that's not true."

I wasn't sure if I believed her.

"His wife is like you," she said. "A witch."

"Am I a witch?" I asked, deciding to not assume I was or wasn't anything at this point.

"Not a normal one, no. But that's the closest thing we could call it. She's a pureblood witch, though," Narcisa said.

Valentin interrupted. "Does your family, do you call yourselves witches?" he asked.

I laughed. "No," I said. "But I don't know why we hadn't thought of that. Are the Winter children *nosferatu*?"

"No," she said hesitantly. "The child of a shape-shifter and a witch produces something else..."

Then I realized it. "*Vieczy*," I said. I suddenly understood what they'd been trying to tell me all along.

"That's what they call them in Russia," she said.

"But really?" I asked.

She bit her lower lip and looked at the ground. It was very human of her. "Vampires," she said. "Warrior vampires." She waited for me to react, but I did not. I didn't believe her. "We had to warn you. They are very dangerous. That's why we brought you here, to get you away from them."

I didn't say anything. I had no reason to believe them at all.

"They like violent kills, and they're very excessive. There are countless tales of covens no bigger than your friends' taking out whole villages in one feed. Their bloodlust is indecent. They're notorious for that," Valentin said. "And if you were going to mate with that boy, we had to warn you. We couldn't let you go on, create monsters from your own womb unknowingly," he added. My stomach lurched. *My womb.* Was this the genesis of my fear? Had I avoided mating for so long because I didn't know what I would produce? I dismissed this as soon as the thought came to me. Because how would I have known this? The cause for my unease must have stemmed from elsewhere.

Narcisa's heart was sad for me.

I sighed. I should have known. Ritka had described the other vampires to me clearly—the temperature and texture of their skin, their skills. It fit the Winters perfectly. The only thing that didn't fit was the image I had conjured of vampires since hearing about them in the human world. I thought of fangs and bats and capes and darkness. Men with blood trickling down their lips. The haggard old *eretica.* The sparkling, pretty, human-like creatures in the most recent versions. None of it applied to the Winters. They didn't drink blood. They didn't have red eyes. They lived on the California coast, for God's sake! They ate regular food. They lived among humans. They loved each other like humans. Setting aside Mark and the violent images of them all fighting the lynxes, they were normal. So I couldn't trust what Narcisa and Valentin were telling me.

But the Winters had been hiding something. That had been clear all along.

I struggled to bring myself into a sitting position. I managed to get slightly upright with my knees bent in front of me. I let my body hang over them.

"How can your kind be killed?" I asked them, finally returning to the reason for my quest in the first place.

"Not unlike the way you might kill a lion. We're mortal through and through, but you would have to have strength to do it," Valentin said.

"But the vampires do have that strength," I said.

"Yes. It is a hierarchy," he explained. "We are just below them in strength, typically matched evenly with witches."

"And how do you kill witches?" I asked.

Valentin hesitated a bit before speaking, but then he allowed himself to continue. "They can be killed in some of the same ways humans can. But they won't die from basic deficiencies. They won't get sick. From injury, they'll heal quickly and easily. I obviously don't know the specifics, but most basic ways of murder would do the trick," he said. Unconsciously I thought back to my first year living among humans—a terrifying, lonely, and uncertain time before I had come to Nashville, before I had met Corrina—when all I wanted to do was die. I tried every "basic way" I could think of to do it. When none of it worked, that's when I began looking for more obscure ways to destroy myself, my kind. In remembering, images flipped through my mind—of drowning, of driving a car off a cliff, of tasting arsenic, and of tightening a noose around my neck. Narcisa looked at me, horrified. She had just seen my weakest, worst moments of life. I felt invaded.

"How do you kill a vampire?" I asked, completing my mental list of tactics.

Neither of them responded at first. I pressed them. It was interesting to me that they didn't want to tell me this one when they had told me about the *nosferatu* and witches. "Surely you must know," I urged. They kept their minds blank, quiet.

I sat there for a long time thinking over all they had told me.

Narcisa was watching me closely, appraising each of these thoughts as I generated them. She repeated them in her mind so Valentin could hear them. I could feel her softening as I began to turn my thoughts to Everett. "You should know," she said slowly, "that he didn't lie to you. His family has bound him to keeping their secrets. He couldn't break that trust. Family is everything to him. Just like it is to you." She was trying to comfort me, but it wasn't working. "There is more to their story," she admitted, despite disapproving looks from Valentin. "You'll have to hear it, and then you can make your own judgments. I'd give them that at least."

"I thought you said they ran off. How do you suggest I find them?" I asked coldly.

Narcisa looked questioningly at Valentin. *We've done what we could to warn her,* he said.

"We'll take you to them," Narcisa said. "We promised your safe return if they would wait for us instead of coming after you themselves. We knew you would want to face them."

Every part of my body was a little more alive at the idea that I could see them, that I could see *him* again.

But what if Narcisa and Valentin had told me the truth? What if Everett and the Winters were not who, were not even *what* I thought they were?

Narcisa eyed me as she saw the next thought flash across my mind. She reached in her woolly boot and pulled out a dagger. "I understand the need for proof," she said. "You see for yourself."

I took the cold piece of metal in my hand.

15
ANSWERS

Narcisa carried me on her back as she ran across the mountainous terrain. As the cold air whipped past me, I tried to rationalize everything I knew about the Winters against what Narcisa and Valentin had told me, but I kept coming up short. I did not want to consider the possibility that Everett had lied to me—not only about being a vampire, but about who he was at his core.

A murderer.

I may be self-destructive, but I had never harmed another creature. Despite all that had happened and all I had become, I was still just a girl born in a simpler era, who trusted God as the point of absolute truth. I might have been fuzzy on a few things—like how creatures like those around me existed in God's world—but I was not fuzzy on this: You don't take a life that God created. Murder made it to the Commandments.

So much of what I had felt for Everett—love, I guess you could call it—was clouded by the stories I had heard and doubt I felt deep inside. I wanted to believe he was the man I had fallen in love with, but I wasn't sure. I couldn't forget that Anthony had put a blockade between us for a reason. Nor could I shake the image of Everett's predatory crouch and exposed teeth, to say nothing of Mark Winter ripping out a giant lynx's throat with his teeth.

But still, part of me felt good running toward them. When I saw Ginny's flash of blonde hair before the fight, I instinctively felt safe. I had spent months wondering where they were, and even in such a terrifying situation, they were the ones I ran to. For reasons I could not explain, I thought of them as my family. I had felt hollow since Narcisa lied to me and told me they had gone. I was ready to be whole, and I was certain only the Winters could fill that void.

The morbid part of me—the same part that got a rush every time someone from an obscure tribe in Central America tried to kill me—*that* part wanted proof that Everett and his family were *vieczy*, as Narcisa and Valentin had claimed. Unfortunately there was only a violent way to prove such a thing.

We had reached the point where the hills sloped off toward flat plains when Narcisa slowed to a stop and let me off her back. Valentin was about to pick me up, but I stopped him.

"Let me see if I can walk," I said.

"Your side is very badly injured. Please let me carry you," he urged.

"How far away are we?" I asked.

"Not far. Just over that hill," he said.

"I can make it," I said. "I want to be on my feet when I see them." This satisfied them.

But each step I took jarred something inside of me. In the past, my wounds had only hurt while I was getting them, then the pain vanished. I couldn't imagine how bad this one was still to be hurting four days later.

As we reached the top of the hill, the smaller lynx with the darker fur came quickly toward us. She spoke in her mind, but we could hear her. She had apparently been in charge of keeping track of the Winters.

I could see them at the bottom of the hill. They had a big fire going, and they were circled around it. My mixed emotions flooded me. I wanted to run toward them yet at the same time run the other way screaming. I took a deep breath, the icy air stabbing at my lungs as I began my slow descent.

Narcisa and Valentin remained in their human forms, so I knew they weren't here for a fight. Valentin wanted me not to believe anything they said. Narcisa urged me to hear them out. I was shocked at how they could face the Winters considering their huge losses in the battle. I felt certain that mortality alone would not make one's attitude toward death so casual, but never having that perspective myself, I couldn't be sure.

They heard us coming, as I had expected them to. Ginny was the first to rise, undoubtedly hearing my thoughts as I neared her. She was the only one I could feel.

Oh, thank God, she said.

Everett jumped to his feet, running ahead of his family as they gracefully shot to their feet to walk toward us. Patrick and Mark caught him and pulled him back. I raised my hand to them, signaling them to stay back. "Stay close to the fire," I said. "It's so cold."

I picked up my pace, needing to get answers now. As Everett's face came more clearly into view, my throat closed up. I closed my eyes for a few seconds, trying desperately to make the surge of love I felt toward him dissipate. It wasn't easy to hate him when my skin got hot at the thought of him, my pain numbing as I neared him.

The Winters stood close together as we approached. When Everett saw that I was not going to embrace him, he stepped back until he was among his family again. I exerted all the control I had not to let him see the love in my eyes. I could see the love—and pain—in his.

Anthony stepped forward and spoke to Valentin.

"We thank you, brethren, for bringing back our Sadie unharmed," he said. It both angered and excited me to hear his possessiveness.

Narcisa sneered. "She is not yours." Anthony narrowed his eyes at her, and she growled softly. I looked pointedly at Anthony, and told Narcisa in my head to lay off.

He spoke again. "We have been very worried about her."

"I didn't come to ease your worry. I came because I want answers," I said. "It's time you tore down the walls and gave me some." They knew I knew more than they had intended for me to find out. I let my icy gaze rest on Everett.

"I've spoken with my friends," I indicated Valentin and Narcisa, "and they've given me some insight into their heritage," I said coolly, "and yours."

The Winters glanced at each other nervously.

"I am not sure if I believe them," I said loudly, "but they have offered me many more answers than you have."

Sorry, Ginny said in her mind. *And he is, too,* she added.

"I don't want to, believe me. They've told me terrible things," I said. "If you are what they say you are, I fear my time with you will end here."

Everett's face shot up, horror in his eyes. Patrick pulled Madeline close to his chest and looked at the ground, as if grateful that he wouldn't lose his love in this battle. *No, Sadie!* Ginny screamed silently. *That isn't how it's supposed to end! You're supposed to love him! You're supposed to be my sister!*

I know, I said back to her. *But I didn't cause this.*

"Everything we've done was to protect you," Everett cried.

I ignored him. "I want the whole truth," I said. They didn't answer, so I provoked them. "Why don't you start with what happens when you mix a witch and a shape-shifter," I said, tired of playing games.

Adelaide put her hand over her mouth as tears streamed down her cheeks. I was shocked to see the tears. She was surely not like them.

Anthony spoke again. "I know you want to satisfy your curiosity, but there are things you can't know yet for your own safety. If you come home with us, we'll explain them in time. We are willing to give you another chance," he said.

That was it. Give *me* another chance? All the anger and resentment, the despair and blackness of three months of separation came rushing to my surface. "Stop this now! I am stronger than you think I am," I yelled. "I don't need you. I don't need any of you!" I seethed.

"Sadie, don't!" Everett's voice cried.

"Let her leave us, Everett," Anthony barked.

"Sadie is supposed to be a part of this family. You've seen it! We cannot let her walk away!" Ginny cried. "And I don't want her to leave," she added. "I love her, and I want her with us, where she belongs."

"Then tell me what you are," I hissed. "Tell me what you've been hiding."

The silence was maddening. I couldn't bear it anymore. I pulled the dagger from my waistband and charged at Everett. I swung my arm over my head then drove it toward his chest with as much force as I could. I screamed as I did it, and rough, tearless sobs erupted from my hollow core.

It was so obvious then. The dagger came crashing down against Everett's strong frame with a loud clatter, the sound of metal against metal or metal against stone. It was like a car crash.

Again and again I drove the knife at his chest until the blade was mangled in my hand, bent further back with each morbid drive to his chest until it wrapped around my own palm, slicing into my flesh. When he could tell I was at my breaking point, Everett grabbed my arm to stop me. I couldn't force myself loose from his grasp, no matter how hard I tried. "Sadie..." he said, his voice full of pity, full of remorse.

"You wretched vampire!" I screamed. "Murderers! All of you!" I backed away. "Of course I can't stab you! You have impenetrable skin, undefeatable strength—just like the lynxes told me!" I yelled. I stumbled backward, the pain in my hand beginning to register. "It's all true. You're bloodthirsty warriors. Gluttonous vampires who murder innocent people for sport!"

I was hysterical. "You all lied to me. And you," I cried, charging again at Everett, crashing my wounded hand against his mountainous chest. He inhaled sharply at the scent of my blood. "You're the worst! You betrayed me. You let me fall in love with you thinking you were a good man when you're loathsome. You let me think you deserved me! Let me believe you were worth loyalty!" I cried, beating his chest over and over. But I couldn't hurt him, no matter how hard I tried. Despite how much stronger I was than a human, he was still more powerful.

I stumbled backward again and lost my footing. The pain in my side flared, searing all the way to my throat. I clenched my hands to my stomach and fell to my knees. They all leapt toward me. "Stay back," I warned.

Everett dropped to the ground and stroked the hair out of my face. I was too weakened by the pain to stop him. "Look at me," he said. I kept my eyes on the ground. "Look at me!" he roared, forcing my chin up to meet his gaze. "I am the same person you have always known. I am the same soul," he said. "We'll tell you everything. Just, please, don't leave."

I sat back on my heels. "The whole truth," I breathed. I raised my head slightly and Everett took my face in his hands and kissed me. I tried to remain strong under the crippling power of his touch. But I couldn't. I couldn't fight him. He seemed to suck the pain from my mouth. My insides liquefied and my head spun. For just one moment, I could feel what he was feeling. Bulwark or no bulwark, love—real love—surged out of him the way it had from Felix the night before he married Corrina.

I took his hand for support as we walked toward the fire.

Narcisa and Valentin approached me. "We tried to warn you," Narcisa said, "but you have made your choice. It is time for us to go."

Valentin brought my bag and set it down next to me. "Strength and virtue will always be yours," he said.

Narcisa looked at the Winters, communicating with me silently. *Vile in the winter, grievous in the summer, not ever any good,* she said. I recognized the line from *Works and Days.* Ginny heard Narcisa's ominous parting and stiffened. I nodded toward Narcisa in silent thanks. They took off into the dark.

"They told you of the *nosferatu?*" Anthony asked.

I nodded. "That you are one of them," I said.

"You have heard the legends, then, of witches like Adelaide mating with the likes of me," he said.

"*Vieczy*," I said.

"That's not what we call ourselves, but yes," Anthony said.

"What are you then?" I asked.

"We call ourselves the Winters," he said, "as your family calls yourselves the Survivors."

I wasn't following. "Winter is your surname," I said. "That's not a species."

"Isn't it? The *eretica* are only able to hunt in autumn and spring. They hibernate, more or less, in the other two seasons," he said. "We are like that. We have a stronger desire to feed in winter, and so it is our namesake."

"You mean murder," I said, my tone hostile. Ginny and Everett both stiffened.

"It's more complicated than that," Anthony said.

"Make it simple for me," I said.

"We limit the damage as best we can," Anthony explained. "We take precautions. We live in California—a temperate climate year-round. Sometimes that can help us stave off the most intense urges," he said. "And we eat human food—mainly vegetables, of course. The chloroplasts in the green vegetables burn up and into our veins, and it gets into our eyes and turns them green, the same way blood would turn them red. It lets us blend in with humans."

"But Everett's eyes just turned brown," I said, turning to him. I looked at those eyes. They were darker even than they had been the last time I saw them, almost a burgundy.

"Because I wasn't eating enough human food since I was following you around," Everett said. "They start to fade."

"They fade to brown?" I asked.

"To red," he said. "They're naturally red, whether we drink blood or not. Brighter, certainly, if we do. Brown is just a stop along the way. Think color wheel." He smiled. His smile looked different with the darker eyes, but it was still just as pleasant.

"Does that make you not *need* blood?" I was hoping he would say something reassuring like they didn't even *like* blood.

"Of course we do," Mark shot. "We're just good about how we get it. We hunt the bad guys, drink donated blood when it will suffice, and learn to go without it for as long as possible."

I was getting tense. "That doesn't make you dangerous?" I asked.

Everett said, "We make sure we aren't dangerous to humans by not being around them when we're thirsty." They seemed to think they had me convinced that I was going to be okay with them now that they had explained themselves. Everett was the only one who could sense it wasn't that simple. He could feel what I could—*us* hanging by a thread.

"So do you actually murder people?" I asked. They all hesitated.

"Rarely," Anthony said frankly. I bit my lip. That was still too often for my taste. "You know, we thought you were one of us," he said.

"What made you think that?" I gasped.

"Your powers are similar to ours," he said. "You don't have a heartbeat. You aren't warm. And your eyes."

"What about them?" I asked.

Madeline spoke for the very first time. "They are like mine," she said. "The pretty violet," she said. "They thought it was blue contacts to cover red eyes. That's what I do." I realized her eyes were red for a reason. She hadn't learned to quench her thirst in moderation.

I looked at Everett. My pretty purple eyes. "I'm not one of you," I said firmly.

"I know," he said apologetically.

"When did you know?" I asked.

"The second I could smell you," he said. That felt...weird.

"Where do you get your powers?" I asked. "From what I've read, most vampires don't have powers."

"Not all of us have them," Anthony said. "I've had the gift of premonition, of foresight forever. Ginny could always mirror to an extent. It got more powerful once she stopped aging, until she could fully mirror powers from all matter of supernatural creatures—from her siblings, from witches, from you."

"And the rest of your powers?" I asked. No one answered. "You do something," I said. "That's it, isn't it? That's what you don't want me to know. You kill some poor people, do something violent and terrible..."

Mark answered me, unwilling to play their game, it seemed. "It's called acquisition," he said. He looked to Everett, whose eyes were heavy. He knew whatever they were about to tell me could make me walk away from them forever.

"Tell me about acquisition," I said.

"You kill a vampire with the power you want, then their power becomes your own," Mark said.

And it clicked.

"You can kill vampires," I said. "You could kill me." All the answers I had been looking for they had known all along.

"Are you scared?" Patrick asked, misunderstanding.

"Of course she's not," Everett said, pain in his voice. "She wants to die."

The family looked up at me, waiting for me to deny Everett's accusation. I didn't.

"And of course you won't tell me how to do it," I said.

"No. Why do you think we have to keep you out of our minds?" Everett asked.

"Don't you think that's my decision to make?" I argued.

"We will not kill you," Anthony said. "Not with our hands, not with our knowledge."

"Sweetheart," Adelaide said, approaching me, "we got the bulwark to protect you. We love you." She pulled my face to her, and she kissed my forehead. "We always will."

Always implied I would *always* be alive. That I would never find mortality. That I would never be free.

"Sadie, look," Everett said. "Before you were at our front door in Pacific Grove we knew that you would come, and we knew that you would find a way to love us."

"So my fate is to live among you and condone your murders?" I said coldly.

"You have to understand. What we do is about protection. Kills are strategic. The vampire with the mental bulwark that Mark and Anthony killed—he had killed five humans that *day*. Do you understand, Sadie? It's collateral damage."

"I don't know if it really matters. How can I trust you? How long will you keep secrets?" I asked.

"As long as it takes to protect you," Everett responded. I looked at the others. They nodded, confirming this.

I sat down to think. I had seen Mark be violent, yes, but it had been righteous. It didn't bother me because I understood why he was killing the man he killed. He had saved a girl's life.

I understood what Everett was saying, that the benefits of their vigilantism outweighed the cost of their bloodlust. The softest part of my heart was urging me to forgive them, but I steeled myself.

There were still parts of my mind screaming for me to run away, but they were quieting. My instincts were telling me to stay. It felt wrong, but I existed—I *survived*—entirely by trusting my instincts. They hadn't led me astray so far.

And I couldn't deny that the heat I felt came not from the fire in front of me but from the stone cold *vieczy* behind me. Where Everett's palm cupped my uninjured side felt white-hot—the physical burn of how much I wanted him, how much I needed to be close to him, how much I loved him. Each moment with him was more potent than the last; our love would grow more intense as time went on. I smiled a little, happy for a moment—just a moment—with my immortality if what we had would only get better.

Then Ginny plucked a thought from my mind and spoke quietly to Anthony. "Ask her what the *eretica* told her," she said.

"Sadie?" he asked.

"She called me a witch," I said. "But then she said I wasn't like other witches. My blood was different."

"How did she know?" Anthony asked, his eyes narrow.

I sighed. "She tasted it," I said. Their eyes went wide. "She said that it burned her."

"You let a vampire taste your blood?" Everett asked frantically.

"Sadie, what if she changed you?" Mark asked.

"Changed?" I asked.

"Relax. The *eretica* aren't venomous. They don't have the power to transform others into their own kind," Anthony said.

"Do you?" I asked. It surprised me that I hadn't yet realized they were poisonous. If Everett had inadvertently bitten me in a kiss, would it have turned me into a vampire? That was a big risk for him to take. Reckless, even.

"The children can, yes," he said. I was suddenly hit with violent and painful images from Madeline's head. I realized then that she must have been human, that Patrick had changed her. I wanted to know how much I was in danger of becoming like them.

"What do you think it means that the *eretica* could suck my blood but it...tasted wrong?" I said.

"It means that I don't know what you are," Anthony said. "Your family comes from witches like Adelaide. But the *eretica* would have been able to drink your blood if you were a witch."

"Could you change me if you wanted to?" I asked, trying to calculate how much I was risking by going with them.

"We can change anything," Madeline said. "We're stronger than all of you."

That was the moment when I knew I had to decide. Either I would risk everything to be with Everett, or I'd have to leave the Winters behind me now. And it seemed so stupid to want to go with them. I was seeking mortality and they were even less human than I was.

But I had been in love with these people from the moment I met them. They were exactly the balance of what I was and what I wanted—supernatural creatures who acted like humans. They were like a human family, and I had never had that. I loved each one of them around this circle more than I loved some of my own family members, and I had no reason to feel that way. But I had never been reasonable. Not since I saw Everett's face. Not since I felt Adelaide's protectiveness. Not since I connected to Ginny's mind. Not since I sat in their sunny living room in California and pretended I could have a normal life. I loved them beyond reason, without reason—exactly the way humans loved their families.

Feeling Everett's arms around me, I knew I had made my choice. It was perhaps the stupidest one I would ever make, but I couldn't walk away from them.

"If I want to come with you," I hesitated, "does it mean I can't see my family?" I hadn't, of course, heard from any of them since the night I sank in Swan Lake, the night this had all started to go wrong. But I would still like to have the chance.

Anthony rose to his feet. "I guess," he sighed, pausing to look at Adelaide, who seemed pleased. "We can't ask you to stay away from them. We understand that family is as important to you as it is to us." He extended his hand to me to help me up.

I smiled up at him, relieved, but his face was severe.

"Sadie, it's time to show you some things about our future," he said gravely. "What's going to happen is unavoidable."

We walked slowly out into the dark land. Anthony kept a tight grip on my arm—possibly because he was worried about me losing my footing, possibly so that I couldn't escape. It didn't matter why. The part of me that was in love with Everett would not go anywhere.

Anthony stopped in the middle of a broad expanse of land. "I hadn't wanted to tell you this yet," he began. "But I understand now that you need truth or you will leave us. We would hate to count you among our enemies when we want to count you as our family," he said. I decided this was more about listening than talking, so I nodded.

"I can see the future," he said. "There are plenty of creatures—humans, even—who have the gift of foresight. Many, still, who can see vivid flashes of impending events. There are rumors of those who can control it more thoroughly, who can choose to see one person's future over another's, but that's nothing more than street-corner fortunetelling as far as I'm concerned. Though one day I may be proven wrong.

"But my gift is special. I make prophecies. That means my visions are rare, but they exist independent of factors that might change the future—apart from anyone's will or intent, apart from even unchangeable forces or conditions." He hesitated. "And it means I have never been wrong. Everything I've ever foreseen has come to fruition.

"Nearly a century ago, I had a vision that involves you. I didn't know you would be the catalyst for the event, but having met you, I know now. When I tell you of this prophecy, I want you to promise you will not blame yourself. You must treat it as something that was going to happen one way or the other, since long before you started dreaming about leaving your family over a century ago. The future was already certain. You cannot find yourself at fault."

I waited. "Five years before Mark was born, I had a vision of Adelaide giving birth. We were thrilled. Once Mark was born in 1912, I had a strange vision that has stayed with me for all these years.

"I saw a battle. A war between creatures like us. There were a few hundred fighting in my vision, but I couldn't imagine it. I had no idea how that many would end up in one place all together. All the creatures we know, they travel like nomads or they exist in small covens. Valentin's pack here—before we fought them—was the largest we have ever come across. With one exception, of course," he said.

I understood. "My family," I said, my voice a whisper.

"Yes," he said. "When we met you and heard your story, I realized who you were. We have spent almost a hundred years planning for a war we knew would one day come, but we had no way to know when to expect it. But I knew the time had come as soon as I saw your beautiful face," he said. "The foundation has been laid, Sadie. The war is upon us."

16
EVOLUTION

"You're going to fight my family?" I asked, scared. "You're going to hurt them?"

"You're misunderstanding. We're going to fight with them. We're on the same side," he said.

"How can this be? We've always been peaceful!" I asked. I could feel the panic rising through my body.

"It will be a civil war. There is a group of rebel Survivors that will threaten your family," he said.

"Anthony, they're not going to rebel. No one but me has left in 319 years," I argued.

"They've already left your family. It happened while you were apart from us. When we heard about it, I sent Everett to you. I wanted him to bring you back to us so we could explain, but then I saw a vision of the lynxes hurting you, so we came here instead," he said.

"But what will cause this battle?"

He sighed. "I feel partially responsible. I now know that your family was safer inside the walled city. I didn't know that letting them disperse would be dangerous until Ginny told me that they do not marry. When I found out, I realized what a terrible mistake I had made."

"Why does that make them unsafe in the outside world?" I asked.

"Because they will evolve into something terrible among humans," he said. "It is a matter of genetics, so to speak. We knew your family a long time ago. Adelaide's family lived in Pickering in Yorkshire in England five centuries ago. They were pureblood witches. Many generations after Adelaide left them, families from their village—other families of witches—migrated to Salem. We would check in on them from time to time. When we learned of the witch trials, we assumed that they were executed and that the line had met its end. We didn't know that your elders had been exiled. They are pureblood witches. Though many in Salem were innocent and wrongfully accused, many—including your ancestors—*were* witches.

"But since your elders have continued to extend their line, and since they do not marry, all their children are illegitimate," he said.

"Not all," I corrected. "John and Rebecca married, so their children would be legitimate. And some in the later generations have chosen to marry."

Anthony scrubbed his face with his hand, the mannerism I now knew was a trademark of all the Winter men. "That only clarifies what we already believe. Your family has become a mix of creatures now. If two Survivors were to mate and have a child illegitimately—like your elders did—and then two of those illegitimate Survivors had a child together, again out of wedlock, that child would be a *nosferatu*," he explained.

"There are no shape-shifters in my family," I argued.

"There wouldn't appear to be. Shape-shifters, vampires—it takes humans to bring out their powers. So long as they were living in isolation from humans, their traits wouldn't be present," he explained. "And if the pureblood witches from John and Rebecca's line mated with the *nosferatu*..."

"They would be *vieczy*, like your family," I said, shock spreading across my face. "And if they go outside the walls and encounter humans..."

"Then they will kill them. The activation of their hunting instincts would be instantaneous," Anthony said.

"But we have been a peaceful people, always," I said, trying to will his explanation untrue.

"Because you have never lived among humans. The elders have kept the family contained to protect them. They would change if they spent time with humans, as you did. But you changed for the better. They would not be so lucky. If a fully matured vampire of our kind who has never learned to control his impulses comes into contact with humans, it will not end well," he said. "I am so sorry, Sadie. I couldn't have known it when I stood up in front of them and urged them all to see the world, but we understand what it means now. This rebellion will end in massacre."

I understood why he didn't want me to blame myself, then, but I could only see it as my fault. Anthony might have encouraged them, but I knew they would never have left if it weren't for me. I opened the door. I showed them the way.

"Who will be massacred exactly?" I asked.

"Humans, for one," he said.

"But in the war?" I asked.

"I am not sure what prompts them to do it, but these rogue Survivors will come back to your family, likely to destroy them once they realize that they can acquire their powers if they kill them. I have seen many cultures of supernatural creatures around the world murder each other for acquisition of powers. It is not uncommon," he said.

"And we are going to fight against them?" I asked.

"We are," he said. "We'll stand along with your family. We cannot leave them defenseless against a pack of *vieczy*. They'd have no chance."

I pressed my hands to my face and closed my eyes tight.

"All we can do now is warn your family that the war is coming," he said gravely. "We will protect them, Sadie."

"The same way that you rid the world of violent creatures," I said.

"Yes," Anthony said.

"Because now, my family, some of them are evil," I whispered.

"Yes," Anthony said.

I swallowed hard as another wave of guilt hit me. I didn't care what Anthony said. I had started this all.

And I felt so stupid! I had fought tooth and nail trying to convince the elders that we needed to see the world around us. Condemning their behavior. Accusing them as tyrants. And all along, they had merely been protecting us.

"Why didn't this happen to me?" I asked. "Why didn't I become one of you?"

"You are different," he said solemnly.

"In what way?" I asked.

"I'm not entirely sure. But whatever the reason, I would be grateful for it if I were you," he advised.

I said nothing. Anthony called out for Ginny, who flew to his side. "I need your mind," Anthony said. "It's time to show her."

Ginny nodded. "Focus on my mind, Sadie," she said. I closed my eyes and obliged. Ginny focused on Anthony. The bulwark in Anthony's mind did not limit her, so she could read him. He conjured up his vision of the war, and I could see it through her mind.

I shuddered when I saw the horror of it. I saw blood, bodies—some of family members and others of creatures I had never seen before. Mark was a powerful, central warrior in the battle. All of the Winters, all of the elders, in hand-to-hand combat with other members of my family and with strangers I didn't know. I had been searching for mortality, and now that I was faced with images of the dead, I was shaken to my core.

Anthony quickly unfocused, the vision fading. I opened my eyes and looked at Ginny and Anthony. "Will it really be like that?" I asked.

"It will," Anthony said.

"What do we do now?"

"We go home," he said, "to your family. And we prepare. You should take some time, though, Sadie. They've already gone, and so there's nothing we can do today that cannot wait a few weeks. You need to focus. Use this time to mentally ready yourself."

"How do we prepare?" I asked.

"We need to train your family to fight. My family has been preparing for this war since Mark was born. I knew he was the powerful warrior of my vision. I've spent the last hundred years training him, acquiring for him as many powers as possible, all so he could be ready to fight this battle," he said. "It's why we named him Marcus."

"Destroyer," I said quietly. "How much time do we have?"

"In the vision the sky is bright grey, and there is no snow," he said.

"There will already be snow on the ground there now this far into October. The snow won't melt until April," I said

"So we have six months," he said. "At most, a year."

I was quiet. Anthony and Ginny were patiently waiting for me to respond. I tried desperately to keep the images of the broken bodies of my family members out of my mind, but it was no use. Ginny hovered close to me, her presence protective.

"I think you should show her the vision of Everett and her," Ginny said after a while. She had been able to follow my thoughts as they swirled darkly into self-loathing. She wanted to distract me.

Anthony nodded once more. "Focus," he said to us both as he flipped through the images of his visions.

And then I saw it.

We were on a beach. My hair was in soft waves from the salty air, a long, white, gauzy dress flitting around my calves, my shoulders and arms bare. Everett was beside me, his arm locked tight around my waist, a loose-fitting button-down opened halfway down his chest, rugged khakis rolled up so we could wade in the water. His eyes were rich golden green again, his smile sparkled in the moonlight, and his hair was messy from the ocean breeze. He pulled me close to him and kissed me, and then he whispered something that made me laugh. Laughing, too, he darted down the beach, and I ran after him, slinging my arms around his neck as he pulled me off the ground and spun me around. Laughing, he stumbled into the water, and we fell to the ground. Warm water lapped up around us as we lay kissing in the surf. Then I rested my head on his chest. He kissed my head and whispered that he loved me. I kissed his chest and said I loved him, too. My left hand was fiddling with his open shirt, a beautiful diamond on my ring finger.

It was a more detailed version of the vision I had had in Twin Falls the moment I touched Everett on the hillside, only the locale was different; this water was warm. At the time, it had felt like a fishhook in my stomach for how impossible it seemed. But now it was here, in Anthony's vision, a promise that it would occur.

Anthony's vision continued where mine had stopped. I watched as Everett lithely sprung to his feet, never letting me out of his grasp. He kissed me once more, set me down, and then we ran slowly back up the beach. There was no one there; there were no houses or shops along it as far as the eye could see, except for one—a stunning mansion. I knew then that the beach, the house—it was all ours. We crossed the sand toward the majestic home, the kind I had only ever seen in movies. It was three stories high, and the back of the house was covered in broad windows and balconies overlooking the water. Everett and I ran up to the porch and into a living room. I couldn't tell how I knew, but I knew it was many, many years in the future.

We were so happy. Our love was so real—I could feel it. It was so warm and light that for one solitary second it sucked from me all my morbid desires for death, along with my fears about the Winters and even the war, all my trepidation about love and touch. For one second, I loved Everett in a way that made me feel like an entirely different being. Then the vision faded out.

I opened my eyes and was disappointed to see the cold, barren landscape around me.

17

FOREVER

Everett and I took off together running toward Moscow, but before we even topped the first hill, I collapsed from the pain in my side. I relented and let Everett tuck me close to his chest and run, holding me, all the way back to Moscow. There was no other way.

We didn't make my usual stop at a drug store before returning to the Hotel National, so there were gasps and stares and cross thoughts as we walked, rugged and filthy, through the hotel lobby and up to the suite. I didn't care. I had at least convinced Everett to stop outside the city and get a taxi so I could arrive on my feet and walk to the elevator. There were some lines I would not cross.

The minute I was inside the suite, I felt better. I had forgotten how luxury soothed me. I pulled off my rugged traveling coat and let it fall to the floor, then wiggled out of the high boots and grimy socks. I shed my sweater, too, leaving my arms bare in a sleeveless undershirt, and swapped my muddy jeans for clean track pants from my suitcase in one fluid movement out of Everett's line of sight. I wanted to bathe, but I wanted to look at him first.

I caught a glimpse of myself in the mirror, and I looked positively terrible. My shirt had rips and holes along my side from the lynx's teeth, and red gashes underneath each tear. My eyes were sunken and rimmed in dark circles, the color in my face was off, and my hair was matted. My skin was covered in a rough layer of grit. A lovely picture.

Everett came up behind me, and slid his cold hands along my arms, wrist to shoulder. He kissed the side of my face, my jaw, my throat. "What is it?" he asked, kissing along my neck, across my shoulder.

"I'm dirty," I said.

"Then take a bath," he said, his sterling lips reaching the tip of my shoulder. His lips retreated, tracing back up the path they had made. "We have forever," he smiled.

I smiled, mine a weaker smile than his. "All right," I swallowed. I pulled myself into the bathroom and started running hot water.

Forever. I knew the gravity of forever. I had already lived longer than most people's forever. I knew how long it would be.

And I was painfully aware that every moment I spent with him like this—vulnerable, my defenses down—was bringing me closer to him, and making it more impossible to live without him. If he were going to promise forever, he'd better mean it. I would have to tell him this.

I slid into a very hot bath. The water stung my wounds. I submerged my body completely at first, lying on the bottom of the oversized tub and looking up at the ceiling through the water, but I couldn't relax. So I sat up and washed quickly.

I hadn't brought any clean clothes in with me, so I wrapped up in the giant hotel robe. When I emerged, I saw that Everett had turned the bed down and had soft music playing. The Harvey Nichols bag from London was sitting on the edge of the bed. "I hope you don't mind," he said. "I was trying to find you something soft and comfortable and...sleeplike," he said. The pajamas I bought when I was going to spend the night with Cole were inside.

"Everett," I said, "You can't sleep. I can't sleep. What are you doing?"

"You need to rest, and I wouldn't mind being close to you," he said. "I know it is not very nineteenth century of us, I'll admit. But I promise to be a perfect gentleman," he smiled and kissed my forehead. "My turn to get clean. You get comfy, and I'll be back in a flash."

I pulled out the pajamas and put them on. Having an affinity for soft fabrics but also a desire for modesty considering the circumstances under which I bought the pajamas, I had selected a deep navy Calvin Klein pants and long-sleeve shirt set. I examined myself in the mirror. I tugged uncomfortably at the sleeves. It had been so long since I had felt comfortable with my arms—my scars—exposed that I hated to cover them up now. I changed into a soft, grey, ribbed-knit tank top. I didn't want to hide anymore.

I was kind of alarmed with how badly my side still hurt. When I was still, it only ached, but when I moved it felt like harpoons were piercing my torso. After three years of letting people try to kill me, it was ironic that I had been wounded seriously when I wasn't even trying.

Everett returned quickly to find me standing next to the bed. He looked worried that I didn't want to lie down next to him, but, really, I just didn't want to be already lying down when he returned, and it hurt too badly to sit. I smiled at him reassuringly, and he relaxed.

He looked gorgeous. His hair was damp and slicked back out of his face. A relaxed-fitting pair of green and grey pajama pants sloped off his hipbones, a fitted, plain white T-shirt stretched across his muscular chest. The sleeves clung to his biceps, a V-neck dipping down past his collarbones, baring the hardened lines of his body. He looked like he was carved out of stone.

It felt strangely domestic to me. I was not entirely comfortable with the situation, but it felt far less illicit than I thought it would. I felt capable of lying next to him and resting, talking.

"This is a good look on you," he said as he crossed the room to me. "You're usually so put together. It's nice to see you deconstructed," he smiled.

"I suppose that is my intent," I said. He ran his hands along my bare arms again. He had not missed that they were a symbol of my trust in him.

"I like this better," he said. "You are such a perfect canvas, you don't need to cover it the way you do sometimes." I looked at the floor, embarrassed. He gently put a hand to my cheek and raised my face up so I was looking at him once more. "You're so beautiful," he said. "It takes my breath away every time."

"You don't need your breath," I said, "so is that saying much?"

"I suppose I shouldn't say my heart stops when you look at me this way either," he laughed.

"You're going to have to be more original than that," I said. "Clichés just won't cut it when you're immortal." I smiled back at him.

"How about this," he said. "When those pretty purple eyes look at me the way they're looking at me now, I feel heat radiating from my toes and fingers all the way into my chest. When you get this close to me, I feel every bit of skin on my body come alive, like each atom holds an intense electric current you're conducting." He was slowly leaning closer in to me, my face still in his hand. "And when your lips touch mine," his voice now softer than a whisper, "I'm connected to a part of my soul I had never been able to reach until you let me touch you, like there's a light in the midst of my darkness I couldn't see till you showed me, like the world outside the space between us has disappeared. And I've found the way I'd like to spend eternity. You," he breathed, "are my personal heaven."

Then he kissed me.

"You need to lie down," he said. "I know you're playing brave, but I can tell you're in pain." I hated that he could see that.

He motioned for me to climb into the bed. I slid between the covers, the soft sheets gliding over my skin. Everett was beside me, propped up on his side, in a fraction of a second. "How is it?" he asked.

"The bed or the injury?" I asked.

He laughed. "Both, I guess."

"Well," I sighed, "the bed is soft and comfortable, and I suddenly forget why I don't spend more time here." He laughed again. "And the injury is...bearable," I said. It was the best I could do without completely lying.

He furrowed his brow. "Can I see it?" he asked. "I want to see how bad it is." I thought it would be good for another set of eyes to look at it to determine if I needed to do anything about it.

"I guess you should look at it," I said. "Unless you get skittish around blood," I joked, smiling deviously, the first time I was able to use humor when referring to his...kind.

"Very funny," he said, rolling his eyes.

I lifted the hem of my shirt and pulled it back over the wound carefully. He helped me, sliding the part of the shirt underneath me out of the way so he could see the entire wound. His eyes studied it carefully, clearly very concerned. It was evident that it was much worse than he had anticipated. He leaned in to look more closely at each puncture wound. Most of them were bright red, open patches of skin. Others had blackened around the edges.

"This is not good," he said.

"I'll be fine," I said. He moved his face close enough to the wounds that I could feel his breath, dry and cool, on my skin.

He looked up at me. "I can fix them," he said.

"You what?" I asked.

"I have the ability to help them heal a little faster," he said. "You'll have to trust me," he said, his face pained.

"Okay," I stumbled. I had no idea what I was agreeing to.

He leaned in closer to my stomach. My anticipation of his touch mixed with fear of whatever he was going to do to me. Tentatively, he opened his mouth and gently ran his tongue over the wound closest to my ribcage. My nerves were instantly electrified by his mouth on my bare skin. I knew this effect wasn't his intention, but I had stopped breathing entirely. He looked up at me to make sure I was okay. I nodded, encouraging him to go on to the next one. Again, his cold tongue slid delicately over the opened wound. This time I could see a pale, shimmery, gold residue where his tongue had been. He continued downward across each of the individual puncture wounds until he got to the lowest one, near my hipbone. When he pulled away, next to the lowest one I saw a trickle of thick gold, metallic liquid, more opaque than the sheen over the wounds. He quickly rubbed it away with his finger. Another shock to my system came as his cool fingers brushed my soft abdomen.

He seemed to be struggling. One of his hands was gripping the bed so strongly that it looked like the material was giving way underneath his grasp. Was this causing him pain, trying to alleviate mine?

"Is it helping?" he asked, hopefully.

"It tingles kind of," I said, "but it hurts less."

"I need to get the rest of them on your back," he said. He put a gentle hand on my hip. "Can you roll on your side?" he asked. I nodded and obliged.

He let out a very low growl. He was just as careful with my back, but he seemed to be hurrying. The pain in his face was still there.

He rolled me onto my back and then sat up. He pulled my sliced hand to his face and repeated the same process. His face was still pained.

"What is it?" I asked.

"Nothing," he said, but I pressed him to tell me. "It was just a little harder to control that than I thought it would be," he said.

"What was that?" I asked. He looked down, embarrassed. I got the impression he thought I understood what was happening, and now felt guilty having done it without me fully understanding it.

"My venom," he said.

My breath caught. "Doesn't that mean..."

"No!" he said quickly, moving to lie down next to me and position his face in front of mine in one quick motion. "No, no. I wasn't doing anything that would hurt you," he said. "I never would! Venom has healing capabilities in very, very small quantities like that. It's just a delicate balance."

"Between you alleviating my pain and me becoming like you?" I asked, a little heated.

He bit his lower lip, the golden glaze still on them. "I was being careful," he said, dejected.

"Is there venom when I kiss you?" I asked.

"Not enough to hurt you," he said. He was getting very self-conscious. I hadn't meant for that to happen, but I hadn't really realized I would actually come into contact with his venom. The idea troubled me significantly.

I decided I needed to be honest with him. "Everett, I want to tell you something," I said. "I don't want you to think I mean any ill toward you or your family when I say this, but it's something you should know."

"Okay," he said, fighting to keep his voice even.

"I don't want to become a vampire," I said. "I'm already immortal, and that's bad enough. I don't need to add moral conflict and a new set of instincts to my plate. It's difficult enough for me as is." In reality, I didn't want to be any *harder.* I was already inhuman enough.

"I assumed as much," he said. "But there is a fairly large risk, you know."

"Is there any less risk because I'm not human?" I asked, hoping.

He shrugged. "Sort of. You're more human than I expected you to be, though," he said, nodding toward the wounds on my stomach.

"What do you mean?" I asked.

"Your blood tastes so much like, well, blood," he said.

"Did you taste my blood just now?" I asked, my voice cracking. I hadn't considered that. I didn't like that image at all.

"They're open wounds, Sadie. What was I supposed to do?" he asked, clearly offended. I deflected my gaze in apology. "You just...tasted more human than I would expect."

"So what, now we have to be more careful?" I asked.

"I hate to admit this," he said, his eyes on the ceiling, "but in my vision of you and me forever, I assumed you'd be like me at some point."

"I'm already immortal!" I said, angrily. "That's not enough?"

"If you're sure you don't want to risk becoming like me..." he trailed off. I gave him time to work up the courage to finish his thoughts. "Then that's going to limit us," he said.

"Does that mean we can't be together?" I asked, frantic.

"No, no, that's not what that means," he said quickly, caressing my face. "Nothing will keep me from being with you," he said. "You know that, right?" I looked down. I wasn't sure if I knew that. "Sadie, come on. You saw the vision. You have to know!" he cried.

"But you thought I'd become like you if I needed to," I said.

"I just thought it wouldn't matter if it happened," he clarified. "Like you said, you're already immortal. You wouldn't be losing a heartbeat or a normal life. It would be much the same," he said. I hadn't considered it from that perspective, but it didn't change my mind.

"Talk to me about these limits," I said.

He didn't want to talk about limits. "It's just..." he stopped and thought about it. "Maybe we can talk about limits later," he said.

"Give me a ballpark," I said.

He grimaced a little. "I suppose," he said slowly, "they are limits that would only arise if we abandoned the nineteenth century and moved closer to the twenty-first." He pulled his bottom lip into his mouth after he said this, embarrassed and uncomfortable.

"Oh," I said, understanding. We were quiet for a little while.

"That's how it happened to Madeline, isn't it?" I asked.

He nodded. "She was a human," he said. "We all thought he was crazy for trying to be with a human, and that she was crazy for trying to be with him," he said. "But Pat was so in love with her. Theirs is one of those great loves, the stuff they write romances about. But even that couldn't change the animal in him, I guess."

"What happened?" I asked, probably overstepping some bounds.

"It was after they were married," he explained. "Patrick's very traditional, so I guess it didn't come up before then," he said. His features were painted in pain. "He couldn't control himself. He called us in the middle of the night after the wedding, an absolute mess. He had already bitten her, and it was too late to do anything about it. She was still under when we got there, but her eyes were already red." He closed his eyes and rubbed his forehead. It was obviously a traumatic memory.

I didn't say anything. I didn't know what to say. I didn't want to tell him how that terrified me, or that I never wanted to do *anything* that might cause him to lose control with me like that. But I didn't want to mean that either. I sensed he wouldn't like a forever limited only to the kind of private moments we had experienced so far. And though I hadn't considered it explicitly, having spent close to a century and a half recoiling from the touch of others, likely neither would I.

This was such a complication. When I envisioned the obstacles to my finding a happily-ever-after, I thought of the qualities in men that would keep me from loving them. I hadn't included venomous in that list. And, perhaps, rightfully so. After all, his venom wouldn't keep me from loving him, but it would keep us from normality.

I closed my eyes and tried to think of something else. I was pleasantly surprised to realize how much less pain I was in. I tried to convince myself this meant he was not all bad, that his uniqueness was, perhaps, not all evil as I had envisioned.

I thought of something pleasant. "You haven't seen the vision, have you?" I said.

"No, I haven't. Some of us can't see inside people's heads," he joked.

"Well, I can't see inside everyone's," I said, flicking his head. Some drying hairs fell out of place and into his eyes.

He pulled himself back up onto his side, so he could look at me. "Can you tell me about it?" he asked nervously.

"Of course," I said. "First we were on a beach," I said.

"Which beach?" he asked.

"I don't know," I said. "The water was warm, and the beach was private, ours." He smiled, and I went on. "And first we were walking. You had me tight against you, my head tucked into your neck," I said.

"Your favorite spot," he smiled. He had noticed.

"And then you said something silly, but I don't know what it was. But it made us laugh, and you ran down the beach, but then I caught you—needless to say. You grabbed me, lifted me up and spun me around. You kissed me, of course," I said, smiling. Everett clung to the story. He was watching my eyes for every emotion, my lips to make sure he got each word the way I said it. He was totally enthralled.

"Kissed you how?" he asked.

I grinned at him. "Kissed me hard. So hard we fell down into the water." He laughed and leaned in, one hand sliding effortlessly under my neck and one hand reaching around my waist. He lifted me gently, bringing me toward him. And then he did kiss me hard. The length of his body pressed against mine as he pulled me closer, tighter. I wrapped my arms around his neck. After a few moments, I pulled my mouth from his and kissed along his jawbone and down his throat, the way he had kissed me earlier. A soft purring sound escaped his lips. His lips found mine again, and he pressed me back into the pillow, his body suddenly on top of mine. I was in a frenzy, unsure of how to balance how amazing he felt and how wrong I thought going too far would be—including a new fear about what could come from such an escapade.

But it was hard to focus on that. The intensity was stronger than I could have imagined, getting better all the while as I thought it would. I kept pulling him against me, wanting him to be closer, wanting there to be no walls.

He suddenly broke our lips apart and pressed his forehead to mine, his breathing short and ragged and powerful. I didn't move, unsure of what to do. I relaxed my grasp a little, and he relaxed his. Then he rolled onto his side, his arms still wrapped around me.

"And then what happened?" he asked, his voice breathy. I realized that he had been well on his way to losing control, and that's why he'd stopped. It was probably for the best.

"Then we laid on the beach," I said. "You held me like you are now, and I put my head on your chest," I said, moving my head exactly as it had been. "Like this."

"And then?" he asked, a playful grin in his voice.

"And then you kissed my forehead, and you said..." I trailed off. I didn't want to say it when we had never said it.

"I said what?" he asked.

"Nothing," I said. "And I had this..."

"No, Sadie," he stopped me. "Said what?" I didn't answer. Just then, he kissed my forehead and purred, "I love you."

I shot my face up to his. "What?" I asked.

He smiled. "I love you," he said again. I smiled, too.

"How did you know?" I asked.

"That that's what I said in the vision?" he asked. I nodded. He put his hand on my cheek. "Because that's exactly what I would have said. Having you here in my arms, your head on my chest, just lying here together...what else could I possibly do but tell you how much I love you, how you've made me happier than I've ever been?"

"And I, you, of course," I said quietly. He smiled contentedly, I could tell. I felt so safe in his arms, images of an impending war, of a treacherous future, of a search for death far from my mind.

"And we have forever," he said softly.

I hated, still, that he would not understand why this didn't please me the way it pleased him. All I wanted was a lifetime. One lifetime of the kind of happiness he and I were going to feel. I knew that was enough. Any more than that felt like greed. I just wanted my piece of happiness, and then I would know I had my share. Everett would never understand this, of course. He would continue to feel pride in his immortality, excitement at the possibilities it held for him, for us. And I would continue to feel trapped.

All at once, I felt a pungent wave of love. It was just the same love I felt at the rehearsal dinner when I thought I may never have what Felix and Corrina did. But here I lay, covered in the same kind of love. It had seemed so impossible, but it had come to fruition just the same. I kissed Everett's chest where I lay, and he stroked my hair.

"It is possible," I said, "that I love you more than life."

"Sadie, you're a strange girl, so I say this with love," he said, his voice sincere. "I need you to love me more than death," he whispered. "Can you do that?" he asked, still stroking my hair.

I felt a pang deep in my stomach. It wasn't easy for me to love him how he was, but I understood now it wasn't easy for him to love me knowing what I was capable of either. We were both living in fear.

"I can try," I said. I could try, and I would. He kissed my forehead once more, and I began to feel an unfamiliar lull. My eyelids grew heavy, my breathing slowed.

"I love you more than all of it, more than anyone. You're everything to me, Sadie. You will be forever. I promise," he whispered. His voice added to the weight in my eyelids, to the peace in my body, to the stillness in my mind.

"Mmhmm," I sighed softly. His thick arms hugged me tight to his chest.

I took another long breath. And then, against Everett's strong, cool body, I drifted peacefully to sleep.

Epilogue: God's Work

Salem, Massachusetts
June 1689

The men's voices were hushed. They were meeting under the cloak of darkness. Young Lizzie Godric would be persecuted if ever it were revealed that she was meeting alone with seven men while her parents slept a few houses down. She understood this was a risk she had to take.

Lizzie Godric knew she was different.

She'd known it for years, understood that something about her was strange. To begin with, she hadn't slept in 647 nights.

"You understand what we have told you, Lizzie?" he asked, his voice urgent.

Lizzie nodded. "Once they take us to the West, we must stay away from all other people. Isolation is the only way to keep ourselves safe and to keep the people safe," Lizzie said, repeating what they had told her.

"Very good," he said. "I mean this. If you listen to nothing else I have told you, listen to that."

"When will it begin?" she asked.

He did not hesitate. He had seen it clearly. "In three years' time. It will likely be winter or maybe even spring when the first accusations begin, but it will not be until the next winter that you leave. That's when all will leave," he said. Lizzie looked around the table at all seven men. "All but me," he said, his voice quiet.

"Why not, sir?" Lizzie asked, fearful. He, the strange prophet, had been her mentor throughout her body's strange hardening, her mind's heretical betrayal. She hated to think he would not come on their treacherous journey.

"I cannot explain it now," he said, the pain clear in his voice, "but they will never choose exile over execution if I volunteer to go. It will have to be these six," he said. "But I will come for you. If you do as I say, I'll come for you."

Lizzie nodded, terrified and overwhelmed by all that she had been charged with, especially since learning of her companion's vision of a witch hunt in Salem.

"Just remember that all that we do will be to protect you. We'll accuse as many as we think may be like you, like me, though there is some chance we will overestimate. It's a risk we have to take," he said. Understanding Lizzie's expression, he added, "We're meant to do God's work, Lizzie. Please do not forget that is our purpose."

Just then, his daughter came into the room in her sleep clothes.

"Daddy?" she asked, rubbing her eyes. She was surprised to see the gathering in her kitchen.

"Go back to bed, Hannah. I'll look in on you in a while," he said. His daughter did as she was told.

Seattle, Washington
November 2, 2011

It was early November when Everett and I met up with the rest of the Winters in Seattle to travel back to Montana. I tapped my fingers nervously against my leg as I sat in the lobby of the Four Seasons awaiting their arrival. I was unhappy to be back to reality after spending two weeks of perfect quiet in Moscow with Everett. If I had not loved him before, after two weeks of sleeping and eating and kisses and quiet moments, I surely loved him now.

But now I was here, facing an uncertain future, the familiar tension having returned to my body and my mind.

It had begun in the British Airways lounge at JFK after our connecting flight landed when I flipped on my cell phone for the first time in nearly three weeks. There were messages from a concerned

Corrina, citing no Twitter updates, text messages, calls, or voicemails in nearly a month. There was a voicemail from the beautiful and heart-broken Cole Hardwick that had been sent not long after our ill-fated meeting in London. He apologized, but he also pleaded with my voicemail, reminding me of his gut feeling that we had a future. "I can wait," he had said. "I know one day the time will be right. Until then, enjoy your life, and I'll enjoy mine." He hesitated before adding, "Until we meet again."

And then there was the message I never expected to receive. I had programmed the numbers for the five cell phones I had given to the Survivors into my phone as "Family 1" through "Family 5," and when I turned on my phone in New York, there was a troubling one-minute-and-seventeen-second voicemail from Family 4. It was Lizzie. She didn't give any details, but I already knew what had happened. She asked me to come home. She said that things were changing, that they needed my help, and that I might be their only hope.

So Everett and I met the Winters in Seattle to go together to Montana. I left my prized CL 63 in the parking garage of the Four Seasons and purchased two SUVs to traverse the terrain between Seattle and Montana, knowing the roads would grow treacherous in the coming months. Winter was upon us.

When we arrived at the Survivors' City gates, there was less animosity than the last time we had arrived there. Lizzie, Sarah, and Hannah were waiting for us. Lizzie swung her arms around my neck.

"I am so glad you've come back," she said.

"I've come to help. That's not the same thing as coming back," I clarified.

"For the second time, I thought I had lost you forever. Just knowing that you would come when I called puts my mind at ease," Lizzie said.

John and his loyal following came not long after we entered the city gates. Hannah had not warned him that we would be returning. His hostility toward me was clear; it radiated all the way to my bones. Sensing my tension, Everett walked hand-in-hand with me through the city. The Winters followed close behind us, obviously guarding me. I was grateful to see my two families coming together, even under such terrible conditions. I doubted they would ever be friends, but everyone seemed to realize the magnitude of the situation that lay before us.

We went directly to the special room off the church. Once we had all crossed the threshold of the church, I stole a glance at the Winters, who seemed unscathed by being in a church. Ginny laughed, hearing my thoughts. Another vampire myth debunked.

Andrew spoke. "Sadie, friends of Sadie, we assume you know the tragedy that's occurred in our community," he said. His voice sounded thin; this was taking its toll on Andrew.

"How bad is it?" I asked.

"Four of the last generation took off together. We thought they might be exploring, but when they didn't return for several days, we knew something was terribly wrong. Soon after that, six more across two generations left in the middle of the night," he said. "We had protection at the gates and around the walls. They stole the keys and took the vehicle you brought us," he explained. There was a pang in my stomach. I had enabled them—first in spirit, now for real.

"So it's ten who have gone," I said. It was worse than I had envisioned.

John could be silent no longer. "Ten is where it started," he scoffed. "Twenty-eight have gone, Sadie. Twenty-eight from your family have left because of you! Because of your wretched ideas, your dark ways!" he shouted.

I shrank in my chair. Twenty-eight? So much worse than I had imagined! Everett squeezed my hand again, leaning into me protectively and instinctually. Everett already hated John, I could tell. I feared the animosity would only grow in their coming interactions. I let my eyes hang on the edge of the worn marble table, fearing John was right.

And then it hit me, and I froze. John could have said any number in that moment and none would have mattered to me like the number twenty-eight. I filtered through my memories until I came to an image of Noah and me in the snow. There were twenty-nine Survivors who had still hearts. Having already left myself, I knew without a doubt that those other twenty-eight were the ones who had gone. It was too much for a coincidence.

I wanted to hear their names anyway. "Who has abandoned you?" I asked, careful of my word choice. I closed my eyes as Andrew listed the names, each a name I had carved into a tree nearly two decades before, a list I had written in my journal, a list that had lingered in my mind. He paused before the last one, but I didn't have to hear him say it to know it was Noah.

There was a heavy silence in the room, and for that I was grateful. I knew that they were ambushing me in their minds, and was glad not to hear the angry voices of many of the elders who blamed me for what had happened. That's why I wanted to meet in this room. It grieved me to see them like this, in anguish over their family. I didn't want to hear their internal pain as well.

"What would you like me to do?" I asked.

"Find them," Andrew said. "Reason with them. See if you can convince them to come back just to speak with us. Maybe we could come up with a system for them to live out there but come back sometimes," he went on, emotion thick in his voice. This idea of compromise with the rogue Survivors was shocking to me. I looked at the Winters and saw that they, too, were uneasy with the idea of compromise. It was so clear that Andrew had no idea what the risk was. He just wanted his family safe and together. He began again. "You've got to help us. All we have is each other. We understand the choices you have made. We can make our peace with those choices now that you come back every now and then. We will dedicate ourselves to peace with the Winters if it means you will still count yourself among the Survivors. But, Sadie, we cannot lose family members like we're losing them now. We will have no family left."

Hearing the pain in Andrew's voice, I knew I couldn't tell them, not yet. I couldn't tell them what had or would become of their children, what monsters they would be.

I looked at the hardened faces of the fourteen Survivors and realized that this could be what would keep them from surviving after all.

Later that night, Everett and I went for a walk on the farthest edges of the city where the woods were thick. The moon overhead was bright and almost full, though little of the light made it to the ground where we were. Snow was falling.

"I'm afraid to tell them," I admitted to him. "They are already so weakened by their family betraying them."

"They do look heartbroken," he agreed. "News of the prophecy won't help that."

"Do you think it's possible we're wrong? That they're all just like me, and, though it's devastating to my family, they've just run off and there is no danger?" I asked.

"My father would tell you that the future is certain," he said. "But I know you don't trust that yet, so I'll say this: We will find your brethren, and we will determine what they are. Then we'll know whether it is as bad as we've imagined."

I sighed. "We've been a peaceful civilization for three centuries. The walls of the city have never been protected. I don't know how to tell them that that's all over, that the destruction of the outside world has found them, even here," I said. "I'm scared."

"You've spent three years trying to kill yourself, and now you're afraid?" he asked incredulously.

I shoved him. We headed back toward the square. "I'm afraid for my family. I'm afraid for your family," I said.

"I'll protect you," he said. I creased my face in disapproval. I didn't need protection. I needed a way to stop the inevitable.

The moonlight danced off the newfallen snow. I lay down on the ground and he followed me, wrapping his arms around me.

"They're going to think they'll survive it," I said, putting my head on his chest. "My whole life I've heard them say we're doing God's work. They'll think this is just a part of that. Surviving is all they know how to do."

Everett stroked my hair and kissed my forehead. "I don't know if it's that they've survived so much as that they've fought for their lives. And they will all fight again, that much I know," he said.

If the time came, would I fight for mine?

"You'd never fight for yourself, of course," he said grimly, zeroing in on my thoughts. "I'll have to fight for you."

I said nothing. He pulled me up so my face met his.

"I know my purpose in life," he whispered. "It will be to keep you alive, no matter the cost. That's my part in God's work."

I knew he meant what he said.

Acknowledgments

First and absolutely foremost, I have to thank my parents, Cade and Anneal Havard, for everything they've ever done for me. You have opened so many doors, broken all the falls, and put me on a pedestal I never deserved but appreciate every day of my life. You are the reason I believed anything I dreamt of could and would become a reality. This book is tangible proof of my dreams having been realized. I could never thank you enough, but I'll continue to try.

A giant debt of gratitude to Meghan Hannigan, the greatest co-conspirator of all time. Thank you for every edit, for every idea, every name, every Rina-tweet, and for every 4 AM IM conversation about the kind of pajamas they sell at Harvey Nichols. Thank you for being such a dedicated fan and such a fabulous brain to pick. I may never have gotten past Isabel on a paper tablecloth if it weren't for you.

A heartfelt thanks to Jane Cavolina, the first person in publishing to give me a chance. Thanks to your patience, guidance and wise editing pen, I can craft a story into a book. I look forward to the many more to come.

Much love to Danielle Thienel for being the most enthusiastic progress reader that ever lived. Thanks for helping me see the vision come to life and never doubting me for a second.

I'm grateful, also, to Gaby Román, Alison Wood, Elizabeth Middlebrooks, and Jane McKee who were all a part of the whirlwind of consulting, creating, writing, and editing this thing.

Thanks to all the others who helped along the way: Steve and Iris Dart for getting us wired in to the book world; Trish Jones and Michael Newman for all the support from Chafie; Grant Harling for cover art (and patience), and Sara Schork for bringing the cover together beautifully; Erica Erwin for the million little things; John Maddox, Nathan Maggard, and Elle Woodward at Market Me Tennessee for creating the coolest web platform ever; and to Nicole Papa Gaia for connecting the world to my vision.

Thanks as well to Anna and Austin for getting married in Tupelo.

A special thank you to every teacher who taught me to write, create, or trust myself at Parish Episcopal and Hockaday in Dallas. I got it from y'all.

This book would not have happened without the intense energy and creativity I received listening to fantastic music. Super-special thanks to Coldplay, whose song brought me the idea for this series, and to Sara Bareilles, Regina Spektor, Ingrid Michaelson, Muse, Augustana, Franz Ferdinand, and The Killers.

And, finally, to the women who paved the way for me, teaching me to love storytelling and trust my imagination: J. K. Rowling, Curtis Sittenfeld, Janet Fitch, Stephenie Meyer, Sandra Cisneros, Gillian Flynn, and Isabel Allende.

Catch a sneak preview of the
next installment of THE SURVIVORS series:

THE SURVIVORS:
POINT OF ORIGIN

I

THE CAVE

I had begun to stir. I could hear young Survivors in the distance, laughing, running. The sound of chopping wood from a few houses down reverberated in my ears. I knew that, like every morning for the last 319 years, since their forgotten exile from Salem, Massachusetts, the 14 original Survivors were gathered in their chapel, holding a service. Andrew, our patriarch, would be standing in front of them, murmuring their Puritan prayers. And they'd all be following him, by habit if not by faith. They attended these services more often than they would have done in Salem—as if the accusation of witchcraft had stalked them for all these centuries and remained a cause for repentance. The morning ran routinely as it always did. I heard the youngest Survivors scurry past our door, a mixture of bare feet and boots crunching hard snow, reciting passages from their ancient Bible. It was as if I'd never left at all.

I rolled to my side, not wanting to wake up just yet. Eyes still closed tight, I sent one hand out to feel the other side of the bed. It was empty.

It was empty most mornings. In recent months, Everett had lain with me until I'd fallen asleep, but then he'd slip from bed. The Winters and I had spent the last three months living with the Survivors in their city, and though it wasn't my favorite arrangement, they loved being here. For one, Everett and his younger siblings, Mark and Ginny, had strong-armed their mother into allowing them to forgo their usual human routine now that they lived in a community full of immortals—none of whom needed sleep, many of whom couldn't—and so the nighttime had become their playground. They sometimes used it for making practical preparations for our dismal future, but based on the number of mornings one or more of them came back with eyes brighter and redder than when they had left, I was sure they indulged, during their darker waking hours, in activities they were still keeping secret from the Survivors.

I hadn't pushed to determine if this was the case exactly. I was still learning how to carefully balance loving someone and hating a part of him—a defining, integral part—at the same time. Asking Everett and his siblings fewer questions about midnight murders helped me walk this tightrope more effectively.

I finally opened my eyes. From the light, I could tell it was still very early. In the six months I had gone without sleep, I had forgotten the significance of mornings. I hadn't remembered what it felt like to exist in human-length days. There was peace at night, then welcome morning sun filtering through the bedroom windows, and a bit of newness each day. I had fallen in love with these things in Moscow, just before I had come here, to the Survivors' city, and I had been sleeping ever since. I could only fall asleep, of course, if Everett Winter's arms hugged me close to his cool core. Candidly, I did not like that I depended on him like this. I didn't like to depend on anyone for anything.

The Winters had realized they would need a place of their own in the Survivors' City if we were to spend a long time here. So one day not long after we had come back to tell the Survivors of their grim fate, they had brought supplies for a house, and, in days, they had one built. It was modest by their standards, but it was still out of place here. It sat at the end of a row dilapidated houses off the main square of my family's city, taller than the others and certainly newer, its fresh layer of commercial paint taunting the old cabins that made up the place I once called home. I was embarrassed that we were living in a home nicer than the other Survivors'. It made it apparent to them that there were classes— that some people in this world were more privileged or had more resources than others. This had never been made known to Survivors before because no one from the outside had ever invaded, as the Winters were doing now. And I had brought them. It was just one more thing to feel guilty about.

And, so, I didn't spend much of my free time among my Survivor peers. This morning, like every morning, when I climbed out of bed and sensed that no one else was in our house, I sank into an antique armchair I bought in Bigfork that stood in the corner of the room Everett and I shared. I put my feet up on the rickety ottoman and reached for a book from the stacks of them scattered on the floor. I was hopeful when Andrew had promised me that they—that the Survivors—would make peace with the Winters if it meant I would help them. I ignorantly assumed this meant that my family as a whole would accept the Winters and, more importantly, would accept my return.

And they did accept the Winters, to an extent. I could read it off of them. Young girls had crushes on each of the Winter brothers, and young men longed to be like them. Patriarchs respected Anthony's ferocity and firm hand. Many women and men alike revered Adelaide for all she could teach them about their powers and abilities. Every boy lusted after Ginny, even after Madeline when she came; they became symbols of glamour, of femininity. Of the beauty of the world outside.

But they hated me.

This was easier to forget when I was alone in this room, in a chair from the outside, with books from the outside. But I could not forget it entirely. I could, after all, feel every emotion, hear every thought of every Survivor inside the city walls.

So, as a distraction, I continued my research as if this were any other room I'd lived in anywhere in the world, ignoring the fact that my entire family lived just yards outside my window. And hated me.

I had purchased nearly every book on vampires and other modern supernatural creatures I could find—from an early edition of Dracula to textbooks dissecting the myths, and even every book off the teen section's "supernatural table" at a bookstore in Kalispell—and I had read them over and over again. I picked up one whose spine had already cracked and reread sections of it. I was always struck by how these fictional creatures who so closely mirrored the Winter children were characterized with such romance. When my boyfriend returned to me with glowing crimson eyes and a fresh vigor that I knew only came from consuming human blood, there was no romance in it. There was only pain in it. Only disgust. Only the gut-wrenching truth that we were not alike as immortals but rather so unalike as creatures. He could kill. I could not.

I shook my head to break the thought process. I could not dwell on this about him, about the Winters. This I learned. So I pretended not to notice.

Then I heard noises outside and below me, and I was grateful for the distraction. I rose from the chair and crossed the cool wood floors to the window overlooking the expansive backyard, a picturesque winter wonderland. Mark and Everett were wrestling in the snow. I heard Ginny rustling in the kitchen downstairs, making food of some kind at her supernatural pace. I knocked gently on the window, and both boys froze instantly, turning around to see me in the window. In seconds, Everett was in the house and up the stairs.

The door to our room flung open. He was disheveled, his dark chocolate hair was windblown, and his ivory skin was absolutely cold as ice, but Everett Winter was still as beautiful as the moment I'd met him. Only now, he was mine.

"Morning, gorgeous," he said, putting his icy hands on my cheeks as he kissed me. I shivered a little, from the cold or kiss I couldn't be sure. He pulled me closer.

"Mmm," I said softly, "Good morning to you." I had already seen from across the room that his eyes were a deep burgundy today and not the bright, glowing red they would be if he'd eaten overnight. I learned that the burgundy color was almost as bright as his eyes got in the wintertime, especially in weather this cold. No amount of green vegetables could turn them green—photosynthesis in the eyes, his father had once called it—in the tundra of winter in northwest Montana. "What have you crazy kids been up to?" I asked. I unbuttoned his thick coat and slid it off his arms, and then I put my arms around his neck and began to relax. It was a signal. A fraction of a second later, he had swooped me up into his arms, his favorite thing to do. I would only let him when I was feeling particularly lazy, lovable, or, like now, just wanted to be close to him.

"Where to, mademoiselle?" he smiled.

"Bed, perhaps," I said. I wouldn't mind dozing for a little while longer, held tight against him. "Or we could go see what Ginny's making if you want some food," I said, stroking his smooth face. He grinned at me, a little sideways. I sighed. "Okay, food it is." He was such a boy. "But make it quick. We've got a plane to catch!" I said. He grinned again and sped quickly down the stairs and into the kitchen with me tucked close to his chest.

"Morning," Ginny said. She didn't turn around as we entered the small kitchen.

"Morning," I responded. "Down, please," I said to Everett. He always looked a little disappointed when I said this. I pretended not to notice.

"Sleep well?" Ginny asked, flipping pancakes.

"Would have slept better if you didn't steal Everett in the middle of the night," I joked.

"Don't blame me," she said. "It was all Polly."

"What was all Polly?" a voice from outside echoed. It was Mark. Polly was their affectionate—read: emasculating—nickname for him, supposedly because his middle name was Apollo. I tend to believe they just liked calling him Polly.

Ginny responded in a normal tone of voice, and then Mark spoke quietly again, his words too soft for me to make out. I could hear things from far away, but the Winters could hear everything. It never ceased to amaze me.

"Order up," Ginny said, sliding the pancakes onto a plate and handing it to Everett. Suddenly Mark swooped into the room, taking the plate from an unsuspecting Everett's hands.

"Hey!" he barked, and smacked the back of Mark's head. Mark slapped back at him, laughing.

Ginny and I leaned against the countertop, watching their antics. "They're five-year-olds," she breathed. I laughed. I adored them like this. I looked around the room at three of my favorite people in the world and was suddenly much happier.

I put my arm around Ginny and rested my head on her shoulder. "I love being a part of this," I said.

"Too bad. We hate you being a part of this," she joked, her arm around my waist. "You all packed and ready to abandon us for those human friends of yours?" she asked.

"Of course. I can't wait to get away from you, naturally," I kidded, nudging her.

Gin? I said in my mind.

Yeah?

Were you the one who told him I wanted to see Corrina for her birthday? I asked.

Actually, it was all him, she answered. I smiled. That made me love him even more.

The boys eventually stopped scuffling and sat down to eat. Mark had narrowly escaped a crushing blow from his big brother. This is how it would always end: in a draw. Everett was stronger; Mark was faster. Or maybe it was just a draw because neither would actually hurt the other.

"Mmm," Mark said. "Sis, you've outdone yourself." He leaned over and kissed Ginny's cheek. He turned to me and kissed my cheek, too. It was the first time I was close enough to see that his eyes were a glaring crimson red. "Morning, little one," he said.

"I hear you're to blame for stealing Everett," I said, nibbling on a few berries to distract myself from Mark's eyes.

"Guilty always," he smiled.

"She's going to fight you for that one of these days," Everett joked.

Mark was smug. "I'd like to see her try." I shoved him and he made a grand gesture of falling backward, but then he snapped himself up off the ground when he was only inches away from it. It was a very inhuman movement.

"Where is everyone else?" I asked.

"Mom and Madeline are at Lizzie's, I think," Ginny said. "Crazy how Mom and Lizzie have bonded, isn't it?"

I shrugged, thinking it wasn't that odd to me. I quite enjoyed that they liked each other. "What about Anthony and Patrick?" I asked.

"Dad and Pat are at the Canada house," Mark said, now tackling a basket of green vegetables to fade his eyes.

"Will I ever get to see this place?" I asked.

"Maybe," Everett said. "Depends on if we like you enough to keep you around." I stuck out my tongue at him. I blamed Mark for my newly acquired unceremonious tendencies.

"When do you guys have to get out of here?" Ginny asked. I drank some hot tea to warm myself.

"Our first flight leaves from Kalispell at 1:40," Everett said. "It will take about an hour to drive up there, I think. We'll leave around 11:30, maybe?"

"You're driving to the airport? You could run so much faster," Mark said.

"Oh, believe me, brother, I know. But I'm just guessing the princess won't want to run in couture, and I can only imagine how dressed she'll be to see her fashionista partner-in-crime," Everett said. A good guess. I had already laid out a newly ordered outfit: Carolina Herrera cowl-neck fur, Alexander McQueen stiletto booties, and a knee-length Derek Lam leather skirt. No running for me.

"You know, you only get to call me princess if you say it in a loving way," I chided.

"Okay, *princess*," Mark chimed in, his voice high-pitched and mocking. I smacked him.

"We're going to miss you!" Ginny squealed. "We haven't been apart for this long in months!" The boys rolled their eyes. "Are you excited to see Corrina?"

"I am, but that doesn't hold a candle to how excited she is that I'm bringing a boy with me," I said, imagining Corrina's tendency to bounce when she was happy.

Everett laughed. "I'm excited to meet the ginger cheerleader," he admitted. Everett had formed a bond with Corrina and Felix though they've never met. They'd been speaking for months on Twitter after I'd once let it slip that I was no longer traveling alone. "Think she and Fefe are upset you're not skipping home hand-in-hand with the fair-haired boy?" he asked, winking at me. He was asking about Cole Hardwick, whose face I had last seen as I walked out on him at a Thai restaurant in London almost four months ago. I had left him heartbroken, and I felt miserably guilty for it. It was not my favorite topic of discussion, something Everett definitely knew. I narrowed my eyes at him and didn't respond.

So Ginny did, always looking to squash our tension. "I think she's more upset about 'getting so old,'" she said. Each of us laughed, the youngest among us was Mark, who'd be 100 in just a few short days.

But Corrina was upset at "aging." She frequently talked about it on Twitter. She was turning 24, which seemed impossible since I'd met her when she was only 21. She was aging so fast, and in that short time that I had known her, it appeared she had actually grown up. She graduated from college. She got married. I was 145, and though some days I felt 1,000, I usually felt sixteen for how little I'd done, for how little I'd learned about myself. I couldn't understand how Corrina had surpassed me in this way. How she'd figured out so much about herself, her life, and what she wanted when I had figured out so little.

"Think we have time for another round?" Mark goaded, punching Everett in the ribs.

"Hey!" Everett snapped.

"You can only have him if he's already packed, and if he will be clean and pretty and ready to go in two and a half hours," I said.

The boys were already on their feet, racing toward the door. "Done packing. I'll be pretty!" I heard Everett call as he tailed after Mark. I crossed my arms and frowned. Then Everett ran back in. "Forgot something," he smiled. Ginny rolled her eyes as Everett leaned in and kissed me. I kissed him back.

I put my hands on either side of his eyes. "If you two do anything that turns them red, you better come back here and eat your weight in vegetables. Deal?" I said as sternly as I could.

He laughed. "Deal." Then he flew out the door.

It didn't take us quite an hour to get to Kalispell, but it was close. We absolutely could have run faster, but I wanted to drive. The highway to the airport was clear enough for me to drive my CL 63, which I had missed, having been forced to drive SUVs in the snow for the last three months. And I did want to look nice to see Corrina. Everett wanted to drive, having found a spot in his heart for the AMG engine and perhaps feeling a deep pang of separation from his Maserati, but I refused. My car. My drive.

On the plane, Everett held my hand while he read a book at a human pace, a method he practiced to enjoy the literature and also to look inconspicuous. I closed my eyes and tried to focus. Having spent a good deal of time with my family over the last three weeks, my sensing abilities were growing. I was now able to sense minds from a distance with better accuracy, even read the thoughts of minds I knew from great distances. This was turning into a very useful talent, albeit disconcerting to quite literally hear voices in my head all the time.

But despite the increase in my powers, I had been unable to do the one thing I was trying to do lately: find the missing members of my family. It was mid-October when Everett and the rest of the Winter family followed me to a hillside in Romania to help fight the *nosferatu* shape-shifters I'd met there. And it was then that everything changed for me. That's when Anthony told me of his vision of a war between supernatural creatures—in fact, a war between Survivors. He'd seen members of my family who had gone rogue bounding over the city walls, and attacking the members of my Survivor family they'd left behind. In early November Andrew had asked me to track down the twenty-eight Survivors who had gone AWOL. Andrew just wanted to find his family, but our motives ran deeper. I believed that if we could find them, then we could stop the war before it began—even if it meant killing them to protect the rest of the family. The Winters believed that nothing could prevent what Anthony saw in a vision once he had it, but they thought we should find the dangerous, rogue Survivors anyway.

But this was proving to be difficult. Being a skilled tracker with unique senses, it should have been easy for me. I could find almost anyone, anywhere, but these twenty-eight were off my radar entirely.

It was now the last days of January, and I was frustrated I had made so little progress. In the air, in a quiet first class cabin with Everett's presence to soothe me, I centered my mind and filtered through all the humming and buzzing and voices in my head, scanning every mind I came across on the ground below. I did this for the entire plane ride from Kalispell to Seattle, then for the first two hours of our flight from Seattle to Dallas. Frustrated, I found nothing.

Abandoning this, I began flipping through books on my electronic reader. In addition to my foray into supernatural literature, I had also bought many classics. Plato's *The Republic.* Sun Tzu's *The Art of War.* Machiavelli's *The Prince.* Karl Marx's *Communist Manifesto.* Histories of the early American colonies, and philosophies from Hobbes, Locke, Payne, Calvin, Rousseau. Every one of Shakespeare's histories. Any works on world mythology I could find.

In my life, there were always questions I was researching. I wanted to know where we came from, and I wanted to know how and why the Survivors were the way they were. And, however shamefully, I searched because I wanted to learn how we could die. But my desire for my own mortality could no longer be at the forefront of my quest. Now that 28 of my siblings had evolved into violent *vieczy* versions of themselves who were undoubtedly roaming the earth murdering humans at an alarming rate, I needed to know—we all needed to know—how to kill a Survivor. We were simultaneously searching for them and searching for a way to kill them. Everett hated this. He knew that if we found a way to kill one of them, I'd have a way to kill myself, too—if I wanted to. And for 128 years of my life, I'd wanted to. I just wanted one, normal life. That would be enough for me.

I settled on Plato's *The Republic.* His famous depiction of Utopia scarily mirrored the Survivors' society, right down to a description of how the community could be stronger if loyalty was to the Republic as a whole instead of to the individual family. Clearly, the fourteen original Survivors believed this to be a necessity: They pointed to it as the reason that none of us knew who our parents were. It made me feel less like a freak that there had already been theories of cultures like my family's in place for thousands of years, but it angered me that Plato would call our world a Utopia. But the Survivors, too, had always called paradise what I had called a prison.

I reread the Allegory of the Cave. It had happened to me just the way Plato said it would. I had first broken free of the chains my family placed on me. I ventured into the world outside and saw the enlightened existence. And then I had come back to my family, who had lived in such isolation, who had spent their existence in the proverbial cave, and tried to show them the virtue of the outside world.

But they resisted.

They liked the world they knew. They hated that I threatened that world, that the Winters, too, threatened their world because we had each experienced a world they pretended never existed. Until I came back.

There was merit to their hatred, though. They blamed me for the 28 rogue Survivors leaving. They were, after all, only following my example. And they knew now that Survivors who left our world and ventured into the unknown turned into something terrible, something evil—even though I had been able to escape this evil for reasons unknown to us all. So the other Survivors could remain forever inside these walls, condemning all those who tried to show them the light outside as heretics. Plato had no rhetoric for what to do when you finally got the Unenlightened to turn their heads long enough to see the outside world at precisely the moment it proved itself unworthy, but that's just what had happened here. The Survivors could live on, satisfied that their world was better than the world outside. But it wasn't better. It was just safer. They could never understand the distinction. (What's the old parable? Ignorance is bliss?)

And then in the twist of all twists, going against everything Plato wrote, I, the enlightened one, wandered back into the cave and resumed my spot in the darkness, lined up among those in chains. And I'd hated every minute of it. The closer I got to Corrina—and to my nearly human life—the lighter I began to feel.

But it didn't change anything. I let the book reader fall on my chest. My throat felt tight and the bridge of my nose stung. My breathing was ragged and hiccuppy. Though no tears fell, I was crying.

"Princess?" Everett asked, having sensed my tension.

"I'm fine," I said.

"What..."

"Why did we come back?" I sobbed. "They hate me so much!"

He sighed heavily, as if he'd known this conversation would come. "They'll never understand the sacrifices you've made to go back. They'll never understand what it means for you to give up your freedom, to risk your life for your family. They're taking you for granted, but you know you're doing the right thing," he said.

"I wish none of this had happened. Just last year I was existing as a human. Living in that world. Doing stupid human things like being a bridesmaid. When did this happen, Everett? When did I give it all up?" I asked.

"You didn't," he said. "It's just on hold right now. We'll get back to normal some day." He pulled me close to him. I didn't want it to be on hold. I didn't want any of this.

Everett took *The Republic* out of my lap. "Rereading this will not help," he said.

"I didn't think it would," I admitted, unable to look him in the eye. Instantly, I was uneasy. I rose to my feet quickly, startling him. "I'm going to go touch up. We'll be landing soon, I'm sure," I said.

"Okay," he said. He looked worried. Really, I just needed to be alone.

I fumbled down the aisle and into the tiny airplane lavatory, and looked at my perfect espresso hair and my glowing isabelline skin. I stared into those violet eyes, more tired now than they'd looked in 145 years.

I'd ruined my life.

2

VISIONARY

When we walked off the plane in Dallas that Monday night, I could hear Corrina's excitement all the way down the corridor. She was screaming in her head, *Sadie has a boyfriend! Sadie has a BOYFRIEND!* Then, seeing the scene through her eyes, I watched as the world in front of her began to shake violently. She was jumping up and down. I laughed out loud.

"What's funny?" Everett asked, nudging me as we walked down the corridor at the super-busy DFW airport. This was my first trip to Texas. From Corrina's love of the place, I was excited to see it.

"Corrina's freaking out," I said. "Like a lot."

He smiled. "What's she saying?"

I rolled my eyes and let my voice take on Corrina's enthusiastic pitch. "Sadie's got a boyfriend! Sadie's got a boyfriend!" I mused. "Over and over and over again," I said, returning to my normal voice. "I think it's really more of a squeal than actual speech."

Everett laughed, too. "This is going to be great. I can already tell how much fun it is to be around someone who calls me your boyfriend," he said.

"How's that?" I asked. As we got closer to baggage claim, Corrina's mental screams grew deafening.

He paused and turned toward me. "Have you ever even once called me your boyfriend?" he asked.

I thought about it. "Maybe when I told Corrina about you?"

"You did no such thing!" he said, jokingly offended. "I was there, Sadie. You specifically said 'Oh, by the way, I've been traveling with this guy, Everett. He's...cool.' It was so romantic."

I rolled my eyes again. We had come to a stop in front of the giant revolving door that would take us out to baggage claim and toward the bouncy Corrina. "Okay, *boyfriend,*" I said, dragging out the emphasis. "You ready for this?"

He smiled his most devious smile and grabbed me by the waist so my feet just skimmed the ground and kissed me. I realized too late he was pushing through the revolving door so that Corrina got a full view of this. She screamed out loud.

"Eeeeee! Sadie!"

"Oh, I'm sorry..." Everett said, pretending he hadn't realized she'd see us.

I shot him an icy stare. *Couldn't resist,* he said in his mind. Then he smiled again, flashing his beautiful teeth. I could not resist that smile. Everett had acquired the ability to shield me from his mind—a bulwark, he had called it—but over the past few weeks, he had learned how to push specific thoughts outside his mental armor so I could hear him when he wanted me to. Conversely, I had learned to crawl over the top of the mental rampart and graze a few things—sometimes thoughts but, more commonly, feelings and strong emotions—from his mind. He didn't know that, though. I knew he would not like me doing this. I even knew it was sort of...wrong. But I was making so much progress with my powers! I was beginning to have faith that one day I'd be able to dance back and forth across the bulwark at will.

"Corrina!" I said. She jumped into my arms just the way she had the last time I had met up with her days before her wedding in Tupelo, Mississippi. That was less than six months ago, but my entire world had shifted, shaken, and reshaped since then. The clearest evidence of this was the striking presence of my supernatural *boyfriend* being introduced to my only human friends.

"You're here! You're here!" she said, clapping her hands together, the giant fur collar of her Malandrino coat and her giant red hair overtaking her tiny frame. "And *you!*" she said, directing her gaze at Everett. An awestruck expression quickly appeared itself on her face. Her eyes went soft, and the sides of her mouth curled up into a syrupy smile. "Hello, there," she said. I got the impression she was trying to refrain from whistling at him. As Everett smiled back at her, she had only one clear thought: *Oh. My. God.*

Everett ate it up. "Corrina, it's so good to meet you. I feel like I already know you from everything Sadie's told me!" he said enthusiastically as he reached out and hugged her tight. She blushed furiously. I elbowed him. Hard. *So much fun,* he said in his mind.

"Honey," I said, my voice light but with an edge only Everett would pick up on, "why don't you get our bags?"

"Sure, babe," he said, matching my game. We had never called each other "honey" or "babe" before. He sauntered away toward the conveyor belt but not before he had time to run one hand through his soft brown locks and wink over his shoulder as he went. Corrina swooned.

"Sadie," she said urgently, "Where did you find him?"

"California," I said. "Epic, isn't he?" I grinned. The comment was more than a little uncharacteristic.

"Epic," she agreed, dazed. She hadn't taken her eyes off him.

"Where's Felix?" I asked.

Oh, no! she thought. She closed her eyes and exhaled through her teeth. "Right, Felix," she said. I laughed. "He's in the car," she said.

And he can't make fun of me for wearing fur when it's sixty degrees anymore because she is too! she thought, satisfied.

I smiled. "Well, looks like Everett's got the bags, so let's not keep Felix waiting."

Corrina had lost her focus again, and stared at Everett from across the room, even though he wasn't facing us.

She's still checking me out, isn't she? Everett asked me.

"Of course," I whispered low. He'd hear me.

"You know, I'm not sure which is getting me more," Corrina said. "That he's the most beautiful man I've ever met in person, that he's wearing a Gucci purple velvet sport coat and still looks stunning, or that he is so madly in love with you that it like radiates out of his skin," she said. I smiled sheepishly. "I cannot believe you didn't tell me about him sooner," she said, smacking my arm.

"Let's go find Felix," I said as Everett walked up with the bags.

Corrina, Felix, Everett, and I spent the evening touring Dallas. Every place we drove, Corrina gave us an extensive social rundown of who lived where and what sort of shopping could be done there. I was giddy when, in one of Dallas's nicest neighborhoods, Corrina pointed out Highland Park Village—which was essentially a glorified strip mall—and from the road I could see Chanel, Tory Burch, Prada, and about a dozen other places I could get lost in for hours.

"Can we go shopping here?" I asked, my voice cracking with excitement.

"Of course!" Corrina said. "We'll have to abandon the boys first, though. I'm assuming they won't swoon over a Berkin bag the way we might."

My ears perked at Berkin bag. "Hermès..." I whispered, so softly only Everett could hear.

He watched as I took all of this in, my excitement growing exponentially. He seemed thoroughly amused as he kissed my hand. "Princess," he breathed, winking at me out of the corner of his eye.

"Felix," I asked, "what will you boys do while we shop?" I hadn't considered that we might split up, but I should have seen it coming. I was instantly grateful for the unseasonably mild Dallas weather. It would not go well if Corrina and Felix discovered Everett's...predatory tendencies. At least, not on this trip. I looked at Everett's eyes—a cool hazel with obvious green highlights coming out in the slivers of city light. It was the greenest I'd seen his eyes since he arrived in Moscow six weeks before. I breathed a sigh of relief.

"Not sure," Felix said. "It depends on what your man is into. Do you golf, Everett?"

"Absolutely!" Everett enthused. I looked at him dumbfounded. I had never heard this before. "But I don't have my sticks with me, man."

"Not a problem. I've got a spare set if you don't mind playing with borrowed clubs," Felix said. There was testosterone-tainted excitement flowing through the air. The boys had connected.

I turned to Everett. "Golf?" I mouthed.

Sadie, I live 500 yards from Pebble Beach—the golf destination of the U.S.—and it never crossed your mind that we might be into golf? he asked. I shook my head. He smirked. *You know, before we got mixed in with you and the crazy Survivors and all this impending war nonsense, we were pretty typical—golfing and all.*

Even in his thoughts, I heard the tinge of regret in his words. He wasn't like his brothers and his father. He didn't have brutality pulsing through his venomous veins. I sensed that Everett wanted nothing more than the two of us to be together in a world unclouded by bloodlust and violence; all he wanted was for us to end up together in a peaceful existence. He was waiting for Anthony's vision of the two of us on the beach—happy and relaxed and uncomplicatedly in love—to come to fruition. He would do whatever it took to get us there.

"All right, it's settled," Corrina exclaimed. "Tomorrow morning, we'll go our separate ways. Felix, you get a tee time at the club so you boys can have your fun, and I'll show Sadie why I call Dallas a shopping mecca."

"Sounds like a plan," Everett said. He squeezed my hand. I smiled. This trip was the first time since I'd met him that we'd had a chance to act like a normal couple. I realized that our Dallas vacation was exactly what we needed to counteract weeks of stagnation in the Survivors' City, preparing for a battle we knew little about, and trying to track members of my family we couldn't find. For just these few days with Corrina and Felix we were allowed to feel like normal people—like humans.

The next day with Corrina was beyond enjoyable. Though I was growing just as close to Ginny as I was with her, Corrina had a special place in my life. She'd taken me under her wing when I needed it most. She had nothing to do with anything negative or stressful in my life. So as we flipped through racks at Prada or perused the tables of scarves at Hermès, she was blissfully unaware of danger and complication, of all the things in my supernatural world. And it showed. We had so much fun together, worrying only about the questionable choice of Ferragamo continuing the coral trend into winter or whether Corrina's loving husband would notice that she spent more on a pair of Louboutins than their mortgage payment. And we laughed all day long. I had missed her. I had missed passing for a human.

Near the end of the day, Corrina and I made it back to her Uptown condo to get dressed for dinner. I used this opportunity to wear my newly-purchased long-sleeved, Rebecca Minkoff dress that cut halfway up my thigh and hugged my body closely. It was a daring number for me, even with the opaque tights I had on underneath it. I slipped into an adventurous pair of red Fendi heels that made me Everett's height. I would not need to fit into the crook of his neck—my favorite place to be—sitting at the dinner table with Corrina and Felix.

When Everett saw me, his eyes widened. "You look beautiful," he said, a little stunned. As he leaned in to kiss my cheek, in his mind he added, *Anyone ever tell you that you make it hard to be a gentleman?*

My breath caught; my stomach tingled. Everett Winter was starting to affect me in ways I had never experienced.

We drove in Felix's Audi convertible to Nobu in downtown Dallas. I loved the feel of the mild air as it spun around us. Having spent all my time in the wilderness lately, I was dazzled by the city lights. I missed the pace and even the plastic pretense of the city.

We had knocked out four courses and two bottles of wine when our dinner was winding down to the perfect mellow pace. Everett and Felix were talking about playing a few courses in Southern California together. Corrina was leaning into Felix as he talked across the table, her own thoughts quiet. I held Everett's hand, but I was leaning back and quiet, too.

It was right then that the buzzing in my head erupted into violent screams, faintly familiar voices, and terror.

I heard Felix ask, "If you're used to ocean courses, have you played Trump National yet?" as my vision moved from the subdued ambience of Nobu and into a different kind of darkness. It was the last thing I heard before all five of my senses were immersed in a different place.

I was moving and turning and talking like I was a player instead of an onlooker.

I was unaware, at first, of who was talking around me. But the familiar voices matched faces I knew like my own. They were the faces of eight Survivors from my generation, all men, scattered in appearance as each of them had stopped aging anywhere between 15 and 50 years of age. They hissed at each other in low, cold voices. Their eyes were blood red, their skin paler and smoother than it had been the last time I had seen them. Their brows were tightly creased into venomous stares.

I couldn't read the minds around me, but I understood what was happening. They had herded a group of four young women into a dark, damp place. I tried to look around, tried to see where I was standing, but I couldn't move. I could only watch helplessly.

"Noah, you get this one's legs. Make her stop kicking," Derek, one of my gruff brothers, barked.

"I can't," Noah's voice said. But the words had come out of my mouth. "Hurry up and finish her off. The venom's what's making her thrash like that." I understood then. I was inside Noah's body. Inside his mind.

In horror, I watched as Derek's mouth moved back to the flailing girl's throat. The other three terrified girls were sobbing hysterically, screaming, watching my deformed brother drink the life out of her. Unable to contain himself, another brother, Peter, snarled and latched onto the other side of the girl on the ground, sinking sharp white teeth into her leg to drink from another artery. I could feel a desire building inside me, one I couldn't explain or empathize with. I swallowed—Noah swallowed—hard as a white-hot searing pain built up in my throat. The longer we watched this happen, the hotter the burn became. It began to feel like swallowing knives. Or fire.

The others must have felt it, too. The remaining brothers pounced on the three girls. Despite his greatest efforts, Noah gave in, too, and I felt helpless as he—as I—jumped toward one of the dying girls. In seconds, their bodies were limp as greedy mouths—my own included—sucked warm blood out of each of them, quieting their cries of terror. The part of me that was still *me* was physically sick, tormented by an image I already knew I'd never be able to erase. But a part of me was fully inundated in Noah's head, feeling what he was feeling, ignited by the hot human blood cooling the burn in my throat. His whole body reacted in a lusty mixture of relief and stimulation. The blood was warm on my tongue.

Then it all went black.